PRAISE FOR *SHATTERED*

"Robin Wasserman's writing cuts straight to the bone, even when it's metal! This series is mind-bending."

—Bestselling author Tamora Pierce

"Fast-paced . . . A thought-provoking bioethical conundrum that raises difficult questions about the definition of life, this text will intrigue and entertain readers."

—*Kirkus*

"[*Shattered*] is a wonderful follow-up to [*Frozen*]. The world Robin Wasserman creates is creative and fascinating, and even though the main characters are mechanical, many still find a way to be dynamic and evolve during the story. [*Shattered*] is the second in a planned trilogy, and I, for one, can't wait for the conclusion."

—teensreadtoo.com

"This installment in the trilogy has intense action, a fast-paced plot, and interesting characters. . . . Give it to fans of Mary E. Pearson's *The Adoration of Jenna Fox* (Holt, 2008) or Nancy Farmer's *The House of the Scorpion*."

—*SLJ*

ALSO BY ROBIN WASSERMAN

The Cold Awakening trilogy
Hacking Harvard
The Seven Deadly Sins series

SHATTERED

The second book in the Cold Awakening trilogy

ROBIN WASSERMAN

Previously published as *Crashed*

Simon Pulse

NEW YORK LONDON TORONTO SYDNEY

ᗰ

SIMON PULSE

An imprint of Simon & Schuster Children's Publishing Division
1230 Avenue of the Americas, New York, NY 10020
This Simon Pulse paperback edition October 2011
Copyright © 2009 by Robin Wasserman
Previously published as *Crashed*.

Also available in a Simon Pulse hardcover edition.
For information about special discounts for bulk purchases, please contact
Simon & Schuster Special Sales at 1-866-506-1949 or business@simonandschuster.com.
The Simon & Schuster Speakers Bureau can bring authors to your live event.
For more information or to book an event contact the Simon & Schuster Speakers Bureau
at 1-866-248-3049 or visit our website at www.simonspeakers.com.
Designed by Mike Rosamilia
The text of this book was set in Edlund.
Manufactured in the United States of America
2 4 6 8 10 9 7 5 3 1
The Library of Congress has cataloged the hardcover edition as follows:
Wasserman, Robin.
Crashed / by Robin Wasserman
p. cm.
Sequel to: Skinned.
Summary: Living with other "mechs" since her wealthy parents transplanted her brain into a
mechanical body to prevent her from dying in a horrible accident, Lia becomes a pawn in a
religious leader's movement to outlaw "mech" technology and eradicate machines such as Lia.
ISBN 978-1-4169-7453-6 (hc)
[1. Science fiction.] I. Title.
PZ7.W25865Cr 2009
[Fic]—dc22
2009003271
ISBN 978-1-4424-2039-7 (pbk)
ISBN 978-1-4424-3360-1 (eBook)

For David Mayer, Ruth Wasserman, and Philip Wasserman, whom I never knew, but suspect I would have liked.

SHATTERED

I see . . . a new and commanding breed rising up, fearless and fabulous, unsparing of blood and sparing of pity, inured to suffering the worst and to inflicting it and ready to stake all to attain their ends—a race that builds machines and trusts machines, to whom machines are not soulless iron, but engines of might which it controls with cold reason and hot blood.

—Ernst Jünger, *Copse 125*

LIFTOFF

"There was no fear."

When I was alive, I dreamed of flying.

Or maybe I should say: When I was alive, I dreamed.

Sometimes it was flying; more often it was falling. Or burning—trying to scream, trying to run, but frozen and silent and consumed by flames. I dreamed of being alone. Of my face melting or my teeth falling out.

I dreamed of Walker, his body tangled up in mine. Sometimes I dreamed I *was* Walker, that my hands were his hands, my fingers the ones massaging soft, smooth skin, getting caught in long strands of blond hair. Awake, people talk about becoming one—but in dreams it can really happen. His lips, my lips. Our lips. Our bodies. Our need.

In dreams you can become everything you're not. You can

reverse the most fundamental truths of your life. You can taste death, the ultimate opposite.

I can't. Not anymore. Machines can't die, can't dream.

But we can fly.

From inside the plane, jumps don't look like jumps. One second there's a figure in the jump hatch, fingers gripping the edge, hair whipping in the wind, wingsuit rippling. Then the wind snatches another victim, an invisible hand yanking its prey out of the plane. Leaving nothing behind but an empty patch of murky gray sky.

Quinn and Ani jumped first, hand in hand. The first few times, I'd watched them fall, linked together and spiraling around an invisible axis, two whirling dots red against the snow.

But the novelty had worn off. These days I kept my seat.

Riley went next, and I was glad. Never speaking, never changing expression, eyes drilling through the floor. Until he thought I wasn't looking, and then he'd fix me with that stony, unblinking stare. I wasn't impressed: None of us blinked.

In another life I would have thought he was going for the dark, tortured thing, that whole moody, broody, aren't-I-deep-and-soulful trip. I might even have fallen for it. But the new Lia, version 2.0, knew better. Riley could sulk and skulk all he wanted, but whatever his problem was, he could deal with it himself.

It was like Jude said: *Orgs are weak and need each other. Mechs only need themselves.*

And then Riley jumped and I was left alone with the mech I needed least. Jude stood at the hatch with his back to the clouds and his amber eyes on me. The sun glinted off the silvery whorls etched into his skin. I traced my fingers along the metallic streaks staining my face and neck.

I'd been convinced by Jude's reasoning. We needed to puncture the illusion that we were human, that beneath the self-healing synflesh, hearts pumped, lungs breathed, organs throbbed and cleansed and churned.

I believed in the honesty. I wanted my outsides to match what lay within, the circuits and the energy converters and the twining networks of wires carrying artificial nerve impulses to an artificial brain. But that didn't mean I wanted to look like *him*.

He reached out a hand, as he always did. His lips curled into a smirk, like he knew I would yet again say no—but that eventually I would say yes.

His lips moved, and—thanks to my latest upgrade—the word bubbled inside my head. "Coming?"

I waved him away. He shrugged and let himself drop into the sky.

I edged toward the hatch.

The first time I jumped, the fear almost drowned me. That was the point. To let go of the steel frame separating us from a five-mile drop, let go of the rigid, rational, *controlled* mode separating us from the blood-and-gut orgs. Absolute control yielded to absolute release. The artificial sensation of fear released artificial endorphins, stimulated artificial nerve endings, unleashed a flood of artificial panic. And in the rush of wind and speed and terror, it all felt real.

But the danger was an illusion, which meant the fear was a lie, and my body was beginning to figure out the truth.

Pausing in the threshold, I raised my arms, and the woven aeronylon of the wingsuit stretched beneath them, silvery filaments shimmering. Then I stepped into the empty.

Buffeted by the wind, I maneuvered myself flat, facedown, limbs outstretched. The suit's webbed wings acted as an airfoil, harnessing the updraft to slow my free fall. Beneath me, snow-capped mountains drifted by at a leisurely hundred miles per hour; above me, nothing but soupy sky.

Here's the thing about flying: It gets old.

I processed the sensations—*processed* not felt. The temperature, fifteen degrees below freezing, frosting the few patches of exposed artificial skin. The thunder of the wind. The silver sky, the blinding white below, the specks of red, violet, and black, circling and swooping in the distance.

The air had no taste, no smell. Orgs had five senses; mechs had three.

The suit's instruments recorded a speed of 105 mph horizontal, 67 vertical, but this far from the ground, there was no fast and no slow. Despite the rushing wind, I felt like I was floating down a river, ambling and aimless.

There was no fear.

I let my body drift horizontal to the ground, and the wind sucked me into a flat spin, swinging me around at a dizzying speed. For orgs a flat spin was death. The body whirled like a centrifuge, a crushing 20g force sending rivers of blood gushing toward the head, the hands, the feet, starving the heart until it gave up beating. But for mechs, flat spins were just another perk, a way to turn the world into an incomprehensible smear. Without a puddle of fluid jostling in the inner ear, dizzying speed wasn't even dizzying. For mechs, "dizzy" was just a meaningless expression. Like "thirsty," or "nerve wracked." Or "bored to death."

I pulled abruptly out of the spin. Quinn and Ani swooped up, flanking me.

"Looking good. As always," Quinn VM'd, her digitized voice clear, her meaning more so.

I shifted my body weight and let a gust of air blast me off to the right, buzzing past Quinn with enough force to spin her upside down. "Obviously I'm a natural." Natural: the joke that never got old.

"Naturally annoying," Quinn shot back, regaining her balance. She dipped down, dive-bombing Ani, who squealed as she wriggled away, flipping in midair. Quinn grabbed her wrist and pulled her into a vertical drop. "Catch us if you can!" she called back to me.

I could; I didn't. I activated the lifting jets, let my legs drop, and began to climb, past fourteen thousand feet, past twenty thousand. Higher.

"Going somewhere?" There was something metallic about Jude's voice, sharp and brittle as his features. It was strange the way the digitized voices took on some character of their owners.

"Away from you." But even ten thousand feet below, he was in my head.

"Good luck with that."

I climbed higher, leveling out at twenty-eight thousand feet. *I could stay up forever,* I thought, letting my body carve lazy circles through the clouds. No more struggle to feel—or not to—nothing but a body and mind in motion, simple and pure. Jude would approve.

"You're too high, Lia." Jude again, a violet dot against the snow. Always telling me what to do. As he spoke, the jets sputtered out in the thin air and my webwings lurched, losing their lift.

"I can take care of myself." I tilted forward into a dive, arms pressed against my sides to streamline the suit. I was done flying.

I was a bullet streaking toward the ground. Critical velocity came fast as gravity took over, sucking me down. The mountains rose below me, snowy peaks exploded from the earth, and *now* came the flood of fear. The others blew past, smears of color. Screaming.

"Pull up, you're coming in too fast!" Ani.

"What the hell are you trying to do!" Quinn.

"Again?" Jude.

Riley, a black shadow against the snow, said nothing.

The ground came up fast, too fast, and I barely had time

to level out before I was skimming powder, slicing down the slope, a white cloud billowing in my wake. Something was wrong. The slope too steep, the angle too sharp, the snow too shallow, and I heard the impact before I felt it, the sharp crack of my head crashing into rocky ground, my neck nearly snapping free of my spine.

And then I was rolling down the side of the mountain, blinded by snow.

And then I felt alive.

And then all motion jerked to a stop, a wave of white crashed over me, and the snow filled my mouth, my nose, my ears, and the world went very still and very silent.

And very dark.

I couldn't see; I couldn't move. I was a statue under the snow.

"We're coming for you." That was Riley in my ear, puncturing the silence. He felt so near, like we were alone together in the dark.

I didn't answer.

They began to argue about how to reach me, and I cut the link, retreating into the quiet. The GPS would pinpoint my location, and my fellow flyers would eventually show up with snowfusers to dig me out. It didn't matter how long it took; I could bide my time for centuries, arise icy but intact to a brave new world. It wasn't so different from flying, I decided. Substitute dark for light and still for speed, but in the end, it was the same. Empty.

Once, I was afraid of the dark. Not the bedtime kind of dark, with dim moonlight filtering through the shades and shadows playing at the corners of the room, but absolute dark. The black night behind your lids.

I'd been trapped there for weeks after the accident, dark, still, and alone. A prisoner in my own body. And then I opened my eyes to discover that my body was gone. That I—whatever part of "I" they'd managed to extricate from my flesh-and-blood brain and input into their quantum cerebral matrix—was trapped after all in a body that wasn't a body. There was no escape from that. Not into my own body, which had been mangled by the accident, flayed by the doctors, then burned as medical waste. Not into death; death was off the table.

After that, darkness seemed irrelevant. Temporary, like everything else.

With snow packing my eyes and ears, there was no warning. Just pressure, then a jolt. Fingers gripping me, hauling me upward. I dropped back flat against the fresh powder. System diagnostics lit up behind my lids: The network was intact, already repairing itself. Synflesh knitting together, ceramic bones and tendons snapping back into place.

A hand brushed the snow from my eyes. Riley knelt over me, his fingertips light on my cheek. Behind him, Ani, worried. The sky had faded to a purplish gray. "You okay?" Riley asked.

"She's fine," Jude said. "Just a drama queen in search of an audience."

"Shut up." Riley took my shoulders and propped me up into a sitting position. "Everything still working?" The mountains loomed over us, white and silent. Years before, this had been a vacation spot, a haven for insane orgs who enjoyed hurtling down slopes at breakneck speeds even though their necks, once broken, stayed that way. But when the temperature plummeted along with the air quality, mountain gliding and its attendant risks were cancelled for good. Leaving the snow free and clear for those of us who needed neither warmth nor unfettered oxygen; those of us who just wanted to be left alone.

I knocked the snow from my shoulders and shook it out of my hair. The rush had faded as soon as I slammed into the ground—I was back in mech mode now, cool and hollow.

I pulled my lips into a half grin. It had been hard, relearning emotional expression in the new body, twitching artificial cheek and eye muscles in search of something approximating a human smile. But by now I had total control in a way that orgs never did. Orgs smiled when they were happy, the motion automatic, a seamless reflex of muscle reacting to mind, neural and physiological systems so intertwined that forcing a smile was often enough to boost a mood. Like a natural b-mod, its behavior-modifying effects were brief but instantaneous. My smiles were deliberate, like everything else, and no amount of curled lips and bared teeth would mod my mood.

I let the grin widen. "Who wants to go again?"

Abruptly, Riley dropped his arms, dumping me into the snow. It was Jude who hauled me to my feet and Jude who bundled me up and strapped me into the waiting plane, while Quinn and Ani cuddled in the next seat and Riley sulked in a far corner.

"Have a nice fall?" Jude asked, as the plane lifted off and carried us back toward the estate. The thunder of the engines wrapped us in a soundproof cocoon.

I leaned back, pointing and flexing my toes. Everything was in working order. "I've had better."

Jude arched an eyebrow. "You know, you continue to surprise me."

"Because?"

"I didn't expect someone like you to be such a quick study."

I didn't have to ask what he meant by "someone like me." Rich bitch Lia Kahn, spoiled and selfish and so sure she's better than everyone else. "Someone like the person I *used* to be," I reminded him. "That person's gone. You showed me that."

"And I'm still waiting for an appropriate demonstration of gratitude."

"You expecting me to buy you flowers?"

"Why would I need flowers when I have your sunny disposition to brighten my day?"

"What can I say?" I simpered at him. "You bring out the best in me."

Jude stripped out of his suit, balled it up, and tossed it across the plane. "Funny how I tend to have that effect on people."

"Oh, please." I stabbed a finger down my throat. "Do *not* start lumping me in with your groupies."

"They're not groupies."

But I could tell he enjoyed the designation. "What would you call them?"

"They're lost, searching for answers—can I help it if they come to me?" Jude crossed his arms, pleased with himself. "I suppose I'd call them wisdom seekers."

"And they're seeking it in your pants?"

"So vulgar." Jude tsked. "When the problem is your body, it's not so difficult to imagine that the body is where the solution lies." He reached for my hand, but I snatched it away.

"Save it for the groupies."

"What?" he asked, amber eyes wide with innocence.

I turned my back on him, watching the clouds stream by. Even now there was something disconcerting about being up in the air without a pilot. Self-navigating cars were the norm—these days, only control freaks drove themselves—but the self-piloting planes were fresh on the market, powered by some new smarttech that, according to the pop-ups, was the world's first true artificial intelligence. Unlike the smartcars, smartfridges, smarttoilets, smarteverything we were used to, the new tech could respond to unforeseen circumstances, could experiment, could *learn*. It could, theoretically, shuttle passengers at seven hundred miles an hour from point A to point B without breaking a sweat. It just couldn't smile and reassure you that if a bird flew into the engine, it would know what to do.

Not that there were many birds anymore.

Especially where most of the AI planes were destined to fly, the poison air of the eastern war zones. This was military tech; action at distance was the only way to win without having to fight. Thinking planes, thinking tanks, thinking landcrawlers equipped with baby nukes saved orgs from having to think for themselves. Saved them from having to die for themselves. Not many had credit to spare to snatch up a smartplane of their own for peacetime purposes—but as far as Quinn was concerned, no luxury was too luxurious, especially when Jude was the one placing the request.

The ground was hidden beneath a thick layer of fog, and it was tempting to imagine it had disappeared. "Flying's getting old," I said, keeping my back to Jude.

"For you maybe."

"We need to find something better." More dangerous, I meant. Wilder, faster, steeper. *Bigger.*

"You want better?" He slipped a small, hard cube into my palm. "For later."

"You know I don't do that crap." But I closed my fingers around it.

"For later," he said again. So smug.

I just kept staring out the window, wondering what it would feel like if the plane crashed. How long would we stay conscious, our mangled bodies melting into the burnt fuselage? Would we be aware as fuel leaked from the wreckage, lit by a stray spark? What would it feel like at the moment of explosion, our brains and bodies blasted into a million pieces?

I would never know. The moment this brain burst into fire,

someone at BioMax would set to work retrieving my stored memories, downloading them into a newly made body, waking me to yet another new life. That "me" would remember everything up to my last backup and nothing more. No flying, no crashing, no explosion.

For the best, I decided. Maybe when it came to dying, once was enough.

DREAMERS

"Natural is hell."

Orgs prefer not to think about it, but machines come to life all the time. Always have, always will. A machine's not a machine without an engine, a power source, an on switch, *something* to turn screws and bolts and gears and whatever into purposeful motion. Mechanical life—it's the difference between *sculpture* and *machine*. Coming to life is just what we do.

But some of us do it better than others.

In 1738, French inventor Jacques de Vaucanson built a life-size mechanical duck that could, supposedly, consume and digest food. The copper fowl crapped on command for admiring crowds all over Europe. But Vaucanson cheated. If anyone had bothered to look inside the defecating duck before its performance, they would have discovered that the duck—like its creator—was already full of shit.

Forty years later a mechanical wooden chess player known as the Turk faced off against Frederick the Great, Ben Franklin, and Napoleon. Checkmate, times three. The Turk wore a turban, puffed on a clay pipe, and was a suspected repository of mystical forces. It turned out to be the repository of a contorted chess-playing human, curled up in a wooden cabinet beneath the board, magnetically guiding the Turk's every move.

The past is irrelevant—that was Jude's law, and we lived by it. But he meant our past as living, breathing humans, the kind that were born from a womb and would end up rotting in the ground. There was no rule against exploring our other past, the toasters and steam engines and microchips strung up on our family tree.

There were the karakuri ningyō, eighteenth-century Japanese mechanical serving girls. "Dr. P's fornicatory dolls"— mute and anatomically correct, just the way his nineteenth-century customers liked them. ELIZA, the twentieth-century computer that could analyze your dreams, and Deep Blue, not as good a conversationalist as the Turk, but better at chess. Forty years ago there were Spot and Patch, animatronic dog and cat, all the fuss without the muss; then came the Nanabots, mechanical nursemaids equipped to administer a feeding and change a diaper, popular with the weak and infirm on both ends of the aging spectrum. Two thousand years ago, there were mechanical birds that chirped, mechanical snakes that slithered, mechanical men that spoke and smiled. All of them an illusion of life—all of them hiding gears or cogs or wires or shit beneath their artificial skin.

And now there's me.

There's us.

"Organic isn't better, it's just *different*," I told the meek little group of mechs traipsing after me. Hard to believe I'd ever been like them, clueless enough to imagine I had a choice. "Orgs are weak in body and mind. Your new life may feel like a punishment, but it's not. It's a gift."

The speech, like everything else, was getting old. I'd shown them the guest houses, the orchards, and the manor itself—steering clear of only the pool, full of zoned-out mechs tripping on digital hallucinations. I'd played the good little tour guide, a live-action pop-up for Jude's estate. (True, it was Quinn's fortune, Quinn's property, but after all these months, none of us thought of it as anything but Jude's.) They were intrigued, I could tell. Tempted, even if it meant giving up the last, desperate hold on their old lives. They just needed that one final push.

Thus, the speech. I gave it the way I gave the tour, mechanically, out of habit, the words dribbling out without my help. Sometimes it felt like this was all I did: tow new recruits across the estate, schooling them in life according to Jude. It seemed so quaint and retro now, the old way, infiltrating BioMax support groups to find the few and far between who weren't interested in being *normal*. There were more of them, a lot more, now that the download had been reclassified as a voluntary procedure, easy to qualify for as a genetic tweak or a lift-tuck. At least, as long as you were between sixteen and twenty-one—above the age of consent, below the age when the download would fry your neural circuits and leave you a mess of frozen limbs and scrambled brains.

"The orgs demand that we imitate humanity, they *designed* us to do so—and then they attack us for claiming an identity that's not our own. They call us skinners, mech-heads, Frankensteins." The words bored me, but I kept going, because I was good at it, and because Jude trusted me enough to let me speak for him, and that gave me power.

And because the more I delivered the speech, the more I believed it.

"They tell us we've stolen the lives of the dead—that we're nothing but a mechanical copy of the people we used to be. People who died so that we could live. Or whatever it is we do. And you know what? They're right."

There weren't any gasps this time around. But of the six mechs following me through the grounds, four looked ready to bolt. The other two were calm; voluntaries always were. It's easy to be calm when you don't care. They were curiosity seekers, probably fame whores beaming back to their favorite stalker zones. Let them try. Jammers locked the whole estate behind an impenetrable priv-wall. We'd been burned by voluntaries before. Now, we let them in, we let them listen, but we never expected them to stay.

"You can tell yourself you're the same person you always were. But you know that's a lie. You know nothing feels the same. Sometimes it probably seems you barely feel at all."

Feel. Such a ridiculously imprecise verb. What was a feeling? The scratch of something rough against your skin? The sensation of a toe dipping into water, the deep, wordless truth of *this feels cold this feels wet.* Then there were the feelings that happened inside your head, the whirring hamster wheel of *happy sad angry bitter jealous bored scared happy.*

Whatever orgs chose to believe about us, mechs had both types. We felt wet—or, at least, we *processed* wet, the artificial nerve endings in our synflesh sending a coded impulse to our neural networks. We processed all environmental conditions with precision. Much as we processed everything else: *Wrecking the car, burning alive, waking in an alien body that wasn't a body* equaled *bad. Angry.*

Sad.

But there was something else, wasn't there? The connection between the two types of feelings, the thing that bonded the feeling inside your head to the feeling inside your body. The thing that made your palms sweat when you were nervous, your stomach clench when you were afraid, your lungs heave and your eyes drip when you thought too long and too hard about what you used to have.

Mech bodies functioned perfectly no matter what was going on beneath the titanium skull. Heaving and dripping would indicate a malfunction. And when that happened, we just returned to BioMax and got ourselves fixed.

"The orgs set us up to fail. They punish us for imitating humanity; they punish us for rebelling against the illusion. Too bad. You can lie to yourself and pretend they don't hate you—"

"My parents don't hate me," one of them argued, a blandly pretty mech with long brown hair and a high-pitched voice. "They love me. That's why they brought me back."

This was an easy one. "They don't love you." Harsh, but better now, before the damage had been done. "They love their *daughter*. Who's dead. What do you think happens to you when they figure that out?"

She didn't look convinced; I hadn't been either. Sometimes they had to figure it out for themselves. Then they came back.

I had.

I led them down the shallow, grassy slope toward the greenhouse. When I'd first come here, it had been a decaying wreck, scabby with rust and shattered glass, much like the rest of the estate. With Quinn's parents long dead and Quinn herself an amputated, bedridden lump living only on the network, there hadn't been much call for home repairs. Once Quinn had downloaded, she'd been too busy smelling the roses and screwing everything in sight to deal with clogged plumbing.

Things were different now.

The main house gleamed, its stone face polished to a shine, its grounds lush with well-trimmed gardens and fruited trees, the greenhouse a crystalline temple exploding with purple and green. I stopped the group just outside the glass door, pulling a pressed purple flower from my pocket. "This is a Quinn," I said, then paused just for the pleasure of watching them wait. Sometimes it was a snooze mouthing the same thing to an unending stream of rebels without a clue. But sometimes, posing under their unblinking stares, it was a power trip.

"Quinn's parents had the flower designed for her on the day she was born—it's part orchid, part hyacinth, impervious to extreme temperatures, and capable of going three weeks without water. Man-made. Org-made. We know it's alive because it can die." I crumbled the flower to dust. "But it's not natural. There is no natural anymore." I paused again, this time to let them see it for themselves, the clouds thick with microscopic toxin scrubbers and ozone patchers, the grass designed to suck moisture out of even the driest desert air and stand tall against frost and drought, buzzing and rippling with new populations of genetically modified bumblebees and squirrels. Let the mechs who were still missing Mommy and Daddy flash on Mommy's lineless lift-tucked face or Daddy's anabolically enhanced biceps and the roid martinis that shot his testosterone through the roof. "*Natural* is hell."

Hell as in the miles of dead zone, underwater or under quarantine, as in the death of summer and the permanent cloud masking stars most of us didn't believe were there. As in the ruined bodies littering the cities, bodies without gen-tech or med-tech, all scabbed and lumpy and rotting.

"*Natural* is weak, like orgs are weak," I told them, opening my hand and letting the purple dust drift to the ground. A little drama queeny? No doubt. But effective. I could see it—not in their blank faces but in the way they stood, frozen and silent, forgetting to put on the little "aren't I human?" show we all used to play at, pretending to fidget and flop and blink. I fixed on one of the girls, Ty, her fuchsia hair pulled into a knot behind her right ear. She'd made it clear that she hadn't wanted to come, that her friend had dragged her along. And that she knew I was full of crap.

This was the one we'd get. I would have Jude invite her on our next cliff dive, and even if she said no at first, she'd eventually give in. Join his movement. Whatever it was moving toward.

"You want to talk natural?" I said as the girl stared me down. "It's the job of civilization to improve on nature. To perfect it. Which makes *us* inevitable—perfected bodies, perfected brains, without defects or weaknesses, without an expiration date. We're the *natural* end of the line."

`"Impressive. I think you're even starting to sound like him."`

I swatted my ear. Mosquitoes might have been extinct, but there were plenty of other pests still going strong.

`"You were watching?"` I asked silently, knowing my voice would find Quinn wherever she was hiding. I'd gotten the VM chip—illicit tech courtesy of Jude's illicit sources—installed only a week before but I already hated the way the computerized voice wormed into my head. Implanted in the access node at the base of my skull, the Voice/Mind Integrator intercepted the signals sent from our brains to our artificial larynxes, digitized them into a robotic monotone before we could make a sound, and sent them out to anyone within a three-mile radius, as long as they were tuned into the right frequency. I couldn't have been the only one who cringed at the way the v-mod replaced the rise and fall of familiar voices with flat computerized tones, the same disembodied voice we'd all spoken with in rehab before learning how to use our new mouths and tongues.

But then, that was the problem with the "improvements" Jude served up, doling them out at sporadic intervals, crediting only vague sources and underground suppliers. Few of them were an improvement on anything, and I would have been happy enough to go without. But I wasn't about to get left behind. I might have renounced my past and embraced a new and improved me and all the other empowering soulsong crap that, true or not, still sounded like bullshit when we spewed it out to the newbie mechs, but I had enough in common with the old Lia Kahn to know where I stood on the concept of loops. That's *loop* as in *do whatever's necessary to stay in the*. So the majority ruled. If the majority wanted infrared vision or internal GPS or strangers' voices crawling through their brains, then I wanted them too. So what if every addition carried us further away from normal?

"Normal" was just one more thing better left to orgs; one more thing we'd left behind.

Quinn was the only one who used the VM with any regularity. Maybe it reminded her of the voice she'd spoken with since childhood, each word selected by the flicker of an eye, one of the few body parts left intact after her accident. We all held on to a few things it would have been easier to forget.

"I'm always watching." There were micro-cams all over the estate, left over from Quinn's predownload years. "By the way, that shirt makes you look like a whale."

I smirked, forcing myself not to seek out the camera. It would be hidden in a branch or a gutter, likely invisible and definitely out of my reach, which meant there was no point in tipping her off about how much the eye-in-the-sky act creeped me out. "It's Ani's shirt," I said, plucking at the skintight mesh rippling with bucolic scenes yanked from the network. At the moment, there was some kind of galactic nebula unfurling across my chest.

"Was her shirt. Who do you think made her get rid of it?" Quinn's low chuckle sounded almost authentic. Even after all these months in the mech body, I still hadn't gotten a handle on laughter. Ani told me I was imagining things, but I was convinced my spastic barking made me sound like a wounded seal. Quinn had mastered it back when we were still in rehab. And she loved rubbing it in. "If I were you, I'd ditch it immediately."

"As in strip down right here while you're watching?"

"Now or later," Quinn said with a soft giggle. "Remember what I said."

I'm always watching.

I started heading back to the house.

"Wrong way," Quinn said. "I have something for you."

"What?"

"Just a little treat. Trust me."

"Busy," I said.

"Don't you think Jude's ass could use a break from all that kissing?"

I stopped walking.

"You don't want to give him a rash," Quinn added.

"Meaning?"

"Meaning back when you thought we were all freaks, Jude was enemy number one, and now you prance around here like his trained monkey."

Thanks to the VM, I could answer even with gritted teeth. "Jealous?"

"Of you?"

Jude liked his toys new and shiny, that much I'd figured out. I suspected that Quinn had started to look a little rusty by the time I showed up. Besides, he may have been a mech, but he was still a guy—and when it came to guys, no toy was shinier than the one they weren't allowed to play with.

"It's not sucking up if I actually agree with him," I reminded Quinn. "We all want the same thing, right?"

"I know what I want," she said. "What about you?"

"You first." Not that I was avoiding the question. The question was irrelevant. What I wanted I couldn't have, so I'd decided to stop wanting it.

"I want you to come play with me," she whined.

"Ask Ani."

"Ani's busy."

Hard to believe. Quinn's attention span was half the size of Jude's—out of sight, out of mind was a way of life. And Ani knew it. "I guess Ani and I have that in common."

"Somehow, I think the vidlifes can get by without you for a few minutes," Quinn drawled.

"You know, I do have a life outside the network," I lied. Living on my own with no parents, no school, and no obligations was a freedom the old Lia Kahn would have killed for. Freedom to hook up with Walker, to party all night dosed up on Xers and zone the days away on a cloud of chillers and chocolate, to dance in the moonlight with Cass and Terra while the randoms watched our flickering shadows, wishing they could steal our lives.

Now Walker was hooking up with the sister I hadn't spoken to in half a year, and b-mods modded nothing. Music was just noise to me, the same way Cass and Terra were just names of people I used to know. My own life had taken a permanent trip to the department of dull. Who could blame me for preferring someone else's?

It's not that I'd become a total vid-head. I wasn't one of the wastoids who spent all day and night whispering directions into the ears of the vidlifers and watching a bunch of strangers act out my wildest fantasies. I didn't need to pull any strings to watch my dark and shameful fantasy unspool across the screen. Because it was there for me at any hour of the day, in infinite variations: the vidlifers themselves, head cases who had given up their identities, their wills, their *lives* to the masses. They spoke no words that weren't piped into their ears, made no choices that weren't chosen for them by randoms spread across the network. They'd erased themselves.

"Come on," Quinn wheedled. "You don't want to miss this."

I gave in. "Fine." The only thing more embarrassing than watching vidlifes was envying the vidlifers. I wasn't about to put myself at Quinn's lack of mercy. "Where are you?"

"Everywhere," she hissed in a deliberately spooky whisper. Then cackled. "But right now? Down by the pool."

I groaned. "No swimming, Quinn, you know that." She just didn't know why. No one did, except for Jude. And he was keeping his mouth shut; it was the one thing I'd let myself ask him for.

"Who goes down there to swim?"

"Not that either," I snapped. But the small black cube was still in my pocket. *Just for emergencies*, I told myself. Like I always told myself.

"You're just endless amounts of fun," she complained.

"Feel free to go bother someone else. It'll be hard, but I'll get over it."

There was a pause. "Just get your ass down here," she said. "Oh and, Lia?"

"Yeah?"

"Seriously. Lose the shirt."

Like Quinn said, swimming wasn't exactly the only reason, or even the main reason, to trek across the grounds to the neo-mod steel-and-glass erector set that housed the pool. Nor was it the only reason I stayed away. The solar panels along the ceiling served double duty as net-linked screens, so you could fine-tune your zone and your backstroke at the same time. Or, as was mostly the case these days, so you could project a dizzying strobe show of light, color, and sound that made the perfect cooldown for anyone coming off a dreamer.

That's what we called them.

Of course, usually when you dreamed—or should I say when orgs dreamed—they dreamed alone. Even cradled in each other's arms, they were alone in the dark inside their own heads. For orgs, sleep was the ultimate isolation. Dreamers, on the other hand, didn't require sleep. They required nothing but a tiny black cube, an ocular uplink, and the will to disappear into madness for anywhere from five minutes to forever. Thanks to the dreamers, mechs could, in their own way, regain their dreams. And thanks to the dreamer links—yet another of Jude's "unofficial" updates— they didn't have to dream alone. Hence the mechs sprawled across the pool deck, twitching and keening, and the bodies lining the pool floor, amorphous shapes wrapped together in the rippling water, their brains melting into a shared madness.

You didn't have to touch to have a linked dream, but I heard it helped. Water too made things more intense. At least, that's what I heard. I'd never tried it myself. These days water made things a little *too* intense—and the idea of dropping a dreamer in public repulsed me.

Quinn was waiting outside, and she wasn't alone. I scowled at Jude. Typical of Quinn to drag him along. "What's he—" I stopped.

It was Jude, but also . . . not Jude.

"Seth, this is the girl I was telling you about." Quinn shot me a wicked smile. "Seth's not interested in staying, but . . ." She raised her eyebrows. "I figured you could change his mind."

He had Jude's face—the harsh, angular lines, the bland beauty we all shared sharpened by raking cheekbones, hooded eyes, full lips built to smirk. But he wasn't smirking, and his eyes—slate gray, not Jude's flashing amber—darted from Quinn to me to the ground and back again. His flesh was an unbroken plane of creamy peach without any of Jude's swooping silver circuitry, and his long, muscled arms looked like org arms, without the transparent panel Jude wore on his left bicep, showing off his internal wiring like a badge of honor.

This guy, this *Seth*, looked normal, in a way all of us on Quinn's estate had accepted we would never be. But he also looked like Jude.

"Don't zone on me, Lia," Quinn warned. "It's only weird for a minute. You get over it."

Easy for Quinn to say. She had a custom-made body and face, tailored to her exact specifications. Unlike Jude, who'd been plucked from life in the gritty city to serve as one of Bio-Max's first experimental subjects—it was strictly off-the-rack for him, a body and face the corporation now kept in reserve for emergency procedures, the downloads that no one saw coming. Downloads like mine. It was one thing to know the doubles were out there—somebody else's brain behind your face, some random's words coming out of your mouth—it was something else to see one.

"What's the point?" I VM'd to Quinn, knowing no newbie would have access to the illicit tech. "You track him down just to freak me out?"

"First of all, Seth found me," Quinn said aloud. "He wanted to take your little tour, but I figured he'd get a better impression one-on-one. He just woke up a few weeks ago. Still figuring out how everything works, right, Seth?"

He smiled with that awkward grimace of a newbie mech trying to fake something that used to come automatically. "It's kind of weird at home these days," he said, slow and steady. I remembered that too. It was hard work, figuring out how to control the air flow and the self-lubricating tongue and the artificial larynx to produce something approximating human speech. From his nervous smile as the words stumbled out, I figured he was fresh out of rehab, still expecting his gold star.

"And second of all?" I prompted Quinn.

"I knew you'd like him," she said.

"And I thought you could use him," she added.

"For what?"

Seth looked cluelessly back and forth between us. It must have looked like we were frozen in a staring contest or some equally inane battle of silent will.

"Look at him," Quinn shot back. "Everything you want, without all the complications."

"I don't want him," I said, disgusted. "Either of them."

Quinn pulled a dreamer from her pocket, tossing it from hand to hand. "Seth can't wait to try it," she said aloud. "Can you, Seth?"

"She won't tell me what 'it' is," he said. "But . . ." He trailed off, spreading his arms wide like he was helpless not to put himself at Quinn's mercy.

"I get it," I said. It wasn't my job to keep some random out of dreamerville. "Have fun."

"It's linked," Quinn told me, "so we can all play."

"Forget it."

"Not even tempted?" Quinn grinned. "You're tempted."

"I'm leaving." I forced a smile at the newbie. "Nice to meet you, Seth. You'll be welcome if you decide to stay. This is a home for every mech who needs it."

He shook his head, hard. "I was just curious. Just visiting, you know?" he said. With Jude's voice. "I'm not like— I mean . . ."

"Not like us," I said, biting back the *If you say so.* "That's okay. I really do get it. Been there, done that." I traced my fingers along the silvery streaks rimming my neck. I hadn't embraced the freak-chic thing as much as the others. But to the newbie, I knew it was irrelevant. I was one of them; he wasn't— he thought. "Maybe you'll make it work."

Maybe you'll be back.

Absolute control, Jude always said.

If I'd had that, I could have stopped thinking. About Jude's double. About my double. Out there somewhere with the same body I'd have until I got up the credit and the nerve to trade it in for a new one, custom-made. About whether Jude's double was right: if it was different for him and if that meant it could have been different for me. Which inevitably led where every-thing always led, straight back home to the damage I'd done just by being me—or, more accurately, *not* being me: perfect daughter, perfect sister, perfect girlfriend, perfectly breakable. The crash broke me; I broke everyone else.

Control meant never looking back, never questioning why I had walked away. Wiping out the memory of their faces: My father, pretending he didn't look at me and see a corpse. Auden, bandaged and pale, his eyes willing me away—first from the room, then preferably from the planet. And Zo's face the last time I saw her. That was the one I kept coming back to. *Tell me I'm your sister,* I'd begged that last day. I kept seeing it: Zo's face when she didn't answer. And I kept wondering: What if I had waited? What if I had stayed?

But that would have been selfish. I had accepted that.

Forcing myself into my old org life, into my old org family—it would have ruined all of us. If I'd understood that earlier, Auden would have been safe. And if I'd ignored it, if I'd stayed, given Zo a chance . . . she might have been next.

So don't think about it, I told myself every day, all day. *Forget.*

I had control, I thought, imagining Seth and Quinn writhing in the pool, locked in the shared dream that would give them a few hours of escape. I had control but not enough of it.

My room was nearly bare: just a chest of drawers, a flat-screen ViM striping the wall, and a bed. The latter was unnecessary; I could shut down just as easily with my back against the wooden floor. All it took was an internal command, and the world went away. For a while, I'd experimented—shutting down while standing up, hanging upside down, dangling out the window. In the end, I preferred the bed.

I lay down and took out the dreamer Jude had given me. The dreamers were nothing more than code, bits of data that overrode our neural homeostasis and threw our systems into a chaos that simulated physical and emotional response. Almost like jumping out of a plane, but more effective. Because they were just programs, they should have been reusable, but for whatever reason, no dreamer ever had much of an effect after the first few uses. Just one of the things no one, including Jude, understood about what they did to us. We all had our theories, but in the end, we just crossed our fingers and flicked the switch.

I hadn't had a fresh one in weeks. I'd promised myself I wouldn't, not anymore. It was too easy—and it made waking life too gray. Like nothing was as real as the world inside your head.

I flicked the switch.

When I was alive, I dreamed in stories.

They weren't real, of course. Org dreams are nothing but random neural firings, spurts of color and unprompted emotion. The story comes later, in that instant before waking, your muddled mind making sense of the chaos by stringing the randomness into a narrative.

Mech dreams were different. There was no once-upon-a-time. No faces, no nightmares. No flying.

There was:

Rage.

Soft.

Wild.

Scared.

Bliss.

Raw jolts of emotion as if there was no body, no bed, no Lia Kahn, only the roiling froth of *joy grief terror pain joy.*

There was no "I."

"I" was an illusion, evanescent, a null spot at the eye of the hurricane, an emptiness that drew its reality from the storm swirling around it.

There was want. A surge of need, pain and pleasure welded together, craving, and the sweet excruciation of denial, giving way, finally, inevitably, to satisfaction.

There were no stories and no faces, but then I saw his face, amber eyes flashing, spiraling silver making his flesh shimmer in the light, lips curled, knowing.

Lips.

I reached out. I wanted. I *needed*.

"Sweet dreams, I take it?" he said, catching my wrist just as my fingers grazed his cheek.

I was awake.

DAMAGE

"I have seen the truth."

I yanked my hand away. "What the hell are you doing?"

"I should be asking you that," Jude shot back. "I just wanted to see if you were in here—no one asked you to molest me."

I sat up, trying to shake off the effects of the dreamer. After, everything felt hollow. Shadows flickered in corners, like the dream was lurking out there somewhere, waiting to reclaim me.

"As you can see, I'm here," I snapped. "Now you can get out."

Jude smiled and perched on the edge of my bed. I hopped to my feet, keeping the bed between us.

"If you really hate me as much as you like to pretend, why move in with me?" he asked.

"You and twenty other mechs," I pointed out. "It's not like we're playing house."

"We're playing something." He shook his head. "At least you are."

"That's exactly your problem. You think this is all just a game."

Something flashed across his face, gone too quickly for me to interpret. "If I thought you were stupid enough to believe that, you wouldn't be here. Or at least, I wouldn't be here with you."

"So being stupid is the key to getting you out of here? I could give it a try."

He stood up and headed for the door. "Don't start shaving IQ points on my account. There was just something I thought you'd want to see."

"I'm sure it can wait."

"Not quite an *it*," Jude said. "More like a he."

"I've had enough new people today," I said, wondering how much time had passed, if Seth and Quinn were still down at the pool together. Wondering whether the dreamer had somehow known what I was thinking—or was I only thinking it now because of the dreamer?

"Not quite new either," Jude said. "But if it makes you feel better, I doubt he'd want to see you either."

"Who?"

"Auden."

The vidroom wasn't off-limits to the randoms, not exactly, but it was known who belonged there and who didn't. When

Jude and I arrived, Riley was sitting on one of the two red couches, stiffly upright and awkward with the usual black cloud hovering over him. It made a certain perverse sense that he and Jude claimed some kind of no-holds-barred, for-richer, for-poorer, in-sickness-and-in-health, not-even-death-did-part-them friendship: One never bothered to speak for himself, while the other couldn't shut up.

Quinn and Ani were sprawled on the other couch, Quinn's hand casually resting on Ani's knee as if to say, *This is mine.*

When I feel like it, that is.

I wondered if she'd told Ani about Seth, or invited her to join in. I doubted it.

If you're planning to live forever, monogamy is an impractical standard, Jude liked to say. How convenient for him.

"Where is he?" I peered around the room as if he'd be hiding behind the furniture.

"He who?" Jude asked.

"You know who."

He didn't say anything.

"Auden." I'd barely spoken his name since it happened.

"Did I say he was here?" Jude gave me the wide-eyed innocent act.

I wanted to punch him.

"I'm out of here."

"Wait." Jude's smile vanished. "You really do need to see this." He nodded at Riley. "Play it back."

Each wall of the vidroom was covered with a ViM screen,

flickering with a constant stream of images that the Virtual Machine interface yanked from the network. Most defaulted to random, but one wall was programmed to pull up any vid that mentioned the words "mech-head," "download," "Frankenstein," or "skinner."

It seemed important to know who was talking about us.

Usually it meant a haphazard collage of muted video: Faither protests, fame-whore newbie mechs selling whatever was left of their souls for a shot on a vidlife, the latest ruling on what we could do, where we could go, what we could own, how human we were. The usual. But when Riley swept his finger across the console, the jumble of images gave way to one large, familiar face, paler than I remembered, his dark eyes like black voids in his flesh.

"It posted about half an hour ago," Jude said. "While you were . . . *sleeping*. The 'Honored' Rai Savona has found his calling." His mouth twisted around the word "honored." Understandable. I could have thought of a few choice adjectives that would have better suited the sanctimonious nutjob. "Honored" was the one he'd chosen for himself.

Savona was standing at a podium, and when the camera panned back, it was clear he'd assembled an audience of hundreds to hear whatever it was he had to say. "Honored friends," he began, smiling out at the crowd. "Today marks both an ending and a bright beginning as I say farewell to the cause I have served willingly for the last ten years and turn the page to a shining future. As of this morning I am stepping down as the leader of the Faith Party." Mumbles percolated in the crowd. "It's with great sadness that I leave behind such a loving community—"

"I'd be sad too if I got fired," Quinn muttered.

"But I'm unable to turn a deaf ear to my true calling—"

"Obsession," Jude spit out.

"Which is why I'm pleased to announce to you the formation of the Brotherhood of Man. Providing social services to the needy, a place of peace and solace for lost souls, and dedicated, above all, to defending the unique glory of God's creation over those who seek to encroach upon it."

Jude scowled. "Translation: Even my crazy Faither friends aren't crazy enough to declare war on download tech, so I'm going it alone. Because I'm going to prove I'm the biggest crackbrain of all, if it's the last thing I do."

It wasn't a surprise; in fact, now that it had happened, it seemed inevitable. After the religious wars a few decades ago, the whole God thing became a serious fashion don't. Some people just couldn't let it go—but that didn't mean they were spoiling for a fight. The Middle East was a crater and Italy was toxic; the world was running out of places to blow up. Smart move for the Faithers to ditch Savona once he started waving his pitchfork.

"We will destroy the technology robbing our nation's youth of their very lives and souls, deceiving heartsick parents across the country with the illusion that their departed children have come back to them, seducing the whole and healthy into throwing away everything, and for what? A false promise of immortality! Hell on Earth, trapped forever in the purgatory of iron and steel."

In person, Savona's stare was magnetic. I'd found it impossible to turn away even when he was telling me I shouldn't—and by his standards *didn't*—exist. But the advantage of watching him on-screen was that we could turn him off. "Tell me again why we're watching this crap?"

Jude frowned. "Wait for it."

Ani shot me an odd look, equal parts pity and concern, then turned away the moment I caught her eye.

"I have seen the truth," Savona said, peering into the camera. "And I have seen the danger. Not just to our souls, to the very fabric of human society, but to ourselves, to *yourselves*. The danger is *real*, and it is imminent, and this is why we must *act*. Self-protection is a moral imperative." He hung his head. "But words are empty. *Words* are meaningless. I offer you more than words. I offer you evidence of the danger. A young man who's faced the abyss and barely lived to tell the tale. This brave young man's story called to me, as it will call to you. As the Brotherhood moves forward, we will all look to him as a beacon. A light in the darkness, a reminder of what we stand to lose if we fail."

I knew. Before the camera panned across the stage, settling on a thin figure emerging from behind the curtain, tracking him as he hobbled toward the podium, I knew. He shook hands with Savona, then looked out over the audience, his eyes finding the camera. Finding me. They were a brighter green than I remembered—then I realized he wasn't wearing his glasses. He'd been the only person I knew who wore glasses, because no one in their right mind would turn down the simple med-tech to fix myopia. But then, no one in their right mind would allow that kind of defect to slip into their child's genetic code in the first place, not when they had the credit to fix it. As I understood it, his mother hadn't been in her right mind, not with all the talk of preserving God's natural plan. When she died, he'd kept the glasses, a tribute to the woman, I thought, not an embrace of her insanity.

Except here he was, embracing the Honored Rai Savona. No glasses.

"I'm Auden Heller," he said, his voice raspy and hoarse. "And this is the story of how I almost died."

I could feel them all staring at me, waiting for me to react. But I kept my face blank. That was the serious advantage to mech life—when you were disconnected from your body, it couldn't give you away.

They've already watched this, I thought. *They all know.*

Which meant it would be useless to run away or shut it off. I would only look weak. I would stay; I would listen. It was no more than I deserved.

And I wanted to see him. Even like this.

Auden eased himself into a chair next to the podium. His movements were slow and careful, as if to protect brittle bones. "I hope you don't mind if I sit," he said, his voice amplified by a hidden microphone. "I get tired so easily now. Rai wanted to do this over the network, so I could speak from my home, but I told him no." His voice rose, some of the color bleeding back into his pale face. "It's important that we be here together, in person, celebrating one another's humanity. Without electronic barriers, without *machines*, keeping us apart."

"Impressive ventriloquism, isn't it?" Jude murmured. "You can barely see Savona's lips move."

I jabbed an elbow into his side. "Shut. Up."

"I used to think this was my fault," Auden said, gesturing down at his ruined body. His cheeks were hollow, his face etched with scars that he must have had the doctors leave intact for effect. He was thinner than he'd been before, and, bent by a twisted spine, his left shoulder dipped below his right. He wore short sleeves, and the skin on one arm was markedly darker than on the other, the telltale sign of a transplanted limb. His hand lay in his lap, its fingers half-curled, and I flashed on the last time I'd seen him, when I rested my hand in his and he hadn't even realized it. The nerves transmitting the sensation had dead-ended at his severed spine. "I was naive," he continued. "When I met the skinner, I believed its disguise. I thought it was my friend. It's very good at simulating human emotion—they all are. And emotional exhibition stimulates emotional response. That's how we're built. If someone smiles at you, you instinctually smile back. Even if that someone is a machine. You forget." He broke off coughing, his whole body spasming. Savona took a step toward him, but Auden got himself under control. And he told the story.

Our story.

I couldn't look at him while he spoke. Telling the world

how he'd befriended me after the download. Telling thousands of strangers how he'd assured me I was human, I was still *me*. Telling Ani and Quinn and Riley about the day I'd leaped off the edge of the waterfall. How he'd nearly died trying to save me, the mech who would never need saving.

My fault, for letting both of us forget what I really was. Jude had helped me see that. I couldn't blame Auden for seeing it too.

"I believe it didn't mean to hurt me," Auden said. I wondered if he knew I was watching. If he thought about me at all— but then I realized he must think about me every day, every time he collapsed after walking up a flight of stairs, every time the nerve implants jolted his muscles into action with a painful blast of electricity or his transplanted liver failed. I'd spent a lot of time pumping the network these past few months. I knew what doctors could fix and what they couldn't. "Just as I believe the skinners don't want to damage society. They honestly believe they're harmless. But I learned that motives don't matter." He raised one arm and used it to lift the other one, the limp, discolored one. "The skinner I took as my friend didn't chop off my arm. But I still lost my arm because of the skinner. I nearly lost everything." He left out the part where he'd wanted the download for himself and been denied, thanks to a genetic tendency for mental instability that might never manifest itself—unless it already had. Believing that, at least, would have made it easier for me to watch.

Auden began coughing, his face going red and flushed with the effort to suck in enough air. When he spoke again, his voice was ragged. "It doesn't matter that the skinners mean us no harm. Some things create danger just by existing. But our eyes are open. Our spirits are willing." The crowd began to cheer. "Together, we will face the threat!" he shouted over the roars. "And together we will defeat it!"

Jude muted the applause.

"He doesn't mean it," I said, though even I was aware how lame it sounded. "He's been brainwashed by that lunatic."

"Or he's just trying to hurt you," Riley said quietly. "The way he thinks you hurt him." He was the only one not looking at me. His eyes were still fixed on the screen, where Savona was helping Auden off the stage.

"You don't know anything about it," I snapped, but of course he did. They all did now.

"He's an arrogant little bastard," Jude said. "Always was."

"Shut up," Ani and I said together. She brushed Quinn's hand off her leg and stood up. I backed away. Ani was into hugging, and I didn't want anyone touching me.

"I'm going to my room."

Jude raised his eyebrows. "Twice in one day?"

I shrugged. He thought he knew everything. Let him.

"Stay," Jude said. "This is going to get ugly, fast. We need to be ready."

"You be ready. I'll be in my room."

Jude ran a hand through his shock of dark hair. "Why can't you just—"

"Let her go," Riley said. He still wouldn't look at me.

"She shouldn't be alone," Jude said in a low voice.

"Let her go," Riley said again.

I went.

Alone was easier said than done.

"Go away!" I shouted. The knocking stopped. But then the door eased open, enough for me to glimpse a patch of blue-black hair through the crack. "Unwanted visitor," I told the room. "Terminate."

The room didn't respond, nor did it deploy countermeasures to keep Ani out. Apparently the new smartchip tech had its limits. Quinn had had the house fully equipped the month before, moments after the AI chips hit the market, promising us it would change all our lives. Like the automated plane, it was a perk of excess credit, a luxury the rest of the world would enjoy only through vids. So far it had been less than earth-shattering, learning who liked what when it came to lighting, temperature, noise level, all the little things that can make life so irritating. When you were walking around with a computer in your head, it was hard to be impressed by an artificially intelligent doorbell. Especially one not intelligent enough to keep out unwanted visitors.

Ani paused in the doorway, as if waiting for the termination order to be carried out. "Since I'm still alive—"

"Don't let Jude hear you say that."

"Since I'm still *intact*," she clarified. "Can I come in?"

"Would it stop you if I said no?"

"Not really. But you might hurt my feelings." She flashed

me that strangely shy smile, the one that always made me wonder how she'd hooked up with Jude and Riley in the first place,
much less how she'd managed to score even a minimal quotient
of Quinn's attention. Not that she wasn't pleasant enough, even
sweet. She was just there—but she was *always* there, and somehow that made the difference. She was a little like a fungus, I'd
decided. She grew on you.

"I don't want to talk about it," I warned her. "The past is
irrelevant and all that, remember?"

She stepped into the room and sat down on the floor, her
back against the wall. "No talking. Got it." She pulled her knees
up to her chest and latched her arms around them. "So what do
you want to do?"

I wanted to know what she thought of me, now that she
knew what I was running from.

No, I thought. *Not running.* Running away was for cowards.
I'd run *toward.* I'd chosen a new life. And I'd done it to protect
everyone else, not myself. I knew that—and not just because
Jude told me so.

"Whatever." I flicked on the ViM screen, calling up my
zone. Strange to think there was more raw computing power in
my head than in the ViM, but then, that was the beauty of Virtual Machines—no one needed a computer anymore, not with
your whole life stored on the network. All you needed was a
screen and a password, and you were good to go.

My zone was pretty bare these days—a few pics, a couple
texts from randoms I'd never met who didn't realize I'd pretty

much dropped off the network. In the old days, I'd basically lived my life on the zone, along with everyone else. Now it was just another reminder of all the crap I'd decided to forget. "What should we do?" I asked.

"You're asking *me*?"

"I was asking the room, actually, but you'll do."

Ani pulled herself up and wandered over to the room's AI port, tracing her fingers along its outer rim. "You think it can understand us?"

I tried to keep the irritation out of my voice. "I was *joking*."

"No, seriously," she said. "Artificial intelligence, right? So what if it really is intelligent? Maybe it has, like, a personality in there. I mean, if they shoved our brains into a house somehow, we'd still be us, right?"

"Would we? How do you know?" The idea creeped me out enough that I didn't want to think about it. "Anyway, it's not the same thing. AI computers are fast, and they're—I don't know, *clever*, but they can never be *smart*. You know they can't build consciousness from scratch. It's why they're stuck with us— exact copies of the real thing."

"The *real* thing," Ani echoed quietly, still examining the port. "Yeah. As opposed to us fakes."

"You know what I mean," I said, starting to get seriously annoyed. "Anyway, wasn't the whole point to be focusing on something that *wasn't* insanely depressing?"

"Right." Ani turned to face me again, her game face on. She grinned. "So what'll it be?"

"Something normal," I suggested. "Something . . ." I didn't want to say, *Something that lets us forget for five seconds that we're the trailblazers to a new and brighter technological future, or whatever it is we're supposed to be calling ourselves instead of chip-brained freaks.* That was the sort of thing we weren't supposed to think, much less say. Besides, which of the "normal" activities— shopping, gaming, zone pumping and dumping—on the agenda would be up to the challenge? Even if, and it was a big if, I could picture Ani and me pumping the network for the latest trend killers the way I used to do with Cass and Terra, or even just sitting around and playing Akira, the way Walker and I wasted time when we were too tired or too lazy for our preferred way of passing an afternoon, none of it would be the distraction I needed. There was a reason I spent so much time blanked out in front of the screen watching vidlifes. There was a reason for the dreamers.

I shrugged. Let Ani figure it out. She was the one supposedly determined to cheer me up. I was ready for some cheering. "What kind of stuff did you do with your friends? Before?" I asked.

Mechs don't have lungs, and we don't have capillaries or pulses, which means our skin doesn't change color when we get upset, nor does our breath speed up and slow down. We don't blink or shiver or do any of the other things that an org body does when it's giving away a secret that its owner would prefer to keep shut up inside. Our secrets belong to us.

But once you know what you're looking for, there are things

you can see. An awkward jerk in a step that should have been smooth. A blank expression, because the mind behind it is suddenly too busy to remember to infuse the lips and eyes with some simulacrum of life. Sometimes just a stillness.

Ani went still.

"Sorry," I said. "Forgot." Hard to do stuff with friends, or do much of anything, when you're a genetic malfunction, abandoned by parents who realized nine months too late that they shouldn't have had you in the first place, warehoused in some kind of "facility" that was basically a loading zone on the curb of death. Ani was lucky that she'd been carried away not by starvation or infection or madness, like everyone else she knew, but by the helpful hand of the BioMax research team, seeking test subjects for the download technology and eager to recruit anyone with the right biospecs who was desperate enough to volunteer.

Or, as Ani put it, with the requisite air quotes, "volunteer."

Ani had shown me a pic of her with Jude and Riley, who she'd met in the hospital before they got the procedure. In the pic, their teeth were crooked and cracked, their cheeks sunken and sallow, Ani's malformed torso and Jude's withered legs giving Riley's malnourished but intact body a glow of health. In the pic, their skin flowed the spectrum from coffee to chocolate, warm browns—as opposed to the pale synflesh they'd been poured into, flesh white by default, ready for the majority of customers who had come calling once the "volunteer" stage was over and the download went on sale.

"Race is an extraneous category when it comes to us," Jude

liked to say. "What's race when your skin is synthetic and your bodies disposable? What are you but mind and mech?"

What he meant: It was easier just to forget.

Add it to the list of things we weren't supposed to talk about.

"Brahm's party," Ani said finally, looking like she regretted the words as soon as they were out of her mouth. "Want to?"

"Do *you* want to?" I asked, skeptical. It's not that I had anything against Brahm, a mech who'd joined up about the same time I did. Brahm was the former heir to the largest wind-farm fortune in the midwest, one of the first to download as a paying customer. Blind since he was a year old, he now walked around with a perpetual squint, as if afraid of seeing too much, too soon. His parents had tossed him out the day he committed to the procedure. Like me, he now had nowhere else to go; unlike me, he wasn't shy about sharing the details to anyone and everyone who'd listen. "Talking" to Brahm meant listening to him rant—about his parents and the Faithers who'd convinced them to disown their apostate mechanical son, about the weather, about the lack of closet space in his first bedroom, and then the lack of southern exposure in the room he'd replaced it with. But ranting or not, he'd come to us with a sincere desire for refuge and plenty of credit to contribute to the cause.

This was the point never included in our newbie speeches, never raised at all, not explicitly at least, but always effectively communicated by Jude to each and every new recruit: Contributions weren't required—but they were always welcome.

"I wasn't invited," I said, stalling.

Ani whacked me lightly on the shoulder. "Come on."

Okay, so everyone knew d-day parties were open to all. And I'd long since gotten over my aversion to celebrating download anniversaries, at least when it came to other mechs. I planned to let my own slip by without the streamers and linked dreamers and rousing choruses of "Happy Death-day to You."

But I suspected Ani wasn't going to leave, not unless I left with her—and maybe disappearing into a noisy crowd wasn't the worst idea. In the quiet, it was too easy to hear Auden's voice. *I believe it didn't mean to hurt me.*

He'd never been a good liar.

Quinn's estate was an odd mix of ancient and modern, brick and stone mingling uncomfortably with glass and solar-paneled steel. It wasn't that unusual these days to see structures that straddled the architectural ages. Tacky owners remaking a perfectly good house in their own image, a jumbled mash-up of trends past their sell-by date, plus a little old-school charm to offer a hint of respectability. But Quinn's parents had had plenty of taste—unfortunately, they'd had significantly less luck and had died before the renovations were completed. *I like it this way,* Quinn told me once, explaining why she'd never finished the job. *Like it doesn't care about being one thing or another. It's okay being everything at once.*

The mansion didn't have a fairy-tale ballroom, but the domed observatory in the south wing came close enough. Nearly thirty feet across with ceilings almost as high, the observatory offered a superb view of the night sky through its windowed walls and dome, even if the stars had long ago disappeared behind a layer of thick red clouds. Now the dome was lit up with flickering projections—not, I was relieved to see, glamour shots of Brahm's nude mech form (a new trend in d-day commemorations). Instead, it was a live feed from the pool house, the writhing bodies of linked dreamers smeared across the sky.

Music pumped and a few mechs twirled in the center of the observatory, their rhythmic movements mirroring the wild gyrations of the dreamers projected above them. Several others were playing at slam, a mech riff on rugby that forewent the ball and the scoring in favor of mass tackles, often propelled by sneaker jets. Points were awarded for style and speed of collision; losers were often required to relinquish an article of clothing. Judging from the flesh on display, they'd been playing for a while.

"Should we congratulate the death-day boy?" I asked, scanning the crowd for Brahm.

"I think he's busy," Ani said sourly, jerking her head at the wide metal stump at the center of the room, which Quinn claimed had once held a massive telescope, before the cloud cover rendered it useless. Only the base had been left behind, a vestigial artifact, its metal skin glowing in the flickering lights, an altar to the party gods. And perched on top, two bodies in their death-day suits, swaying in time to a music none of us could hear—the divine offering.

"You want to get out of here?" I asked Ani, as Quinn stuck her tongue down Brahm's throat.

Ani shrugged. "Everyone deserves a d-day kiss, right?"

"You want me to go up there and drag her off him?" I said, only half-joking. "Because I will."

Ani shook her head, her face a rictus of pleasant disinterest. I dragged her across the room, dodging the slam players and positioning us against the windows, hoping she'd have a strong enough self-preservation instinct to turn her back on the room and look out at the night.

When she didn't, I put my hands on her shoulders and did it for her.

"Tell me this doesn't bother you," I challenged her.

Ani met my eyes without flinching. "She does what she wants."

"And that's okay with you?"

"Jude says—"

I pressed my palm flat against the window, blotting out a hand-shaped chunk of the orchard spread beneath us. The window was ice against my synflesh—Brahm liked his temperatures extreme. "Forget what Jude says."

"But he's right," Ani said quietly. "Monogamy's an org thing. We shouldn't be trying to make it work for us. We're better than that."

"Fine, let's say you're right. So who else is on your list?" I turned my back on the window and peered into the crowd, trying to pick out faces in the murk. But the only person I recognized was Jude, leaning against a wall, arms crossed, eyes on me. Even from this distance, even in the dim light, I saw him see me, smile—and turn away.

"I don't have a list," Ani said.

I shook my head and faced the window again. "Exactly. So why does Quinn get to have one?"

"It's not like that," Ani insisted. "She missed a lot. She's just . . . enjoying herself."

"So what's Jude's excuse?" I muttered under my breath.

Too loud—she heard me.

"He missed a lot too," Ani said very quietly. She refused to ever speak about Jude's past, or Riley's. It was the only thing she wouldn't back down on. They'd been there when she needed them, protectors, Jude especially. Like the big brothers she saw in vid-lifes, she'd once confessed, the kind of no-questions-asked reliability that she'd always assumed was imaginary, and beyond even the realm of imagination for someone like her. She would, and did, talk about this unseen aspect of Jude ad nauseum. *You don't know him like I know him*—it was her go-to explanation for everything. "But I don't think it's about that for him. I think he's just—"

"A man whore?" I suggested.

She laughed, looking around guiltily as if he could hear us. "He's trying to prove something," Ani said.

"Whatever. As long as he doesn't try to prove it to me." Apparently mech guys were as disgusting as org ones. You'd think BioMax could have improved on the defective male brain, but if you believed what they said, they wouldn't know how to even if they wanted to. Apparently, replicating was easier than altering. It was hard, getting people to change.

Ani looked surprised. "You mean you two haven't . . . ?"

"Are you kidding?" I shuddered. Resisting the urge to turn again, check to see if he was watching me. "Not. Interested."

"If you say so."

"Look, I realize you all worship him or something, but—"

"Not worship," Ani cut in. "Admire."

Right. *Admire.* That's why they all followed him around like groupies, doing and saying anything to weasel further into his favor.

They?

I told the voice in my head to shut up. It was different with me. I understood what Jude was trying to do, and I believed in it. That was different than believing in *him.* Believing in people was nearly as useless as believing in some invisible all-powerful guy who lived in a cloud. People were unreliable, even the mechanical ones.

"So." I leaned forward. "Since you think he's so great, does that mean you—?"

"No!" Ani recoiled at the idea.

"At the rate he's been going, I guess that makes us the only two left."

"Three."

"Doubtful."

"Not Quinn," she said. "He promised."

"Promised that he hasn't? Or that he wouldn't?" I asked, glancing up at the pedestal out of the corner of my eye. Quinn and Brahm were still going at it. I wondered what she would do if she knew Ani had come to the party. Or if she'd expected nothing less.

"Hasn't and wouldn't," Ani insisted. "Won't."

"If you say so."

"*He* says so," Ani said. "That's good enough." She tipped her head forward and pressed it to the glass. Just for a moment. And when she looked up, she was smiling. "I'm in the mood to slam something," she said, jerking a thumb at the idiots barreling into each other at full force, their skulls knocking with audible cracks. "You in?"

I'd played once before. It required no skill, unless you counted a total lack of restraint and a willingness to eventually find yourself crushed beneath a wriggling mass of sharp elbows and flailing feet. It was, when played right, like becoming a human pinball, ricocheting from body to wall to body again, limbs twisting and tangling. Hurling yourself into a stranger, hearing their bones crack against your head or their surprised grunt as your weight smashed down on their shoulders and sent you both toppling to the ground, left little room for rational thought. The world became pure matter in motion, action and reaction. It was brainless and stupid. I couldn't think of a better way to spend the night.

ALL FALL DOWN

"Everyone was happy."

T he days had no shape. They passed, which was good enough.
It was a Friday when Jude sent me to the corp-town, not
that it mattered, because when you didn't have school or a job
or contact with the world beyond the bounds of the estate,
when the seasons only shifted from cold and gray to colder and
grayer, when you didn't age and the sentence of your life had no
foreseeable period, marking time became a formality.

But I remember it was a Friday.

He was in the vidroom, pumping the Brotherhood's zone.
It was all he ever did anymore, scanning the texts and vids they
posted, Savona testifying before congressional subcommittees,
Auden meeting and greeting fellow victims who'd suffered at the
mechanical hands of the skinners, testimonials from new members,

rigged debates with purported supporters of BioMax, who mumbled and stumbled their way through a halfhearted defense of the download technology before bowing to the inevitable, conceding that Savona was right and vowing to do everything in their power to take down the tech from within.

That was the party line: Eliminate the download, not its recipients. Hate the sin, not the skinner. Savona didn't want to destroy us, he just wanted to strip us of our credit accounts, our citizenship, our identities, ourselves. He wanted it known that we were machines, and just as machines had their place, so did we.

It was beginning to rain when I got summoned. Riley was already there, slouched on a couch, his legs kicked up on one of its arms. Quinn and Ani were there too, not much of a surprise since Quinn had been hanging around Jude more than ever lately, and where Quinn went, Ani was sure to follow.

"I need you and Riley to run an errand for me," Jude said, barely lifting his eyes from the screen. "He'll fill you in. If you leave now, you should make it back by tonight."

A road trip with Riley, the wordless wonder? No thanks. "Did I miss a memo? Since when do I take orders from you?"

Jude turned to me, miming surprise. But he knew exactly how much I hated the glorious dictator act. "Let me rephrase: Dearest, most valued, exceedingly busy Lia, can you do me this minor favor? Pretty please, with a cherry-flavored dreamer on top?"

"Forget it," Quinn said, standing up. "I'll go."

Jude shook his head once, sharply. "Lia's going."

"Why?" Quinn and I said together. She glared at me.

Jude looked back and forth between the two of us, a smile playing on his lips. "Because I trust her."

"And not me, right?" Quinn slumped back down on the couch. "Very nice."

Ani rested a hand on her back, rubbing slow, wide arcs along her spine. "I trust you," she murmured. Quinn shrugged her off.

I wasn't sure which would be worse: leaving with Riley and enduring endless hours of his sulky scowl, or staying to bask in the stench of Ani's desperation.

"How about you go yourself?" I suggested.

"Busy," Jude said, turning back to the vidscreen.

"So send Riley alone," I said. "Or are we working on the buddy system now?"

"One to pick up the package," Jude said. "The other to watch the drop."

Much as I hated it when Jude pulled the need-to-know spy crap on us, I couldn't help it; I was intrigued. "The package of . . . ?"

Jude shrugged. "Could be dreamers, could be new tech. Hell, for all I know, they're giving us wings. Ours is not to ask, but to receive and enjoy."

Quinn, Ani, and I all gaped at Jude. For months he'd been producing new, easily installed tech for our mech bodies—nothing major, a VM hookup here, nanojected titanium bone-knitters there, a microplayer that piped music inside your head. All untested, all unlicensed by BioMax, whose technicians—on the rare occasions when one of us showed up for a scheduled monthly tune-up or the more frequent emergency trips post-collision, crash, or other such self-inflicted catastrophe—eyed the tech with badly disguised suspicion and fear. The suspicion I got. Jude didn't have to spell it out: He obviously had a connection at BioMax, some employee or former employee who'd decided to field-test the newest toys. But I never understood the fear. Especially since they didn't even know the whole story. They saw the tech, because that was impossible to hide. But they didn't know anything about the dreamers.

Of course, neither did the rest of us, if "anything" included where they came from, why they existed, or how they did what they did. Letting Jude believe he could order me around seemed like a small price to pay to find out.

Riley spoke six words on the drive.

One and two: *You'll see.*

Three: *Yes.*

Four: *No.*

I asked my first two questions—*Where are we going? Have you been there before?*—as the car sped past the fields bordering the estate, spotted free-range cows grazing in a sea of genetically engineered green. I figured Riley would insist on driving manually, since he seemed the type, but he left the car in automatic, keyed in the mystery destination, and settled into the driver's seat, apparently content to silently watch the road stream by.

"You ever learn how to drive manual?" I asked after half an

hour had passed. That earned me word number four, a quiet "No." Paired with a cool gaze that efficiently transmitted the message: *You're dumber than I thought.*

Asshole, I thought. But I was the asshole. As if anyone learned to drive growing up in a city. Like there were any working cars in a place where energy was rationed so carefully that no one got more than a couple hours of electricity to spread out over a day. And what would he have needed a car for, anyway? Anywhere you needed to go in a city, you could get to on foot—not that there was anywhere to go except for the central distribution facility for the occasional ration of food. I'd heard sometimes they even handed out meds, mostly the experimental ones, but sometimes there was a surplus of something useful but defunct. When it came to disposing of unwanted waste, better the city than the garbage.

"The government could afford to supply med-tech to the cities," Auden had once told me. Another of his conspiracy theories. Back then they'd seemed almost charming. "They just don't want to. They figure people who are sick and starving don't have time to be angry."

"But wouldn't being sick and starving give them *more* reason to be angry?" I'd pointed out.

"You just don't get it," he'd said that time, like he'd said whenever I called him on one of his elaborate plots. It was why—aside from the fact that it bored the hell out of me—we usually tried not to talk politics. I couldn't help feeling like Auden, who usually listened to me more intently and less judgmentally than anyone I'd ever known, was dismissing everything I had to say under the basic theory of: *You don't get it and you never will.*

I had to admit that had been one of the benefits of dating a brainburner like Walker. However much care his parents had put into selecting the genes destined to give him that perfect smile, those eminently strokable biceps, the scruffy brown hair, the square jaw and the cleft chin, they'd overlooked certain other aspects of his development. Which is to say, if you're going to be dumb but pretty, you'd better be *really* pretty—and willing to let your girlfriend take the lead. Walker was both. Of course, dumb had its drawbacks too. It made it harder to understand the subtleties of situations like your girlfriend getting her brain dumped into a machine—and easier to fall into bed with her sister.

Though even brain-bulging Auden hadn't been smart enough not to follow me to that waterfall. Lose a liver, gain a new conspiracy theory. The most successful one yet, so maybe it had all worked out for him in the end. *Maybe he should be thanking me.*

Just when you think you can't hate yourself any more, a thought like that slithers through your brain.

But before I could look around for a helpful self-impalement tool, the car stopped, and Riley spat out words number five and six.

"We're here."

Synapsis Corp-Town was twice the size of the only other one I'd visited, my godfather's corp-town about a hundred miles south.

I was nine when my father decided it was time for me to see how the other nine-tenths of the country lived. "This is why I make you work so hard," he'd told me, resting a heavy hand on my shoulder. "Take your eye off the prize, just for a second, and you could end up in a place like this." But even then I knew it would never happen. I was young not stupid: Even if I morphed into a zoned-out, brainburned loser, my father would never let me sell myself to a corp-town. Imagine the humiliation—the *public* humiliation—were a *Kahn* to end up working a line twelve hours a day, administering gen-mods to soy crops or keying data for the credit crunchers, then going home to corp-supplied housing, feeding her family with corp-supplied food, staying healthy with corp-supplied med-tech, voting for the corp-supplied candidates, obeying each and every corp-supplied rule lest she have it all stripped away from her and end up in a city. My brain may have been a computer, but the corp-towners were the ones who ran on a program, their lives prescribed, their every word and move coordinated by a central processing unit. The corps were machines, and the corp-towners were just the cogs, the gears, the fuel that made them run.

The corp-town stretched across more than fifteen square miles, but most of that was taken up by manufacturing and agricultural concerns. According to the schematic that greeted us at the entry gate, the eastern half of the compound was reserved for farmland, acres of modified corn and soy crops that would eventually be ground into the tasteless nutri-grain that formed the bulk of nearly all corp-town food. We'd all gotten a taste of it in elementary school—one full day of nutri-pops, nutri-shakes, nutri-burgers. It had been enough to last a lifetime. They say corp-towners develop a taste for the stuff, that they'd prefer it to real-world food if they ever got a choice. But no corp-town had ever tested the theory.

Riley swiped an ID card across the scanner at the gate, and our faces popped up on the screen with two unfamiliar names scrolling beneath them. He shot me a quick look, like I'd be dumb enough to protest where the corp authorities might be listening. But I kept my mouth shut, resolving later to find out where Jude had gotten his hands on such ridiculously good fakes. Add it to the list of things I'd probably never know.

A light flashed green and the gate swung open.

"End of the line," Riley said, hopping out of the car. I followed. Corp-towns were car-free zones—ours would presumably find its way to a nearby lot, while we tooled around on the blue solar-powered cart that was already waiting for us. We climbed into the narrow vehicle, which noticeably shuddered when it took on our weight. The rusty thing looked like it hadn't been replaced—or even retooled—since the corp-town was first built.

"Destination?" its nav-system requested.

"Residential, A-three," Riley said.

I felt like a child—or, worse, like a *pet*, towed around on a leash. Following obediently and unquestioningly after my master.

"Ever been to one of these before?" Riley asked as we sputtered into slow, lurching motion.

I grunted something that could have been a yes or a no. Just because *he* was suddenly and inexplicably in the mood for conversation didn't mean I had to oblige. Despite the leash, I was no puppy.

The corp-town wasn't quite *pretty*—it was too manicured for that, its stacked cubes of productivity too regimented and too concrete—but it wasn't quite the wasteland I remembered from my childhood. The large pool of waste water dotted by mirrored solar-collecting lily pads was nearly beautiful, especially with the reflection of purple-tinged clouds unfurling across its still surface. Of course, I was lucky—being a mech, I didn't have to deal with the smell.

The heart of Synapsis, like all corp-towns, was the housing complex, a cluster of ten massive glass cubes, each about thirty stories high. Glassed-in skyways spiderwebbed from these to the outlying factories, where Synapsis workers repaid the corporation's beneficence. I didn't know enough about Synapsis Corp to guess what was going on inside the concrete block buildings (the glass walls of the housing cubes sucked up plenty of solar energy, but privacy apparently took precedence over energy efficiency when it came to protecting industrial secrets). Not that it mattered, since these days all corps did pretty much the same thing. Plenty of programming and systems maintenance, a dash of information processing, a smidge of chem- and bio-engineering, probably even a pinch of manual labor for flavor. Yes, machines could do almost anything, but human labor was just as efficient, half as expensive, and, especially when it came to exceedingly toxic waste or toxic working conditions, 100 percent more disposable.

"Why would anyone want to do that?" I'd asked my god-father, confused by the pale, ashen-faced workers spilling out of their underground burrows.

"No one *wants* to," he'd said, and left it at that.

So it fell to my father to explain: Not all corp jobs were created equal. Which was why jobs were assigned rather than chosen. It was easier that way, more orderly, more efficient. Joining a corp-town meant free housing, free food, free med-tech—and it meant accepting the job you were given. Whatever job the corp-minders judged you to deserve.

"People like choice," my father had said. "But they like food even more." And it was easier on everyone to have a nation of employees than a nation of beggars. So everyone was happy.

The few who weren't, the few who preferred to make their own rules—have too many children, vote for whoever they wanted, eat more than their ration of soymeat, use more than their ration of power—well, they were welcome to move to a city and see for themselves how freedom tasted. If they were good enough, they might even get out again. This was America, after all. Anyone could get ahead.

That's what my father had always told me.

The residence cubes were identical and unmarked, leaving us no choice but to trust the cart when it deposited us at an entrance. Behind the transparent walls, thousands scurried back and forth through a multileveled atrium, denizens of an oversize ant farm. Towering above our heads were the hundreds of privacy-free residential units, cubes within cubes, complete with all the comforts of a 15 x 15-foot home.

Riley led us into the ground-level atrium, its carpet of artificial grass gleaming green in artificial sunlight that belied the dark gloom beyond its walls. Corp-towners worked on a three-shift system, one-third working while the other two-thirds slept or played, so even in the middle of the day, there were more orgs than I'd expected milling about the plaza, toting bags of food and clothes and whatever other crap they wasted their corp-credit on. Orgs everywhere, cozying up to one another on park benches, strolling hand in hand down paths lined with fake stepping stones, people crowding in and out of the elevators that would speed them up or down to their housing module. Maybe it wasn't more people than I'd ever seen in one place, but knowing that there were thirty levels above us and another twenty carved out of the ground below, all of them equally packed, made me want out.

Not that any of them came near us. As we walked down one of the curving paths, a vacuum opened in the crowd, as if an invisible force were clearing our way. And as they edged backward, they stared. And whispered. At least, some of them whispered—some insulted us in raised voices, unashamed.

"What are *they* doing here?"

"It's uglier than I thought."

"What do you think it's thinking?"

A laugh. "As if it thinks."

"Mom, it's looking at me." That was a whiny kid, pink hair, baggy overalls hanging over a matching pink hug shirt, the kind I'd loved when I was a kid. For a few blissfully simple months, trading hug shirts had been the perfect declaration of best friendship: You had only to wrap your arms across your chest and, no matter where she was, your best friend would feel the hug. We'd all dug them out again in junior high—boyfriends made the tech infinitely more entertaining. There was nothing like sitting through an intensely boring biotech lecture and suddenly feeling the warmth and pressure of invisible arms wrapping you in an invisible embrace.

Two men, not old, not young, scruff blotting their faces like a rash. One to the other. "Would you? For a thousand?"

The other. "*Ten* thousand. Maybe. But only the girl one."

"Hell, I'd slam it for free. Try anything once, right?"

An old woman, her tan, dry skin taut from one too many shoddy lift-tucks, the best you could get in a corp-town. "You shouldn't be here."

Not all the stares were hostile—there were plenty who watched us closely, neutrally, like little kids watching an anthill, placing bets on which insects would wander off and fry in the sun.

Riley deposited me on a bench just opposite a small fountain flickering with water and colored light. "This is where you meet him," he said. "I'll be watching from up there." He pointed to the level above us, where two girls a couple years younger than me were leaning against a railing, making a pathetic show of ignoring the boys goggling them from beneath. The floors, like nearly everything in the atrium, were made of glass; the girls were wearing skirts and had apparently decided to put on a little show.

I raised my eyebrows at Riley.

He scowled. "Over *there*," he said pointedly, nodding at an open spot on the railing, suitably far from the giggling exhibitionists. "If anything seems off, I'll VM you."

"How am I supposed to know who 'him' is?"

"He'll find you," Riley said. "Just take the package. Don't tell him I'm here. Don't ask any questions—and don't answer any."

Stay with me, I almost said, watching the orgs watch me. But that would be paranoid and weak, and I was neither. "So get out of here before 'he' shows up."

With Riley gone, the whispers grew. It was like his silence had been loud enough to drown them out, but now they were all I could hear. Or maybe now that I was alone, the people were getting bolder. I waited for one of them to take the next step.

If something happened, would any of them try to stop it? None of the tech upgrades we'd gotten had made us any faster or stronger. No martial arts savvy downloaded directly to the motor cortex, no superhero skills whatsoever. Just a titanium head and some bones that were nearly impossible to break.

Nothing's going to happen. No violence, that was rule number one in every corp-town, and violating it was the fastest way to get yourself ejected. One of the vidscreens flashing overhead made the point in stark terms, broadcasting a looped vid of two men wrestling, a knife flashing in each of their hands. As the

69

background shifted from the corp-town plaza to a desolate city street, blood spurted and the men fell backward, still. The moral of the story scrolled across the screen—*Live like an animal, die like an animal*—and then the whole thing started again.

The rest of the vidscreens were flashing pop-ups for corp-produced goods and services to be bought with corp-credit—corp-towners got paid in play money that was only good within the bounds of the corp-town, forming a neatly closed circle between corp and employee. Within the corp-town, everything went cheap; play money let the poor playact at being rich. You could trade in your corp-credit for real credit, but only if you wanted to sacrifice all your purchasing power, foregoing a corp-supplied wardrobe or a kitchen full of corp-supplied food in favor of one box of real chocolate or a slab of real organic beef. I never understood why any of them would have bothered trying to buy anything in the outside world—but then, I never understood why they would set foot in the outside world in the first place. And most of them didn't.

"It's easier that way," I'd told Auden once, cutting into one of his rants. "Why would they want to see what they can't have?"

"It's easier for *us* that way," Auden had replied. "We pen them up, like we pen up the city people, and then we don't have to think about them. Or see them. We can just forget they exist."

"No one's stopping them from leaving the corp-towns—or the cities, for that matter. But why go where you don't belong?"

Leaving a corp-town was logistically almost as hard as leaving a city. Regulations restricted corp-towners to public transportation, and the last bus and train lines had died out years ago. What was the point, when the minority had cars of their own and the majority was better off staying put? There were a few jobs that required leaving the corp-town regularly on corp-transport—the shippers were always traveling back and forth, and the security-operations force were a regular presence, standing guard over the rest of us with their badges, their thermobaric grenades, their stunshots, and their don't-screw-with-me scowls that couldn't mask their boredom. Not to mention their bitterness at protecting a life they could never afford themselves. Small wonder that secops was as low on the desirability spectrum as wastewater management and human resources. At least the data-entry grunts got to stay hidden away in their glassy cubes—ignoring us, I'd always assumed, just as happily as we ignored them.

There was one recent exception to the stay-put rule—the Brotherhood of Man had begun sending buses to area corp-towns, offering residents a field trip to the newly completed Temple of Man. I wondered how many of the hostile faces surrounding me had witnessed Auden's little martyr show live and in person. How many looked at me and were afraid.

Twenty minutes passed, and Jude's mystery man didn't show. Another twenty, and still nothing.

I glanced up at Riley. He was resolutely ignoring the giggling girls—who were now taking turns boldly flashing their net-linked lingerie at *him*.

"Is he usually this late?" I VM'd.

"Never," came the answer. "Stay put. I'll voice Jude."

Of course, I thought in disgust. *Jude always knows what to do.* The all-knowing, all-powerful Jude had all the answers.

Then the sun went out.

Darkness, and then the world blazed red. I stood up as the alarm sang out, a single scream at the top of the octave. The crowds froze, faces tipped up toward the vidscreens, which all flashed the same useless message: *Alert. Biohazard. Alert.*

The red strobe flashed on, off, on. Glowing faces burst from the darkness, then dropped into shadow. The fountain bled pink, the rippling pool of water at its base a bottomless red.

I was staring at the fountain when I realized the noise had stopped. Not the alarm, which was still singing, but the sounds beneath it, the rustling, mumbling, shrieking, crying chaos of the crowd. Gone.

Ring around the rosie, a pocketful of posies.

The inane rhyme whispered through my head as they began to drop. They fell silent and still, their eyes bulging and mouths convulsing, fishlike, open shut open. Soundless. The two men with their dirt-beards, the old woman. The giggle twins, their giggles silenced, their skirts askew. Down, hard and ugly, heads cracking against plastic stone, arms jutting at odd angles. Down went the little kid, fingers clawing at her pink shirt. And her mother, down without a fight, her back to the kid.

Ashes, ashes.

Someone told me once that the nursery rhyme was about

the Black Plague. That the ring of roses referred to the disease's trademark red rash; the ashes to the burning bodies of the dead. But that was a lie: I looked it up. The words were nonsense; they meant nothing.

The red light pulsed rhythmically. I tried not to count the faces, hundreds of faces. Some of them twitched, chests heaving, sucking in air and whatever poison hid inside of it, whatever *biohazard* had touched off a useless, too late *alert alert alert*.

Some of them—one of the men, the girl, three women with chunky ankles and identical rings on their stubby fingers—prostrate, frozen. Askew. Their eyes open, their chests still.

Faces red, then pale, shadowy, *non*, then red again.

"We have to get out of here!" Riley's voice in my ear. Riley's shirt absurdly pulled over his face as if he had anything to fear from the poisoned air. Riley's hands on my shoulders. Riley, there, but seeming very far away. Riley alive and in motion, seeming wrong in the still, empty room. Empty until you looked down.

"Lia!" Riley grabbing me. Dragging me out of the plaza.

Running, stumbling over something lumpy and large that didn't make a sound as our feet sank into its chest.

Running without looking down, just step over them like stones, just go, Riley said, don't stop don't look just go.

Running and standing still, leaving a piece of myself in the empty atrium, still watching the red light pool in the whites of their eyes.

Ashes, ashes, we all fall down.

TOGETHER ALONE

"We're all better off now."

The red light turned to tears, trickled down pale, still faces. Their eyes were bleeding.

Alert! Biohazard! Alert! screamed the vidscreens, although there was no one left to warn.

"Get it together!" Riley's hands were rough on my arm and back, pushing me forward. "We have to get *out.*"

What's the hurry? I thought, a mad giggle rising in me. *No bio equals no hazard. Safe and sound.*

But I shook him off and I ran with him, down the dead, empty hall, the corp-town in lockdown, its residents hiding or evacuated. Or neither. Steel shutters had dropped to shield the glass walls, trapping us inside, in the dark. The biohazard protocol had locked even the glowing emergency exits, sealing the corp-town tight—no nasty microorganisms would escape to the outside world. And no mechs.

Riley went straight for the control panel to the right of the nearest exit and ripped off the cover. He began messing with the wires, stripping two of them with his teeth and winding them together, then touching them to a third, and before I could ask what the hell he was doing, the steel slid up toward the ceiling, and he pushed through the door. His hand gripped mine, tugged hard, and I followed.

We cut across the matted astroturf surrounding the residential cubes, ignoring the solar-powered cart that had carried us here—even if it wasn't on lockdown with the rest of the compound, it was too slow and too easily tracked by the secops. Alarms were blaring across the campus, and steel shutters had dropped across all the residence cubes, turning them into bunkers, a fitting accessory to the corp-cum–war zone. The air split with distant sirens. Thunder shook the sky. Except it wasn't thunder; it was a squadron of helicopters dropping toward the glass cube as the emergency vehicles, the fire trucks and ambulances, appeared on the horizon. Next would come the secops looking for someone to blame. I suspected we'd do.

"We didn't have to run," I said, my brain finally starting to work again, though I was still running, because he seemed so sure and I was so not. We passed the wastewater ponds and trampled through deserted soy fields. The workers had presumably all been hustled away to the underground safe houses dotting the perimeter, and only the reaping and spraying machines remained to witness us tearing through the knee-high fronds of sallow green. "We could have stayed—maybe we could have helped."

Riley sped up. "We're helping ourselves."

We ran for miles, quickly crossing the boundaries of the corp-town into open country. Security at the borders was light—in most spots nonexistent—and it would probably take at least an hour before the secops had a chance to cover the grounds. In the meantime, the more distance we could put between us and them, the better. Mech bodies didn't tire, so we just kept going. Through industrial wastelands and past smokestacks puffing purified clouds into foggy sky, beyond the boundaries of the corp-town, away from the sirens, through flat fields and more fields, staying off the road, feet tramping through the high grass, another mile and another stretching between us and the corp-town. I'd been a runner, before, and I knew my stride. Counting paces was easier than thinking, so I focused on the wet thump of our shoes on the soggy ground, marking off five miles, then ten, then twenty. Until a cloud of green mushroomed on the horizon, resolving itself, as we drew nearer and nearer, into a wide, dense grove of trees. We'd reached the border of a Sanctuary, twenty square miles of unspoiled wilderness, off-limits to orgs. Which meant, except for the birds and squirrels and deer, we were alone.

"Here," Riley said, letting himself slam into a thick trunk, wrapping his arms around the tree and pressing his cheek to the bark. "This is good enough."

"For what?"

"For keeping our heads down." He sank to the ground, hands plunged into the layer of dead leaves swimming beneath the trees.

"You act like we did something wrong." *And maybe we did,* I thought, remembering the faces. Eyes open, watching me, watching nothing. *We could have stayed. We ran.*

"Wake up, Lia," he snapped. "You think it was an accident, that happening when we were there?"

"I don't think anything. I don't even know what *that* was."

"It was a setup."

"You think that was about *us*?" *Because* of us, is what I meant to say. Is what I didn't want to say.

He shrugged. "If not, we have some pretty shit luck."

"What else is new?"

"I'm staying," he said with sullen finality. "Do what you want. I don't care."

As if he would leave me behind. It didn't matter how much he sulked, I could tell: He wasn't the type. "If you don't care, how come you didn't just leave me there?"

"Wasn't thinking," he said. "Now I am."

I sat down next to him. The ground was spongy. Dry leaves crunched beneath my weight. "Those orgs," I said, quiet. "People. You think they . . ."

"Yeah." Riley looked down at his hands, still hidden in the leaves. "Some of them, at least. I don't know."

Some of them what? Died, or lived?

"I never—" I stopped, about to say I'd never seen a dead body, but that was wishful thinking. I'd seen my own, burned and broken, brain scooped out for slicing and dicing and scanning.

"What?"

"Nothing."

Sometimes it was useful being a mech, staying blank and keeping things inside. The problem came when you wanted to get them out. If I'd been trembling, if I'd been sweating or pale and cold or shivering uncontrollably, if I'd puked until there was nothing left but bile, if I'd felt anything in my body, then maybe my brain could have taken a break. Of course, if I was in a position to do any of those things, I wouldn't have been sitting in the dark, rain beginning to patter against the leaves. I probably would have been dead.

Riley wouldn't let me link in to the network. "They could use it to track us."

"We don't even know if 'they' are looking for us," I argued. "And even if they are, you can't track people through the network."

He gave me a weird look. "Who told you that?"

"No one had to *tell* me. Everyone just knows."

"You want to link in, you do it somewhere else," he said. "Away from me."

I didn't want to go anywhere. "How long you think we need to wait?"

"Couple days maybe. To be safe."

"Here?"

He almost smiled. "You got somewhere to be?"

Nowhere to be, no need to eat or sleep, nothing to do except find a way to stop seeing what I'd seen. And I had to admit, he'd picked a good hiding spot. All Sanctuaries had periodic ranger sweeps to make sure the orgs stayed out, but the odds of anyone finding us in the next day or two were pretty minuscule.

"You can shut down if you want," Riley suggested. "I'll keep watch."

And lie there unconscious, trusting him to make decisions for the both of us? "I don't think so."

He tipped his head up, as if there were anything to see but dead branches. "Whatever."

We sat there silently for a while. I almost laughed, remembering how much I'd dreaded having to spend a few hours in a car with him. Now here we were, playing at being alone in the world. But I didn't laugh—thinking I'd been right not wanting to come.

Weird how tiny, stupid decisions make all the difference.

"You want to talk about it?" Riley said suddenly.

"What?"

"You know. What happened."

Now I did laugh.

"What?" he asked, looking almost hurt.

"Since when do *you* want to *talk*?" I asked, still laughing, but only in my head, where I couldn't stop. *This is hysteria,* I thought, my mental voice wracked with giggles, my body still and calm. Riley rested a hand on my upper arm, like he knew, and somehow it quieted the noise. He pulled his hand away.

"I didn't say I wanted to talk," he said. "I asked if *you* wanted to."

"Fine," I said. "But not about that."

He nodded.

"Tell me something," I ordered him. It felt good to boss a guy around. Normal, almost.

"Like what?"

"I don't know. Anything."

He looked more blank than usual.

"Like, tell me how you did that back there with the door," I suggested. I didn't particularly care, but it was something to say.

"I used to do a lot of that stuff," he said. "It came in handy."

I didn't have to ask him *when*. It was the same nebulous *before* we all had and never talked about. Jude's law. *And Jude knows best, right?*

"Okay, but *how* did you do it? Who taught you?"

He shrugged. "I just figured it out."

"Fine." I crossed my arms. "Great."

"What?"

"Nothing."

"Why do you always look at me like that?" he asked.

"Like what?"

"Like I'm saying something wrong. Usually when I'm not even saying anything."

"You're *never* saying anything," I pointed out.

"I am right now," he said. "You've still got the look."

"Maybe because you're still not actually saying anything. Not really."

"You're strange," he said. "Anyone ever told you that?"

"Not really, no," I said coolly. Strange meant not fitting in; I defined *in*. "I saw a pic of you," I added, turning it back on him. "You and Jude and Ani. From before."

Jude had freaked out when he'd heard that, when I threw in his face that I knew what he'd been, *before*. Riley didn't react.

"It was a long time ago," he said tonelessly.

"Less than two years. Not so long."

"Long enough."

"So you and Jude, you were friends?" I asked, even though that much I knew. "Before?"

Riley smiled, a real smile, one of the first I could remember seeing on him. Sometimes, with mechs, a smile could transform the face into something even less human—the expression somehow incongruous on the synthetic lips, a quaint and unsettling party trick, like a dog propped at the dinner table with a fork and spoon. But Riley's smile was natural enough, and it made the rest of him seem more real. "You know Jude hates talking about the past."

I glanced over my shoulder as if making sure. "Yeah, Jude's definitely not here," I said. "So?"

"So nice try," he said, then grimaced like he couldn't stand *not* to answer. "But yeah, we were. Best friends."

"Funny that he didn't ditch you along with the rest of his past," I said. "All part of embracing our bright new mech future, right?"

But Jude's friendship with Riley apparently fit into the same category as our org names, one of the few things we weren't obligated to dump in the garbage as a testament to our new lives. In its own way, continuity was as important as discontinuity, Jude maintained. The radical break from our past, from our old families and old values, could only have meaning if we kept some core piece of ourselves intact—and then, of course, there was the small practical matter that keeping at least a tenuous grasp on our old identities was necessary if we wanted access to our zones and credit. And so the past was irrelevant . . . except when it suited him. When he needed it to pay the bills or to guarantee loyalty. Or to throw it in my face, remind me how I'd ended up with him and why. That was the thing about Jude. He spoke with conviction, but sometimes the distinctions he drew seemed arbitrary, invented ad hoc to serve his own purposes. Then he turned preference into principle, and his particular conveniences became our general rule.

Though Jude would just say I wasn't seeing the big picture, and that's why I needed him.

I gathered Riley would agree. He raised his eyebrows. "You don't buy it. That we're all better off now."

"So what if I don't?"

"Let me guess . . ." He tapped a finger against his lips as if he were choosing his words carefully, but the pause was too studied to be natural. He knew exactly what he wanted to say. "You go along with it, and you don't talk about what you miss, because no one else seems to miss anything, and you figure that's the way to go. It works for them, so it should work for you. Or it will. Till then, you keep your mouth shut."

"What makes you think that?"

Because that was less of an admission than *How'd you know?*

He didn't bother to answer either question. "Ever think they don't miss anything because they don't have anything to miss?"

"Well, obviously," I spit out. And at the beginning, I'd taken refuge in that. *I wasn't like you*, I'd told Quinn. *I was whole.* "I'm not saying I don't have anything to miss, I'm just saying it's pointless. It's better to just forget."

"That doesn't make it easy," he said.

It was getting dark. And probably colder too, but temperature wasn't something I noticed anymore. I registered it—or, at least, the body registered it—but I didn't even feel it in the dim, distant way that I "felt" the ground was soft and wet, the bark rough against my back. It was a fact, an irrelevant one I'd learned to dismiss.

"In the pic, you were . . . you looked healthy," I said, not really expecting him to do much more than nod. He did. "But I thought all the volunteers—" I cut off the word. "The early test subjects," I corrected myself. "I thought you were all . . ."

"Defective?" he asked wryly. "Injured or diseased, without any options? Desperate?" He pressed his lips together in a thin, tight line. "Some of us had options," he said after a moment. "Just not good ones."

It was so irritating, all this ridiculous secrecy. "What's the big deal?" I said, frustrated. "Like I really care about where you or Jude came from."

That smile was playing on his lips again. "Could've fooled me."

"You don't want to talk about it, don't. Whatever. I just don't get the big deal about saying what happened."

"Like what happened with Auden?" he said.

I froze. We stared at each other, and it was clear Riley knew he'd won, but it wasn't a Jude-like smirk on his face, acknowledging the inevitability of his triumph. It was just something patient and watchful.

"Chocolate," I said finally, turning the clock back to an easier question. "I miss that. And running."

"You didn't get enough of that just now?" he said lightly.

"Not the same."

"If you say so. What else?"

Walker's lips—anyone's lips. The pleasure-pain of fingers tickling down my spine. Chillers, about a half hour into the dose, when everything made sense and nothing mattered. Crying. Boring Thursday night dinners, mocking my mother, preening under my father's praise.

Yelling at Zo.

"No," I said. "Your turn."

"Fine. Sweat." He laughed. "Stop looking at me like that."

"You're going to have to clarify: Is this 'the look' you claim I always give you, or some new look? It's hard to keep track."

"The look that says you think it's weird."

"You miss sweat? That *is* weird," I agreed. "But there's no look."

It wasn't that weird. I was a runner. Had been a runner. I understood about sweat.

"And burgers," he added. "A night on the roof with a perfectly grilled soy burger—"

"Soy?" I wrinkled my nose. "If it's not beef, it's not a burger."

"I wouldn't know." His voice was frosty.

Right, because once they'd stopped mass-producing beef, there wasn't enough to go around. I'd done it again: forgotten the obvious. Who I was. Who he'd been. I vowed to myself that I wouldn't do it again.

"Would you go back?" I asked. The forbidden question. But the rules didn't apply here.

He stretched his arms behind his head, grasping the trunk he was leaning against as if he wanted to uproot the tree. "I don't ask myself that."

"I don't believe you," I said. "You weren't like them. You were whole. Healthy. You had a *life*."

"Like you?" he said. "Before whatever happened, happened?"

"Before my *accident*," I said loudly. One of us wasn't afraid to say it out loud. "And yes, like me."

"I wasn't like you."

"Why not?"

"You think you deserved it?" he asked. "Your accident? This?"

"Of course not!"

"Well, maybe I did." Riley stood up and walked a few trees away, then sat down again. Close enough that we could still see each other, far enough that there would be no more talk. So we watched each other, and we watched the clouds drift across the wine red sky, and we waited for things to be safe.

"You sure?" I asked, hesitating over the link. The flexi ViM screen was only a few inches across with a strip on the back that adhered to the underside of my left arm. At its maximum length, which it was set at now, it fit perfectly in the stretch from my wrist to my elbow—but with slight pressure it would compress to a palm-size screen I could wrap around my wrist or slip into my pocket. The image quality wasn't great, but I didn't need a hi-res reminder of the death we'd escaped.

"Not really," Riley said as my finger hovered over the screen. It was set to link in whenever I swiped a Z across its face—after managing the first two slashes, I'd frozen before the third. It was Riley's fault. I'd spent two days chafing at his paranoia, and now that—based on no evidence whatsoever aside from the fact that time had passed and we were still here—he had decided it was safe, I couldn't help feeling like linking in to the network would call the darkness down on us. Or at least the secops.

We didn't do anything wrong, I reminded myself.

"It's time, Lia." The rangers would eventually catch us in a sweep; the longer we waited, the more inevitable our discovery became.

We linked in.

The news zones were lit up with updates about reports of the bio-attack. We picked a zone at random, setting the vid filter for most watched.

42 dead, 231 injured, the cap read.

Suspects at large.

Skinner slayings stun nation! That one was in bold.

Riley played one of the vids, a grainy aerial shot from the eye in the sky, and there I was. Upright and still as three hundred people collapsed around me.

"Shut it off," I said, my voice as cool and even as ever.

The skinner stands alone, read the cap.

The me in the vid wasn't panicking, she wasn't kneeling down to help the victims, she wasn't doing anything but watching it all play out, calm as if she'd expected it.

Riley froze the vid. "You don't have to watch these," he said. "I can fill you in later."

Because he was strong and I was weak? No. "Just play the next one," I ordered him. This one we watched all the way through. Along with the one after that.

We heard how the attackers had slipped past the security system, easily evading the biostat sensors, because, of course, they had no biostats. They'd released an aerated form of Naxophedrine into the air vents leading to the plaza. The toxin had been a favored weapon of choice back in the bad old days when you could barely walk down a city street without getting hit by, among other unpleasantries of modern life, shrapnel, radioactive dust, or weaponized squirrel flu—this before everyone wised up and got the hell out of the cities. Naxo had been one of the milder weapons—usually aimed at creating mass chaos rather than perpetrating mass murder. Among its known effects: heart palpitations, seizure, lung paralysis. All temporary.

Usually.

Authorities concluded that the attackers must have used an enhanced or unusually concentrated version of the chemical. Whatever it was, it had killed forty-two people. And then the attackers, the skinners, had slipped out as easily as they'd slipped in. Just like us.

Recriminations flew, and the Brotherhood of Man was doing its best to fan the flames. An unthinkable tragedy, but an inevitable one, the Honored Rai Savona said, repeating himself in infinite variations. Lax security despite the thousands of skinners set loose on the country, determined to transform their existential threat into a flesh-and-blood one? It was a miracle, Savona said, that something like this hadn't happened sooner. And given the fact that the skinners could slip through a security web designed to snag organic terrorists—criminals with finger- and eyeprints, with DNA-laced epithelia, with bodies they could alter but never abandon—it would be a miracle if it didn't happen again.

Issuing his edict of I-told-you-so doom, Savona did his best not to smile.

We watched the aftermath of the attack: spidercrawlers trawling the scene, their metallic tentacles snapping pics, searching for hidden explosives and time-release toxins, scrabbling over the bodies to triage the victims. And then the humans took over, alienlike figures, their faces distorted by thick biomasks, loading the wounded onto stretchers. We watched the secops swarm the atrium, stepping over and around the bodies that remained—intact bodies, healthy and whole, except for their pale skin, their open eyes blurry with blood.

We watched the attack from every angle, watched the orgs fall again and again, and each time, even though we knew what to expect, it came as a surprise—they were moving, they were laughing, they were fighting, and then they weren't anything.

We watched as the secops finally dealt with the dead. Shoved them into bags, zipped them up, dragged them out like trash. Watching it all play out on-screen made it less real and more real at the same time. It was no longer something that belonged to *us,* something chaotic and terrible and private. It was an *event* now, neat details packaged into a comprehensible narrative; it belonged to the world. It wasn't life—it was *news.*

Riley paused over the next vid, which hadn't been posted until the day after the attack. "Maybe we've seen enough," he said. Trying to protect me again? Not his job.

"Play it."

The vid was grainy and without sound. The camera bounced around and for a few seconds, it was hard to make out anything but shadows and blobs of light. The lens focused, revealing a group of masked figures. The camera panned across their faces, each covered in black. Then zoomed in on a smashed console emblazoned with the biohazard symbol. A quick cut to a grate, a hand holding an aerosol sprayer, a bluish mist drifting into an air duct.

A blur as the camera spun around, landing on the person holding it. She was the only one without a mask. Her face swam in and out of the frame as she set up the shot. Then she was clear, and she smiled.

A message from the mechs, read the cap.

Riley reached for the screen. One swipe of his finger and the face would disappear. I grabbed his wrist, squeezed it. Didn't meet his eyes; didn't want to see them rest on my face, then dart back to the face on the screen, her face.

Our face.

"You orgs want a war?" a murderer said in my voice. She smiled again, and it was my smile. "You got one." An alarm sounded. Her smile grew. "You know what happens next."

I did.

CITY LIGHTS

"I wasn't pretending to be human. I was over that."

Riley cut the link.

"That wasn't me," I said.

"I know."

"That *wasn't* me," I said again.

He nodded. "I know."

"But it wasn't—"

"Lia, stop." He put his hands on my shoulders like he was holding me steady. Like I was shaking. Which I wasn't. *"I know,"* he said. Slow and firm. "It wasn't you, it couldn't have been. You were in the atrium when the alarm sounded. I saw you. Besides, other than her face . . ." He didn't have to say the obvious. She'd had shorter hair, different clothes—black from head to toe, a killer and a cliché. She'd stood differently, moved differently. She was a physical copy, nothing more.

Riley was still holding on to me. I couldn't look at him. Instead, I linked in again, flipping through the vids until I found what I was looking for. It was cross-posted from the Brother-hood's zone. "I would never have expected *this*," Auden said in response to tepid questioning from some unseen interviewer. "But that's exactly the point, isn't it? You never really *know* a skinner. You only see the self they want you to see."

"Do you understand me?" Riley said, fingers tightening on my shoulders. "That. Wasn't. You."

But it had my face. My voice. My smile. Auden believed it was me. Anyone watching, anyone I'd ever known, would think it was me.

My father would think it was me.

"Just stay calm," Riley said, like he could see behind my steady gaze, steady hands, into the storm inside my head.

He cut the link again. "Take it nice and slow," he said. Sounding like my old track coach when we'd pushed ourselves too hard for too long and needed something to lean on. Strug-gling to fill our lungs.

Breathe in, breathe out, I thought, the hysteria creeping in again. *If only.*

"None of this is your fault." Riley leaned close, his voice warm and steady in my ear. "You didn't do this."

"It wasn't me," I said again after a long, silent moment, and this time I wasn't trying to convince him, or myself. It was just the only fact I had, a starting point.

"It wasn't you," he said in the same tone, and I could tell he got it. Crisis averted. For the moment. "I know that. But no one else will."

"What the hell is that supposed to mean?"

"Don't freak out," he said.

"Sorry, but did you not see the same vid I saw?" I snapped. "Because this is me freaking out."

"We have to voice Jude and—"

"And what?" I grabbed his arm as he was reaching for the ViM. "We leave him out of this."

"He'll know what to do," Riley said.

"Right. Because Jude always knows what to do."

"This is not a joke," he said in a low voice.

"You think I don't know that? Was that *your* face on the vid?"

He looked down at his arm, and I realized I was still holding on. I let go.

"Jude's the one who forced us to go to the corp-town," I reminded him. Forced *me*, specifically. No one else would do.

"So?"

"So if someone's setting us up, it hasn't occurred to you that Jude—"

He stood up abruptly. "He wouldn't do that."

"I'm not saying—"

"You better not. Or I'm out of here."

"Fine. I don't think he would ever do something like that." So I didn't want him to go; so I lied.

"Good. Because he wouldn't." Riley kept his eyes fixed on a low-hanging branch. There were still enough leaves clinging to the trees to block out most of the dim sunlight. The first night had been hard, huddling in the darkness, listening to the unfamiliar chitterings and hoots of the Sanctuary's protected species, wondering if there were wolves or bears or some other fanged predator of an earlier age prowling for fresh blood. Nothing seemed quite as dire once the sun came up, but after two days trapped in the trees, all I wanted was some sunlight and an open sky.

"I just said that, didn't I?" Best friends was one thing, but it was like Riley thought if he said one bad thing about Jude—or let anyone else release a single criticism into the universe—he'd be struck by lightning.

Jude's not God, I wanted to remind Riley.

But not as much as I wanted not to be left alone.

"The point is we shouldn't bring anyone else into this," I said. Thinking: Jude sent us to Synapsis Corp. Sent *me*. To meet a mysterious contact who never showed up. Thinking you'd have to be a moron not to wonder. Or an acolyte, blinded by faith. Same difference. "You said yourself, they could track us through the network—and now we know they're looking for us." Looking for *me*. "If we get in touch with Jude, we'd only make him look guilty. Bring down the secops on everyone."

"I don't know . . ."

"It's my life, right?" I said. Only one mech had turned her

face to the camera. A few shots had caught Riley running away, but he'd been the smart one, covering his face with his shirt. No one was looking for him. "If we're going to take a risk, it should be my decision."

"And you don't trust him," Riley said sourly.

"Right now I don't trust anyone."

"Including me." It wasn't a question.

He's Jude's best friend, I thought. *Riley would do anything for him.* But not this.

I had no way of knowing; I knew. He'd stepped over the bodies with me. He'd been there. And he was here now. Probably I should have suspected him. But I didn't want to.

"If you're out to get me, you're not doing a very good job of it," I pointed out, only partly for his benefit. "And you're already stuck with what happened. Jude isn't."

Riley dropped down to the ground again, looking a little lost. "You're right. Just us, then."

I didn't want to say it. The old Lia Kahn would never have said it. But she was dead. "They're looking for me, not you."

"So far," he said darkly.

"I mean, this doesn't have to be your problem."

"You want me to go?" he asked.

I hesitated. Then shook my head. "But you can. If you want."

He hesitated too, longer than I had. "I'm in this."

"But you don't have to be."

"Yes. I do."

• • •

We needed somewhere that no one would bother to look for us, where no one bothered to look at all. "I know a place," Riley said, "but . . ."

There were plenty of buts.

But I haven't been back since the download.

But it's not safe.

But I don't know if you can handle it.

"I can handle anything," I told him.

It's not that I convinced him. It's just that we couldn't come up with a better option. So we went with the last resort.

Riley's city was a day's walk—a day and a half by back roads, which was how we went. We walked through the night, navigating by the dim glow of our ViM screens and occasionally switching to infrared. We reached the city's crumbling edge just as the sun was peeking through the jagged skyline. I'd been there before, but only at night, when the dead buildings were just ragged shadows, the city people all hidden away, in bed or in shadow. At night, the sky's dim red glow gave the place a weird dignity. Maybe it was the illusion that the city wasn't dead after all but just a sleeping monster that would wake when the lights switched on.

Now that the lights were on, it was easy to see that the monster wasn't sleeping; it was dead. Unlike most of the cities on the eastern seaboard, this one was still habitable, but just barely. The streets were paved with rubble and dogshit, lined with broken cars so old they still ran on gasoline (or would have, if they ran at all). Small clumps of orgs—their teeth rotting, their faces pockmarked, their insides and outsides racing each other toward decay—gathered in burnt-out buildings with broken windows, staring slack jawed at vids playing across giant screens. None of them noticed us as we passed.

"The vids play all day," Riley explained. "When you're a kid, you're supposed to watch the ed ones, learn to read and all that. After, you can do whatever you want. But there's nothing else to do."

There was no wireless web of energy here, which meant no one had ViMs to watch the vids of their own choosing. It also meant our mechanical bodies would be powering themselves on stored energy, good enough to last three days, four if we pushed it. Riley was convinced that would be enough. And if it wasn't, we could always sneak back to the Sanctuary for a quick recharge. There was no network either, at least no wireless access—they jammed the signal in the cities. Instead, communal ViMs let residents link into the network for a few minutes each day. According to Riley, most never bothered.

"How did you *live* here?" I asked as Riley led us down widening streets. The squat, brick structures gradually gave way to cement monoliths, their faces the color of ash.

"What was the other option?" He slowed down, his eyes tracking the broken windows we passed. Once he knelt to pluck a glittering scrap of metal from a small pile of trash. He held it out to me, proud of the find. "A real coin," he said. "You can find them all over if you know what you're looking for."

"So?" I didn't need him playing tour guide. "It's not like they have any value anymore."

He slipped it into his pocket. "Maybe not to you."

Shadows flickered behind the glass. I turned my face to the ground. We'd agreed we shouldn't bother trying to disguise ourselves—no disguise would hide what we were. Even if my picture hadn't been all over the vids, two mechs traipsing through a city was a dead giveaway we were doing something we shouldn't. Riley had claimed it didn't matter. "There's no law in the city, not really. You just do what you can until someone stops you." Meaning no law but the unspoken kind, expressed only in the native language you absorbed growing up in the city, in favors and blackmail and protection money, in the unforgiving thresher of Darwinian selection. You either figured out how to survive, or you went extinct.

"What are we waiting for?" I asked now as we passed building after building, all of them identical except for the designs sprayed in black and gold across their faces. Sensing our presence, the graffiti rippled and swirled, occasionally emitting a piercing blast of noise, the artist's primal scream embedded in the electropaint. "Can't we just pick one and get off the street?"

Riley shook his head. "Even in a city, everything belongs to someone."

He stopped suddenly in front of a building capped by two forty-story towers, its doors scarred by deep fissures running diagonally across their length as if giant claws had sliced through the metal. A thick layer of grime had turned the facade a dark, earthy brown. The windows at street level were all boarded up, but through the cracks I could see figures moving around inside.

"There are *people* in there," I hissed as Riley started toward the door.

"Yeah?"

"*Yeah*, well, shouldn't we go back the way we came? What about all those empty houses?"

"You don't get it," Riley said.

"So explain it to me."

"Now?"

I crossed my arms. "Now or never."

So he did. Some of the buildings we'd passed probably were empty, he explained, but in the city, empty was death, home to roving bands of the desperate and hungry, as bestial as the outside authorities made them out to be. We couldn't be killed, but we could still be attacked, robbed, dismembered . . . he left the rest to my imagination. There was safety in numbers as long as you chose the right numbers. Which was why most of the city crowded into the skyscrapers at its center, seizing a place as either protector or protected. Every gang had its own territory, some owning whole towers, others sharing space in a precarious balance of power, as in this building, *Riley's* building, where west and east towers coexisted as uneasy allies and occasional combatants.

We entered the lobby, a long, narrow space with ceilings that towered three stories over our heads. At ground level, the windows were boarded up with jagged-edged wooden boards. But above, a latticework of steel beams and broken glass let in the light and—judging from the puddles, the rust, and the mold—the elements. Facing the entrance, a sleek wall of black marble rose from floor to ceiling, small holes smashed into it at regular intervals like hand- and footholds for a mountain climber. And at the point where the marble met the ceiling: the climber himself, hanging from a narrow cable, his long rifle aimed out at the street. There was a matching sniper at the other end of the lobby—one to guard the west tower, I decided, the other to guard the east. On the ground, two clumps of sentries mirrored the division, each protecting the entrance to one of the towers, all with their weapons trained on us.

Riley had called them "sentries," but they were children, alongside a few decrepit and aged men and women. All carrying guns, all settled into wheelchairs or leaning on crutches and canes.

"Not enough power to run an elevator," Riley VM'd. "So either you climb the stairs . . ."

Or you didn't.

Apparently, in a tower everyone had some job to do, even the ones forced to stay on the ground.

"Which floor did you live on?" I asked him as if I could somehow gauge where he'd fit into the vertical hierarchy.

"The ground," Riley murmured aloud. "With them."

"But—" I stopped myself. Of course. Jude had stayed on the ground; Riley had stayed with Jude. "You sure about this?" I asked, nodding toward the nearest weapon—too near for my taste.

"Ground level's neutral territory," Riley said. "Just keep your mouth shut."

I bristled at both the implication and the tone. But I did as I was told.

Riley strode up to one of the younger boys guarding the west tower. The kid sat malnourished and one-legged in a rusted wheelchair, a long, black gun laid across his lap. *"Skinners?"* he said, fingers rigid on the arms of the chair. "You don't belong here." One hand dropped casually, almost as an afterthought, onto the handle of his gun.

"Let 'em stay," gargled an older man leaning on a crutch. "We can have some fun."

"Shut it, Ches," Riley snapped. When he spoke to the boy, his voice was gentler. "It's me, Jay," he said. "Riley."

"Yeah, right. Prove it."

"Fine." Riley slipped his hand into his pocket and drew out the crushed coin he'd found, then tossed it to the kid. "For your collection."

The boy's eyes widened. With a furtive glance at his fellow sentries, he shoved the coin into his pocket. Then, never taking his eyes off Riley, scrawled something onto a piece of paper and shoved it into a long tube that ran up the side of the wall, disappearing into the ceiling. The page whooshed away.

"Pneumatic tubes," Riley VM'd. "Works on compressed air. Best way to stay in touch without power."

"Since when do you know how to write?" he asked the kid.

The boy scowled and hocked out a mouthful of thick, yellowish saliva. "Gray made me. New rule. Reading too."

Riley grinned. "Since when does Gray make anyone do anything?"

"Things change," the kid said without matching his smile. "You should know."

The response arrived a few moments later. The boy retrieved a crumpled piece of paper from the tube, read it over slowly, his lips moving as he pieced the letters together into words. Then he nodded. "Fifteenth floor," he told Riley. "They're waiting for you."

Riley gave him a half shrug, half nod, then pulled me past the group of guards toward the stairs.

"Hey, Riley!" the kid called after us. "So what's it like, anyway?"

"Quieter," Riley called back, and then the stairwell door closed behind us and we were on our way up.

"Quieter?" I repeated as we climbed the steep, narrow flights, stepping over piles of garbage. The stairwell was a windowless concrete chimney stretching endlessly above us and echoing with the clatter of pounding feet.

"What'd you want me to say?" Riley took the stairs two at a time, keeping me at his back. "That while he's stuck in shit for the rest of his life, I'm rich and safe and never hungry?"

"Just wondering what you meant," I said. "Quieter."

"There's always people around in a city," Riley said. And as if to illustrate his point, a crowd of slummers pushed past us on the stairs without pausing, their pupils wide and faces streaming with sweat, telltale signs of a shocker trip. They probably hadn't even seen us. "Nowhere belongs to just you."

The door marked 15 released us into a long, gray hallway lined with doors, windows at either end letting in little light. Three orgs were waiting for us, their limbs bundled tight into thick sweaters, their breath fogging in the chill air. The two guys were a couple years older than me, while the girl looked about my age.

"It's hotter than I thought it would be," the shorter of the two guys said, looking me up and down, his ratface scrunched like he was trying to pick up my scent.

The other shoved an elbow into his gut. "So this is the guy claiming to be Riley? What's the game?"

The girl shook her head. "No game," she said, her eyes laser focused on his face. "It's him."

The taller one spat out a bitter laugh. "Says who?"

"Says me." The girl took a step toward him, then stopped with a foot of distance still between them. Riley stayed silent.

"How do you know?" the ratface asked.

"He voiced me a couple times. And sent some pics. After." The girl blushed and ran a hand through her spiky red hair. She was wearing makeup, I realized. A red smear across her lips and something sparkly over her lids—compensating for her lack of genetic perfection with a layer of paint. As if she could make herself pretty through sheer force of will. Add to that the baggy clothes, no tech anywhere in sight, just plainprint on the shirt and, from the look of it, shoes that didn't even conform to her feet. She looked like a total retro, which made sense, since the retro slummers my sister hung out with were just shoddy imitations. This girl was the original. *Zo will be glad to know she's doing it right,* I thought instinctively, before remembering that I wouldn't be telling Zo anything any time soon.

The taller guy scowled at her, and she blushed again, harder. Then she moved to his side, slipping an arm around his waist. Next to me, Riley stiffened.

"She right?" the guy asked Riley. "It's you?"

"Yeah, Gray," Riley said. "It's me."

"Prove it."

"You sure you want me to?" Riley asked. "Because I didn't think you'd want Mika and Sari to know about that time we were crashing at Bo's place and freaked out on shockers. What'd you declare yourself? Emperor of Piss and—"

"It's him," Gray said abruptly. Mika snickered. "Heard about your new look," he said to Riley. "But seeing it . . ." He shook his head. "Always had to be different, didn't you?"

The girl, Sari, kept her arm around Gray but pulled her body slightly away from him—it was subtle, probably too subtle for any idiot guy to notice, but I did. It was a move I'd pulled myself, one that said to anyone watching, *I'm with him . . . unless you've got a better offer?* "I think what Gray means to say is that he's glad you're not dead." She drove a steel-tipped boot into Gray's ankle. "Right, Gray?"

"Right, baby," he said, wrapping an arm around her shoulders and pulling her into him again. Maybe he wasn't such an idiot after all. "Didn't think you'd be back," he said to Riley. "After you and Jude disappeared, we all—"

"You knew Jude?" I asked.

Gray jerked his head toward me. "Who's this one?"

"A friend," Riley said. I noticed he was keeping his eyes on Mika. Worried about what he'd do next, I wondered, or just trying not to watch Gray pawing his old girlfriend?

"Right." Gray sneered at me. "Didn't know you had a thing for blondes."

"Maybe it's true what they say," Mika said. "I hear skinners—"

"Mechs," I corrected him. It shouldn't have mattered—sticks and stones and all that—but it did. Words counted.

"'Skinner' works for me," Mika said. "Computer brain shoved into some fake skin, walking around like you're a real person, stealing the identity of some dead guy—or girl, in your case. I assume."

"I didn't steal anything." Orgs just didn't get how something could be true and not true at the same time. In every way that mattered, I was the same Lia Kahn as I'd always been; in every way that mattered, I was completely different.

But I wasn't pretending to be human. I was over that.

"Whatever," Riley said. "It doesn't matter. We need your help."

"Figures that's why you're back," Gray said. "You and Jude

105

score big, and you disappear, but now that you *need* something—"

"You know why I stayed away," Riley said in a low voice.

Gray cocked his head at me. "But *she* doesn't, does she?"

Great. More secrets. "Why—"

"Lia." Riley shook his head at me, slightly. As if he was in
charge of whether and when I shut up.

"Why'd he stay away?" I asked Gray.

He shrugged. "Ask him. Besides, doesn't really fit in anymore, does he, looking like *that*."

Riley hugged his arms across his chest like he was trying to
cover as much of his skin as he could. Like he was ashamed. In
the corp-town, he'd stared down all the whisperers and gapers,
silently daring them to do their worst. But here he slumped and
covered up, looking like he wished he could rip the synflesh off
his body, strip by pale pink strip.

"We just need to crash here for a while," Riley said. For the
first time, he met Sari's gaze. "Please."

"You're in trouble," Mika said. "We've got enough of that."

"And if Jude and me had said that last year, you'd be dead
right now," Riley said. "You owe me."

"We owe *Jude*," Gray said. "Don't see him here." He grinned
at me. "Unless he's feeling a little more *feminine* these days. That
you in there, kid?"

"Let us stay here, keep it quiet, and you and Jude'll be even,"
Riley said. "You know I speak for him."

Sari gave him a shy smile, then perched on her tiptoes to

whisper something in Gray's ear. His eyebrows knit together in a ragged V, but then he nodded. "Fine. Sixteenth floor, unit six, vacant for emergencies. It's yours. But only for a few days."

"You're fucking kidding," Mika spat.

"I'm fucking serious," Gray said. Ratface shut up.

Riley held out a hand to shake, but Gray didn't move. After a moment, Riley dropped his arm. "Thanks," he said.

"Nothing personal," Gray said. "I get that you're still the same guy, somewhere in there, but . . . you know."

"Yeah, nothing personal." Riley jerked his head at me. "Come on, let's go."

"Just for a few days," Mika reminded us as we tromped behind him up the decaying stairs.

"Yeah, then what?" I muttered.

"Can't hide forever," Riley said. "We deal with this, then we can go."

"Home?"

"Wherever."

We trekked up to the sixteenth floor, where we got a room of our own. A room with three blank beige walls and a pool of piss on the floor. A fourth wall of cracked windows cast the room in dying light, enough to see the film of grit coating the rickety table and chairs.

Foregoing the broken furniture, Riley slumped on the floor with his back to the wall and his feet a few inches from the urine.

I found a place on the other side of the room. Mika reappeared a moment later and tossed us a wad of clothing. "Gray said you'd want it," he growled before slamming the door shut behind him.

A grimy pair of pants had landed nearest me. I nudged it with my foot, half expecting a cockroach to crawl out from beneath. "We want *these*?"

Riley was already scooping up the jeans and a black rag that might once have been a shirt. "We don't want to be wearing what we wore in the vids," he said. "Just in case."

"Plausible deniability," I said, flashing on the image that bothered me the most, my still, upright form at the center of those sprawling bodies, the only vertical in a horizontal world. "Got it." I lifted the gray pants between two fingers, glad I couldn't smell them, trying not to wonder what had caused the rust brown stain spread down the right leg. The T-shirt was of indeterminate color, the bastard child of mold and puke.

Riley turned his back on me, slipping out of his old shirt and into the new one in one smooth, swift motion, revealing only a glimpse of the skin underneath. Bodies were bodies, Jude always said. Shame was an org thing, a pointless leftover from the Garden of Eden. But I turned away as Riley went to work on the jeans. If he was so repulsed by the sight of me, I wasn't about to watch him. Besides, taut abs, bare ass, whatever. It was nothing I hadn't seen before. Instead, I focused on my own city gear. The pants were baggy, at least two sizes too big, but they knotted at the front, and I cinched them as tight as they'd go.

The threadbare shirt was probably see-through, and I imagined I could feel a colony of insects swarming across my skin, burrowing deep into their new nest.

Regretfully, I dropped my own clothes on the floor, aiming squarely for the pool of urine, knowing it was the only way I wouldn't be tempted to put them on again. Riley still had his back to me, waiting.

"A true gentleman," I teased. "Unless you snuck a peek while my back was turned?"

"I wouldn't do that," he snapped, like he couldn't imagine why anyone would want to.

"Fine. You can turn around now," I said. "Your eyes are safe from the hideousness of my bare skin."

"That's not— I wasn't—"

It wasn't like him to stammer. I let the awkward moment drag on as his gaze strayed involuntarily down my body. Then I put him out of his misery. "What now?"

"We wait till dark," Riley said. "Then we get on the network and see what we can figure out."

"But what about—"

"Doesn't matter if they track us to the city," Riley said. "We're protected here. Someone comes for us, there are warning systems in place."

"*Gray's* systems." Like I was going to trust my life to a total stranger.

Like I hadn't already.

Riley nodded. "I'll link in from a public zone."

"If it's that easy, why wait?" I didn't ask exactly what he expected to do once we *got* on the network, since the options— voice Jude, watch and rewatch the vids of the attack, give myself up—were all varying degrees of useless. But even a bad plan was better than no plan. I pulled out my ViM.

"You crazy?" he snapped. "Put that away."

I was tired of him treating me like a defective. Was it my fault I hadn't grown up in his precious little concrete hell? "What'd I do now?"

Riley rolled his eyes. "Signal's jammed here, remember? And you don't show off what you've got, unless you want someone to grab it."

Someone, like the trigger-happy losers he'd chosen to entrust with our lives. "Nice friends you've got."

"Who said they were friends?"

I slammed my head back against the wall. Hard. "Great. Just great. So who the hell are they?"

"Some guys who owe me," Riley said. "Around here, that's what you get."

"So Jude's just some guy who owes you?"

Riley looked down. "That's different."

"And Sari?"

He curled his fingers into a fist and ground his knuckles against his lips. "What about her?"

I allowed myself a small smile. We were back in my territory now. "You tell me." Not that I cared about what Riley was or wasn't doing with some random slum case, but—aside from the not insignificant satisfaction to be gained from getting the prince of silent sulking to actually reveal a byte of information—I was bored. "I didn't know you kept in touch with any of your old . . . not-friends."

"Why would you know?"

"Does Jude know?" I asked. "Doesn't seem like he'd approve."

"You think I need his approval?"

"You're the one who nods along to whatever the hell comes out of his mouth," I said.

"Maybe I'm loyal."

"And that means never questioning anything?"

"Not the big things," Riley said.

"That's not loyalty, it's blind faith."

He just shrugged. "Says you."

We'd gotten way off topic, and I suddenly wondered whether Riley was smarter than I'd given him credit for, steering me away. "So you miss it here?"

He swept his arms out before him, showing off the peeling, stained walls, the yellow puddle. "What's not to miss?"

"I'm serious," I said. "You could have come back after the download."

"Thought you said you were serious," Riley said, cracking a half smile. "And even if I'd wanted to . . ." He shook his head, turning his left hand over as if examining its smooth surface, free of identifying creases and whorls. "Wouldn't have worked."

"Just because you're a mech?"

"Partly."

"What if Jude had wanted to move back?"

Riley paused. "He didn't."

Before I could explain the meaning of a hypothetical, the door opened. I froze, but Riley leaped to his feet, assuming a fight stance, knees bent, fists drawn.

"Am I interrupting something?" Sari asked, stepping into our cozy little hideaway.

It took a moment for Riley to drop his fists.

"What do you want?" he asked, his voice gruffer than the one I was used to.

"Honestly?" Sari took a few steps toward him. He backed against the wall. "Just to get a good look."

"You got one," he said.

"Also this." Before he could react, she'd crossed the room and her arms were around him, her cheek pressed to his chest. He hesitated, and then his arms crept around her. His eyes met mine, over her shoulder, then closed.

It wasn't an easily categorizable hug. There was no sex in it, barely even a spark, but there was still something about it that made me feel like I should leave the room, leave them alone.

Then she let go and slapped him across the face.

"Did that hurt?" she asked.

He shook his head. She slapped him again—or tried to, but he caught her wrist just in time. She twisted away from him.

"What the hell?" he shouted.

"You tell me," she shot back. "Where'd you go?"

"I'm right here."

"Before!" She took a couple deep breaths. "You stop voicing me. Or answering any of my texts. You totally disappear! So you tell me: What the hell?"

"Sari, come on."

"You never came back." She looked up at him, eyes clear and dry, mouth pinched to a point. This was a girl who didn't cry. "Two years, and you never came back—until one day you just show up again? With *her*?"

"You know why I couldn't come back," he said.

"Even if you wanted to, right?" Sari snapped. "But you didn't. Why would you? Better life, better girls, better everything, right?"

"Nothing's better," Riley growled. "And I'm not the only one with a new life. Since when are you and Gray so tight?"

"It's not like that," she said, the lie so obvious on her face that she must have intended it to be. She wanted him to know the truth behind the denial—to hurt him. I had to admire how well she played the game.

"So tell me how it is," Riley said.

Her eyes narrowed; her voice tightened. "Like you care."

"Since when do I ask, if I don't care?"

She reached out her hand again, and Riley moved to intercept it. She gave her head a quick, sharp shake. He dropped his arm. Sari touched his face lightly. Her fingers flickered across his cheek, his chin, the bridge of his nose. "It's really you?" she asked, peering into his eyes like there'd be some leftover in there, something familiar tying him to the face she'd known. A waste of time. But that was the thing about orgs. If they couldn't touch it, see it, hear it, they concluded it didn't exist.

Riley closed his hands around hers, removed them from his face. They stood that way, connected, for a long moment, then separated. I couldn't tell who'd let go first.

"What do you want, Sari?"

She hesitated. The iron expression wobbled. Then stiffened again as she made her decision. "Just to talk. Like we used to."

Riley looked like he wanted to argue, but instead he nodded. "Yeah. That'd be good."

Sari shot me a nasty look. I couldn't blame her. "Not here," she said. "Not in front of *her*."

"She's okay," Riley said.

"I don't know her."

"I do." Riley said.

Do you? I thought, skeptical.

But Sari was convinced. She glanced back and forth between us. "Yeah. Obviously. But *I* don't, and I don't want her listening."

"I'll go," I said. "It's fine."

Sari snorted. "Where *you* gonna go?"

"She's right," Riley said. "It's not safe."

He was doing it again, acting like I was some fragile blossom needing protection from the elements. And not even in a marginally flattering, she's-such-a-beautiful-flower kind of way. More in the I-don't-want-to-clean-up-the-inevitable-mess kind of way. On the other hand, as far as I could tell, this claustrophobic, stained, piss-ridden room was a pretty good stand-in for the city at large. And I wasn't in the mood for sightseeing. "Fine."

"You want me to go?" he asked, like he'd asked in the woods.

He'll come back, I told myself, and I nodded. Just like last time, he looked hesitant.

Unlike last time, he went.

"That was quick," I said, irritated by my relief as the door swung open. Only a few minutes had passed. "I figured you two would—"

I jumped to my feet as Mika and two other guys I didn't recognize—*big* guys—stepped into the room, shutting the door behind them. *Knees bent, fists clenched,* I thought, trying to imitate Riley's instinctive don't-mess-with-me pose. The look on their faces suggested I wasn't doing it quite right.

"Didn't realize I was having company," I said brightly. "You should have told me you were stopping by, I would have cleaned the place up."

One of the musclemen paled as he looked me up and down. "You didn't say it was going to be one of *them.*"

"We don't have time for this shit," Mika snapped. "Just do it."

"It's not natural," he whined.

"Who's supposed to be intimidating who here?" I asked Mika, trying to figure out how to get past four hundred pounds of muscle (plus a few pounds of Mika's scrawn) to make it to the door. "Because I don't think it's working out the way you planned."

"*Do* it," Mika ordered like a guy who's never given an order before.

"Do what?"

Instead of answering, the less chatty of the two musclemen darted toward me and twisted my arms behind my back. "Sorry," he murmured, and before I could ask him sorry for what, something hard slammed into the back of my head and the transparent pane of glass between me and the world—between my artificially constructed reality and the vivid, visceral, *live* experience of org life—shattered into a thousand bright shards of pain.

CITY DARK

"Why not just stop being afraid?"

Hit me again, I almost said—and that scared me more than the musclemen, more than wild-eyed Mika, who looked totally freaked out to see me still on my feet, eyes open, brittle grin firmly in place. But the pain made the world seem real—made my *body* seem real. Extreme pain, at least, the kind that overwhelmed my conscious awareness that every sensation was just a string of little ones and zeros assembled into patterns specifying *hot, cold,* or *ouch.*

"Again!" Mika shouted, saving me from choice, and the hand smashed down, touching off another explosion of light and pain behind my eyes, and this time I think I screamed, although it was impossible to hear anything, not with the thunder in my head.

And then it drifted away, and I was still on my feet.

"Seems like someone didn't do his homework," I taunted Mika, slowly inching away from him as a plan—a crazed, stupid plan—began to coalesce. "We can do this all day, but I should probably mention that my skull's made out of a reinforced titanium alloy. It can survive five hundred g of impact. You're strong, but I'm guessing not that strong." I had the back of the chair in my grip. A rickety piece of junk that wouldn't stop them from coming at me again, but—I stole a glance at the wall of windows, already spiderwebbed with cracks—might just get the job done. If I had the nerve.

"Mika?" the guy said. I could see why he kept his mouth shut—his voice was about three octaves higher than any self-respecting muscle-bound thug would want it to be.

"You're not scared?" Mika said, looking at me like I was his science project.

"Of what?" I tried to laugh. "You want to kill me? Good luck."

"It's true," said the first muscleman, he of the lower voice and higher fear factor. "I saw it on the vids. You knock one off, they just download it into a new body."

Mika glared at him. "Who cares?" he asked. "You know that's not why we're here."

"Gray promised Riley we could stay here, *safe*," I reminded him, and tightened my grip on the chair. Any second, they could come at me again. *Just do it,* I told myself. *Do it.* "You want to piss them off?"

"Riley's not here," Mika said. "And Gray's an idiot."

I rolled my eyes. "Yeah. *Gray's* the idiot."

"Just finish this!" Mike shouted at his goons, my cue that it was now or never. As the 'roiders lurched toward me, I hoisted the chair, whirled around, slammed it through the window, didn't flinch from the explosion of glass. Instead I ran *into* the storm of razor-edged crystals, into it and through it and past it, jagged glass carving my palms as I grabbed the frame and threw myself, without pausing, without thinking, without fear, into the sky.

Life is a physics problem. Bodies in motion. Bodies in free fall, at a constant rate of acceleration, gravity dragging them down and down and down.

Thirty-two point two feet per second per second, down.

Sixteen stories between jagged glass and stained pavement.

Three seconds. Three seconds to live—if you're an org.

If you're a mech, three seconds to decide.

Headfirst, brain crushed on concrete, life downloaded to something new and fresh and far away.

Feetfirst and there was a chance.

In the dark there was no ground, no building, just the wind, just the clock, seconds ticking down. My body had no org instincts, no reflexes to act on. There was only thought put into action. There was only what I knew.

Two seconds.

I knew a lot: You learn how to fly, you learn how to fall.

Relax, I thought, angling my body, head up, feet down. Muscles loose. Toes gently pointed, knees bent. *Relax*.

One second.

Tense up, and the impact would jolt through rigid muscles, straight to the energy converter in my chest, the computer in my head. The wind was thunder, the ground was coming, my brain was raging, but my body obeyed. Relaxed. Prepared.

The ground slammed into me with shattering force, sending a shock wave that blazed up my spine. It felt like my bones were liquefying. It felt like being crushed to an infinite point. But I ignored the feeling, focused on the act. On letting the fall drag me into a roll, my arms tucked under my legs, my head to my chest. Down and then up again, bouncing like a child's ball, arms covering my head, elbows arrowed forward, knees tucked. Protect the soft spots. Twist hips to the right, shift body, land sideways, another explosion, radiating from head to toe, roll over, and over, just let it happen.

Until it ends.

I was on the ground. Arms worked. Legs moved. I twisted my head, gently, from side to side. Everything intact. And I was still thinking, I was still *I*, so the brain was safe. Which meant my chance to throw this body away and escape to the safety of a storage computer, a new download and a new machine, had slipped past, and somewhere up there, Mika and his thugs were on their way.

This is wrong, I thought, slowly, gingerly testing the arms, then the legs, pushing myself upright. Jumping out a window shouldn't make you feel more alive.

On my feet, I spared only a second to look up at the path I'd fallen, tracing the line of the building, searching for the broken window, but the tower was too tall, the night too dark. And they would be coming for me.

Everything looked different in the dark. Thanks to Jude, I could see in infrared, but there was nothing to see but towers and shadows. The dim red glow of the sky was enough for that. I didn't need to see where I was going—I needed to know where to go, and without Riley, there was no hope of that.

"What the hell is going on?" I VM'd Riley, half expecting that the network jammers would jam this too.

"Lia?" His voice sounded so close and so calm. Too calm. He didn't know.

Or that's what he wants me to believe, I thought.

"Lia, where are you? What's wrong?"

If I told him where I was, and he was a part of it . . .

"You need to get out of there, *now*," I VM'd. "Your friend Mika's crazy. I'm—" I trusted him. Even if I shouldn't, I trusted him. "I'm outside. They're coming. Which way should I go?"

He didn't hesitate. "West six blocks, then turn right, go another ten blocks, and there's a vacant lot behind the tower. Lots of broken-down cars. Pick one, get in, wait for me. I'll be—"

"You'll be what?"

Nothing.

"*Riley? Riley!*"

But he was gone.

Three figures emerged from the tower, and I ran. West, like he'd said, pounded down the street, silently as I could, but the streets were abandoned after dark, and I was like a neon target in the empty city, and they gave chase. I kept to the edges of the sidewalk, trying to disappear into the shadows cast by the towers, then veered to the right and darted into an alleyway. The narrow dead-end passage was lined with piles of trash, and I squeezed between two of them, frozen. I could hear them out there, pacing the streets, calling for reinforcements.

"Maybe she went down there," someone said. "No way I'm following."

"The tunnels?" Mika's voice. "Bitch can't be that stupid."

I waited for them to give up. They would have to eventually, and I would find my way home. I'd navigated the city at night before, for fun, for a *game*, and I could do it again. Even if this time I had no light, no pack of daredevil mechs at my back. I could do this alone.

Then: White eyes in the darkness.

"I saw you jump." A small voice. Young.

"Shhh!" I hissed. He crept closer. It was a kid about half my height, harmless. Except that with one shout, he could send us both to hell. "Please."

"They're looking for you," he whispered.

"Hide and seek," I said desperately. Kids hated me. All of them. Even when I was an org. I knew how this would end. "So let's hide."

"Gimme your shoes." He pulled back his lips like he was baring fangs, but there were more gaps than teeth.

"What?"

"Your shoes!" he said, too loud. "Or I tell them where you are."

I didn't bother to ask why he wanted them, or what he'd do with shoes two sizes too big. I just stripped them off and shoved them at him. He hugged them to his chest and grinned. "I saw you jump," he whispered again. "I want to jump."

"No!" I hissed, shaking my head wildly. "It wasn't the shoes—"

"She's in here!" he shrieked in a shrill, almost feminine register. "Over here!"

Just a kid, I told myself, suppressing the urge to wring his scrawny neck, but I was already in motion, shooting out of the alley and pinballing across the street. Bare feet slapping cement, I ran. Something sharp sliced my heel. I kept going. Mika and the others were already responding to the kid's cry, running at full speed, about a block away. I knew I could outlast them, but only if I could outpace them, and they were fast. The alleys were dead ends. But just in front of me, the ground opened. Cement stairs led down into a dark maw: the tunnels.

Bitch can't be that stupid, Mika had said.

Watch me.

It was dark down there, pitch-dark, but I had the infrared, and the underground cavern lit up in deep blues and purples. The stairs emptied onto a thin platform running along the edge of a long pit that tunneled into the distance in both directions. And in the pit, streaks of orange and yellow light scampering through the navy blue. Heated bodies scurrying through the cold dark. I pressed against the gritty tile wall of the platform as more yellow shapes streaked through the darkness, a couple on the platform angling toward me, their tiny claws feathering across my bare feet.

The rats, or whatever they were, didn't scare me.

It was the other lights in the darkness, deep in the tunnel but creeping closer, bodies outlined in pulsing orange and red, the colors of life, the size of people, but people with twisted, gnarled shapes, backs hunched like horseshoes, limbs askew or absent.

I could hear voices above me, Mika shouting at the head of the stairs, urging his thugs down into the deep. Escape meant venturing into the tunnels, wherever they led. Whoever was waiting there for me.

The lighted bodies advanced. I shut down the infrared; I needed to see their faces. Mech eyes needed no time to adjust to the dark. The orange figures faded to gray shadows, and I saw: They were human, barely, stooped and ragged, their skin so layered with black soot that they melted into the tunnels.

For a moment I allowed myself to nurture the fantasy that they, whoever they were, poor but kind, would envelop me in their fold, spirit me away to safety, and then bask in the glow of my gratitude as I gifted them with a new life, safe and aboveground, their lives saved in return for saving mine, a happy ending.

And then I saw the glint of the knife in a raised hand, a long shard of broken glass clasped in another, heard a low, gutteral roar. The rats streamed away, seeking the safety of darkness, like they knew what was to come.

I should have jumped headfirst, I had time to think, just as a hand clamped down on my shoulder, yanked me backward. Someone grabbed my arm, nearly pulling the shoulder out of its socket, and dragged me up the stairs, my feet scrabbling for purchase as my ass thudded against the concrete. "Should've left you down there for the carvers," the guy grunted, dumping me in a heap at the top of the stairs. Compared to the dark of the tunnels, the night sky seemed to blaze pink.

Mika leaned over me. I threw a wild punch, but he caught it, his scrawny grip deceptively strong. "Thanks," he said, a creepy smile stretching across his face.

"For what?"

"For making this fun." And he shoved a gag into my mouth. Pulled off his T-shirt and wrapped it twice around my head, leaving me in the dark. Someone tied my wrists together, then—after I landed a few kicks, yielding some mildly satisfying grunts and yelps—my ankles. Hands hauled me off the ground and slung me over a shoulder, my head dangling toward the ground, my blindfolded face plowed into someone's ass. They carried me away.

When they pulled out the gag and ripped off the makeshift blindfold, I'd come full circle: another room, as featureless as the first, only without windows. The thugs were gone, leaving Mika and me alone.

I was tied to a chair.

"Go ahead," I told him, steeling myself. My hands were bound behind my back, and my ankles knotted against the legs of the chair. They'd turned me into a piece of furniture. "Just do it."

"What?"

Like I was going to give him ideas. "Whatever it is you're going to do."

"That's what you think?" he asked, sounding disgusted. No—offended. He walked over to me, stroked a finger along my jawline. I jerked my head away, then thought better of it. *Bring it a little closer,* I urged him silently. *I'll bite it off.* "You think I brought you here to . . . *do* things to you?"

"You're right, that's crazy," I said, straight-faced. "You probably just want to chat."

"You think we're all animals, don't you?" Mika poked me in the shoulder. Hard. "*Don't* you?"

I shrugged.

"Penned up like dogs. Fighting each other for scraps." He shook his head. "Who are *you* calling an animal? I'd rather be a dog than an *it.*"

"Not a dog," I muttered. "Dogs are housebroken."

"What's that?"

I just smiled at him. He slapped me, snapping my head back so hard it slammed on the back of the chair. The jolt of pain was like a mouthful of milk chocolate—sweet in the moment, but not rich enough to make much of an impression.

"Why aren't you scared?" he asked.

"Of *you*?" I sneered. "Maybe because you're too stupid to notice that I'm a *mech*. You can't kill me. And I don't care if you hurt me."

"I could make you care," he said. "You don't want me to do that."

"Doesn't seem to matter what I want."

He circled the chair a couple times, then stopped in front of me, his legs straddling mine. He slapped his hands down on the chair back, long, hairy arms locking me in, then sat down, his ass heavy on my knees. He lowered his face to mine, and I wondered what his breath smelled like. Sour, I imagined, concentrating on his chipped front teeth. Or maybe sickly sweet like rotting fruit.

It's just a body, I thought, watching his hands creep along my bare arms. *It's not me. It's got nothing to do with me.* Tiny, curly black hairs dusted his knuckles. His ragged nails were dark with grime. Long fingers, a strong, tight grip. *It's just wires and microreceptors and synflesh. Not me.*

He pushed himself back to his feet. "I'm not an animal," he snarled, backing away. "Whatever you think."

I didn't want to feel relief, because that would be an admission I'd felt fear. I was supposed to be beyond fear. Secure in mind, fearless of body, that was the idea. "Fine," I said, steady. "So now what?"

"Now we wait."

We waited for more than an hour. Me in my chair, Mika's eyes darting from me to the door and back to me again. When it swung open, and Sari sauntered in, I allowed myself one moment of willful ignorance before accepting the obvious. This wasn't a rescue.

I glared at her. "Where's Riley?"

She raised her eyebrows. "Worried? There's nothing I can do to him anymore, right?" Sari whispered something to Mika, who nodded. "Besides, how do you know Riley's not the reason you're here?"

I just stared at her.

She laughed bitterly. "Oh, that's right, you know him so well."

"Like you used to?" I reminded myself that she was no different from any other stuck-up bitch who thought she was in charge. And that was something I could use.

"No one knows Riley," Sari said. "You'll figure that one out yourself."

"Seems like a pretty pathetic attempt to get him back."

She snorted. "Why would I want him back?"

"Right, you've got Gray now."

Sari rolled her eyes. "Gray was convenient. Now he's not. A girl like you probably understands exactly how that goes."

"Don't pretend you know anything about me." There had been guys who were toys, guys who were power plays, guys who were placeholders or just something to play with before I got bored, but that was over now. Mechs played by different rules. And I didn't play at all.

"I know freaks like you and Riley belong together," she said. "I've moved on."

"To what?" I glanced pointedly at Mika. *"Him?"*

Sari burst into surprised laughter, then cut herself off as Mika's face flushed red.

"What's it feel like?" she asked abruptly.

I struggled against the rope binding me to the chair. "A little tight, actually. Feel free to untie—"

"Not that. You know. Sitting around, knowing you're not going to die. Never get ugly. Sick."

None of the orgs in my world—my former world—got ugly when they got old. It's like the pop-ups said: a nanojection a day kept the wrinkles away. And there was always a lift-tuck every few months when things started to sag.

"At least you're starting out ugly," I said. "So you've got nothing to lose."

Sari bared her teeth, but before she could do anything, the door eased open. A thin, vertical strip of face appeared through the crack. An inch of pale lip, split by a deep red scar, a sharp nose, hooded brown eyes. "Let's go!" the mouth commanded. "Things to do."

Mika scrambled, tipping me off. This was the final puzzle piece, the alpha to their pathetic betas. Riley's replacement. Sari glanced at the door, eyes shining. She smirked at me. "This is all Riley's fault, you know."

"I doubt that."

She jerked her head toward the shadow behind the door. "You piss off Wynn, you pay. Riley knew that then, and he knows it now. Ask him. If you ever see him again."

She left me alone.

"Riley?" I VM'd. But again there was no answer. Possibly he was out of range. Gone to get help. Or just gone.

Mechs feel fear, just like orgs. Sharp, imminent fear, a red, flashing danger sign, like when you're hurtling toward the earth at a hundred miles per hour. And when the fear's sharp enough, it overpowers that annoying voice, the one wanting to know *If I'm afraid, why aren't my hands shaking? Why aren't my teeth chattering? If I feel fear, why don't I feel fear?* You don't think about it, because when the danger sign's flashing brightly enough, you don't think at all.

Fear I felt. But not the thing that comes after the fear, the thing that shows up when the door closes and the noise stops and you're just waiting—and waiting—for something to happen. The tight-chest, stiff-neck, rigid-muscle, can't-breathe thing that serves as a constant reminder that Something Bad is on its way.

I never noticed it when I was an org—that's part of being an org, having the luxury not to notice anything—but some emotions are more inside your head than others. *Happy*, that's a brain feeling. But *sad*? That's in the body. In the gut and the throat and the jaw. *Anxious* too. *Worried. Nervous.* All the feelings your brain would escape from if it could. So your body grabs hold and doesn't let go. Org minds can go to as many happy places as they want, but their bodies always drag them back down to sweaty palm–ville.

Org bodies. Not mine.

So when I forced my mind to something else—clothes, in

this case, and the new morphdress I was considering, almost solely for the pleasure of watching Jude's face fall as its skirt transformed from mini to maxi before his eyes—it went.

I can't escape, the train of thought went. *And they can't kill me. They can't hurt me in any way that counts.*

So why think about what was going to happen next?

Why not just *stop* being afraid?

And then the lights went out.

I'm not afraid of the dark, I told myself, then repeated the words out loud. My voice sounded strange, floating through the black. Disembodied.

It was just curfew, I thought. Nothing more mysterious or dire than that.

I'm not afraid of the dark.

It was what the dark meant. The cities were primitive. Energy ran through wires, snaking through the air or buried in the ground, safe from those who would steal it, abuse it, use it up. Unlike out in the real world, where energy was wireless and, as long as you could afford to pay, there for the taking, as much as was needed. That was the world I was built for. That was the world that powered the converter in my chest.

I'd last three days, maybe four. But that was it. Then no more power, which meant . . . what?

As long as the artificial brain was intact, it sent out a signal that interfered with the functioning of any other brains with the *Lia Kahn* pattern. It was how BioMax ensured that I remained

Lia Kahn, the one and only. The memories I stored every night were guaranteed to stay locked away in storage. Until the brain in my head was destroyed and the signal failed, giving BioMax the automatic go-ahead to download Lia Kahn into a brand-new body. No harm, no foul.

But power failure meant I stayed in this body, even if it was useless. Maybe indefinitely, an unconscious lump of parts. And maybe that was the plan. Toss me out with the garbage—or keep me around, a life-size doll, to do with what they would.

None of the mechs I knew had played around with power failure. Maybe my brain would stay active while they did whatever they did. Maybe it would be like being trapped underground, blind and frozen, forever.

I said I wasn't afraid of the dark.

I say a lot of things.

"Lia." It was Riley's digitized voice in my ear, low and urgent. The VM link only worked within a few miles, which meant they hadn't taken me too far away. "Where are you?"

"Trapped." I wiggled my fingers. If I'd been an org, they probably would have gone numb by now. "I don't know where they brought me."

"I shouldn't have left you alone. I never thought Sari would—"

"It's done," I said. "Where are you?"

"They tried to . . ." A pause. "It doesn't

matter now. I got away. It was too easy—I think they let me. You okay?"

"They can't hurt me."

"They won't try." He didn't sound as sure as I would have liked. "They're not after that."

"So what do they want?"

"It's complicated."

It was always complicated.

"There's this guy Wynn," he said. Then stopped.

Keep talking, I thought. And not just because I needed to know. His voice, even in this monotonic form, was warm, something to hold on to in the dark.

"He thinks he runs things around here," Riley said finally. "And I . . . pissed him off."

"I heard." Sound tough, be tough. That was the rule. "So he wants some kind of revenge?"

"He wants me," Riley said. "And Jude. For you. That's the trade."

"He *had* you," I pointed out. "He took me instead."

"Because that was easier."

Because he knew you'd fight back, I thought, disgusted with myself. *Because he knew I couldn't.*

"And he needs me to get Jude," Riley added. "He wants both of us."

"Why?"

There was another pause so long, I was afraid he'd gone.

"So do we have a plan?" I asked. "I assume Jude's

not just going to walk in and give himself up?"

Say yes, I thought. *Say Jude's already here, ready to play martyr.*

But Jude didn't do martyr, any more than I did damsel in distress. Self-preservation was his defining quality. Like it was supposed to be mine—I just wasn't proving to be very good at it. Maybe Jude would sacrifice himself for someone else. For Riley, maybe—I was sure Riley thought so. Maybe even for Ani. Never for me.

"It's complicated," Riley said again, like I didn't know what that meant. "But we'll find you. Wynn's got the top thirty floors of the east tower. Security's good but not perfect. We can get through. Find you."

"Take your time," I said, wondering if sarcasm could travel through the VM line. "Not like I'm in any—"

The door eased open.

"Lia? What is it, what's wrong?"

"Later. Company's here." A tall, slender figure stood in the doorway. It was too dark to see his face.

"I'll get you out of there, I promise."

Feel free to hurry, I thought. The man stepped into the room, slamming the door shut behind him. "Wynn?" I guessed.

A hard laugh. "Not as dumb as they said." His voice was deep but hoarse, like the words scraped his throat on their way out.

"This is insane."

Another laugh, more genuine this time. "Damn right. Welcome to the city, skinner."

"I've never done anything to you." It sounded lame, even as I said it, like I was starring in a vidlife, reciting someone else's script, forced to play out the scene, though we all knew how it would end.

"You picked the wrong people to be friends with," he said. "Bad luck. And they owe me. So now you pay up."

"Whatever you want. I've got plenty of credit, I can—" But even in the dark, I could see he was shaking his head.

"Eye for an eye, baby." His face was an unnerving blank in the dark. "Life for a life."

Jude would never give himself up, not for me, I thought. And even if he did, this guy might never let me go. Everything in a city belonged to someone, Riley had told me, and you never gave up what you had, not if you were smart. Wynn wasn't stupid, not if he'd set this whole thing in motion. I belonged to him.

"I never had a skinner before," he said, approaching me. I couldn't move; I couldn't do anything but watch the shadow loom, the dim outline of a hand swoop toward my face. He dragged his knuckles across my cheek. Softly. Rested a hand on the back of my neck. Gently. Bent his head to mine, his lips feathering across my ear. "This could get interesting."

The door exploded. There was a burst of light, someone screamed—maybe it was Wynn, maybe it was me—and a thud. Wynn's body, smacking the floor. The man who'd shot him, his green uniform and black faceplate illuminated by dancing flashlights, ducked back into the hallway, leaving me alone again. Out there it sounded like a war, or at least the way war sounded on the vids: voices shouting on top of one another, boots pounding, thuds and thumps like punches landing, bodies falling, "Fucking animals!" someone yelled, another shot, and then silence. In the room, just one mech tied to a chair, an org sprawled at her feet.

A phalanx of secops marched in, stunshots drawn. "Lia Kahn?" the lead guy said.

It wasn't a real question, so I didn't bother answering.

"You're coming with us." Though the unidirected sonic blast of the stunshot could knock an org unconscious in seconds, we both knew it wouldn't have any effect on me. Not that it mattered. I was outnumbered, outpowered—and almost as eager to get out as they were to bring me in.

As two of them began to untie me, a third kicked Wynn out of his way. His body rolled a few feet, then stopped, one arm flung over his head, palm up, fingers slightly bent as if he were holding an invisible hand. I couldn't tell if he was breathing.

I never saw his face.

DEAD END

"Do you want a war?"

They wore the standard green uniform of secop foot soldiers, a Synapsis logo swooshing across their chests to mark where their loyalties lay. Less a fashion statement than a fail-safe, the logo housed tracking and recording tech, relaying all data back to their corp-town bosses. For the lawless, it meant that once one secop had found you, they all had. For the secops, it meant Big Brother was always watching.

For me it meant there was no point in fighting back or running away, not unless I wanted my face on record as resisting a security action, which meant automatic detention. Given the other things my face was on record doing, detention no longer seemed much of a worst-case scenario. But there was the small matter of being tied to a chair.

Three of the men in green swarmed around me while two others guarded the door, their stunshots aimed at the hallway. There was no movement out there, no noise. Meaty hands untied the knots around my wrists and ankles.

"Hold still," one growled, and without giving me a chance to obey, yanked my arms out in front of me. He clamped my wrists together in his large grip.

I reminded myself not to knee him in the groin. "You don't have to— Hey!"

With his other hand he slipped a pair of cuffs from his belt and, with a smooth, practiced flick, snapped them around one wrist, then the other. The metal edges chewed into my skin.

"It only hurts if you fight it," he muttered.

Nothing hurts me, you crackbrain. But I stopped straining against the cuffs. "How did you find me?" I asked, not expecting much of an answer. I didn't get one. I didn't get anything: no concerned questions, no reassurances, no urgency, just silent efficiency as they hoisted me out of the chair like I was an object. I got it. This wasn't a rescue operation. It was a retrieval.

But how did they know where to find me?

The burliest of the secops slung me over his shoulder, treating me to another ass in my face, another upside-down ride. This time I wasn't blindfolded. So I saw Sari and Mika as we passed— saw their bodies, that is, faces planted into the dirty floor, limbs twisted at wrong angles. A gun lay on the ground next to Sari; a knife glinted by Mika's shoulder. The four bodies laying next to them, all strangers, rested next to equally useless weapons.

The privatization of security operations meant no more guns, I reminded myself. At least not the bullet-shooting kind that drilled bloody holes in your head.

And there was no blood.

Just unconscious, I told myself. The secops would have stunned them like they did to Bliss Tanzen's boyfriend that time he took too many Xers and tried to set the school on fire.

But that guy's father had been VP and part owner of the Freetower Corp, and the secops knew it. We were in a city now, where no one owned anything. And the bodies weren't moving.

"Are they dead?" I forced myself to ask as my head bounced against the secop's back. I could feel his shrug; my body rose and fell with his jerking shoulder.

He grunted. "What's the difference?"

Another room. Another lock. Another chair. At least I wasn't tied down, even if I was still trapped. And this time, I wasn't alone.

There were six of us. All with the same blond hair, the same blue eyes, the same pale hands with long, tapered fingers, the same pert nose and full lips. I was beautiful, there was no arguing that.

Just not unique.

It was one of those impersonal, featureless waiting rooms—beige walls, beige tiling, uncomfortable beige chairs—and it should have been easy to imagine that we were just waiting for a doctor's appointment or some kind of disciplinary encounter with the school principal. But there were little touches—the lack of a ViM screen on the wall, of windows, of anything that wasn't nailed down, the uniform glowering by the door, the small Synapsis logos engraved into the ceiling tiles—that made it impossible to forget where we were. This wasn't the kind of place in which people waited by choice.

"What?" the girl next to me said suddenly. "You're staring."

"No I wasn't," I said, quickly looking away. But everywhere I looked, there I was. In sonicshirts and net-linked hoodies and Zo-style retro gear, in full-on org drag and in silver-streaked mech mode that even Jude would be envious of. And still, all of them so much like looking in a mirror that when the girl turned to me, I had to touch my own lips to make sure they weren't wearing the same scowl. I kept my eyes on my lap, which seemed safer. "You know what we're doing here, anyway?"

"Quiet!" the secop at the door snapped.

The girl with my face just shrugged, unintimidated. "Don't you watch the vids?" she whispered. "They called in every F-three-one-six-five in a two-hundred-mile radius of Synapsis. Can you blame them, after what happened?"

It hadn't been difficult to memorize my serial number: *F3165-II*. It popped up on the glowing readouts that scrolled across my eyescreen whenever I performed a self-diagnostic check. F for female; II for my place in the production line of identical models. I'd never bothered to ask what the other numbers meant, since all I needed to know was that they meant *me*—along with everyone else in the room.

Called us in, she had said, but no one called me. They *found* me—they must have known where to look. *Riley?* I thought. Maybe he'd decided it was the only way. Maybe I'd been stupid one too many times, trusting my life to a near stranger who'd made it very clear he only cared about two people: Jude and himself.

"So you think one of them did it?" I asked, eyeing the other Lia's. *Not Lia,* I reminded myself. "What's your name?" I asked abruptly, before she could answer my first question.

"Why?" she asked. "You think *I'm* the one who did it?"

"Sorry, I just—"

"Kidding. I'm Katya." She held out a hand for me to shake. But I couldn't force myself to take it. "So was it you?"

"No!"

"Quiet!" the guard barked again, loudly enough that we both flinched.

"Trank out," the other girl advised. "They just want to talk to us and then they'll let us go home."

Not all of us, I thought. *Not the one they're looking for.* I was innocent—but how was I supposed to explain where they'd found me? Of course, if Riley had told them that much, maybe he'd told them everything. They could already know I'd run from Synapsis.

"And you believe them? That they'll just send us home?" I asked.

The mech shrugged, looking like she didn't have time to care. With her smooth, blond hair, self-assured smile, and immaculate clothes, she looked more like me than I did. It was like watching myself in a vid, acting out a scene I had no memory of performing.

"Why not?" she asked. "I didn't do anything."

"Yeah. Me neither."

The door swung open, and a woman in a dowdy tech-free suit with the telltale Synapsis logo stencil across its collar poked her head in. "F-three-one-six-five-eleven," she said, glancing at a ViM that fit discreetly in the palm of her hand. "Lia Kahn."

"So you were nowhere near Synapsis Corp-Town at the time of the attack." Detective Ayer's voice was nearly as flat as that of a newbie mech, but she was org all the way. You could tell by her dry, flaky skin, pulled too tight by some cut-rate lift-tuck and not helped in any way by the stiff copper curls molded around her face. I knew the corps screened kids around the age of ten, tracking them for manual labor, for data entry, for the factories, wherever their aptitude would allow them to excel, and I wondered what it was about Detective Ayer that had screamed secops. Obviously it had been the right verdict—the corps only farmed out their best officers for off-site work. So she was either unusually good or unusually determined. Or both.

"How many times are you going to ask me the same question?"

"Until I get the truth."

The car, I thought suddenly in alarm. What if they'd found our car at Synapsis and somehow traced it back to me? I tried not to panic. The car belonged to some mech I barely knew, who had contributed it for general use when he arrived at Quinn's estate. There was nothing connecting it to me.

And that's all you care about, right? Jude taunted in my head. *You. Who cares what happens to anyone else?*

"Were you in Synapsis at the time of the attack?" the detective asked impatiently.

"Of course not," I said. *Think frivolous,* I told myself. *Think oblivious, superficial, bitchy.* In other words, *Think Lia Kahn.* If I could will myself back to that person, the org Lia Kahn, who would never have been caught dead hanging out with Jude and his lackeys, much less running errands for him in a slummy corp-town, if I could convince myself, then I could convince her too, and she would let me go home. Or wherever. "Why would I be slumming in a corp-town?"

"Why slum in a *city*?" she countered. "Odd choice of field trip for a pampered little rich girl like you."

"Um, because the city is wow?" I suggested with a giggle. "You can do *anything*." Wide eyes, dim smile.

And maybe it was working. Because Ayer gave up her pacing and sat down across from me at the narrow metal table. The interrogation room was small and spare, without the mirrored wall I expected from the old-time vids. But the mini-cams posted in each corner got the message across pretty clearly: Someone was watching. Ayer propped her elbows on the table and folded her hands. She rested her chin on her knuckles. "So you just snuck into the city last night to have a little harmless fun?" she prompted, almost kindly.

I nodded.

"And things got carried away?"

"It was like, I just wanted to take a pic and post it on my zone, you know?" I babbled, as if I was too nervous to filter my words. "Because last time I snuck into the city, Cass and Terra didn't believe me, like I'd just make something up, and okay, it's not like I actually went *into* the city, but I think it should count if you just, you know, get close enough to see. And smell it, if you know what I mean."

"I thought you mechs couldn't smell," Ayer said thinly.

"Right. Um. I mean, that was before. But I'm a . . . skinner now, right? So I figured I could do it, and I just asked this guy if I could take a pic of us together, and he totally freaked out and went all crazy on me, like he was on some kind of schizo shocker trip, and then I'm, like, *tied to a chair*."

"Must have been pretty scary," Ayer said.

I nodded again, eagerly—maybe too eagerly. "So can I go now?" I asked. "I mean, I don't want those city guys to know I got them in trouble or anything, so . . ."

"Just to be clear, you went sightseeing in the city by yourself. To play at slumming for a few hours. For *fun*," the detective said, standing up again. The sympathy was draining from her voice. Fine. As long as she thought I was a repulsively self-absorbed rich bitch and not a mass murderer. Let her hate me all she wanted. "And you're certain you went nowhere near Synapsis Corp-Town?"

I forced myself to laugh, hoping it didn't sound as artificial as most of my attempts in that direction. "Who's going to be impressed if I go to a *corp-town*?" I scoffed. "I mean, the city, that's one thing. That's slamming. But a corp-town?" I wrinkled my nose. "That's just, like, where they grind fish crap into food or something. What would I do in a place like that?"

"I can think of a few things," the detective said in an icy voice. She stroked a finger across her ViM. The gray wall lit up with images of the corp-town attack. I looked away—then abruptly looked back, confused. How would an innocent person react? Was I supposed to be so horrified I couldn't stand it? Or should I act fascinated, like someone who hadn't seen it in person, who hadn't stepped over bodies while trying to escape?

I am *innocent,* I reminded myself. *I shouldn't have to act.*

Somehow, the more time that passed, the less I believed it.

"Don't I get a lawyer or something?" I asked.

She narrowed her eyes. "Have you done something that would require a lawyer?"

I wondered how many noobs actually fell for that one. "Do you know who my father is?"

"We know a great deal about you, Lia."

"Then you know I'm not some idiot city slummer you can bully into giving up my rights."

Detective Ayer raised her eyebrows. "What kind of rights do you think you have?"

"Same as everyone else."

"Same as every *org*, you mean?"

I kept my face blank.

"'Org.' That's the term you and your friends like to use, am

I right?" she asked, too pleased with herself. "And you skinners prefer to call yourselves 'mechs.'"

I shrugged. "So?"

"Seems rather hostile," she said mildly. "Inventing a slur for everyone who's not like you?"

"More hostile than 'skinner'?" I shot back. "Or how about 'Frankenstein'? That one never gets old."

"Call yourself whatever you want. But 'org' . . ." She shook her head. "I don't know, I hear that word, and it sounds to me like you're trying to denigrate humanity. Convince yourself that you're somehow superior."

"That's a lot to get from one syllable," I said.

"Context counts," the detective said, swiping her ViM again. The mech vid popped up on the wall screen, my face smiling into the camera, delivering her succinct manifesto. *You orgs want a war?*

Detective Ayer froze the frame. "Do you want a war, Lia?"

"Of course not!"

"Is that you in the vid?"

"I already told you it's not! I've never been to that corp-town or anywhere near there." No DNA, I reminded myself. No fingerprints, no biomatter, no nothing that could connect me to the corp-town.

"It must be strange, sharing a face with a murderer," she said casually. "Or maybe it doesn't bother you, the murder of forty-two *orgs*?"

"It bothers me."

"But maybe the ends justify the means?" she suggested.

"What ends could justify *that*?"

"You tell me."

We glared at each other. There was no way I'd look away first.

"Let me lay it out for you, Lia," the detective said finally. "It might not be you in that vid. But I think it is. I can read people—"

"I'm not people," I said sourly. "I'm a *skinner*, remember?"

"A skinner who was picked up in a *city*. Tied to a chair by a bunch of city rats? Now tell me, what's a sweet little girl like you do to get the slummers so angry?"

"You'll have to ask them," I said.

Her lips quirked. "I'm afraid they're unavailable for questioning."

I didn't let myself dwell on that one.

"Some people—some *orgs*—don't need a reason to hate me," I said, the "you should know" clear in my voice. "It's enough that I'm a mech."

"Just to be clear: You're refusing to explain your activities of the last three days?" she asked. "You're aware how that looks?"

"Like I care. What I do is my business, not yours."

"Maybe." She sighed, tugging at the cheap material of her corp-provided suit, the wrong cut and a size too small. I could have told her that shoving herself into the beige sausage casing wasn't working and that she should go back to pinching her pennies to save up for her next lipo—lift-tucks and the like were rarer in corp-towns, more of an occasional splurge than a fact of daily life, but no amount was too much to pay to stave off age and fat. Too bad for her, I wasn't really in the fashion-favor-granting mood. And for all I knew, pleasantly plump was the latest trend in her corp-town, the better to make clear you weren't an underfed city rat. Besides, at least she still got to *eat*. Let her deal with the consequences.

"But here's your problem," she continued. "It's my job to decide what's my business. And right now, I say it's you."

"I want a lawyer," I said.

"Tough."

"I have rights," I reminded her.

"Oh, really?" She smirked. "What are they?"

I hesitated. The ins and outs of the criminal justice system weren't exactly a hot topic of study at the Helmsley School. "I know you can't just lock me up here when I haven't done anything wrong. If you won't let me voice a lawyer, at least let me tell someone I'm here."

"And who would that be?" she asked.

"None of your business," I said. Thinking: *No one*. I hadn't talked to my parents in months. So who did I know that could fix this kind of problem. *Jude?*

Riley, I thought. But that was idiotic. How was he supposed to help? Even if it turned out he wasn't the reason I was here?

"Since you seem a little murky on the facts, let me explain them to you," Detective Ayer said. "One: There has been a major attack on a civilian population. Two: There are indications that this may be part of an ongoing threat. Three: I'm empowered to do anything within my means to ensure another such attack doesn't take place. Four: You're a skinner. Not a person. Just a person-shaped box with a computer inside. Boxes don't get lawyers."

"The *government* considers me a person," I said. "Look it up."

"Five," she continued, like I hadn't said anything. We both knew that the government had outsourced all security matters to the corps. Everyone had agreed it was safer that way. The government couldn't be trusted with unlimited power, they'd made that obvious time and time again. But the corps were, in principle, regulated by the exigencies of the market. They thrived when the customer thrived, and mutual self-interest was the ultimate satisfaction guarantee. So now corporate boards made the rules, and the corporate secops carried them out. No questions asked. "No one knows you're here. And until you cooperate with me, no one will."

I crossed my arms. "Is this where I'm supposed to cry?"

I am a machine, I told myself. *You can't threaten a machine.*

"You can do whatever you'd like," the detective said. "As long as you tell me the truth. Let's start with Friday morning. Why don't you tell me everything you did from the moment you woke up."

"And if I say no?" I asked. "What then?" Even if I could formulate a convincing enough lie about the last several days, how would I remember all of the details on the inevitable second or third time she walked me through it? Why hadn't I spent the last couple days planning what I would do when I got caught? What had I expected, Riley and I would just go on the run forever, playing house in some urine-stained room on the thirtieth floor of west tower, scavenging for spare power and poking around the network once a year to see whether it was safe to come home?

"You don't want to test me, Lia."

"For the sake of argument, let's say I do." Nothing like a good offense, right? Especially when your defense is nonexistent. "What next, you torture me or something? Violate the HRC?" Even at Helmsley, they'd made sure to teach us about the Human Rights Covenant, supposedly some kind of guarantee that the government would never go psycho again, rounding up people by the hundreds and abandoning them to darkness and pain until they vomited out details of nefarious plots they may—or in most cases, may not—have known anything about. All that trouble, and they hadn't managed to prevent Chicago or St. Louis or the Disneypocalypse. It turned out that bio-sensors and facial recognition screeners were more efficient than torture.

The government had signed the HRC back when they still ran security, but the secops were all bound by it.

"There you go again, talking about your rights," the detective said. "*Human* Rights Covenant. What makes you imagine you qualify?"

I could tell her the truth, I thought. Not because she scared me, with her sausage suit and empty threats. But because I was tired, and if I could make her believe me, this could all be over.

She would never believe me. That I'd been in the corptown while, in a stunning coincidence, another mech, one who just happened to have my face, enacted an insane plan I knew nothing about? Odds like that hovered somewhere around absolute zero.

"Do whatever you want," I said. "I'm a machine, right? Machines don't hurt."

"I'm told that's not quite true," she said, smiling. Like she was enjoying herself. "But I'm afraid you misunderstand. I'm not threatening you. And certainly—given you have no need to eat or sleep—I'm not going to waste my time by waiting you out."

"So we're done here?" Like I had any real hope of that.

"I'm starting to think you're misunderstanding me on purpose," Detective Ayer said. A new image popped up on the screen. My sister, Zo. "You don't care about what happens to you, that's obvious," she said. "And frankly, I can't blame you." She swept her eyes up and down my body, then shuddered. "Probably just waiting for someone to put you out of your misery." Another image popped up next to Zo. My mother. "But what if you weren't the only person at stake?" My father. One big, happy, Lia-less Kahn family. "What if your actions actually had consequences?"

I forced myself to laugh. "You're kidding, right?"

"People are dead," she snapped. "Living, breathing, *organic* humans are dead. Thanks to you and your friends. Is that a joke to you? Because it's not to me." Leaving the screen lit, she retreated to the door. "Your coconspirators are still out there. Which means people could die. And I'm willing to do pretty much *anything* to stop that. So why don't you sit here for a while and think about whether you really have nothing left to lose."

She closed the door behind her. I heard the lock catch. *Now they'll watch me,* I thought. *Hoping they'll catch me*—but that was where my imagination failed. Catch me what? Monologuing about all my evil plans? Smearing my finger across the layer of dust on the table, letter by letter spelling out my confession? Or did they just hope to catch the exact moment I broke, staring at the faces of my family, imagining what might happen to them if I didn't give Ayer what she wanted? Strange, the way orgs clung so desperately to this idea that we weren't human, then ditched it as soon as it was no longer convenient. If I was just a machine, then why would I care what they did to a family that, by their standards, wasn't mine? And if I did care, didn't that mean I was human after all?

Apparently not.

It was an empty threat. It had to be. This just wasn't how things worked. Not anymore.

I stayed in my seat as one hour passed, then another, waiting for Ayer to return. I knew how to wait. Hadn't I been doing it for days now? Hadn't I been doing it for months, waiting for something to happen that would change everything? That would *fix* everything, turn back the clock to the time before I left home, before Auden, before the download? If you're waiting for something that's never going to happen—that you *know* is never going to happen—it shouldn't count as waiting. But that's how it felt.

Almost twelve hours passed. When the door opened, Ayer was wearing another, even frumpier suit, blue this time, with the Synapsis label emblazoned in a garish red. New clothes for a new day. And she wasn't the only one. She set a neatly pressed pile of clean clothes down on the table beside me, complete with a pair of shoes. And not just any shoes I realized suddenly, confused—these were *mine*.

"You have a visitor," she said, as the door swung open again.

For a moment I thought I was imagining him. That the pressure and confusion had plunged me into a dreamer flash-back, or maybe some kind of wish-fulfillment mechanism had overwhelmed my neural system.

And then the hallucination spoke. "Hello, Lia," he said, stiff and proper as always. Unreadable. I couldn't look at him. Not without picturing him the way I'd seen him last, when I'd thought I wouldn't see him again.

I forced myself not to get up. He wouldn't want to touch me. But he crossed the room and rested his hands on my shoulders, and his lips brushed the top of my head, and I hugged my chin to my chest and closed my eyes and was sorry and grateful that I couldn't cry. "Hi, Dad."

UNSAID

"That's what happens when your whole life is an oxymoron."

This is over," he said. "You're coming with me."

I glanced at Detective Ayer.

"Don't look at her," he snapped. "She's got no power here."

"Lia, when was the last time you saw your father?" the detective asked.

"I—" I stopped. Trick question, obviously. But knowing she was trying to trick me into telling the truth wouldn't help me come up with the correct lie.

"She's not answering any more of your questions," my father informed her. "And she's leaving here with me. *Now*."

The detective flushed. "M. Kahn, you understand, there's

paperwork to be completed, and even if everything you say checks out—"

"*If?*" My father wasn't the kind to explode. If anything, he did the opposite—as his anger built, he contracted. He fell silent, his face scary white, his voice low, his eyes riveted on the target of his scorn, as if willing his gaze into a face-melting beam. Some people were too dense to notice the shift; true idiots mistook his stillness for passivity. But like Ayer had said before, she could read people, and she read my father. Or maybe she'd read enough of my file to know that a man like him—on the board of several corps, including hers—could get her kicked so far down the ladder that by the end of the week she'd be shipped off to the nearest wind farm to spend her days trolling for power pirates.

"I didn't mean to question your integrity, M. Kahn," she said tightly, each word clipped and precise.

"Much as I appreciate that heartfelt sentiment, your superiors aren't relying on my word," he said. "They're acting on the records of BioMax Corp."

"Just a coincidence that you sit on the board," she mumbled.

"What's that?" my father snapped. "Speak up."

Her shoulders slumped. "Nothing."

"Fortunately for all of us, I suppose, the decision is out of your hands," my father said. "Your superiors haven't seen fit to question the material supplied by BioMax, so unless there's something else . . . ?"

Detective Ayer turned to me, and her defeated expression regained a little of its spark. "You didn't know, did you?" she asked.

"Didn't know what?"

"That your alibi was out there, ready and waiting. That you could have ended this farce before it started."

"Maybe I just enjoyed your company," I said, pride overcoming curiosity.

She shook her head. I could see from her expression that she knew she'd be crazy to push the issue—and she was going to do it anyway. Her last stand. "I don't think so. You asked how we tracked you down. Don't you want to know?"

"Lia, we're leaving," my father said. Like I was still his perfect, darling daughter, who lived in the bedroom down the hall, said please and thank you and of course, yes, whatever you want, Daddy, like I hadn't seen him on his knees praying to a God he'd never believed in, wishing that he'd had the strength to let me die.

He'd done me a favor, convincing me once and for all that I wasn't the same person anymore, no matter how much we both might have wanted it. I'd done him a favor in return: I left.

"No. I want to hear this." Knowing that he was my only option, that if he changed his mind about rescuing me and left me here, here is where I'd rot. Knowing that if I said one more *yes* and walked out the door with him, I'd keep walking, straight to the car, then to the house, to the old bedroom and the old life, the one that didn't fit me any better than all the old clothes in Lia Kahn's closet, custom-tailored to a body that was now a pile of ashes in some biowaste landfill.

"BioMax is tracking you," Detective Ayer said. "BioMax

knows where all you mechs are, every minute of every day. Took a couple days to get them to release the data, but once they did, we would have found you anywhere."

Relief, that was first. No one had turned me in. Riley hadn't betrayed me. Relief, and then disgust—with BioMax, and with myself for not figuring it out.

My father's face was as blank as mine.

"That's your big secret?" I said coolly. "You think I didn't know that?"

As an org, I'd been good at bluffing; as a mech, I was a pro. Empty expression, inflection-free voice—Ayer would never know how much she'd thrown me. "Seems like you're the one who's been wasting time. All that data and you still can't figure out who attacked the corp-town? What kind of detective are you anyway?"

Judging from her expression, the kind that wanted to violate the Human Rights Covenant and throw me into the wall. But she behaved. "BioMax doesn't archive its tracking data," she said tightly. Apparently my father wasn't the only one who could release his bottled-up anger word by bitter word. "They can only tell us where you *are*, not where you *were*."

Lie, I thought. BioMax would never collect the information just to throw it out. Ayer didn't seem dumb enough to believe the line, but maybe she was smart enough to know it was all she'd get.

What else was BioMax lying about? Was it just a GPS tracker, or could they see what I saw, hear what I heard? Could they somehow know what I was thinking? My brain was a computer, after all—a computer they'd built. Shouldn't it have occurred to me that they could read it as easily as I could read the network? That maybe they could write over it as easily as I could update my zone?

"Did you want to hear the rest?" Ayer asked, giving herself away with an inadvertent glance at my father. Because he'd given the secops something they didn't have, I realized. Evidence that had convinced them to let me go—evidence that shouldn't have existed.

"BioMax feeds the tracking data to my father," I said flatly, confirming the guess with one look at Ayer's face. My father remained unreadable. "They may not archive it, but he does."

The detective looked disappointed that I wasn't freaking out. She didn't know him like I did. You didn't say no to my father—if the information existed in the world, it was only a matter of time before he claimed it for himself.

"And according to him, you've spent the last several days at home with your family." Detective Ayer smiled coldly. "I just can't understand why you wouldn't have mentioned that yourself, saved us both all this trouble."

"I'm sure there are lots of things you don't understand," I said. "You must be used to it by now." I could feel my father's eyes on me, sense his approval.

"Unless there's anything else, we'll be going now," my father said. "Once you apologize to my daughter for wasting her time."

Detective Ayer looked like she'd rather die. "If you come

across any information about the attack, I hope you'll come to me," she said. "We *do* intend to solve this case."

"I hope you can," I said. "Oh, and apology accepted."

The clothes felt wrong, like they belonged to someone else. Which they did. They'd come from a dead girl's closet. But I put them on anyway, grateful to trash the city rags. I laced up the dead girl's sneakers. And let the dead girl's father take me away.

My BioMax rep was waiting for us in the parking lot. Just as repulsively handsome as I remembered, even in his tacky suit with its thermo-pulse lapels and gold net-links at each cuff. The first time I met Ben, I'd fixed on the dimpled chin and the full lips, instinctively turning on the flirt even though I was stuck in a hospital bed unable to do anything but blink—and even though, at the time, my skull was stripped bare to expose the tangled mess of circuitry that lay beneath. That was back when I thought we were on the same team, still members of the same species. Before he leaned in close, gave me that sickly fake grin, and said, "Call me Ben," my first tip-off that he wasn't a doctor or a savior but just some guy who wanted to sucker me into trusting him. Even though I saw him every time I went into BioMax for a checkup or repair, I could never be bothered to remember his last name. Call-me-Ben it was. And now, apparently, we were on the same team again.

"Good to see you again, Lia," he said. "Though not under these circumstances."

"Seems like you've been seeing me nonstop," I snapped. "So you like to watch? Seen anything you like?"

Ben raised his eyebrows at my father. "She knows?"

"She knows," I said.

"We don't *watch*," Ben told me. "We keep track of where you go, but that's it. No spying."

I rolled my eyes. "Right. That's not spying at all."

"It's precautionary," he said. "To make sure none of you get into any trouble. Like, say, wandering into a corp-town that's about to become the site of biological warfare."

"What'd you do?" I asked my father. "Pay him off to give the cops fake information?"

"BioMax is not in the business of violating its clients' privacy," Ben said stiffly.

"Especially not if it would prove your clients are a bunch of terrorists," I guessed. "You know who attacked that corp-town, don't you? And you're protecting them."

"We're protecting all of you," Ben said.

"You're protecting your *investment*."

"You don't want to become an object of fear and hatred."

"I didn't want to become an object at all," I snapped. "But no one asked me."

"Enough," my father said. He didn't have to raise his voice. "Ben, thanks for your assistance. Now, if you wouldn't mind . . ."

"Of course," Ben said smoothly. "I'll be waiting in the car."

We walked. In silence, at first, until Ben was out of sight. The secops headquarters looked like a silver pyramid that had been smashed with a giant sledgehammer, leaving behind a crushed jumble of razor-sharp points and jagged edges. The planes of the building jutted at awkward angles, so that wherever you stood, it appeared ready to topple over on your head. Covered in silver-plated panels, it likely gleamed in the sun—but on a day like this, like most days, the sky a swirl of murky grays, it nearly faded into the clouds.

We kept the station at our backs, and instead wandered through its carefully groomed gardens, which burst with the bright purples and pinks of tropical flowers, genetically coded to survive the cold. It was something I never would have noticed before the download, the way the flowers looked wrong, almost plastic, sprouting from the frost-tipped grass. My father stopped abruptly, staring down at a large pink blossom the size of a fist, its stiff petals barely flickering in the breeze. For a moment I thought he was going to pluck it—ill-advised as that would have been, given the fact that despoiling private gardens was illegal and this garden happened to belong to the secops. Besides, what would my father want with a flower?

Finally he looked up from the flower—to me. I didn't like it. It was too easy to imagine what he was seeing, the machine that usurped his dead daughter's life. The mistake.

In his eyes I wasn't some wondrous machine, a marvel of modern technology. I wasn't a mech, I was a *skinner*. A *thing*, just like the Brotherhood of Man said, the thing that the people in the corp-town and the city saw when they glared at me, the thing, the *object*, with the unnatural gait, the unblinking eyes, the man-made brain.

In his eyes I wasn't a miracle. I was a desecration.

His hair was a different color than the last time I'd seen him, black instead of his natural blond. He was a vain man, but not about his appearance—that was my mother's domain, and I could only assume that, as usual, she'd decided to mod her look and changed his to match. It made his skin look paler, throwing the lines ridging his eyes and mouth into sharp relief; past time for another lift-tuck.

There had been a time, when Zo and I were kids, that our mother had insisted we all conform to some Kahnian Platonic ideal. Blond hair, blue eyes, Zo and I with identical waves in our shoulder-length manes, our honey-haired mother towing our father like an accessory, the two of them looking enough alike to be siblings. It was popular in those days, families looking alike, parading their designer genes like a uniform, but Zo and I put a stop to it as soon as we were old enough to fight back. It had been years since the two of us had been a matched pair, and my mother had given up trying to keep pace. But she'd never before picked a look so drastically un-Kahn. Although— given the metallic purples and silvers glimmering across my body—I wasn't looking very Kahn myself these days.

No one watching us together would guess we were father and daughter.

"Do you mind if I . . . ?" He broke off, then folded me into an awkward hug, his body stiff and unyielding against mine. Or maybe it was my body that was unyielding, my arms that stayed at my sides. "That's from your mother," he said, letting go, staring at the stupid flower again.

"Oh. I guess, give her one for me too?" It was hard to imagine. The last time I'd seen them touch, I was lying in a hospital bed. I couldn't remember the time before that.

"You could do that yourself," he said.

So we were done with small talk and onto the main event. "I'm sorry," I said. *I'm not sorry.* "For leaving like that." *But not for leaving.*

"Without saying good-bye?" he asked. "Or telling us where you were going? Telling us *anything*? Yes, I guess you would be sorry."

Now I was the one staring at the ground. "It was easier that way."

"For you," my father snapped.

"Sorry," I mumbled again.

"Your mother thought . . ." He shook his head. "You know how she gets."

I tried to catch his eye, hoping for a smile. It was one of the things that brought us Kahns together—me, my father, and Zo, at least. We all knew how my mother got. But he wouldn't look at me.

"But you knew where I went," I said. "Because you've been watching me."

"Can you blame me?"

"I had to leave," I said.

"I realize you think that."

"This is better."

"I realize you think that too." He frowned. "Though I can't say I understand why."

I wasn't about to tell him what I'd seen, that I knew he felt obligated to treat me like a daughter and pretend everything was the way it used to be, even if it was tearing him apart. My father didn't do weakness. Another reason my leaving was a gift to him. "How's Zo?" I asked instead.

"She misses you."

No, she missed her sister. As far as she was concerned, I was just an imposter, come to steal her sister's identity and life. So Zo had stolen it first. Starting with Walker. But I wasn't about to ask my father if Zo was still sleeping with my ex-boyfriend.

I didn't even care anymore. Walker felt irrelevant. I remembered wanting him, I just couldn't remember why. Zo was welcome to him, as she was welcome to all my old friends and old clothes, my old spot on the track team, my old spot as favorite daughter. Only daughter.

"She didn't want me there," I said.

"She's a child. She doesn't know what she wants."

"She's only two years younger than me," I pointed out. Waiting for the inevitable: *You're a child too.*

You don't know what you want.

Come home.

But he didn't say it.

Your sister misses you. Your mother misses you. Never I *miss you.*

It started to rain. My father glanced up, looking annoyed that the weather would dare interrupt him, then down at his shoes, already spattered with grime from the fat, filthy raindrops.

"Whatever you were doing in that corp-town," my father said, steering us back toward the car, "I know it's because you're mixed up with these . . ." His face twisted. *"People."* He raised his arm, letting his hand fall lightly on my left shoulder for just a moment, like he was choosing arbitrarily from a list of "fatherly gestures," seeking one that felt right. This wasn't it.

Did he think I had something to do with the attack?

Did he think I was capable of something like that? And if he did, why would he be here now?

Just ask me, I thought. *Ask me what happened.*

And I resolved that if he did ask, I would tell him everything.

"I don't want to know about it," he said, hunching his shoulders against the rain. "Just be careful."

I was still a minor; if he wanted to force me to come home, he could. Or at least he could try. I'd been wondering all these months why he hadn't—certainly he had enough credit and enough reach to find out where I was. To drag me home. But he hadn't.

And now it turned out he'd known where I was the whole time. Known, and just left me there.

I didn't miss you either, I thought.

And *I missed you too.*

I never understood it as an org, how a thing could be true

and not true in equal amounts. When we were kids, they always tried to drill it into our heads, the way the universe constructed itself through a simultaneity of opposition: Light is a particle. Light is a wave. Light is both, at the same time it's neither. Every reality contains its own opposite; every whole truth rests on two half lies.

These days, it made a lot more sense. That's what happens when your whole life is an oxymoron.

Now I existed solely thanks to the quantum paradox, my brain a collection of qubits in quantum superposition, encoding truths and memories, imagination and irrationality in opposing, contradictory states that existed and didn't exist, all at the same time.

I am the same; I am different.

But when it came to my family, different won out. *Some things create danger just by existing.* I couldn't go home again, even if he'd asked.

Which he hadn't.

"I don't think the authorities will be bothering you anymore," he said. "But if they do, voice me."

"Thank you," I said. Formal, proper, like a stranger. Like him. "And for today. Thanks."

Like it was no big deal that he'd made it okay, the way I used to think he could make everything okay. I wasn't a child anymore; I knew better. Some things could be fixed with credit and power and properly applied pressure. Most things, the important things— things like bodies on the ground, bleeding from their eyes, things like what happened when the secops arrived and the guns came out and the losers fell, things like me, stuck between being a person and a *thing*—no one could fix. Not even him.

My father patted me on the back, twice. Item number two on the list of awkward "fatherly gestures."

"Ben's agreed to drive you back," he said.

"Oh. Now?"

"Unless there's something else you need?"

As I watched him, trying to figure out what he was expecting me to say, he met my gaze for the first time. But if there was a message encrypted in his blue stare, I couldn't crack the code. "No," I said. "Nothing."

WATCHERS

"It's for your own protection."

I would have expected someone like call-me-Ben to drive
a late-model Trivi or maybe even a Petra, one of those
neutered bubble cars with a rotating cabin and a collapsible gel
body—bland as his wardrobe, suitable for middle-aged trend
chasers who preferred safety to style. But the car was a Taiko,
black and practically dripping with credit, its bullet shape so
streamlined that it was hard to imagine how a human form
could fit inside. The wheels were hidden beneath the frame, so
there was nothing to break the smooth, sleek line. I'd never
seen one up close before, much less ridden inside, but I heard
that with the right patch, you could override the velocity
restrictions and push it to almost two hundred. Walker had
always wanted one, and the fact that I knew anything about

them at all was a testament to how crazy he'd been on the subject. You can't tune out three years' worth of obsession. (Trust me, I tried.)

The paint was supposedly some kind of special alloy that absorbed even infrared light—it looked like someone had carved a car-shaped hole in the universe and filled it with pure nothingness.

The door swung open. Ben was behind the wheel. I climbed into the backseat, hoping to endure the ride in silence. No such luck. He programmed the nav-unit for Quinn's estate, then climbed in beside me. I stared out the window, watching my father's figure recede into the distance.

"You're welcome," Ben said once we'd pulled out onto open road.

"I didn't say thank you."

"I noticed."

I kept my eyes on the window. The land was flat here, sprawling green fields stretching toward the horizon. A herd of cows whizzed by in a spotted blur. The road wove through flower-dotted meadows; clumps of willow trees, their spindly, sagging branches kissing the road; acres of greening corn, bowing to the wind. *Nowhere to hide,* I thought, then wondered how long it would be before I stopped searching for safe harbors.

"No one gets something for nothing, Lia," Ben said.

I faced him. Hard to believe I'd ever found this guy attractive. Not that his features were anything less than perfect—but there was a softness to them, a waxy, malleable quality, like he'd been molded in a factory, the simulacrum of a real live person. Everything about him looked artificial, from his sparkling brown eyes to his artfully tousled hair to his soft, full lips curving up in a sardonic smile. But: *He can be as fake as he wants, and he'll still be more real than me.*

"You're angry," Ben said.

"You noticed."

"That's exactly why you weren't informed about the tracking."

"You mean *spying*."

"I understand it displeases you. But it's for your own protection."

"I can take care of myself."

He laughed softly. "Of course. All evidence to the contrary notwithstanding."

The car vibrated beneath us as we lurched off the highway onto a loose gravel road. "We're going the wrong way."

"Scenic route," Ben said. "You and I have a lot to discuss."

I thought about opening the door and throwing myself out of the car. It would have been a bit melodramatic, but melodrama seemed appropriate. We couldn't have been going more than fifty or sixty miles an hour—it would be a bumpy landing, but I'd had those before. Thick skin, strong bones, titanium skull, just a few of the benefits of being a mech.

But if call-me-Ben wanted me, he would always know exactly where to find me.

Another of the benefits of being a mech, apparently.

"The doors are locked," Ben said.

"No problem." I gave him a placid smile. "I'm getting used to being a prisoner."

"You're not a prisoner, Lia." Ben sighed and leaned back in his seat. He laced his fingers together, inverted his hands, palms facing out, then stretched his arms with a satisfied groan. "You're just possibly the solution to a sticky little problem we've been having."

"I doubt that. What do you want?"

"Your friend Jude," Ben said.

I don't have friends, I was about to say, then stopped myself. Friends were for orgs, just like family. I didn't know what Jude was to me—an ally, a protector, an antagonist—none of the old categories fit. He was simply *like me*.

I smirked at Ben. "Last I checked, he's not mine to give."

"I want the name of his BioMax contact." Ben's voice was steely.

"I don't know what you're talking about."

"Let me tell you what I know, Lia." His features were still just as soft, but his voice, his eyes, were hard. "I know Jude has an inside source at BioMax. That he's stealing information and technology. I also know that Jude was supposed to meet his contact at Synapsis Corp-Town this week, but he sent you instead. For the first time. And just as you arrive . . ." Ben shook his head. "That's some seriously bad timing, don't you think?"

No more secrets. That was all I could think. Not when they were watching.

"How do you know?" I asked, hating how small my voice sounded.

Ben made a sound like a buzzer. "Wrong question, Lia."

I wanted him to stop saying my name. There was a little twist in his voice, a glint in his eye, each time he formed the syllables. Like the name was a secret between us. Like he was silently saying, *We both know you're not* really *Lia Kahn. But I'll play along if you will.*

I waited.

"Why didn't he go himself?" Ben asked. "Why did he need *you* to go? What did he really want?"

I saw where he was going. I'd already gotten there myself. Jude was the one who'd sent me to BioMax, it followed he was the one most likely to have set me up. But he wasn't the only one who'd known about the corp-town trip. Jude's BioMax contact knew too. And he'd known enough not to show. Call-me-Ben wanted me to believe Jude had set me up—and so, for the first time, I started to think maybe he hadn't.

"He must really scare you guys," I said. "Afraid he'll turn us against you?"

Ben arched an eyebrow. "'You' *orgs*?"

"'You' *BioMax*." I was spinning through the possibilities as quickly as I could. BioMax knew where we were at all times—they had all they needed to set us up. But why go to the trouble and then whisk me away from the secops? Why do it in the first place?

He burst into laughter. "Lia, as far as I'm concerned, if

Jude were who he claimed to be, he'd be a hero. Our BioMax clients *need* someone like him, to ease the transition into life post-download." His eyes were gleaming, his movements loose and free, as if some part of him usually tamped down was breaking out. "All that stuff about mechs being superior, about this technology being the dawn of a new era for humanity . . . if I didn't believe that, why would I work for BioMax in the first place?"

"Great, so Jude's a hero," I said sourly. Maybe they were all working together. "Where's the problem? You want me to arrange a meet-and-greet?"

"I said he *would* be a hero," Ben reminded me. "If a tidy little confidence boost was all he was after. But it's not."

"How would you know?"

"Wrong question again," Ben said with another buzzing noise. "What does this boy *really* want? Have you even bothered to ask? Or is it easier to just smile and nod and accept whatever he says as gospel?"

"You know me," I said with as much fake sweetness as I could muster. "Always going with the flow."

"You really think you're all a bunch of rebels, don't you?" he asked, sounding like he was trying not to laugh. "And what, exactly, are you rebelling against?"

"I don't know," I mused. "How about stalker corps that get off on spying on us?"

Nothing ruffled him. He just drummed his hands on the smoky glass of the window, adopting a philosopher's tone. "'Us.' Interesting word, that. And who would 'us' be, in this scenario?"

He ticked the options off on his fingers. "We've got Jude, who appears out of nowhere and charms himself into the heart of, among others, Quinn Sharpe, heir to one of the country's largest fortunes. Not to mention Ty Marian, Anders Prix, Lara Pirendez—none of them in Sharpe territory, certainly, but not too shabby. Sloane Beignet—I'm told *you* were responsible for bringing her in. And then there's Lia Kahn. Whose parents have yet to part with any of their credit—but, if and when they do, will, I'm sure, be donating to the cause."

"What are you getting at?" I knew what he was getting at.

"I'm just wondering whether it's a coincidence that so many of your friend Jude's nearest and dearest acolytes are swimming in credit."

"It's no coincidence," I snapped. "So we're rich—so what?" Not wanting to admit that I'd had the same thought myself. But Quinn had donated her credit freely—they all had—so we could live as we wanted to live. *Jude pays me back in other ways,* she'd told me once. *And not just me, all of us.* It's not like Jude reveled in the luxury—there seemed to be little that he actually wanted for himself. "The download costs. We're *all* rich."

"Not all of them," Ben said pointedly. "At least, they didn't used to be."

"That's really what you want to talk about?" I said. Daring him. "The 'volunteers'?" He could hear it in my voice, that I knew better.

"You're so quick to distrust BioMax," he said smoothly, shifting gears. "And yet so quick to put your faith in someone like Jude. Do you know *anything* about this boy? Where he came from, who he was before the download?"

"It's irrelevant," I shot back. "None of us are the people we were before the download. Those people are dead."

"Excuse my language, but: bullshit," Ben said. "That's a lie *he* needs you to believe, so you'll walk away from the people who actually care about you. Like your family, Lia. Like your father."

"Not that it's any of your business, but my father cares about Lia Kahn, his dead daughter. I'm just an electronic copy. You know it, I know it."

"Does he." Ben shut his eyes and tipped his head back against the seat. As if we were done and it was naptime.

Not that I wanted to hear more of his crap.

Still. "You don't know anything about my father."

"I'm sure you're right." He didn't bother to open his eyes. Instead, he pulled out a tablet-size ViM, passed it to me. It was as black and sleek as the car, featureless but for the slim gray thumbprint in the left corner. No one needed that kind of security on their ViMs—that was the whole point of a ViM, that the data was stored on the network, not on the machine. Nonetheless, the screen stayed blank until Ben reached across me and pressed his thumb to the print. "A greatest-hits selection for you."

The vids were cued up on the BioMax zone, the picture blurry and amateurish, the cameras shaking. All featured my father facing down clusters of suited men and women, various corp logos hanging over their heads or stenciled onto the surface of the tables.

My father, seemingly oblivious to the camera and the hostility of his audiences. "These are human beings," he said in vid after vid. "Can't you see that? People we know. People we care about."

My father, for once asking rather than ordering, asking for understanding. For the download technology. For the mechs. For his daughter.

"These aren't machines," he said, "no matter what they look like. These are our children—my child."

One-on-one in an ornate living room, pounding a delicate glass table so hard I expected it to shatter. "Would this be any less a table if it was made of wood? Of steel? We don't define a thing by what it's made of—we define a thing by what it *does*. A brain isn't a brain because it's a mess of cells and neurotransmitters and organic gunk. It's a brain because it *thinks*. We're all made out of nothing but *stuff*. Our stuff may bleed, but fundamentally? It's still just matter in motion: an organic machine. And fundamentally, if you judge them by how they think, how they feel, how they *act*, they're still human."

Ben, his eyes still closed, permitted himself a small half smile. "He borrowed that one from me. Nice, isn't it?"

"What is this?" I paused the final vid on a grainy shot of my father's face. At the secops station he'd looked older than I remembered, but here he seemed young again, as if fresh off a lift-tuck, the fuzziness erasing the cracks carved into his face and the dark half moons under his eyes. The camera had somehow captured something that never escaped in real life—the anger hidden beneath the tight lips and the carefully modulated voice.

In the frozen vid, his face was still perfectly composed. But his eyes looked wild. "Where'd you get this?"

"You think you're the only one we keep an eye on?" Ben finally opened his eyes and looked at me. "What?" he said with palpably false surprise. "You didn't know?"

I didn't say anything.

Was it guilt? As far as I could tell, my father didn't know the meaning of the word. Guilt required acknowledgment of wrong-doing, and in the world according to my father, everything he did was right, by definition.

Except for the choice to make me, I thought, not wanting to remember.

Remembering.

Forgive me, he'd begged. *If I could do it again . . .*

I would make the right choice this time.

He felt guilty that he'd unleashed me on the world and on his family—Lia Kahn's family, forced to pretend that the dead had come back to life, that an electronic copy could ever replace the real thing.

And yet: "These are our children. My child."

And yet my father didn't lie.

Maybe he was lying to himself.

But what if he just believed it?

"Your father's been running all over the country, trying to persuade his estimable peers to ease the path for download recipients," Ben said. "He's become quite the crusader for mech rights. All behind closed doors, of course."

"Of course." It wouldn't do for a man of his stature to be zone-hopping like a Savona-style crackpot, spilling his guts to the masses. And my father had long made clear his belief that true power acted in silence and shadow.

"He wants you to come home," Ben said.

If he wanted that, he would have made it happen. My father didn't do subtle, and he didn't do voluntary.

"What's your point?" I asked, wondering if I should reconsider the whole jumping-out-of-the-car thing. But that would prove Ben right. Like I was someone who preferred not to ask questions because I was too weak to deal with the answers.

"I think you're a little confused about who your real friends are," Ben said.

"I'm not—"

"It's understandable." His drone was maddeningly calm. "You know, Lia, as an official BioMax rep, it's policy to remain a watchful distance from all our clients, but . . ." He cleared his throat. "Did I ever tell you that you were my first?"

I shook my head. Thinking: *Who cares?*

"It was my job to help you and your family through the transition period, and I can't help feeling as if I've failed you." He pressed his fingertips together, then tapped them against each other, one by one. "I probably shouldn't admit that. But I feel responsible for you, Lia. I worry."

"Good show," I said, giving him a slow clap. "Though next time, you might want to try a single tear rolling down your cheek. Much more effective."

The corner of his mouth twitched. "You're growing cynical in your old age."

"Check the manual," I said. "I don't age."

"Fine." Ben leaned forward and keyed something into the nav-panel. "I'll take you back. Obviously there's no point in discussing this further."

"You noticed."

"Loyalty's a tricky thing," Ben said. "Just because you give it to someone doesn't mean you get it back."

"Funny, this feels like discussing."

"There's nothing to discuss," Ben said. "You've made that clear. You'll go back to the Sharpe estate. You'll do your best to pretend the last several days never happened."

As if I could.

"You'll probably tell your friend Jude everything I've said here, just to prove to him how loyal you are. Or prove it to yourself. And then, once you've had time to think about it, you'll get in touch with me and give me the name of Jude's BioMax contact."

"I think your fortune-telling skills are failing you," I said. "Because there's no way." Not that I owed Jude anything. But I owed Ben even less.

"I'd prefer you do it because you want to," Ben said. "I'd rather convince you that Jude's not doing any of you favors by loading you up with untested tech."

"Well, you can't, and you shouldn't—"

"I'd *prefer* to do it that way," he said over me. "But since that's not an option, we'll resort to plan B. Reciprocation."

"What the hell is that?"

Ben smiled. "You give me the name—and I keep quiet about your unfortunately timed presence at the Synapsis Corp-Town. I keep those records where they are. Buried. Simple reciprocity."

"Blackmail."

He shrugged. "Whatever. Take a couple weeks to think about it. I'm a patient man."

He reached forward and flicked a finger across the car's control panel and—so smoothly it was almost imperceptible, we accelerated, the landscape bleeding past in a blur of color. Even at this speed, the car cornered tightly, veering back onto the highway, flying toward home.

We were running out of time, and he hadn't told me the one thing I needed to know. I hated to ask him for anything. "So if you're tracking us, you must know," I said, so quietly he had to tip his head toward me to catch the words. "You know who else was at the corp-town. Who did it."

"Who killed all those people, you mean? Who set you up?"

Assuming it wasn't you, I thought. "If you know, how can you just . . . do *nothing*?"

Ben smiled thinly. "I know you were there, and I'm doing nothing about that," he said.

"It's not the same."

"I already told you," he said irritably. It was the first real emotion I'd seen from him the whole trip. At least, I assumed it was real. "It's my job to protect you. *All* of you."

"Then what the hell is the point of the tracking?" I countered. "You said it was to keep us out of trouble—what, that doesn't include trying to kill hundreds of people?"

"You don't think I'd do something if I could?" he shouted—then abruptly fell silent.

"Then *do* it," I hissed. After everything I'd seen the last few days, I didn't have any sympathy left. Certainly not for him.

He didn't respond.

"You don't know who it is, do you?" I said suddenly. Just guessing—but I saw on his face it was true. "Your precious spy gear crapped out on you."

"No technology is foolproof," he said steadily. "You'd do well to remember that."

I didn't bother to answer. He no longer had anything I needed. We drove the rest of the way in silence.

"A pleasure, as always," Ben said as the car stopped at the southern boundary of Quinn's estate. He reached across me to open the door. I jerked away just before his arm could brush my chest.

I got out of the car, resisting the temptation to slam the door on his fingertips.

"And remember, Lia." He scratched the back of his head, letting his fingers rest on the spot where his skull met his neck, the spot where, somewhere inside my own head, a microscopic GPS chip was broadcasting my location to his bosses. And to my father. "We'll be watching."

I didn't want to go back to the house. I wanted to stay there, in the green empty, the concrete strip of road to my left and the estate grounds to my right. I wanted to pretend that I was stranded on the side of the road, come from nowhere, with nowhere to go. No one waiting for me. No one watching me.

I hadn't been this free since before the corp-town attack— free to wade through the overgrown grass, find the rambling path that would take me to the house, or to turn in the opposite direction, to the road, and start walking. Toward Lia Kahn's home, Lia Kahn's father, Lia Kahn's past.

Or just walking toward nothing. Filling myself up with nothing, an emptiness that could blot out the faces of the dead, call-me-Ben's voice, my father's hands on my shoulders, his lips brushing against my hair.

I belong here, I thought, trying to convince myself to climb the grassy slope. *I belong with them.*

Jude was up there. Jude, who might have set all this in motion. And when I got to the house, he was waiting for me.

"Took you long enough," he said, leaning against the doorframe of the main entrance. Even Jude looked small beside the columns of marble and steel.

"I'm fine, Jude," I said with a sneer, trying to gauge something from his expression. But there was no guilt, no shame, only judgment. I couldn't have been killed, so why was I making such a fuss? "Thanks so much for your concern."

"They're waiting for you inside," he said.

"Who?"

"Your many friends and admirers," he said, with a go-figure shrug.

"Riley?" I asked.

Jude nodded.

"Is he . . . okay?"

"What do you care?"

"I don't."

Jude grimaced. "He's here, he's fine. He's inside with the rest. Seems everyone wants to know about your adventures."

"But not you."

"I know enough," he said. "I've been watching the vids. It's not pretty."

"No," I said. "But I guess mass murder usually isn't."

Jude shook his head, a look of impatience flashing across his face. "I don't mean that. I mean that vid of you—"

"Not *me!*"

"Right. Whatever. That vid of someone who *looks* like you pumping poison into the system. The whole world thinks we just declared war on the orgs. It didn't occur to you to *voice* me when any of this happened?"

"So *that's* what you're mad about. Can't stand that we actually handled something without you."

"Handled it." Jude snorted. "Right. I've already talked to Riley. *He* wanted to come to me. You stopped him. You let him go back to that place *alone*. It didn't occur to you I could have *helped?*"

"Could you have?" There was something strange about talking to Jude. The conversation felt familiar and profoundly alien all at once. It was the same disconnect that came from looking around at the place I'd been living in for the last six months. Like nothing was the same anymore. I wondered if this was how my father felt when he looked at me. Like he was staring at a two-dimensional copy of something he'd once cared about.

Jude smashed a fist into the doorframe. His face stayed calm. "Go ahead. Ask me."

"What?"

"You know what."

I was too tired for the game. I gave him what he wanted. "Did you set me up?" I asked flatly. "Did you kill all those people?"

He didn't flinch. "You going to believe me if I say no?"

"Say it," I suggested, "and we'll find out."

"If you think I could do something like that, I'm not going to waste my time convincing you otherwise," he said.

"Not much of an answer."

"Why even stay here if that's what you think of me?" he asked. "Why don't you just go?"

Go where? I thought. "Fine." Calling his bluff. "I guess we're done here. I'll pack up and be out by morning."

"Wait," he said quietly. "Ask Riley."

"Ask him what?"

Jude picked at a loose stone in the doorframe, scraping out the sediment between the stone and wood. He turned half away from me, his shoulders hunched, his head angled toward the door. "Ask him, and he'll tell you I wouldn't do this," he said, careful to keep his eyes on the wall. "If you really think . . ."

I didn't know what I thought anymore. "What am I supposed to think?"

He started to speak but choked off the words. Then he shook his head. "Think whatever the hell you want."

"Jude—"

Suddenly, he whirled from the wall, facing me head-on. "I wasn't the only one who knew you'd be at Synapsis."

"What?"

It was like he was fighting a war with himself, the part that didn't care what I thought battling the part that needed me to believe him.

"You think it had to be me, because I sent you there," he said. "That I was the only one who knew. But I *wasn't*." He sounded like a child, denying that he'd thrown the ball, broken the window. I waited for him to blame it on his imaginary friend.

"Let me guess, I'm forgetting about your mysterious contact," I said. "The reason for the whole stupid rendezvous."

"That's not what I mean." Jude hesitated. He slipped down along the wall and perched on one of the stairs climbing up to the entrance. I stayed on my feet. "If I tell you something, will you swear to keep it to yourself?"

"I don't make blind promises." *Not to you.*

"BioMax is tracking us," he said. "GPS. They know wherever we go."

"You *knew*?"

"*You* knew?" He gaped at me. "How?"

"You're the genius, right? Figure it out." I was too angry to look at him. To think that he'd known all along and hadn't *told* us? Hadn't done *anything*?

"You can't tell anyone," he said.

"No, apparently *you* can't tell anyone!" I yelled. "Because you're on such a freaking power trip about being the all-knowing Jude! How *dare* you keep this a secret?"

"What the hell was I supposed to do?" he asked. "If people knew . . . well, look how *you're* reacting. I didn't want to start an unnecessary panic."

"I'm having a little trouble with the 'unnecessary' part— they're *spying* on us, Jude." I started pacing back and forth, trying to force out some of the anger through motion, but it didn't work like that, not in the mech body. My brain just kept whirring, furious at all of them.

Jude was still sitting down, sprawled almost casually against the stone stairs. "BioMax isn't our enemy. Not yet at least."

"You so sure about that? Or you think it was just a *coincidence* that the attack happened while we were at the corp-town? That your so-called source never showed up? Wake up, Jude. Either BioMax has something to do with this or . . ."

"Or I did," he said sourly. "Back to that."

"What the hell am I supposed to think? Especially when you're telling me you trust them. Even after *this*?"

"I don't trust anyone," Jude said coldly. "You think you're the only one who can do the math here? Are you really surprised? Did you believe all the BioMax crap, that they have our best interests at heart?"

"That's exactly my point!"

"No! That's exactly *my* point. If certain elements of BioMax were involved in this, all the more reason not to let them know we're onto their tracking tech. Let them think we're totally clueless. Let them expose themselves for what they really are."

"And until then, what? We just sit around and *wait*?" I asked in disbelief. "How can you even stand it? Knowing—" I shuddered. "Knowing they're *watching* you."

He didn't say anything. His gaze flicked away, just for a second, but it was long enough to reveal that there was something else. And I'd just hit on it.

Just like when I was in the car with call-me-Ben and he'd accidentally let slip that the trackers weren't foolproof.

"But they're *not* watching you, are they?" I said slowly, forcing myself not to yell.

He shrugged but couldn't refrain from cracking a small, sharklike smile. He was actually *proud*.

"They think they are," he said. Boasted. "Streaming live GPS, mapping my every move. And it's all bullshit. I've been feeding them false data for months."

"While you let the rest of us . . ." I stopped, searching for the words. I wanted to get this out right. No incoherent anger or misplaced betrayal, irrational reactions that he could brush off as weak and orglike. "You didn't bother to tell any of us," I said finally. "You let us hang and saved yourself."

"Oh, please." He rolled his eyes. "I see the time away hasn't cured you of your inclination to melodrama. 'Saved myself'?

From what? As if they'll be able to wring any dirty little secrets out of your location." He shook his head. "Trust me, you're not that interesting." He rubbed his hands across his face, a neat little simulation of org exhaustion. "Yes, I can jam the tracking. And *no*, I'm not about to do it for everyone. It doesn't occur to you that there may come a time when we can make the trackers work to our advantage? We don't want them knowing we can screw with the data. Didn't anyone ever teach you that you don't put your cards on the table until you have to?"

I hated to admit it, but he was making sense. That was the problem with Jude—he always made sense. He was too good at rationalizing, turning his whims into logical inevitabilities.

"All I know is you pretended we were all in this together," I said. "And then you did this, on your own."

He's not your friend. But that was Ben's voice in my head. And beneath my anger, there was something else—maybe it was the fact that Jude had voluntarily revealed one of his precious secrets, one guaranteed to make me hate him. Or maybe it was the moment when, for just one second, the mask had fallen away, exposing his need. He *needed* me to believe him innocent. And I almost did.

"You think I don't care about you? Them?" He swept his arms out to encompass the estate. Inexplicably, he was angry too—as if *I* was the one who'd done something wrong. "I'm doing this *all* for you!"

"Excuse me if I can't quite see how you selling us out to BioMax is *helping*."

"Because I'm taking care of it!" he shouted. "I make sure they don't see anything they shouldn't see. I know everything they know. *Everything.*"

There was a long silence as I processed what he'd said. And he realized what he'd revealed.

If it were anyone else, I would have said he looked almost afraid.

"You get the GPS feed?" This wasn't anger. I'd moved beyond anger. The thought of Jude sitting in front of a screen, watching us drift through our lives, watching *over* us like the Faithers' god, probably delusional enough to believe that he was sitting in judgment rather than violation? That was sickening.

"You'd rather they knew everything, and we know nothing?" he said defensively, his voice rising. "Someone has to watch our backs."

"And you love it, don't you?" I said coldly. "Watching."

It was one thing to know that strangers at BioMax were watching over my shoulder—even call-me-Ben was nothing more than a pretty face with a boring name attached, paid to pretend he cared about where I went and what I did. As for my father, he'd always been a watcher, keeping tabs on everything, from the hours I put in at the track to the experimental error rate in my biotech homework. That's what fathers did. They paid attention, even when they weren't supposed to.

But Jude was supposed to be one of *us.*

I felt like he'd stripped off my clothes, exposed my naked body.

Except it was even worse. Because the body was just an object. Eventually it would break or break down, and so what? It would be interchangeable with whatever came next. Only our minds were inviolate—that's what Jude had taught us, wasn't it? The thing that separated us from the orgs, the thing that made us mechs, that made us *special*. We lived in our heads. Unlike the orgs, we didn't fool ourselves into believing that our bodies mattered. Only our minds were alive, and they belonged to *us*.

But now Jude had reached his long fingers inside my head and carved out a space for himself. He'd crawled inside me, without my permission, without my knowledge.

And he'd watched.

There was nothing personal in a location, I reminded myself. GPS coordinates weren't diary entries. They only told him where I was, not who, not why.

But it was my choice whether or not to tell him anything.

And he'd taken that away.

I didn't run. I didn't turn around, skid down the hill of green, back to the road to nowhere.

"You can't tell anyone," Jude said. Nearly pleaded.

"Oh, I'm pretty sure I can." *Even if it means mass panic?* I thought. *Even if Jude's right and we might need this later, when it really counts?*

"I'm not going to try to convince you I'm right—"

"Good."

"I'm going to bribe you," he said, regaining a little of his composure. "You keep your mouth shut, and I'll jam your tracker too. I'll feed BioMax a false stream—no one will know where you go, not BioMax. Not me."

Not my father. Not anyone.

"And let everyone else keep getting spied on?" I asked. "Turn myself into as big a liar as you are?"

"That's right," he said. "That's the plan. Or tell whoever the hell you want and spend the rest of your life with the fine folks of BioMax crawling up your ass, watching your every move."

I wasn't the same self-centered bitch I'd been before the download. But I guess I was close enough. "Okay," I said finally. Hating myself.

At least he didn't smile.

"You really think you'll be able to keep this to yourself?" he said.

I nodded.

He rolled his eyes. "You'll last five minutes. Tops. So here's the deal: You've got such a burning need to spill your guts, spill to Riley. You two are so tight now, so into your little secrets. I'm sure he won't mind keeping another one. Especially for me."

"You're so sure he'll just do whatever you tell him?"

Jude didn't answer; he didn't have to.

"All that time we were in the city, you knew," I realized. "And when those orgs grabbed me, you—" I closed my eyes for a moment, trying to ground myself in the present, to shut out the sickening sensation that I was still tied to a chair, waiting, just imagining that I'd escaped. "You claim we should have called for

191

help, but you knew where we were the whole time—and you did nothing."

Jude stood up, brushing the grime off his jeans, starting into the house. "Not all of us do everything we want, whenever we want."

I recognized the insult. But there was something else buried in there too. I just didn't get it. If he'd wanted to rescue me, what had stopped him?

What's the difference? I thought, disgusted with myself for even entertaining the idea of Jude *rescuing* me like I was some helpless maiden waiting for her noble prince.

He is not your friend.

"What are we really doing here, Jude?" I asked. "What's the point of all this? What do you *want*?"

"At least you're finally starting to ask the right questions." And he turned his back on me and went inside.

I told Riley that night. We sat in my bedroom with the door closed, both of us on the floor, our backs propped against the wall, our knees drawn to our chests, a foot of space between us.

He didn't react when I told him what had happened to Mika and Sari, at least what little I knew. And he didn't react when I told him about the trackers. He didn't say anything until I told him that Jude had known all along.

"He must have a good reason," he said then.

I almost laughed. "Why? Because he's *Jude*, giver of all knowledge and wisdom, keeper of the peace?"

"Because he's Jude," Riley said, and he wasn't joking. "I trust him. I wish you did. Maybe then we wouldn't have . . ."

"You blame me." I shouldn't have been surprised. And I shouldn't have cared so much. "I made you take me to the city. I didn't let you voice Jude. I screwed everything up. Is that about right?"

Riley looked down. He crushed his hands into fists, then brought them together, knuckle to knuckle "I screwed up," he growled. "I shouldn't have taken you there."

"You didn't have a choice."

"They wanted a trade," he said. "You for Jude. And for me."

"I know that," I said. "You want to tell me why?"

"Wynn thinks we owe him something."

"What?" I figured I deserved to know.

"A life," he said. "Among other things. It doesn't matter. I'm sorry you got involved."

"And when they took me, you went to Jude."

He nodded. "Jude freaked. He swore we'd find you. But by the time we did . . ."

"Secops showed up," I said.

"Yeah."

"Except it was all a lie," I pointed out. Couldn't he see? "If he's tracking us, he knew where I was the whole time. Just like always."

Riley didn't answer. He tilted his head back against the wall, staring up at the ceiling. "Never thought I'd be living in a place like this," he said.

"Did you hear what I said? Jude *lied* to you." I wanted to shake him. "He was probably going to let me rot there."

Riley shook his head. "We were going to get you out. He would have done anything."

"So he told you."

"And I trust him."

"Even though he sent us to that corp-town? Come on, you're telling me that you don't even suspect, just a little, that—"

Riley stood up. "Jude wouldn't do that. Not to me."

"And not to the orgs," I prompted him. "You know, the ones who died. You forgot to say he wouldn't have hurt them. Doesn't have it in him or something like that."

"Why are you here?" Riley asked.

"What? I live here."

"But why? If you think Jude could do something like that."

"I'm not here because of him," I snapped. And maybe, deep down, I didn't believe Jude was capable of something so terrible; maybe I wanted to believe in him as much as anyone else. Or I just needed an excuse to stay, because I had nowhere else to go. "He's watching all of us," I said finally. "Maybe I just think someone should be watching him."

"You don't know him," Riley said, and he was already at the door, leaving me. "I do."

"Are you sure?" But I said it under my breath. Quietly, so it belonged to me.

Riley hesitated in the doorway, drumming his fingers against the frame. It was strange—I wouldn't have thought him the type to emulate org shifts and twitches, pretending that his body was anything other than what it was. But there he was, playing out a pantomime of org fidgeting. Jude had encouraged us to embrace our body's natural stillness, its dissociation from feverish thoughts, yet another way to maintain control, another point scored in our game against the orgs. I'd bought it; Riley apparently hadn't. "You okay?" he finally asked.

I thought about my father then, the tightened line of his lips holding back a tidal wave. I'd never thought about what it must have been like to live behind his colorless expression. Caged by self-control, and in that cage, with him, my body after the accident, ravaged first by fire then by BioMax, my body now, the one he'd purchased, the one he'd willed into existence, the mistake.

In that cage, with me: my reflection in his eyes. And their eyes, the eyes of the dead, bloody and sightless. Auden's eyes, staring into a camera, staring out at me, believing I could do anything after what I'd done to him. Mika's eyes, shut tight, as we stepped over him, another body in another hall.

I could lock it all away. Even if it meant locking myself in with it.

I almost broke.

But I remembered that Riley wasn't my friend. That I didn't have those anymore.

"I'm fine," I said.

"Because if you're not—"

"I'm fine." I was intact and unharmed; I wasn't going to jail. I wasn't going anywhere. "I'll be fine."

"That's good," he said, like he meant it.

"What about you?" I suddenly thought to ask.

"Fine," he said.

And hope springs eternal, right? Maybe we would be.

ZONED

"And I was nothing."

Things got back to normal.

Nothing got back to normal.

Normal: Long days without much to fill them. Watching Ani hang all over Quinn, watching Quinn hang all over everyone else. Talking about nothing. Scaling buildings and jumping off cliffs, trying to feel.

Not normal: Ariana Croft, a girl with a stranger's name and my face, arrested for the corp-town attack. My face all over the vids, panic evident in wide-eyed protestations of innocence. The looks I was getting from the other mechs, the same kind of peripheral gaping I'd endured at school right after the downloads, randoms passing me in the hall, pretending to fix their eyes on the ground when really they were soaking me in, absorbing every inch of the freakitude so they could report back to their friends. Now Jude and Riley were the only ones who didn't watch me like they were half expecting me to strike again. Jude because he never looked at me at all unless he had to. Riley because his look was different. *Waiting for me to break,* I thought more than once, catching his eye just before he turned away. *Not going to happen.*

In the not-normal column: not backing up my memories, not once since the attack. Because backing them up would make them permanent—as permanent as I was, at least, which was extremely. If I kept them where they were, trapped in my head, no backup, no record anywhere but in me, then there was always a chance they could disappear. One day, I would wake up in a fresh body, with a fresh mind, one that didn't know how blank eyes could get, or how quickly skin paled when blood pooled, still and lifeless in the veins.

It was a game I'd played before, toying with the idea of forgetting, wiping out a moment like it didn't exist.

Normal: I still wasn't going to do it. My body—Lia Kahn's body—was gone, which meant the only thing left of her, of me, was my mind. And sometimes it seemed like that was nothing more than a long skein of memories. I wasn't about to start unraveling the thread, throwing pieces of myself in the trash. I didn't know where the memories ended and I—whatever *I* existed without all the things that had happened to me—began.

Normal: I was still afraid.

I couldn't stop watching the vids of the attack.

I did it alone, in my room, staring at the screen on the wall, playing and replaying the same shots. I saw it from every angle, in color, in infrared, in black and white. Over and over again, I watched myself in the center of the atrium, standing still, bodies dropping all around me. I watched the girl who looked like me pump the Naxophedrine into the air-circulation system. And smile.

And then, when that got old, the images so familiar that they left me numb, I moved on. I pumped Ariana Croft's zone, just before they slapped a priv-lock on it. I dipped into her friends' zones, but none of them had spoken to her since the download, so they only had stories about a girl who didn't exist anymore. There were plenty of pics showing what she'd looked like before, curly brown hair, violet lenses in her deep-set eyes, a little chunky but in such a way that you knew she was doing it on purpose to seem voluptuous. Totally artificial—a girl with that kind of credit and those kinds of friends wouldn't leave anything to chance. She'd go in for lipo once a week and make sure they left *just* enough fat behind to seem authentic. An extremely noncasual casual oversight, like a carefully tousled mess of hair or a faceful of haven't-bothered-to-shave scruff. But it wasn't sexy, just sad, like a wispy moustache that looked more like a smudge of dirt than a handlebar of hair.

Not that it would have mattered, once she got sick. I even looked up the disease, some kind of bizarre immune-system disorder that couldn't be screened out and couldn't be treated. None of the zones had any pics of that. But I knew it would have made her sick and fragile and, even without the weekly lipos, skinny. Without the download, it would have made her dead.

None of it told me anything, except that this girl wasn't me.

But maybe that was the one thing I needed to know.

There was no chance that BioMax had illegally downloaded a copy of my brain into another body, that the second, secret Lia Kahn had gone insane, taken on a new name, a new persona, and decided to kill a bunch of people she'd never met before. No chance whatsoever.

But it didn't hurt to confirm that Ariana Croft was a real person. A damaged whackjob, maybe, but not me. Even if she looked like me.

Our bodies were just things, right? My body was one thing. Her body, despite the choppy haircut and bad dye job (violet with green streaks), was another. Sometimes I ripped my eyes from the vids and stared down at myself, feeling as disconnected as I had those first few days after the download, untethered from legs, arms, skin, fingers, all of it seeming to belong to someone else. Sometimes I reminded myself that even if there had been no Ariana Croft (which there was), if someone at BioMax had figured out a way around all the safeguards (which they couldn't), and for some nefarious purpose had created another Lia Kahn in body *and* mind, it still wouldn't be me. It would have just been a copy, and by definition, a copy wasn't the same as the original.

Except that I wasn't the original either.

Except that if my brain and body were destroyed, my

backed-up memories would be downloaded into a new brain. Another copy. And it would feel like me. It would *be* me. That was the whole secret to mech immortality, right? When is a copy not a copy? Not much of a riddle, because the answer is obvious: when it's identical to the original.

Maybe. But I didn't trust the logic enough to test it. I could ditch this body for a new one with a new face. This me could die, and an identical copy would live. Same difference, right? Except I was afraid it wasn't.

I was afraid.

These were the kinds of things I tried not to think about when I wasn't busy trying not to think about dead people. Or trying not to think about my father. Or call-me-Ben's daily, and increasingly threatening, reminders of our "deal," which for all I knew was moot now that I was no longer under suspicion—but to believe that would have meant ignoring the fact that there were more shadowy, faceless mechs in that vid, attackers still to be caught. Thanks to the corp-town attack, we were *all* under suspicion, every mech. All of us with no fingerprints and no bio-stats—and according to Rai Savona and his little puppet Auden, no souls, which meant no moral compass or internal censor and thus nothing to stop us from wreaking havoc, sowing chaos by some kind of infernally programmed design, or just destroying everything around us by virtue of our very nature. I tried not to think about Auden too, telling myself that it could have been worse, whatever he'd turned into—whatever bitter, twisted dupe *I'd* turned him into—at least he'd lived. But that thought brought me right back to dead people and sent me straight back to the vids, and the whole thing started all over again.

It was like a cut on my lip that I couldn't help worrying with my tongue. Knowing that I should let it alone, knowing better, but so hyperaware of it every time I spoke, every time I moistened my lips, every time I was sitting around and my mind wandered, just for a moment, away from the constant litany of *Don't do that*, and without intent or even awareness, my tongue slipped back into place, exploring the crevices of the wound until the pain woke me up.

I could have stopped myself. Every morning and every night I looked at the small pile of dreamers I'd hoarded, sitting just beside my bed. I'd gotten them from Sloane, and I knew she could be trusted to keep her mouth shut. I'd met Sloane before either of us came to live at Jude's estate—in fact, I was the one who'd brought her here, who'd convinced her that this, not another boyfriend, not another pointless suicide attempt, was the answer she'd been seeking. She'd spent the last several years, before and after her download, researching methods of escape.

Thanks to Jude—which meant thanks to me—she'd discovered a new one.

These weren't the puny hour-long dreamers that barely topped the buzz of an intense b-mod. These were industrial-strength dreamers, good for days, even weeks, of blissful mental absence. A nice long vacation from everything.

I kept them by my bed as a test. Every time I passed them by I knew I was stronger than that. I wasn't that kind of mech.

They sat there for days, one week, two, and I kept passing the test, passing them by.

Until one day, I didn't.

I wasn't prepared.

Heavy dreamers weren't anything like the lightweight version I'd sampled.

They dragged you down.

Deeper than I'd ever been.

Trapped in a dream inside a dream.

Blind in a white fog.

Existence and nonexistence in one.

Being and non. Here and not. Pleasure and pain.

That was all there was. All I was.

And I was nothing.

Waking up was like breaking through the surface of a deep, black pool of water, emerging from silent depths into the too-bright, too-noisy open air. Everything was sharp edges; everything was off-key. I just wanted to slip back under.

"I thought you hated these things," Ani said, standing over me.

"How'd you get in here?" I mumbled. It felt like the dreamer had blown my body into a million pieces, drifting on the wind, hidden in the crevices of the walls and floorboards, dissipated. I was everywhere and nowhere at once. "I locked the door."

"Quinn had the house open it for me."

Right. Artificially intelligent locks could be fooled. That

was the beauty of dumb, mute technology: You couldn't reprogram steel.

I reached for the next dreamer. It was set to last a week. "Have her lock it again when you go."

Ani glanced at the dreamer in my hand. "Or I could stay. We could talk."

I shrugged. The world was getting too sharp, the fog fading away. The longer I was awake, the easier it became to think. And I wasn't in the mood to think.

"I'm just worried," Ani said. "After what happened—"

"Get out." I didn't want to remember *what happened*. That was the whole point.

She flinched.

"Please," I added. But I didn't say it nicely.

"If you stay under too long . . ."

"I'll be fine," I said. "The dreamers are safe."

"Right. Tell that to the empties."

It was what we called the mechs who dreamed away their lives, twitching and shuddering for weeks on end. Empties because they were nothing without the dreamers; because they were hollow. Bodies whose minds were on permanent vacation.

These days, I only felt empty when I was awake.

I was the center of a storm.

Light swirled around me. Through me. Wind blew in waves of red and purple and black. Color had sound and sound had color. There was no body, but there was pain.

And noise, like metal on metal, like a scream.

And need, and memory, and flesh on flesh, and lips, and the weight of a body on my body.

And weightlessness. And nothingness.

The storm raged, but I was its center, and I was still.

Quiet.

It was getting harder to come back.

When the dreamer died, there was a moment in between. Like the dazed limbo between org sleep and waking when the dream dies away and reality strays just out of reach. It was like falling—but falling so far and so fast, through a darkness without a bottom, that it felt like flying.

When I came back to myself, Jude was there.

"Sweet dreams?" He leaned against the doorframe, arms laced across his chest.

"Very." But there was nothing to remember about what these deep dreamers were doing to me; I didn't have the words to describe it to myself. It was like becoming another person; an unperson.

"Then you must have been dreaming of me." The words rang hollow, a force of habit. Or maybe it was just that the dreamer made the world seem tired, Jude's words dull and empty.

"Worried about me?" I asked.

"Why would I be?" His eyes strayed to the single remaining dreamer. No matter—once they were gone, Sloane would supply more, as many as I needed. She understood escape.

He slung a scuffed red backpack over his shoulder and crossed the room, perching on the edge of the bed. With a cool smile, he swung his legs onto the mattress. I slapped them away. "This came for you." He dropped the backpack on the bed. I reached for it—then jerked my hand away as the bag twitched toward me with a low mewing noise.

Jude shoved a slip of paper at me. "This too."

He misses you, the note said. Typed, so I had no way of knowing who it was from.

But when the bag mewed again, I had a pretty good guess. I groaned and unzipped the bag. A flabby gray cat poked his head through the opening and nuzzled into the back of my hand. "Great. Just great."

"You know her, I presume?" Jude stroked his hand along the cat's head. It purred, arching its back. That was a sign. In a few moments, the cat would get freaked out by all the affection and lash out a claw. I kept quiet—let Jude figure it out for himself.

"It's a him," I said. "Psycho Susskind."

"Doesn't look very psycho to me," Jude said, scratching his knuckle against the scruff of Susskind's neck.

"He loves machines," I said. "Thought the toaster was his best friend. People, not so much."

"She dropped it off in person," Jude said. She. There was only one *she* it could be. "Middle of the night. So does she look like you used to look?" he added. "Before?"

"I thought we weren't supposed to talk about the past," I reminded him.

"I'm just saying, she's hot."

"You would think so." Jude was exactly Zo's type, I realized suddenly. Not on the surface, maybe—there was nothing about him that resembled the creepy, greasy retros my sister used to bring home, their eyes red from a late-night dozer session or wide and twitchy from too many hours locked in a virtual reality circuit, fingers grasping at imaginary demons. Losers, and she knew it. Choices guaranteed to spite our father, sending him into one of his silent, pale-faced rages. But Jude could match Zo smirk for smirk, shoot down her snide crap with crap of his own. Throw in the gaunt, angular features, sharp and chiseled where the rest of us seemed waxy and soft, and he was the complete package. Either her soul mate or her double.

"You like the cat so much, you take it," I said. "He'll love you."

Who was less human than Jude?

"She brought it for *you*," he said.

"So?"

He didn't say anything for a moment, pretending to concentrate all his attention on the cat. But I could see his eyes flashing, watching me from beneath heavy lids. "So nothing." He stood up, scooped the cat into his arms. "You got that from Sloane, didn't you?" he said, nodding at the final dreamer on the nightstand. I reached for it, but I was still moving in slow motion. He swept it away with ease. Jude nestled the small black cube into his palm, rubbing his fingers along its smooth surface. Most dreamers had a series of lines etched into their sides, indicating their duration. This one, which Sloane had been hesitant to pass along, was unmarked. "It's a new one," she'd said. "Something about a neural feedback loop? I didn't really get it. But I guess somehow it works different on different brains."

"You control how long it lasts?" I'd asked.

She had hesitated, then shaken her head. "I don't think 'control' is the word for it."

"What do you care who I got it from?" I asked Jude now.

He smiled thinly. "I'd just suggest that you consider the source."

"Aren't *you* her source?" I said.

"That was for *Sloane*," he said. "Maybe I got tired of listening to her whine about how much she wants to die."

"She's over that now," I told him. A year ago Sloane had jumped out a window in some pathetic attempt to end whatever Great Pain she imagined was consuming her. She'd passed out in a puddle of her own blood and woken up with a mechanical body and a promise from her parents that no matter how many times she tried to break herself, they'd always Humpty Dumpty her back together. And they did, more than once. *You had an accident,* they'd say when she woke up, and she'd smile and nod and pretend to believe them and then try it all over again. Until eventually she gave up; she joined us.

"Whatever you say."

"This is none of your business," I told him.

"What? Sloane's death wish, or yours?"

I pulled my knees to my chest. "Don't talk to me about death." I knew I sounded like a child. "You don't know what you're talking about."

Sometimes, when I closed my eyes, the attack played out in reverse. The bodies climbed to their feet, alive again. But their bloody eyes were still dead.

"*I* don't know? Right." Jude flung the dreamer at the bed. "I don't know why I even bother trying."

"That was *trying*?" I asked. "That's just sad, Jude."

"Don't worry, it stops now." He left the room. Psycho Susskind climbed on top of me, his claws bearing down on my chest, and waited for me to do something. When I didn't, he padded out of the room after Jude. A new acolyte for the great leader.

Apparently Susskind didn't miss me any more than Zo did.

I don't want to think about that, I thought, like a child.

But unlike a child, I had control over my life. I had control over everything—that's what being a mech was all about. I picked up the dreamer from where it had landed beside my pillow.

I didn't want to think about Zo or dead people's dead eyes or anything else.

And I didn't have to.

Time passed—or it didn't.

Thoughts glittered and fluttered. Words flickered bright and sputtered out, diamond sharp and meaningless.

Sweet in the brash and senseless blue and down and down and deep.

The silence of noise, waves made visible, shimmering green and gold. A universe of infinite vibration, quantum strands quivering and shivering.

Bare peculiar lands of majesty in six of purple plasma gray and I am lost.

And I am lost.

And I am.

I am.

Lost.

The world bobbing up and down, that was the first thing.

No, not the world, my head. Shaking, flopping back and forth on my neck.

Then: his hands on my shoulders, fingers gouging flesh.

His eyes, black in the dim light, wide. Scared.

I could feel the dreamer tugging me down. I was in the water again, the deep, black pool, the surface too far, the world through its murky window a soup of distorted shape and color.

"Lia!" His face in my face. My body still in his hands as he dragged me upright, as he pushed me against the wall, shouting, incomprehensible. And then the one sound that wasn't noise.

Lia.

The name like a slap, like breaking through the water into the pain of winter air.

Kicking toward the surface, reaching up toward dry land, toward him.

I could let go, I thought. *Stop fighting. Drift away.*

Maybe this was what happened when you overloaded on dreamers—maybe at some point you didn't need the dreamer anymore, and the brain made its own dreams. Maybe after the dreamer ate away everything else, the dream was all you had left.

But I didn't let go. I held on. To the light and noise. To Riley, my face in his hands, my hands on his chest.

I woke up.

"How long?" I asked.

He let go of my face, eased me to the floor, one hand in my hand, the other at my waist. We sat cross-legged, facing each other. He didn't let go of my hand.

"How long?" I said again.

"Since Jude was here?"

I nodded.

"Twenty-two days." He winced like he was expecting me to freak out.

Three weeks. Plus the weeklong dreamer before that and the three days I'd dreamed away before that. One month below. In the dark. One month gone.

But if you were going to live forever, what was one month? Infinity minus one is still infinity.

"You know, I get it," he said, pulling his hand away from mine.

"What?" But I knew what.

"Wanting it all to go away." He brushed his hands along his thighs, then placed them flat on his knees. It was like he didn't know what to do with them now that he was no longer holding on. "Forget."

211

Normally there was nothing I hated more than someone pretending to understand what was going on in my head. But this time, it didn't bother me.

"I keep thinking that someone should have screamed, you know?" Riley said. "It would have made it seem more like a vid. Unreal. But . . ."

"Yeah. No screaming," I said, letting myself remember. For the first time not fighting back against the images. The dreamers had left an empty space behind them. And the memories rushed in to fill the vacuum.

"There was a girl," I said. "A kid. I saw her before it all happened. She had this hot pink hair and—"

"Yeah." He stretched his arms behind him, leaning his weight back on them. "I saw her."

"She was probably eight or nine," I said, picturing Zo at that age. She'd been experimenting with different hair colors, showing up with purple streaks one morning, rainbow the next. It was before she'd settled on the retro thing, and instead she was obsessed with av-wear—a phase that we all went through, when instead of modeling your avatar to look like you, you turned yourself into a live-action av, complete with neon hair, netlinked morphtattoos, and the occasional glitter wings.

But Zo had gotten a chance to grow out of it.

He leaned forward, his hands uncertain again, on his lap, then on the floor, then cradled, one in the other. "I stepped on someone. When we were running away. I wasn't looking, and then—"

"We both did," I said. I wanted him to stop talking. I wanted to go back to the dream. But it was like we were flying. Like we'd jumped out of the plane, and nothing was going to stop us now, except the ground. "We couldn't help it."

He shook his head. "I looked down," he said. "When I felt it. Something— I don't know. Soft and hard at the same time. You know?"

Soft and hard. The feel of a foot sinking into a chest.

"She was still alive," he said. "Mouth wide open."

"Like she was screaming."

"It sounds stupid," he said. "I know. She was just trying to breathe, but . . ."

"It looked like she was screaming."

"I stepped on her," he said. "And I didn't stop."

"We couldn't have helped her."

"You wanted to stop," he said.

"I didn't know what I was doing," I reminded him. "I froze. *You* got us out of there."

"And straight into hell," he said.

I rested my hand on top of his hands. He stiffened.

"Thank you for waking me up," I said.

He pulled his hands out from under mine. Stood up. "You would've woken up if I was here or not. Just good timing."

"Probably."

There was a loud scratching sound at the door. "Psycho Susskind," he said. "You want me to let him in?"

"*What'd* you call him?"

"Isn't that his name?" he asked.

Yes, but it was *my* name for him, mine and Zo's. Weird to hear it come out of Riley's mouth.

"He doesn't seem too crazy to me," Riley said. "Maybe you weren't feeding him enough."

"Have you *seen* him?" I laughed. "The last thing that cat needs is more food."

Riley grinned. "He never turned me down."

"*You* were feeding him?"

"Didn't think you'd want him to starve," Riley said.

"Sorry," I said. "You shouldn't have to take care of my cat."

So I had a cat again. I hadn't even wanted one the first time around. Zo and I had begged for a puppy. But when our father showed up with psycho Sussie, we knew better than to do anything but smile and say thank you. And then pretend not to be disappointed when we tried to pet him and he hissed and ran away.

"Someone had to. But I think he misses you," Riley said.

"Doubtful. But you can let him in."

Riley obviously couldn't wait to get away from me, and I couldn't blame him. I reminded him of everything we both wanted to forget.

He opened the door and the cat slipped in. A moment later, nodding a silent good-bye, Riley slipped out.

Susskind was gray with thin black raccoon stripes streaking his fur and a long strip of black trickling down his spine and tail, a reverse skunk. If you looked closely, you could see the gray was speckled with white, like a permanent dusting of dandruff. His eyes were a pale, watery green, the color of wilted celery. All of which made for one extremely ugly cat.

He curled up against me, butting his head into my arm. *Pet me,* in catspeak. *Love me.* But every time I gave in and stroked his fur, Susskind would stiffen and creep away. It was only when I gave up that he would return, nuzzling my hand, digging his claws into my leg, giving me those cat eyes, which, unlike a pitiful puppy-dog gaze, bore no neediness or desperation, just a pale green watchfulness. We repeated the cycle a few times, head butt, purr, escape, return, until he judged me worthy and lowered his bulk onto my lap. Now he gave me a different look. *I'm ready,* it said. *I deserve it.*

What are you waiting for?

So I rested my hand on his soft coat, rubbing slow circles into his warm, ample belly. When I was a kid, Susskind's fur had looked irresistibly soft. I'd longed to run my hands through it—but he always ran away before I got the chance. Now the fur barely made an impression. The synflesh wasn't designed to appreciate that kind of subtle sensation.

He let out a guttural purr and clawed my arm. *That* felt good.

"Did you really miss me, you psycho?" I whispered.

He rested his paws on my knee, then lowered his head onto them. His eyes narrowed to slits. Naptime.

"I think I've slept enough," I told him. But I sat there

with him, my hand on his back, rising and falling with the
even breaths.

I hadn't been a cat person back when I was a person. But
then, Susskind hadn't been a person cat. Orgs were as repulsive
to him as they were to Jude. Whatever I was now, he approved.
No questions asked. Even in catspeak.

"I missed you too."

Something to remember about cats: They're not your
friend. If you ever came across a giant dog, some kind of
mutant puppy towering twenty feet off the ground, the dumb
thing might knock over a few trees while it was doing its
yippee-yay-a-new-friend happy dance, but the worst thing it
would do is lap at you with its giant tongue and maybe drown
you in dog slobber.

A giant cat would bat you around for a while between its
giant paws.

And then eat you.

You can't blame them; it's just the way they're built.

TEMPLE OF MAN

"It didn't happen because I was good.
It happened because I was lucky."

My zone was flooded.

I'd dropped out for this long once before—just after the accident. The voices and texts had piled up, digi-gifts heaped on an electronic shrine. Fake presents from fake friends, as it had turned out. But at least I'd been missed. Not that it had given me much comfort at the time. It was hard to remember that Lia Kahn, the one who still thought she was socially invincible. I had what everyone wanted—the right clothes, the right friends, the right look. I had the shiniest toys. And the one with all the toys decided who else got to play.

No one told me that when right turns wrong and your shiniest toy turns around and screws your sister, all that power disappears, along with everyone else. Game over.

I had a new zone now. New zone for a new body and a new life, and this one was sparse. I'd created it with Auden, chosen the avatar that he preferred—blond hair, silver skin, gray eyes, the face a merge of the old Lia and the new one. After Auden had finished with me, I'd kept the av. But it didn't have much to do these days. I wasn't zone-hopping or trying to up my pathetic Akira score. The stalker sites had never really been my thing, and they'd gotten even duller since the election—it was one thing to have a president in and out of rehab, so dropped on downers she barely noticed the difference, but this new guy had some kind of body-worship fixation, and there were only so many nude self-portraits you could gawk at before they just got old, six-pack abs or not.

I may have been watching the vidlifes, but that didn't mean I wanted to link in with other fans, trading chatter about Lara's latest hookup or whether you could still see Cord(elia)'s Adam's apple, post snip-tuck. I had no use for music anymore—this brain, although it was supposed to be an exact copy of the biological version, processed melody as noise. And once I got used to the emptiness, I stopped posting vids and pics. It wasn't just that I had nothing to show off. I had no one to show off *for*. None of the other mechs were any more into their zones than I was. Quinn claimed she'd gotten enough of the network after all those years chained to a bed, seeing the world through a screen. Growing up in the city, Jude and Riley barely had zones in the first place—they didn't seem to get why you'd want them. Only Ani was obsessive, posting pics of everything and everyone, trying to disguise her disappointment when we didn't cross post on our own.

Mostly, I used my zone for the same thing that Jude used his for: finding myself. And not in the weeping, wailing, soulsong kind of way. I had turned my zone into a digital scrapbook, a patchwork of all the vids and rants about how us evil skinners were determined to take over the world. *Know your enemy,* my father used to like to say. When you *are* the enemy, I guess that translates to *Know yourself.*

So once I'd cleared out the fog the deep dreamer had left behind, I linked in, determined not to fall back into an obsessive loop of corp-town attack vids. I would just dip in, see what I'd missed, then cut the link and start living my life again.

The flaw in that plan: Like I said, my zone was flooded. The list of suspects in the attack had been leaked, complete with my name, and in came the hate mail. The standard trash from Savona's brainwashed ex-Faithers calling me an abomination in the eyes of God, plus a few death threats from randoms too stupid to understand the "can't" in "can't die." And plenty of generic mass texts that looked like they'd been sprayed out to every mech on the network, warning that we were all the same, we were all dangerous, and soon they hoped to see us all in the same landfill, shut down, rusted, and busted beside heaps of burned-out cars and broken-down ViMs.

I wasn't about to go weeding through the venomous junk, but a few messages were red-flagged as req texts, meaning that they wouldn't archive until they'd been read. Only the government and a few of the most powerful corp consortiums had that kind of authority:

From Corps United in Regulating Borders, my passport had been revoked. Explicit permission from CURB was required if I wanted to leave the country.

From the Associated Union of Credit Corps, my credit—what little of it I had after leaving home—was frozen.

From the Conglomeration of Transportation Corps, mechs were forbidden to drive without at least one person in the car. There was an asterisk beside "person" and a note at the bottom that clarified, "qualifications for categorization as a 'person' to be at the discretion of the CTC."

And from the Department of Justice—which, despite outsourcing the majority of its portfolio to the private sector and neutering itself in the process, refused to follow its fellow governmental departments into the great blue yonder and instead stubbornly clung to life, no matter how toothless or obscure—notification of congressional hearings to be conducted on a new definition of the word "person," for general legal and regulatory purposes. Buried in the bureaucratic blizzard of words, the heart of the proposed definition: "Resolved: A 'person' will be defined as an organic entity, its brain and body conforming to the biological criteria of the species *Homo sapiens*, its defining qualities including but not limited to birth, aging, and death."

A lot could happen while you were dreaming. It was tempting to just go back to sleep.

Instead, I went to find Riley. Not because I thought he

would know what to do, since there obviously wasn't anything *to* do. Not because I needed him to explain the world to me; I had the network and the vids and, even without watching them, I had a pretty good idea of the whole trajectory, mech attacks orgs, orgs attack mechs, what could be more logical than that? I didn't need him for anything.

But I went looking for him anyway.

The smarthouse was smart enough to tell me that Riley was in the vidroom. It just wasn't smart enough to inform me that he wasn't alone.

"Bastard!" Jude shouted as I opened the door. He was in full VR gear, whacking an invisible hockey stick against an invisible puck. Not that the herky-jerky motion bore any resemblance to an actual hockey play, but I'd spent enough tedious hours watching Walker's virtual reality stick work to recognize the body language.

"Suck it," Riley shot back, grinning and jerking to his right. From Jude's grunt, I figured he must have blocked the shot.

You could play VR sports the couch potato way, lying around and steering the action with your fingers and eye twitches—but most guys I knew preferred the full action, full contact method, cramming a little reality into their virtual.

"Give up yet?" Riley taunted, muscling past Jude with a sharp elbow to the shoulder.

Jude whipped around, raising the invisible stick above his head. "Do I look like that kind of loser?"

"There's more than one kind of loser?"

Jude sent a shot careening past Riley, who lurched for it, then swore under his breath when he missed. "You're the expert," Jude drawled, "you tell me."

Riley ducked, swiping an invisible puck away from his head. "Watch the face!"

"Was that your face?" Jude asked, all innocence. "I get confused—your face, your ass, so tough to tell them apart . . ."

"Staring at my ass now?" Riley sputtered through his laughter, slapping a shot to the left. He raised his hands in triumph. "He shoots, he scores! He's beaten the all-time record! He's—"

"Even more obnoxious when he wins than when he loses," Jude said, grinning. "Even though he gets zero practice."

I realized I'd never seen Jude laugh for the fun of it rather than at someone else's expense; I'd never seen Riley laugh at all. But here they were, no different from Walker and his brain-burner football buddies, assing around like a couple of idiots with nothing more to worry about than whether they could finish the bottle of chillers before their girlfriends showed up for date night.

Riley kept telling me that I didn't know Jude, not the way he did. So was this what he meant? The real Jude, the astonishingly normal, orglike Jude, who dropped the all-knowing guru act as soon as he was alone? Or was it just a mask, designed to fool Riley into thinking that his faith and loyalty were well-founded, even though they were miles and bodies away from whatever ties bound them together.

Or maybe he was both at once; maybe he was neither.

"See something you like?" Jude suddenly asked, taking the VR mask off his face, staring at me like he'd known I was there the whole time. I suddenly felt like I'd been spying on more than just a game. Riley jerked around toward the doorway and pulled off his own mask, wearing that bleary-eyed expression of someone yanked into reality before he was ready.

"I'm just, uh, looking for Ani," I stammered, backing away.

"She's out," Riley said. "Another rally, I think."

Jude glared at him.

"What rally?" I asked.

Riley opened his mouth, then, with a wary glance at Jude, closed it again.

Obedient like a dog, I thought in disgust. *Not attractive.*

It wasn't the kind of thought I wanted to be having about Riley, or any of the mechs. Attractive, not attractive—not my problem, either way. Not that I was oblivious to his broad shoulders or sinewy muscles. And not that he wasn't exactly my type, not just the tall, dark, and monosyllabic thing, but the way he could say all he needed to with a touch or a look or—even though I didn't technically have proof of this, I had no doubt— his biceps tightening around you, curling you into his chest, into that body-shaped hollow created by his open embrace—

No. That was exactly the kind of thinking I didn't need. One disastrous night with Walker had been enough to prove that when it came to mechs, anatomically correct was necessary but not sufficient. I could do anything I wanted—it was the *wanting* that was the problem. There was a reason we had to jump out of planes and dive off cliffs to get a high, to break through the wall separating us from the ability to experience something real. I'd wanted Walker all right, just as much as before the download—but when I had him, his body tangled up in mine, it had been cold and awkward and empty. It had been—why not just say it?—mechanical.

Walker wasn't the only one. That was the renegade voice in my mind, the one that insisted on reminding me of everything I'd prefer to forget, like that afternoon by the waterfall with Jude. But that didn't count. That hadn't been real. Just a moment of desperation. It didn't prove anything other than the fact that I was right about staying away.

"What rally?" I asked again, determined to stop thinking about things there was no point in thinking about.

"See for yourself," Jude said, flipping on the nearest screen and calling up a live vid.

Savona had upped his production values while I was dreaming. What had once been a bare stage with a plywood podium was now an elaborately dressed proscenium, framed by dark velvet curtains that perfectly set off the glowbars lining the stage. The eerie golden glow encircled a central dais, coated with iridescent paint that shimmered under the stage lights. Savona stood at its center, the glowbars showering him in a golden aura. And sitting by his side, as always, his most loyal disciple.

He looks stronger than he did before, I told myself.

An audience of hundreds cheered them on. "Do you want

to live in fear?" Savona shouted at his Brotherhood. "Is that the country you want for yourselves, for your children?"

"No!" the crowd roared back.

"Are their rights more important than our lives?" he shouted. The camera zoomed in on his flushed face. Despite the frenzy in his voice, his black-eyed gaze was ice. "More important than our *souls*?"

"No!" the crowd faithfully called back.

"Friends, we once were lost, but now we are found," Savona intoned. He raised a finger: *Wait*. At his command, they fell silent. Auden planted his hands on the arms of the chair and heaved himself into a standing position. He leaned against Savona for a moment, steadying himself, then stood upright, unassisted. "Our message has been heard," Savona said. He grasped Auden's hand. "Our sacrifices have not been in vain."

They raised their clasped hands. "We are in the right," Auden said, his raspy voice projected over the crowd. "Will we do whatever is necessary?"

"We will!" the crowd thundered.

"Will *you*?" Auden asked, and when the camera zoomed in on him, his gaze was anything but steady. His eyes were wild, unfocused, and at odds with his strangely placid smile. I wondered if Savona had drugged him up before wheeling him out onstage.

"I will!" the crowd shouted as one.

"*I* will!" Auden shouted back. He and Savona raised their hands again. "*We will!*" they cried in unison. The applause drowned out whatever they said next. The vidroom's sound system was designed to be louder and clearer than life; the cheering erupted all around us.

I forced myself not to lunge for the controls and blot it out. *No more dreams,* I told myself. *Eyes open.* So I watched. I listened. Until I couldn't take it anymore, and as if he somehow knew exactly when I would break, Jude shut it off.

"They've been throwing one of these every week," Jude said. "Your little boyfriend's gotten pretty popular."

"It's not Auden," I insisted.

"Sure looks like him," Jude retorted. "So unless you're not the only one with a convenient double floating around—"

"Enough!" Riley held up a hand to each of us, palms out. "It doesn't matter."

"It doesn't matter that she's denying reality to believe whatever the hell she wants to believe?" Jude asked, voice soaked in sarcasm. "Maybe she should go join her boyfriend onstage. She'd fit right in."

"This isn't helpful," Riley said. He and Jude looked at each other for a long moment. Then Jude nodded.

"Fine," he said. "Here's the deal. While you were . . . sleeping, Savona and his Brotherhood ramped it up. It's not just these ridiculous rallies. They're bussing people in from the cities, feeding them, giving them free med-tech, and sending them home with plenty of antimech crap to spread around to their friends."

"That's the part I don't get," I said. "Why would anyone in a city want to team up with *Savona*? He's got everything, and they're—"

"Nothing?" Jude asked dryly.

For a long time, I'd believed my father when he said that the people who lived in cities deserved to be there—maybe even *wanted* to be there, because they couldn't hack the rules of the real world. I'd thought Auden was crazy, going off on all the ways that the government and the corps treated the slummers like nonpeople. "I'm just saying that they should know what it's like. To be told you don't count."

"They do," Riley said quietly. "That's the problem."

"Auden's smart," Jude added. "He's going to the cities, the corp-towns, showing them all the ways their lives suck. They aren't allowed to hate the people who put them there. But they can hate us. Average city lifespan is thirty-seven years. We live forever. You do the math."

I didn't have to. I'd seen the look on Sari's face when she saw Riley and me standing together. Heard the catch in her voice when she'd asked what it was like knowing I'd never grow old. Everything else about her might have been part of the show, but that was real. And they'd all looked at us that way. It wasn't like in the corp-town, all those people staring at us, curious or disgusted or afraid. In the city, there'd been all those things, but there'd also been something else. "They really hate us."

"Why not? Why should they die and we get to live?" Riley asked. But he wasn't looking at me—he'd turned to Jude, like he honestly wanted an answer.

Jude quieted him with a nearly imperceptible shake of the head. "Your boyfriend's smart," he said, returning his attention to me. "He feeds the idiot masses all this Faither bullshit about our immortal souls or lack thereof. But he's working both ends—drowning the network in op-vids and pop-ups about how we're a security risk."

"Because of the corp-town attack," I mumbled, feeling guilty, even though there was nothing to feel guilty about. "But they arrested her."

"It's not just Ariana whatever her name is," Jude said. "It's the fact that she was able to get into the ventilation ducts—no fingerprints, no biometrics. Someone finally woke up to the fact that mechs can be anyone, do anything. Savona's riding it as far as he can. The Faithers—or whatever they're calling themselves now—may be crazy. But Savona's not. He's good."

But Savona *was* crazy. Crazy enough to do . . . anything? "You don't think— Could the Brotherhood have had something to do with the attack?"

"Someone deserves a gold star," Jude said with a sneer. "You're a little late to the party, but better late than never, I suppose."

Auden would never be a part of something like that, I thought.

But maybe he didn't know.

"So what are we doing about it?" I asked.

Jude raised an eyebrow. *"We?"*

I ignored him. "If they're involved, there must be some kind of proof. We should—"

"Start sniffing around?" Jude suggested. "Attend some rallies? Maybe get someone on the inside to find out what's really going on?" He clapped his hands together with a sharp crack. "Brilliant idea. Too bad you were busy napping, or it could have been you."

"So you sent *Ani*? By *herself*?" I asked. Unbelievable.

"She can handle it," Jude said. "Wears a camo hoodie that hides her face. They have no idea what she really is."

"You didn't think to ask me?" I said. "I'm the one who knows Auden. How much more inside track can you get?"

"You haven't quite been available," Jude pointed out.

"You could have—"

"And even if you *were*," he said over me, "you're not objective. You're obviously in denial about your twisted friend."

"And *you're* objective? You've hated him from the beginning. You're probably thrilled to finally have a good reason."

"But you admit I have a good reason," he snapped. "That's the point."

"The point is Ani shouldn't be doing something like this by herself. Next time I'm going with her."

"Well, isn't she lucky to have such a noble protector," Jude drawled, like he knew exactly why I was so determined to go to the Temple, and that it had nothing to do with Ani.

For once I almost wished he'd give me one of his tedious lectures about what was really going on inside my head, because I had no idea. I believed what I'd said about Ani: This wasn't the kind of thing she could handle on her own. After seeing those vids, I wasn't sure any of us could. But she was a big girl, and I didn't owe her anything. So what was it, then? Was I just so desperate to see Auden and—what? Prove that he didn't really hate me? Convince him that we could go back to the way things were?

Could I be that delusional?

"Someone set me up at that corp-town," I said, keeping my eyes on Jude, watching—always watching—for some kind of tell-tale reaction. But there was nothing. "If it was the Brotherhood, I have to know. I'm not going to let Ani do all the hard work."

And maybe that was it: the idea of *doing* something. Any-thing. Even if it meant facing what Auden had become; what I made him. If he and his Brothers wanted to take everything—my credit, my identity, my personhood—away from me, let them try. But this time, they'd have to do it to my face.

"It's not a good idea," Riley said.

Like it was his decision. "Don't think I can handle it?"

"Can you?" Jude asked.

"I guess we'll find out." I glared at both of them, daring them to try to forbid me.

Instead, Jude raised his hands over his head, imitating Auden's motion of victory. "We will!" he shouted in a raspy voice, sounding eerily like Auden. "You will!"

I would.

The Brotherhood of Man held a rally every Sunday.

"I still don't see why you have to go." Ani pulled a camo hoodie over her head. She tossed a second one to me.

"Maybe I'm curious," I said, checking myself out in Ani's

mirror. This was less a fashion don't than a burn-before-wearing situation. Sensors in the hoodie detected ambient color and reflected it, allowing the wearer to fade into any background, an imperfect invisibility. The thick, baggy hood cast enough of a shadow over my face that I could have been any age, any gender, I could have been some gap-toothed, pockmarked med-head from the city. I could have been alive.

The camo tech had been a military innovation before we were born, had filtered into the fashion zone when we were kids, and had quickly drifted into obscurity when it became obvious that fading away defeated the point of style. Now they were cheap novelties, just the kind of thing a tech-deprived city rat might rescue from the trash with a scavenger's glee. We'd fit right in.

Ani strung a thin silver pendant around her neck and fumbled with the chain. Then she held the necklace out to me. "Can you?"

A glowing orb of blue lazulate dangled from the silver chain, a perfect match to the silver blue streaks that trickled down her neck and spine. I'd seen this kind of stone before—Bliss Tanzen had had one that she loved showing off, at least until it became clear she'd lied about receiving it from a dashing young heir to the SunFire fortune. It turned out that after a shocker-fueled all-night encounter, the solar energy baron had blocked her from his zone; the necklace came from Daddy. But I knew from Bliss's incessant boasting before her secret emerged and the necklace got recycled that something like this was worth almost as much as a car. A small, cheap car with a submoronic nav-system that restricted it to preprogrammed routes and major highways, but a car nonetheless. Lazulate was almost as rare as it was useless, which meant its harmless radioactive glow had become a totem of wealth. "Pretty," I said, fastening the chain at the nape of her neck. "New?"

Ani closed her hand around the pendant. "Quinn gave it to me."

"Quinn *Sharpe*?"

She glared at me. "Surprised? What, that she'd bother? Or that she'd bother for me?"

"No, that's not what I meant," I said quickly. "I just— Quinn doesn't seem like the type to—"

Ani burst into laughter. "Joking." She brushed her thumb across the glowing face of the lazulate. "You're right, I guess. But Quinn's changing."

"People do that?" I asked, only half kidding.

"These last few weeks . . ." Ani shook her head. "I don't know. Maybe she's just getting tired of all the . . ."

Screwing everything that moved? "Experimenting," I suggested, experimenting myself with a little tact.

"Right."

"Or maybe she finally figured out who she wanted to be with," I said. Not sure whether I believed it.

"Maybe," Ani said, sounding like she wasn't convinced either. "But I think it's more than that. She never really had a chance to *be* anybody before, you know? She was living on the network—it wasn't real. So after the download, it was like she had to start all over again. Figure herself out. Maybe she's finally doing it." She gave her wrist two sharp taps, and the glowing green numerals of a skintimer appeared. "We should go, or we'll be late," she said. "You sure about this? Seeing Auden like that, it could be—"

"Who knows if we'll even get there," I said with as much nonchalance as I could dredge up. "Could get stopped a mile from the house." The penalty for driving without a human in the car was just a fee, for now, along with confiscation of the vehicle. But our funds were limited. Thanks to some creative accounting, we still had access to plenty of credit under a variety of fronts and assumed names, but the bulk of it had been seized—losing a car was a less than desirable eventuality. And I'd had enough of the secops for one lifetime.

"We'll be fine," Ani said. "They're not enforcing the restrictions. It's just a scare tactic."

"Then let's go," I told her. "Find out if there's anything to be scared about."

Find out what's going on with Auden, I thought.

If he means everything he says about us.

About me.

No, nothing to be scared of at all.

The Temple of Man wasn't a building. It was hundreds of acres of buildings, sprawling, flat concrete blocks spiderwebbed together by tunnels and skyways. Within a mile of the Temple, the countryside gave way to an unbroken stretch of asphalt in every direction. No trees, no grass, no relief from the gray cement, the same color as the dingy sky. Only one structure violated the horizontal skyline, a narrow white tower shooting three hundred feet into the air, widening at the top for a story-high globe of windows. It reminded me of the pics I'd seen of the Middle East, after the war started but before the bombs dropped, ending the war and all the warriors in a flash of atomic fire. In the pics, tall spires had jutted from domed temples, strange, ornate lighthouses dotting the horizon, and as a kid I'd often imagined the bored but devoted keepers who might have lived up there in the sky, tending to their god. I wondered if they'd been the first to see the bombs, fire streaking through the night, and whether they'd had time to wonder or panic—or jump—before the sky exploded.

"It's where they used to track the planes taking off," Ani said, following my gaze.

"Seriously?" Maybe it was a good thing the energy crisis had destroyed the airline industry. A million planes flying around and the only thing keeping them from crashing into one another was a few guys looking out the window? "How many you think used to fly in and out of here a day?"

Ani shrugged, taking in the miles of paved runway stretching to the horizon. "Twenty?" she guessed. "Maybe thirty?"

It was impossible to imagine. Sure, once they'd figured out how to build hybrid biofuel planes, they'd gotten them back in the air, but most were corp-owned cargo flights. If you had enough credit, you could always track down a plane to get you where you needed to go. But if you were unlucky enough to count as "most people"—and most people were—cost and restrictions forced you to go by ground. Or stay home. Just as there weren't enough roads to go around, it had turned out there wasn't enough sky. Which meant the majority gave up their wings so a minority could fly.

"Not much of a temple," I said as we headed toward one of the largest of the concrete block buildings, falling into step with a bedraggled crowd. I kept my head down and my voice low. "I thought these things were supposed to look like fairy tale castles or something. High ceilings, stained glass. *Pretty.*"

"The old ones did," Ani said. "And some of the Faither ones still do. But Rai Savona's not a Faither anymore, remember? Now he says that all those churches and stuff are bad for you, that they make you feel small and unworthy. He likes this building because it's low and unimpressive. The most impressive part of any temple should be the humans inside it, he says. *We're* sacred, he says. Because God dwells inside of us."

"Them," I said.

"What?"

"You said 'us.' But God doesn't dwell in mechs, not according to Savona. Right?"

Ani ducked her head. "Right. Them. Anyway, that's what he says."

"And people actually buy that?" Thinking, *Sounds almost like you* buy *it.*

She shrugged. "Faithers are used to it. Most of them just meet where they can. Basements, cafeterias. Dead buildings are good—libraries, those old vid theaters. And in the cities, they're lucky if they can squat in one of the tower rooms for a few months, before—" She finally noticed how I was looking at her. "What?"

"You know a lot about this," I said. "Faithers."

Ani looked away, pinning her eyes back on the tower. "There are a lot of them in the city. Especially in the Craphole." She rarely talked about it, the place she'd grown up, a dumping ground for children whose parents couldn't be found or, like Ani's, couldn't be bothered. I'd never heard her refer to it as anything but the Craphole. "The government made sure we didn't starve," she said. "But that was it. The Faithers were the only ones who remembered we were alive. They showed up every once in a while with clothes, sometimes even med-tech." She shrugged. "I don't know, I guess they thought God told them to do it or something. Crazies."

"So you didn't become one." I wasn't sure whether I was asking or telling.

"Believe in some invisible, all-powerful guy who was going to fix everything as long as I was a good girl? Or in the fact that, in the end, bad things happen to bad people, and good things happen to good ones?" She shook her head, then stretched her arms wide, fingers splayed. "I believe in this," she said. "This body. And it didn't happen because I was good. It happened because I was lucky."

I hesitated. If she rarely talked about her childhood, she *never* talked about how she'd ended up as a candidate for the download. "Do you know why they picked you?" I asked. We stepped through the doors into an enormous space, thick pillars stretching up to ceilings so high, I felt almost like we were still outside. It seemed to be some kind of clearing zone, with clumps of orgs scurrying back and forth, directed by officious-looking Brothers in iridescent robes. LED screens lined the walls, announcing service times and meal times and scrolling name after name of Brothers and Sisters new to the cause. There were hundreds of them.

"They picked all of us," she said. "The ten of us who slept in my room, at least. We went to bed in the Craphole—and when we woke up, we were in the hospital. All in the same room together that first day, I guess so we didn't freak out. They wouldn't tell us what we were doing there. Just did a bunch of tests. Then started taking us away one by one."

"Do you still talk to them?" I asked, wondering why I'd never met any of them. "Are there any at Quinn's place?"

"I never saw them again," Ani said flatly as we followed the orgs through a series of metal detectors and bioscanners and were loaded onto a narrow moving sidewalk. Fortunately, most of the crowd had rushed ahead of us, and the stragglers barely glanced at us as we passed.

"But I thought you said you spent a few weeks in the hospital before the download and that you could pretty much do whatever you wanted." I knew that was when she, Jude, and Riley had gotten close. The way Ani talked about them, I figured they had sort of adopted her, for whatever reason taken her under their protection. A hospital where a bunch of city kids could do whatever they wanted—even city kids rife with missing limbs and congenital diseases—could be a dangerous place.

"Yeah, I did. And I asked around. The kids I came in with weren't there anymore."

"BioMax sent them back?" I asked, surprised.

Ani shook her head.

"Then what?"

She rolled her eyes, her mouth set in a grim line. The moving sidewalk had carried us through a shimmering silver tunnel and dumped us in some kind of anteroom. Huge golden doors—ridiculously new and shiny compared to the rest of the dump—marked this as the entry to the inner sanctum. It was unsettling the way Ani had guided us here, so smooth and sure, as if she belonged. "Jude and I weren't the first downloads," she said, patience and pedantry mixing in her tone like she was a teacher dealing with a particularly remedial student. "Just the first successes."

"Oh."

Volunteers for the advancement of science, BioMax had called them. Heroes. Submitting themselves to an experiment for the benefit of the greater good.

"I'm sorry," I said lamely.

"It's not like they were my friends. Just people I knew." Ani tugged her camo hood tighter over her head, dropping her face into shadow. "Come on. Let's go in."

BODY TO BODY

"It took a kiss from a princess to wake me up."

By the time we slipped into the auditorium, Savona and Auden had already taken the stage. Several hundred people crowded into the wide, windowless space, crushed against one another in their desperation to get closer to their heroes. Auden's face beamed down at us from giant screens lining the walls. His face, ten feet high, every scar magnified. It was easy, it was nothing, to have a scar brushed away, but Auden had left his intact, thick, pale worms of white crawling across his cracked lips and crooked nose. He looked different than before—not just paler and thinner but almost like a stranger, his nose jutting at a sharper angle, his chin flatter, and I remembered the patchwork of bandages across his face the last time I'd seen him in person and wondered how much of him had been rewired and rebuilt.

His eyes sparkled, pools of black at their center flooding out the green, as if he stared out at a darkened room. Or as if he was zoned. It felt like he was watching me.

But when I turned away from the screens, forced myself to look at the real Auden, a tiny figure on the distant stage, it was obvious he couldn't have seen me in the crowd. From where I stood, I could barely pick out the familiar features of his face or the cane he leaned on for balance—there was no way he could look into the sea of bobbing heads and pick out my hood-rimmed face in the crowd.

"They don't understand," he was saying, alone under a spot-light. Savona stood off to the side, hands folded, nodding with approval. They wore identical iridescent suits that rippled in shimmering rainbow, like light on an oil slick. "Those who stay comfortably at home, watching us on the vids. They think it's all the same. But is it the same?"

"No!" the crowd shouted, barely waiting for the question. They were well-rehearsed.

"No," Auden said again, as quiet and calm as the crowd was manic. "We meet here, we come together in person, *body to body,* to affirm our own humanity. To remind ourselves that being human is about more than the ability to watch a vid, to make a speech, to communicate, to *think*. Are we just minds, dis-connected islands of cognition, connected only by an electronic web?"

"No!" came the enthusiastic response.

"Mind is inseparable from body," Auden said. "When one

hurts . . ." He paused, and the giant screens overhead showed him brushing two fingers against a jagged scar on his neck. "The other screams in pain." He shook his head. "We don't live in our minds. We live in our bodies. There is no mind without body, no body without mind. *Life* is born in their merger. A mind shoved into a machine is—"

"Still a machine!" the crowd screamed. "Still a machine!" I glanced at Ani, who was dutifully mouthing the words. But I couldn't fit my lips around them.

"Dead," Auden said. "Dead thoughts in a dead body, imitating life. But *we* know life," he said. "Life infuses the heart, the liver, the arms and . . ." He paused again, looking down at the cane. "Legs." Auden limped forward to the edge of the stage, peering intently out at the audience. The room fell silent. "The skinners wear a mask," he said, his voice so low it was almost a whisper. "They hide among us. They clothe themselves as human—clothe themselves in human skin, identities stripped from the dead. They prey on the confusion of the grieving." He clapped a fist over his chest in an unmistakable gesture of self-flagellation. "They prey on the sympathies of the weak."

"You're not weak!" someone behind us shouted.

"This is new," Ani whispered to me. "Usually it's just the same old stuff—I've never heard this before."

Auden shook his head. "But I was weak, friend."

Friend? It wasn't just what he was saying, it was the words themselves—it didn't even sound like Auden, not the one I'd known. *What did they do to you?* I thought.

What did I do to you?

"I believed that because it spoke like something human, because it appeared to act like something human, it *was* something human. And why not? In that life, before, I lived a life of the mind. I worshipped at the altar of rational thought. I told myself I believed only in what I could see, what I could touch— all the while *ignoring* the reality of what my senses were telling me. What did I really believe in? An imaginary entity, the *mind*, the *self,* as if that was something that could exist outside of the *brain*. As if it was possible to distill an identity from electrical impulses, suck them out of a skull, dump them into a computer. I told myself I was a rationalist, that the Faithers believed in a fairy tale."

There was a bit of uncomfortable mumbling in the crowd, as if they weren't sure whether they were supposed to cheer or boo.

"But I was the one trapped in the fairy tale," Auden continued. "I was under a spell. And just like in a fairy tale, it took a kiss from a princess to wake me up."

I couldn't shake the feeling that his eyes were resting on me.

"The skinner breathed its dead breath into my body. It gave me life, though it had none of its own to give. And despite everything else, I'm grateful to it for that."

Now the crowd didn't hesitate. The booing and cursing drowned him out for several moments. But then Auden raised his hand, and they fell silent.

"I *am* grateful," he said. "Because when I opened my eyes,

when I *felt* the pain of being trapped forever in this broken body, I knew the truth. That humanity doesn't live in the mind. That I am my mind *and* my body. And no matter what the skinner says, no matter how good a show it puts on, this is the one truth the skinner cannot hide. They can lie—their bodies can't."

Savona joined Auden at center stage, basking in the applause. It was easier when he began to speak. I could ignore his words, the same old Faither bullshit about how only God could create life, about how skinners were abominations, how creating more of them would drive society to its knees, and on and on—it didn't penetrate. I'd heard it all before, empty logic resting on the existence of some ludicrous invisible eye in the sky. It was easier because it wasn't Auden.

At Savona's command the screens overhead began streaming images from the corp-town attack, but even that was easier than listening to Auden. Ani was rapt, but I just looked away. Into the crowd, careful not to meet anyone's eye but helpless not to search their faces, wondering what had drawn them here. What it was about their lives that hating me would remedy.

I didn't find answers. Instead I found too much to recognize, fuel for paranoid imagination. A dusty blond head peeking over the crowd became Zo; a squarish face covered in brown scruff glanced at me with eyes I could imagine bleeding on the floor of Synapsis Corp-Town; a dead girl with pink hair clutched her dead mother's hand. They couldn't be here; none of them could. I wouldn't give in to the delusion. But as if gripped by some disease—the aftereffects of heavy dreamers or heavy guilt—I couldn't erase their impossible faces.

So I shut my lids and shut them out.

"We can't forget!" Savona was shouting. "We can't be lulled into a false sense of security by their assurances that this will never happen again. This *will* happen again! And again! And again! Unless we stop them. Unless we send the message, loud and clear, to each and every skinner. That *you are not one of us!*"

Ani nudged me, and I opened my eyes again, fixing on Savona, ignoring the crowd.

"Today, together, we forge a new beginning!" he ranted. "Your presence here is a promise. Standing here today we enter into a bond with our neighbors, with our Brothers. We celebrate our humanity!"

Auden leaned forward to whisper something in Savona's ear. He nodded. "This is no metaphor, friends. No empty words. We are more than words, remember. More than mind. We are *alive*, mind and body, and we embrace that fact, as we embrace one another. So go ahead!" he shouted. "Embrace your Brother, embrace your Sister, celebrate the bond we forge together!"

The people around us shifted uncomfortably.

"What's he talking about?" I murmured to Ani.

She shook her head. "Don't know. He's never done this before."

"I mean it!" Savona cried. "The network has torn us so far from one another, turning us into a sterile community of words and thoughts. Fight back. Here, now, fight back. Affirm your existence, the fact that you are here, not just in spirit, not just in mind, but in body. You are alive, you are human, as are we all. Embrace it!"

Tentatively at first, then enthusiastically, the audience turned in on itself, stranger greeting stranger, shaking hands, hugging, as Ani and I shrank toward each other, searching for an escape before someone could touch us. But there was no safe path through the crowd. The orgs closed in.

"Don't be shy, honey." A woman with a round, pockmarked face opened her bulging arms and swept me into them.

I felt her muscles stiffen.

Her body pull away.

Saw her eyes sweep me up and down.

Heard her scream.

"Skinner!"

And then it was chaos. A hand yanked the hood off my face. More hands tore at my shirt, pulled me away from Ani, into a teeming mass of writhing limbs, twisted faces. And the chant, *Skinner! Skinner! Skinner!* shaking the room. Gobs of spit splattered against my face.

"You're lucky you're a girl," a man snarled, his fingers clamped down on the back of my neck, his thick, calloused lips peeled back from rotting teeth.

"It's not a girl," the woman beside him snapped. And to prove the point, she drove her fist into my stomach. It didn't hurt, but I doubled over with the impact. Someone grabbed a fistful of my hair and dragged me down to my knees. Behind me, someone grabbed my shoulders, held me down. I could fight back against one, against three, but not against hundreds, and I imagined myself on the ground, trampled by the herd, feet grinding my body into the floor, like my feet had stomped the corp-town bodies, and wondered if it was what I deserved.

"Stop." Auden's voice, amplified and quiet at the same time, somehow cutting through the storm.

At his command, the grip on my shoulders relaxed. I shrugged it off and stumbled to my feet as the crowd dropped back a few steps. A circle of empty space formed around us. Ani sat on the ground, looking dazed, her hoodie torn. Someone had ripped a small patch of blue hair out of her head. Up onstage, Auden nodded with approval. I wondered what would have happened if he'd been closer. If he'd known it was me down here, probably he'd have been happy enough to watch the crowd tear me apart.

"Let them through," Auden commanded, and his followers fell back, opening a pathway between us and the door. Several of them spit as we passed.

Just outside the auditorium, a man greeted us, draped in an iridescent robe that shimmered like Auden's suit. He took my arm, like a gentleman, only his grip was steel. His other hand clamped down on Ani's bicep. "I think it's best that you come with me," he said.

I wrenched my arm away. "Best for who?"

"Maybe we should just go with him," Ani said, shooting a nervous glance at the door separating us from the angry crowd.

"What do you want?" I asked the man. "We weren't doing anything wrong. It's a public event, right?"

"I want nothing," he said with a weirdly serene smile. "I'm just a messenger."

"Oh yeah? For who?"

But even as I was asking, I knew. Who else?

"For Brother Auden and Brother Savona," he said, face lighting up at their names. "They would like to speak with you."

"Then they can come to us," I said, though of course they couldn't, because that's not how this kind of game was played.

"Brother Auden has a message for you," the man said. His hair was blonder than mine, almost white against his ruddy face. It fell in long, wispy strands across his eyes, which had a strange, faraway look, like he was peering through me into the distance at his divine reward. "He says, 'It's time we talk. Unless you want to run away again, Lia.'"

"He said that?" I asked. Stalling. *Lia?* So he knew it was me. Not just some anonymous skinner.

Lia Kahn. The one responsible.

The man nodded. "Ready?"

No.

The office was sparse, with little more than a desk and an oversize ViM screen plastered on one wall. The opposite wall was a touch screen, scattered with notes and scrawlings—but it went blank a moment after we stepped into the room. The desk looked almost antique, left over from the days when they installed screens and network links into the surface of dead wood rather than just building the whole desk as an integrated ViM that knew what you wanted nearly before you'd figured it out yourself. My father had one just like it—he claimed the solidity appealed to him, the permanence, but I think it was just that he didn't like his desk talking back to him. I shouldn't have been surprised that Rai Savona felt the same way.

He leaned against his desk, arms crossed, face unreadable. Auden stood next to him, leaning on nothing, legs quivering with the effort of staying upright. His eyes were pinned on the floor.

Savona cleared his throat. "Since you've intruded on our sanctuary here, Lia, Auden thought you might as well get what you came for."

"Funny how you call me Lia when you've made it pretty clear you don't think that's who I am," I said, grateful for a voice that didn't shake. "Or do you call your toaster by name too?"

"Consider it a courtesy," Savona said. "An undeserved one."

"You look better than you look on the vids," I told Auden. His face was less pale, his eyes less watery, his hands steadier. I'd said it in relief; he took it as an accusation.

"Some things are necessary," he said.

It took a moment for the meaning to sink in. "You make yourself look *weaker*?" I asked incredulously. "For effect?"

Auden pulled himself up straighter, his expression grimly proud. "I'll do whatever it takes."

Savona bared his teeth in a mirthless smile. "He's not as

weak as he was the day you abandoned him," he said, placing a supportive hand on Auden's shoulder. Auden shrugged him off. "But the damage you caused is permanent. Damage to his spine, his organs, his life expectancy—"

"It was an accident," Ani said.

I said nothing.

"But you made him stronger too," Savona said. "You showed him the way."

"Then why can't he speak for himself?" I snapped. "Or is he too drugged up and brainwashed to even know I'm here?"

Auden raised his head. His eyes were paler in person, his pupils still too large. "The only drugs I'm on are for the pain."

He raised a hand to his face, then abruptly dropped it, as if trying to adjust glasses that he'd just remembered were no longer there. Suddenly the last six months dropped away and I was back in his hospital room, standing by his bed, begging him to forgive me, because if he did—if he had—none of it would have happened, I would be home and we would be together, whole and healed, and everything else would be background noise. Something to watch on the vids, and then shut off when it got old.

"What do you want?" he asked flatly.

"Just to talk. You and me. Can't we just go somewhere? Away from . . ." I glanced at Savona.

Auden shook his head.

"Maybe it's not a bad idea," Savona murmured in honeyed tones.

"No," Auden said sharply. "Not going to happen." Savona nodded. I recognized that nod. It was the same one that Jude got from his mechs when he issued one of his edicts. It was a pledge of obedience. Savona was letting Auden believe he was in charge.

Or Auden really was.

As Auden took a few steps, it became clear that the weakened martyr onstage was less of an illusion than he would have liked to think. Slowly, with one foot dragging slightly behind the other, he lurched around the side of the desk. His gait was awkward and spasmodic, almost like mine when I'd first learned to walk in the new body. I tried not to imagine the electrical impulses shooting through his spinal cord, stimulating dead nerves to life, one painful step at a time. He sank into the desk chair with a soft sigh of relief and rested his arms on a stack of papers. It took me until that moment to realize this was *his* office not Savona's. Whatever Auden was, he wasn't zoned and he wasn't a puppet.

"I don't know your name," he said, looking at Ani for the first time.

She looked at me, like I was supposed to give her the answer. Or maybe just permission. "Ani," she finally said.

He nodded. "Ani. You've been visiting us for the last few weeks."

"I didn't mean to—"

Auden held up a hand to stop her. "It's fine. But there's no need for all this sneaking around. The Temple of Man is a public space. We're here to help anyone who needs us."

"Really?" I snarled. "Even us world-destroying soulless monsters? Tell me something—if your God's so impressive and all-powerful, how come he can't give a soul to a machine? He can do anything, just not that?"

"He's not my God," Auden said, and I felt at least a shadow of relief that however far gone he was, he hadn't plunged all the way off the cliff. But then he kept going. "He's just God." He shot a quick glance at Savona, who nodded in approval.

"He can do anything He so chooses, as you astutely point out," Savona put in. "He *could* have created a universe where gravity is repulsive or men walk on their hands or giant lizards rule the Earth. But he didn't. He created *this* universe and does honor to us by His choice. He *chose* to endow humans—only humans—with a soul, to make us rulers in His earthly kingdom. And much as you might enjoy indulging your what-ifs and could-have-beens, this is our reality, yours as much as mine. The sooner you face that, the easier it will be for you."

Shades of Jude, I thought. Funny how eager some people were to accuse you of denying the truth—especially when "the truth" was one they'd invented.

"You really believe this crap?" I asked Auden. "What happened to science? Logic? The power of empiricism, all that?"

"Logic and empiricism dictate that the ability to *mimic* self-awareness doesn't establish the existence of an inner life. Human consciousness transcends computation." He didn't even look at me. "You're not to blame for what you are," he told Ani. "You don't understand, which must be difficult. And when you're ready, we're here to help. Bring your friends, if you'd like. We have nothing to hide."

"What makes you think we need *your* help?" I asked. "Or anyone's?"

"Not we," Auden said. "Just her. She's welcome here whenever she likes. You're not. Ever."

"Because I know who you really are," I told him. "And it's not *this*."

"Tell yourself whatever you want." It was like nothing I said touched him. No emotion, no hesitation, nothing. "But you're leaving and you're not coming back." He pressed a button on his desk console and spoke past us to an unseen minion. "Can you please escort our visitors out of the building?"

"And what if we don't want to go?" I asked.

I wanted to go.

"This will be easier on everyone if you just go quietly," Savona said. "Especially you, Lia."

The door opened behind us. "Let's go," said Auden's faithful minion, her voice sickeningly familiar.

I curled my hands into fists, grinding my nails into the synflesh of my palms, a helpful reminder. *I am a machine. I am in control. Nothing can hurt me.*

Then I turned around to face my sister.

We didn't speak. Not as she led us out of Auden's office and through the corridors bustling with robed ex-Faithers, or Brothers, or whatever they called themselves, and not when she took us on an unnecessary detour through a wide hangar in which orderly lines of city poor waited patiently for handouts of bread and plankton soup, all in the shadow of a rusted airplane, its windows shattered and its fuselage layered with years of graffiti and rust.

Not until we passed through the final door and were released into open air. I stopped, staring down Zo in her shimmering robe, her blond hair nearly as short as Ani's and just as spiky, her face painted not with the retro makeup she used to favor but with a delicate silver temp tattoo on her left cheek, the same stylized double helix that the Brotherhood of Man had emblazoned across its zone, its Temple, and apparently, its servants. "What the hell, Zo?"

"Hello to you too, sis." She smiled, and not her patented screw-you smile. Not even the fake, brittle grimace that she'd shot in my direction for the first few weeks after the download, before we'd declared open war. This was something different, the same creepily serene look as on the faces of all the robed figures we'd passed in the halls. "Long time, no see."

"So I'm your sister again all of a sudden?" What would she need with a sister, now that she had her *Brothers*?

Her face melted into a sympathetic frown, equally unsettling. "You *believe* you are," she said. "The Brotherhood has helped me see that's not your fault. You can't be blamed for the delusions of your programming."

"Delusions. Right."

Ani clamped a hand over my forearm. "Let's just go."

I shook my head. "What if I said you're right?" I asked Zo. "That I'm not the same person?"

"You're not a person at all," Zo said calmly. "I can't fault you for believing you are. But I can help you see the truth."

"How, by sleeping with my boyfriend?"

"He wasn't your boyfriend!" she snapped. Then she took a deep breath. When she spoke again, the calm was back. "That was wrong," she said. "I thought I was protecting Lia. But—" She swallowed hard. "Lia's dead. I can't protect her anymore. I see that now."

Lia's dead. The words didn't sting like they once had. But it wasn't what she said, it was the way she said it—blank. Impersonal. Like she really believed I was nothing to her.

"So you don't hate me anymore."

"I don't feel anything about you," Zo said. "You're a machine."

"Right. You don't hate me. You've just decided to devote your life to the Brotherhood, which, big coincidence, wants to wipe mechs off the face of the Earth."

"You never bother to listen to anyone but yourself, do you?" she said with a flash of the old Zo. "No one wants to do anything to you. We just want them to stop making *more* of you. So that no more families get destroyed."

Like ours, she didn't say. Because she didn't have to.

"We broke up, you know," Zo said suddenly. "Me and Walker."

"How would I know?"

"Well we did." A giggle slipped out. "He's insanely boring."

She had a point.

"I really don't care, Zo. I'm over it."

"I heard," she snapped. "Mechs are too superior to worry about us pathetic little orgs, right? Too *special*? You must be a natural."

"I think this is pathetic, Zo," I said, not sure whether I meant the Brotherhood or our conversation. "But not because I'm a mech."

She twisted the fabric of the robe around her index finger, a nervous habit left over from when we were kids. "So you're not even going to ask about them?" Zo said, a little of the old bitterness bleeding through around her edges.

"Who?"

She rolled her eyes. "Mom. Dad."

Your mom and dad, I would have said. Except I wanted to know. "How are they?"

"Like you care," she said.

"I do."

"That's why it's been six months and no one's heard from you."

So she didn't know I'd seen our father.

A herd of Brothers swept past us, piling onto a blue bus marked ELIXIR CORP-TOWN. There was a fleet of buses just like it, each bus with a different corp logo on it, each presumably awaiting a shipment of corp-towners returning home with full stomachs and plenty of ammunition for their antiskinner campaign.

"Just tell me," I snapped.

"How do you think they are? Their precious little baby disappeared."

"So? Now they can lavish all their attention on their *other* precious baby."

She snorted. "Yeah. Right. There's a lot of love to go around these days."

"Meaning?"

"Nothing."

"Right. None of my business. Not my family. I forgot."

"What family?" she asked. "Mom's so zoned out that half the time she barely remembers her own name, much less that she has a kid and husband. Not that her husband's ever home. Or speaks to either of us when he is." She smeared her hand across her forehead, like she was rubbing away thoughts the Brotherhood didn't permit. "It's too late for us," she said with a new lilt to her voice. "But at least I can help others."

"Savona tell you that?" I asked sourly.

"Actually, it was Brother Auden."

"So I'm not your sister, but suddenly he's your brother?"

"He's my *friend*," she said.

"And you just love stealing my friends, don't you?"

"I didn't have to steal him," Zo said. "He came to me. Said you ran away from him, just like you ran away from us. Explained how we're better off."

"We should go," Ani urged again, tugging at my arm.

"Thanks for the cat," I told Zo as a good-bye.

She flinched. "I don't know what you're talking about."

"Whatever."

Ani caught my eye with a silent question—*Stay* or *go?* I didn't hesitate.

Go.

We walked away—but Zo's voice stopped us after a few steps. "Is he doing okay?" Zo asked. "You know. The cat."

"He's fine," I told her.

She paused. Then, so softly I almost didn't hear: "He missed you."

"Yeah." I kept my back to her. "I missed him too."

"I don't want to talk about it," I told Ani on the ride home, before she could say anything.

Her smile contained far more pity than I would have liked. "I wasn't even going to try."

I pretended to link in to the net, just so I wouldn't have to look at her. But really I was staring past the screen, out the window, counting the mile markers as they streamed by.

Mile by mile, the car brought us home.

The entryway was one of the oldest parts of the mansion and came outfitted with two elaborate crystal chandeliers whose bulbs had apparently been burned out for several decades. Despite the high ceilings and ten-foot windows, the place always felt oppressive to me. Maybe it was the dark mahogany walls or the pillars that sprouted every few feet or the velvet couch inset into the fireplace that inevitably housed some mech or another in the throes of a dreamer fit—but even on a good day, some-thing about the room screamed, *Get out while you still can.* And this had not been a good day.

"Don't," Ani said when I began to head upstairs to my room, to blissful, silent solitude.

"I'm not going back to the dreamers," I said, like it was any of her business if I did.

"It's not that," she said, even though it obviously was. "Just . . . don't you think we should find Jude? Tell him what happened while it's still fresh?"

"If this is your attempt to keep me from crawling off to sulk, it's a pretty pathetic one," I said.

She grinned. "I have no shame. Not if it works. . . . So?"

"So . . ." I sighed. "Someone should get what they want today. Why not you?"

We found Jude the first place we looked. The vidroom. The door was half open. We both heard the moans and sighs at the same moment. Ani shot me an unusually mischievous glance. "We should probably let him have his privacy, but . . . who knows what's going on in there. He could be hurt or something."

"It *does* sound pretty dire," I said, grinning. She was going above and beyond to perk me up. Mission accomplished. "What if it's an emergency?"

"Excellent point," Ani said. "We're just doing what any good friends would do."

She swung open the door.

Jude lay on the couch, his chest bare, on top of a girl with long, black hair, her shirt tangled in her arms as she tried to wriggle out of it. He pulled the fabric out of her hands and yanked it over her head, laughing as it caught briefly on her earring and she smacked his hand away. She was facing away from the door, so we saw only her long, slender neck, exposed when she leaned forward to press her lips to Jude's chest. He wrapped his arms around her narrow waist, mechanical muscles bulging beneath synthetic skin.

I couldn't look away.

I no longer hated the sight of my own body, not the way I once had, but I couldn't imagine reveling in it, not like the two of them, much less exposing it to someone else, pressing skin against skin. The memory of that night with Walker was too fresh—I would never let anyone else look at me the way he had, touch me like I was diseased.

I couldn't see her face, but I could see Jude's, his closed eyes, his faint smile as her hair tickled his cheek. And then his eyes opened—and met mine. He grabbed her roughly and flipped her off the sofa, and I recognized her cry of complaint at the same time I recognized her face. At the same time I heard the small, sad sound escape Ani. It was the whimper of a wounded animal who'd given up the fight.

"You promised," she whispered. Her hand closed over the pendant around her neck. The warm blue glow lit up her pale skin.

Jude leaped off the couch, nearly landing on Quinn. She just glared at him and proceeded to slowly, calmly pull her shirt back on. "I changed my mind," she said.

Jude rushed the doorway, chest still bare, hair rumpled, eyes wild. "Ani, look—"

Ani slammed the door in his face.

"I don't want to talk about it," she told me.

"I wasn't even going to try," I said with a small, hopeful smile. But she just turned away from me and walked briskly down the hall, neck stiff, head erect, arms tight against her sides.

I didn't try to follow her. I didn't try anything.

But I should have.

SKIN TO SKIN

"It was almost like being alive."

When you don't eat, you don't exercise, you don't work, and you don't have to slog through school, there's no obvious start to the morning. Sometimes, especially when you can go back to "sleep" simply by instructing your brain and body to shut down, there's no obvious reason to start at all.

Which is why I figured I might not see Ani for another day or two. But instead she showed up at my door just as the sky was pinking up.

She didn't come all the way inside, just leaned in the doorway. "About yesterday," she said. "I just want to make sure you know it's a nonissue."

"If you want to talk . . ."

Ani flashed a bright, fake smile. "Nonissue means non-discussion."

"Fine." I decided not to point out that she was the one who'd come to me.

She traced her finger along the doorframe like she was examining it for cracks. "Interesting, isn't it? That stuff Savona was saying about how we can't be blamed for what we do, because we have no souls?"

"No one has a soul," I pointed out. "Orgs or mechs. It's a fictional concept. Like unicorns. Or zombies."

"Right." Ani choked out a bitter laugh. "Can't imagine why anyone would believe in the walking dead."

"We're not dead."

"We used to be."

I tried to ignore the image that popped into my head, the gleaming morgue, the burned corpse with my face. "Thanks for the reminder."

"Look, human morality comes from human mortality, right?"

"Says Savona."

"Fine," she granted me. "Says Savona. Life on Earth is unfair, but after you die, God punishes the evil and rewards the good."

I grinned. "Soul is one thing, Ani. You want to start telling me you think there's a *God*?"

"That's not the point," she snapped. I dropped the smile. "If people are good because they *believe* they'll be rewarded after they die, that's all that matters. So what does that say for skinners—"

"Mechs," I corrected her.

"We don't die," she said. "So what do we have to be afraid of? What's to stop us from doing whatever we want?"

"What's to stop anyone?" I asked. "God doesn't exist, heaven and hell are fictions, and only a few crazy Faithers still think otherwise. So under your theory, the whole world should be going crazy with bad people doing bad things."

She just looked at me, like, *Your point?*

I thought of the corp-town attack. Of the reason the corp-town had biosensors to be hacked, all the attacks that had preceded it. The weapons ban. The prison ships that used to circle the continent, and the islands for the cases too hard-core for the ships, and the cities that had replaced them both, a useful repository for nearly anyone who colored outside the lines.

"And no one did *anything* wrong back when the God delusion was still going strong," I said sarcastically, arguing with the voice in my head as much as with Ani. "You don't need to believe in heaven to be good, just like you don't need to believe in hell to know you don't want to go there."

Ani shrugged. "Jude's the one always saying mechs play by different rules," she pointed out. "Maybe things like loyalty, doing the right thing, keeping promises have nothing to do with us."

Keeping promises. Now we were getting somewhere. "And none of this has anything to do with Jude and Quinn, right? Because you don't want to talk about that."

"Monogamy's impractical when you're going to live forever, right?" Ani forced a smile. "No big deal."

I noticed she wasn't wearing Quinn's necklace anymore.

"Ani, look, maybe you should—" I broke off as my ViM pinged with a text from call-me-Ben.

Remember our deal. I don't have forever.

"Lia, I should probably get out of here."

"Wait, I really want to talk to you," I said, keying in a response. **Working on it. Need more time to get the info out of Jude.** Ben had granted me two more weeks to produce the name, but now he was texting me at least twice a day with annoying reminders not to drop my end of the bargain. I was beginning to think that ferreting out his BioMax mole didn't matter to him nearly as much as bending me to his will and forcing me to acknowledge, on a daily basis, that he was in charge.

"I'm out of here," Ani said.

"Wait. Please."

"Why?"

I could have told her about the deal with call-me-Ben. But that would mean making a decision. Because no matter how she felt about Jude now, she'd never let me betray him.

Not that I was planning to. But.

"You heard everything I said to Zo yesterday," I said.

She nodded.

"So you know Zo started hooking up with my boyfriend. After the download."

"I figured," Ani said. "Sorry."

"I saw them." I could still picture the two of them, pressed up against the brick wall behind the school, skin to skin. I didn't care anymore. Walker belonged to a different Lia, and she was gone. "That's how I found out."

"So *what?*" she asked, face twisted in sour anger. "What do you want from me? You tell your pathetic story, and I tell mine? Except that you saw mine, right? You know how it ends."

"I just thought   "

"Sorry," she said. Though she didn't sound it. "But it's different for you. That guy was your boyfriend. Zo was your sister."

"Right, and Quinn is your—"

"Nothing," Ani said. "No labels, no obligations."

"And Jude is supposed to be your friend," I reminded her. "Like a brother, you said."

"Guess I was right," Ani said. "Because look what your sister did to you."

"Yeah, and it *sucked*. I just thought you'd want . . ."

"What?"

A long pause. "I don't know," I said feebly.

She smirked. "Thanks, you've been very helpful." She sounded like Jude.

We just watched each other for a moment, like animals gauging a potential predator, weighing the options: fight or flight. Riley chose for us. He appeared behind her, leaning over her shoulder into my room.

"You busy?" he asked. "I can come back."

"Yes," I said.

"No," Ani said at the same time. "Not busy."

"We're talking," I said firmly.

"We're done," Ani said. "I should go, anyway. I'm late."

"Go where?"

"Back to the Temple," she said. "Savona sent me a message this morning, said he and Auden are willing to talk to me if I want to come in. This could be the way to end all this."

"Then I'm going with you," I said.

"He told me I should come alone." Ani shifted her weight. "He said to remember what Auden said yesterday. About you not coming back."

"I can go," Riley said, looking uncomfortable. "Whatever you guys want—"

"I told you, we're done," Ani said, slipping past him. "I meant what I said, Lia. Everything's fine."

Riley glanced after her. "Doesn't seem fine."

"Tell me about it."

He stepped out of the doorway, tipping his head in the direction Ani had disappeared. "You want to . . . ?"

I shook my head. "You can't force someone to feel better."

Riley rubbed the back of his neck. "Then maybe I should get out of here."

"Wait—Why? What'd I say?"

"Well, you didn't ask me what I was doing here."

"Okay . . . what are you doing here?"

He gave me an embarrassed grin that, for one strange

second, made him look like a little kid. "Came to force you to feel better."

"Exactly how is *this* supposed to cheer me up?" I asked when the car dumped us out at the Windows of Memory. We'd driven in silence, like the last road trip we'd taken together— and like the last time, Riley knew where we were going, while I was clueless. I wondered if he was trying as hard as I was not to think about the last time, and whether he was having any better luck.

"I thought you said you didn't need cheering up," he teased. "I thought nothing was wrong."

"I didn't say it was," I corrected him. "But *if* I was upset about something, I don't see how this is supposed to help."

I'd been to the museum before on class trips. It was the closest dead zone to our school, and unlike most of the dead zones, it wasn't toxic or radioactive, just uninhabitable. Unless you were a jellyfish.

When you're ten years old, wandering through an underground aquarium whose floor-to-ceiling windows looked out on the submerged ruins of a drowned city wasn't a bad way to spend an afternoon, but there was a reason I'd never been back. It should have been creepy, staring into the blue depths at algae-covered buildings lit by the museum's underwater floodlights, schools of jellyfish skittering through the wreckage of abandoned cars, but it was hard to get creeped out when you were safely behind reinforced glass, watching Zack

Bana pretending to jerk off while the tour guide blathered something about early twenty-first-century traffic patterns.

"You'll see," Riley said, steering me away from the main entrance. Most of the museum was below sea level, but visitors entered through a shallow glass dome surrounded by seven glowing crystalline spires. One spire for every ten thousand deaths. A wide plaza stretched around the perimeter, dotted with memorial statues and plaques, wilted flowers and soggy notes cluttering their feet.

The plaza was on a hill overlooking the sea, and a tall barbedwire fence discouraged anyone who might have ideas about testing the water. We walked along the fence until the museum shrank to doll size and the laughter of the tourists faded into the tide. After nearly a mile, the fence turned at an abrupt right angle. But instead of following it around, Riley took a flying leap and landed midway up the fence, dangling by his hands. His feet scrabbled for purchase, and a moment later, he found toeholds in the chain link. He grinned down at me. "Coming?"

I looked up dubiously at the coils of jagged wire running along the top, wondering if it was electrified.

"Nervous?" he asked.

"You're joking, right?" I said, then began to climb. I scrambled to the top in seconds—and not that we were racing, but I made it there first. I closed my hand over the tangle of wire lining the edge, letting the barbs dig into my palm. "No pain, no gain," I said, grinning, and vaulted over the top, letting myself drop the fifteen feet to the ground. My feet slammed into the grass. I let momentum carry me forward into an awkward somersault, feet over head and back to feet again, then stumbled forward and did a full face-plant, arms splayed, mouth in the dirt.

"Graceful," Riley said, climbing safely down the other side and offering me a hand.

I spat out a mouthful of grass and climbed to my feet.

"You've got a little . . ." Riley gestured at my pants, the front of which were covered in a thick layer of reddish brown dirt.

"So?"

Riley raised his eyebrows. "Didn't think you were the type, Lia Kahn."

"What type?"

He shook his head. "Just come on."

We skidded down the shallow grassy hill and found ourselves at the edge of the ocean. It was strange—in all the times I'd been to the Windows of Memory, I'd never actually been anywhere near the water. It had always looked pretty from atop the hill, the floating scum shimmering in the sunlight. But up close, it just looked like sludge.

Still, there was something about this place. The sky seemed bigger here—staring out at the horizon, it was easy to picture a time before the world was round, when the glassy sea stretched infinitely far and flat. The shore curved around, forming a narrow bay, and soon we were standing almost directly across from the Windows, too far to see anything but the glow of the crystal spires.

"Weird to think there's a whole city under there," I said, nodding at the water.

"Yeah."

"Especially since it feels like— I don't know. Like we're at the edge of the world. Like there's nothing left but us. You know?"

There was a long pause, and I suddenly felt like an idiot for saying anything at all. But then: "Yeah."

It was something.

We fell into step together, our arms swinging in sync, our faces turned to the ocean, eyes slitted against the wind. It was peaceful, and not the kind of empty quiet that forced unwanted thoughts into my head. This quiet was full—of rustling grass, of wildflowers, their bright blues and purples suggesting fragrant perfumes I could no longer smell. Full of Riley, forging the way, his head bent, his gait rangy and loose, his facial muscles losing a little of their tightness with every step, something relaxed and almost happy creeping across his face.

But then he stopped. "Here's good."

"Good for what?"

"I borrowed a bathing suit from one of the other girls," Riley said. "I hope that's not weird—I didn't want to ruin the surprise by—"

"The surprise is we're swimming?" I asked.

He hesitated, noticing the anger in my voice.

"I don't swim," I said.

Everybody knew that.

"But you can," Riley said.

"Yes."

"So what's the problem?" He tossed me a ball of material, a garish red suit that looked like something my grandmother would have worn back before they fixed the ozone. Rolled up in it was a small, slim lightstrip with a square of adhesive on the back. "Stick it on your forehead," he advised. "It's good for about an hour of light. We won't be down longer than that."

I hadn't been in the water since that day Auden and I had raced back and forth in the frigid stream, shouting over the thunder of the waterfall. The day I'd been so oblivious that I hadn't noticed how cold it was, how cold *he* was, hadn't noticed anything until he'd drifted away from me . . . over the edge.

"I don't swim," I said again.

"This isn't the same," Riley said.

"Same as what?"

"Same as the waterfall."

"I can see that," I snapped. "This is sludge." The waterfall, and the river feeding into it, were man-made, one of the nature preserves erected a couple decades ago to restore and replace the natural habitats killed off by water shortages, temperature change, and smoggy sky as viscous as soup. But there was nothing to be done about the oceans, especially the coastal regions clogged with remnants of drowned cities. The acidic water had killed off most of the fish, leaving behind only roving schools of jellyfish and a thick layer of blue and red algae, stretching toward the horizon. They called it the rise of the slime.

271

"This isn't about the water," Riley said. "It's about what happened. Isn't it."

So that was the game. Find my weakness and bear down, watch how long it would take until I broke. No wonder he and Jude got along so well.

"It doesn't matter what it's about," I said. "I'm not going in."

"Scared?"

"You think you can *trick* me?" I had a weird, childish urge to shove him in the water and run away. "What, I'm going to say, 'Who, me? I'm not scared. I'll prove it to you!' Like I'm some idiot ten-year-old?"

Jude would have struck back. Riley looked like I'd punched him. He sat down with his back to me, cross-legged in front of the still, dark water, playing his palms across the surface of the slime. It shimmered in the light, iridescent like the Brotherhood robes, colors shifting in the dim sun. "That's not what I meant," he said quietly. "I asked because I wanted to know."

"Oh."

I sat down next to him, not mad anymore. Still confused. "That's none of your business." But I didn't say it meanly.

"I know."

I cupped my hand and plunged it through the layer of algae, into the water. It was the same temperature as my body—or close enough that I couldn't tell the difference. "I used to love to swim," I admitted.

"It was an accident, you know," he said. "It wasn't your fault."

"You only know the story he tells on the vids—"

"Jude told me what happened," Riley said. I swore under my breath. So much for keeping my secrets. "And he told me it wasn't your fault."

"That's not what he told me."

Riley pounded a fist softly against the water. "That's just Jude."

Whatever that meant. "Why'd you bring me here?"

"I thought you'd like it."

"But so what?" I asked. "Why try to cheer me up or what-ever this is?"

I was starting to recognize the crooked smile, one side a little higher than the other, eyes wide. Innocent and knowing at the same time. "That's none of your business."

But he didn't say it meanly.

"Let's go," I said.

"You don't have to."

"I know." I stood up, staring into the sludge. No reflections here. "But I'm not wearing the granny suit."

It was nothing like the waterfall.

It was like nothing I'd ever experienced as a mech.

It was almost like being alive.

The water felt like nothing. But not the same way every-thing else felt like nothing, or slightly more than nothing. It was warm, almost body temperature. Even when I was alive, swim-ming through water like that had meant an absence of feeling, a feeling of absence, no sense of where my body left off and the water began. Buoyant, cutting effortlessly through the water, my body itself faded away.

When I was alive, swimming had been the inverse of running, and yet somehow the same. Running was all about the body, feeling every pound of the pavement, every screaming muscle, every pant, every gasp, running was my mind letting go, my body taking over, sensations flooding everything out, filling me up. Running, before the download, before it became a mechanical exercise in pumping limbs, had been like flying.

But swimming, the body disappeared. Swimming was silent and dark. Null. And somehow in the end, the same release, the same emptiness, this time filled up not with a rush of speed and adrenaline but of quiet. Swimming, before the download, had been like dreaming.

It still was.

Why didn't anyone tell me? I thought, cutting through the water, matching Riley stroke for stroke. It wasn't just the same as before; it was better. Because this time, I didn't have to rise above the surface to draw a breath. I didn't have to ruin the silent still by blowing out bubbles or thrashing around with the last of my air. I could just swim and swim and swim. I could swim forever.

We were built to withstand pressure differentials, so there was nothing to stop us from diving deep, kicking slowly to propel ourselves toward the submerged city.

We played our lights across the algae encrusted buildings poking up like massive coral from the debris-covered seafloor, overturned cars mingling with toppled roofs, tangled masses of traffic signs, the corroded, severed head of a stone statue, strewn clothing billowing in the gentle current, broken glass diamond-bright in the lightstrips' beams. The water had preserved the ruins, enough that it should have been easy to imagine them teeming with life, intact and unsubmerged. But it was too quiet, too still, the contours of its broken buildings fading into the darkness. Hard to imagine the city thriving, even without the rising waters; easy to imagine that decay was inevitable, built into its foundation.

Riley stayed away from the buildings, but I was curious. I drew close. He shook his head, jerking a thumb up, away. I ignored him and swam up the side of one of the tall, narrow buildings, pressing close to the windows, smearing my hand across the growth of algae. Riley tugged my arm, shaking his head wildly. His hair floated like stubby seaweed above his head. I pulled away, catching hold of the window frame, pulling myself toward it—and caught sight of the bodies within. Not skeletons—bodies. Bodies preserved, mummified by the sea, bodies with bloated, waxy skin, bobbing and shaking in a watery prison. Most of the city had been evacuated in time, but there had been plenty who refused to leave. The tour guides at the Windows of Memory always made that very clear—but none of the windows looked in on the results.

I let go. Let myself float.

Down, because there was no air left in my body.

And down farther, until I sank to the ground, a cement

pavement almost completely covered in soft, mossy growth. Civilization reclaimed, permanently.

Riley kicked down to me, grabbing my shoulder, pointing his index finger up to where the sky should have been. Jellyfish darted away from our lightstrip beams, like the light would burn. I shook my head; he nodded. A silent fight, and a moment later, I let him win, launching myself off the ground, my body a rocket, arms straight up, legs straight down. It was a superhero pose, and soon we were flying again.

We stayed a safe distance this time, enough space between us and the dead city that it was just that, dead buildings, dead cars, dead iron and steel and brick. No dead people.

But this time, I didn't forget they were there.

"I'm sorry," Riley said when we finally came back to the surface. "I didn't think— I didn't want you to see that."

I climbed out of the water, using the ugly bathing suit to pat myself dry. I'd gone swimming in my tank top and underwear. Still, Riley turned away until I was dry enough to put my clothes back on. I watched him climb back into his jeans, water still dripping down his bare chest.

"No, it's okay. Actually—thank you," I said. "For bringing me here. For making me— Why didn't you tell me it would be like that?"

"Like what?"

"You know," I said. "Like when we were alive. It felt the same as swimming always felt."

He shrugged and started walking back. "I didn't know. I never went swimming before the download."

"How's that even possible?"

He stopped and glared at me. "You've been to the city," he said. "See any pools?"

I kept doing that. Forgetting we didn't all come from the same place. Forgetting that it mattered.

"I just thought you'd like it," he said, his expression softening.

"I did."

He smiled.

"You come here a lot?" I asked as we began walking together along the shore. "It's kind of a long way to go, just for a swim. Not to mention it's kind of . . ."

"Depressing?" he suggested.

I shook my head. "I know it should be, but somehow it's just—"

"Not," he said with me. Our arms swung in time together, close enough that our sleeves brushed and, once, the backs of our hands. Like the water had loosened something in him, Riley talked. "It's the first place that's ever belonged to just me. It's big here, you know? No walls. And even down there, under the water . . ." He knotted his hands together, then released them. "The city was never like that for me. Before. It's quiet. Safe. Like you said. Being alone in the world. That's why I come." He glanced at me and risked a shy smile. "I never brought anyone here before."

"Not even Jude?"

He shook his head.

I wanted to ask why. But I was starting to get a feel for Riley: He'd tell me when he wanted to. Until then, there was no point in asking. "So how long have you guys actually been friends?"

He looked like he'd never thought about it before. "He's just always been there. Since we were kids."

"But you guys are so different," I said.

He shook his head. "Not so different. We come from the same place. That matters. When it's hard . . ." He sloshed his foot through the sludge lapping at the shore. "You find out who you can count on."

"So what were you like?" I asked. "Before."

"Different." He crossed his arms, brushed his hands up and down his biceps, rough, like he was trying to wipe off the skin. "You saw the pic. You know."

Black instead of white; org instead of mech. "Your face was the same," I said. "I mean, not— Obviously it's not the same face. But something about the expression." I had a sudden impulse to touch his face, to show him what I was talking about, the way his mouth set in a permanent frown, the way his lids hung heavy over his eyes, like he was half asleep, or like he just didn't want to see. "Ani told me what happened to kids in her city, the ones who were . . . sick," I said, thinking of predownload Jude, org Jude, trapped in his ruined org body, sunken cheeks and useless legs. "Was Jude . . . ?"

Riley didn't answer. He turned away from me, staring out at

the ocean. It was gray in the dimming light, fading into the sky. "Jude wasn't sick," he said quietly, glancing over his shoulder as he always did when he neared the edges of Jude's secrets. "He wasn't born that way. It happened when we were six or seven. Older kids. They—" He walked faster, still watching the water. "I was there, but I wasn't big enough to stop them. It just happened, and then it was over. He almost died."

"You took care of him after that," I guessed. "He needed you."

Riley shook his head. "I needed him. He figured things out. He's smart—"

"Not as smart as he thinks."

"Smart enough," Riley said. "He got us food, got us power. Kept us safe. I'm the one who screwed things up. And when I did . . ." He held his hand in front of his face, turning it over as if he'd never seen it before. Searching his fingertips like he was looking for imperfections. Or maybe for prints, the identifying whorls and eddies that mechs did without. "He figured out a way to fix that too."

"*He* got you into the download program?" I said, disgusted. "Just so he wouldn't have to go through it alone?"

"I got shot," Riley said flatly. "And thanks to Jude, I got a choice. Death or . . ."

"This."

"They didn't tell me what I was choosing," Riley said. "They didn't tell me I'd be like this. Or that I'd *look* like this. They didn't tell me I could never go home."

"Why would you *want* to?"

Riley's face was blank. "I don't."

We reached the fence and climbed over, carefully this time, returning to civilization. The crowds milling through the memorial plaza had mostly dispersed, but we still skirted the edges, keeping our faces averted from the orgs. I paused for a moment in front of a glass sculpture of an antelope, its antlers sparkling in the light like the memorial spires. The golden plaque stretched across its flank marked it as one of the Committee for Animal Remembrance and Education's extinction tributes. At every testament to loss of human life, CARE erected one of its own statues, ever-present reminders that, as the plaque said, "In the midst of our human sorrow, let us never lose sight of the greater tragedy, the death of millions, innocent victims of civilization." And then, as the list of extinguished species—the endless Latin names for bears and squirrels and deer and apes, even the ones who'd been repopulated in genetically modified form—scrolled across the LED screen, their final battle cry: *As cities fall, may nature rise again.*

There'd been riots, back when CARE had first started planting these things around dead zones like they were glad to see all those hundreds of thousands of humans knocked out of the way so the animals could return. But by now they were just background noise. It had been years since I'd actually stopped to read the list of names, to rest my hand against the cool glass head of a fantastical animal and wonder if it had been as beautiful in life as the sculptor had rendered it in death. That was the thing about the Windows of Memory, about all these memorials. They made death into something elegant and clean. Even—if you were stuck on a field trip—something boring. They cleared out the bodies, dumped them in another section of the underwater city, sanitized death to make it safe for the living.

"If mechs ever went extinct, you think someone would build one of these for us?" I asked Riley as we began walking again.

"You ask Jude, eventually we'll be building one for *them*," Riley said. I glanced up at his face, trying to figure out if he was joking. He caught my eye and held it. There was something too intense in his gaze, like he was seeing something he wasn't sup posed to, and I wanted to look away. Which is why I didn't.

Which is how I almost stepped on the baby.

I screamed.

"What?" Riley asked, alarmed.

"Nothing." *It's not alive*, I assured myself, picking up the wriggling, crying doll. Some new trend in realistic toys, though I didn't know what kid would want to deal with a squalling infant that stared up at you with creepy blinking eyes, drooled yellowish saliva, and from the feel of the thing, wet its diaper.

"Some kid must have dropped it," Riley said.

The baby's flesh was soft and pliant, almost lifelike, just like ours. Maybe they'd used the same material.

I pictured Zo and me as little kids, playing house, Mommy and Daddy to a bedful of dolls less advanced but just as creepy as this one. And suddenly I wanted to throw the baby as far as I could.

It's as close as I'll ever get, I thought. Playing house. *Mech mommy. Mech daddy. And our mech baby.*

The doll dropped out of my hands. The impact bumped its screeching up another decibel. Somewhere nearby, a child's piercing scream added to the fun. "You hurt her!" the kid shouted, running up to us on short, chubby legs. Brown pigtails flew out behind her. The Mickey T-shirt marked her as a student at one of the Disney elementaries. Surprising, since the doll was a generic. I'd always heard the Disney kids couldn't play with anything but corp-approved toys.

Riley picked up the doll and offered it to her. "What's your name?" he asked.

She burst into tears. Angry tears spurting out of swollen eyes, streaking down her bulging red cheeks. She squinched up her eyes and nose into a little old man face and began emitting a sirenlike wail, the noise cut short every few seconds as she drew in a loud, gasping breath, just enough air for another round.

We backed away. But not quickly enough to avoid the attack of Mama Bear.

"What'd you do to her?" The woman was just as chubby as her child. She snatched the girl's hand, yanking her away from us.

"Nothing," I stammered. "She just dropped her doll, and we—"

The woman grabbed the doll away from the kid, who started sobbing again. "Who knows what they did to it," she snarled. "We'll get you a new one." She glared at us. "Skinners don't belong here—this place already stinks of death. Or is that why you're here? Come to laugh at our grief?"

I opened my mouth—nothing came out.

"Well?" she snapped, shaking the doll in my face. "Are you getting out of here, or should I call the secops?"

The thought of the secops was enough to get my voice working again. "Why don't you shove that doll up your—"

"We're leaving," Riley said quickly, slipping his hand into mine.

Her eyes widened, and her face paled. I saw it. She'd recognized me from the vids. *"You,"* she said in a weak, shuddering voice. "It's *you!*" That wasn't so weak. I could tell she was gearing up for a scream.

"Now," Riley hissed, pulling me away.

He didn't let go of my hand until we reached the car.

"I feel sorry for that kid," I said, reluctant to get in. Surely the woman wouldn't go to all the trouble of calling the secops. And I refused to let her ruin the calm that had descended over the day. Besides, we'd parked far enough from the crowds that the lot felt empty. Riley was right, there was something about this place, the wide open space, the heavy sky . . . I wasn't ready to leave.

"I almost feel sorrier for the mom," Riley said. "Having to listen to that screeching all day."

He was right. Getting stuck with a kid like that would be a nightmare. Any kid would be a nightmare—now, at least. But there was supposed to be a later. A later when we weren't seventeen, when we would want all that crap. The screaming. The diapers. The kid.

We were supposed to grow up.

Riley leaned against the car, arms crossed. He tipped his head back, gazing up at the swirling clouds. It was clearer here, since the wind blew most of the crap inland, and I wondered if at night you might actually be able to see the moon. "I chose this," he said wonderingly. "I chose to live like this."

"You chose to *live*," I corrected him. "Anyone would." I joined him at the car, my back resting on the metal, our arms almost touching.

"Would you?" Riley asked. "If you could go back? If you'd had a choice?"

"I'd choose for the accident not to happen," I said. "After that, there were no more choices."

"Jude loves it. Being a mech."

"You're not Jude."

"He hates talking about this stuff. Thinks we should forget all about it. That we're lucky now."

"You're not him," I said again.

"Yeah." He turned to face me. "He's right, though. It's hard. Talking about it." He shook his head. "So I just don't. But you're different. You get it, right? You miss it too, you know?"

No, I thought. Because that was the answer I gave everyone, including myself. "I miss home," I admitted. "I miss who I used to be. I don't . . ." But that was enough truth telling for the day. I couldn't say it out loud. *I don't want to live like this.*

I didn't say it because there was no point. It didn't *matter* what I wanted. This was reality. This was life.

"Thank you," he said. "For not lying." He leaned forward,

raised his fingers to my jaw, grazing the skin midway between my cheek and chin. So lightly I could barely feel it. "It's good talking to you. Like I can say anything."

I should tell him about Ben, I thought. Riley would know what to do. Whether I should give call-me-Ben what he wanted, whether it my was job to keep Jude's secrets.

I should tell him, because not telling him is a lie.

But telling him would be like telling Jude. Telling him meant no more choices.

Riley rested his other hand at my waist. Drew me toward him. "I don't know who you used to be. But this version isn't so bad."

"Because you don't know me." But I let him hold on, and I let him believe. And when his fingers traced the line of my jaw, down my neck, I pressed my hand over his. Flesh to flesh.

"You don't know me either," he said.

His lips were soft and fit perfectly against mine, as I fit in his arms, huddled against his chest.

His lips were soft, and his kiss was soft, and if I didn't feel it in my body, if it didn't rip me open, leave me trembling, torn out of myself, if the sensors on my lips, my back, my chest, my fingertips registered the pressure of his skin, the temperature, and not the electric shock of raw desire, it didn't matter.

Because we fit together. Because his lips were soft but his arms were strong and they held me up.

And when he let go, I held on, his hand in mine, our fingers linked. And I wasn't alone.

SAFE OR SORRY

"Sometimes talking makes you look weak."

As always: Things got back to normal.

As always: Nothing got back to normal.

But this time, in a good way.

This time, Riley was there.

We spent hours, whole days, walking through the orchards, watching apple blossoms flutter to the ground as we walked, hands linked, sometimes silent but often, more often than I would have expected, talking. Never about Jude, who had barricaded himself in the vidroom, searching for a clue about how to turn the tide of public opinion in our favor; never about Ani, who was rarely around anymore and rarely wanted to talk when she was; never about the Brotherhood-inspired crowds camped out at the estate borders, shouting, spray painting the gate, throwing things over the electrified fence, usually things like rocks and fiery wads of paper and rotted fruit, sometimes things like pig intestines, and once a thing set to explode, a homemade thing with a timer and a defective fuse.

Never about the messages I got daily from call-me-Ben, messages that were gradually turning into threats. He'd given me a deadline. Two weeks to choose: Give up Jude (with information I didn't have), or let Ben give me up to the scoops (for crimes I hadn't committed). To decide whether I wanted to be a traitor or a martyr.

I let Riley believe I had no secrets. I let the time slip by. I deleted the messages.

We talked only about the past. I told him about Zo and Walker and my father and, after a week had passed and my hand felt empty without his hand pressed against it, about Auden.

He asked more than he answered, and there were certain things I still wasn't allowed to know. How he got shot, or why he blamed himself. Why he owed so much to Jude—and it was more than just the mutual protection he'd alluded to by the flood zone. There was something specific, some chain that bound them together—that was clear. We edged near it a few times, but then we drew too close, I asked one question too many, and he would shut down again.

Sometimes it was better not to talk. Sometimes it was good just to lie there with him, under a tree, a cold wind blowing that neither of us could feel, my head against his silent chest, his arms curled around me. It was strange being with another mech.

I could still close my eyes and remember the feel of Walker's arms around me, his body cradling mine. I was used to Walker's steady, even breathing, the rise and fall of his chest, his warm breath misting my cheek. When I lay my head on Riley's chest, it rested there, completely still. When we looked into each other's eyes, we didn't blink.

No one said anything to us about what we were, whatever it was. Not even Jude, who had something to say about everything. They all just accepted it as if it was old news. All except Ani, and she tried only once. "Remember when you asked me what Quinn and I had in common?" she asked. She never talked about Quinn anymore.

"You said it didn't really matter. That it wasn't about that."

"Turns out it did," she said. "And it was. Just so you know."

And maybe that was her admitting that she needed something, that she'd lost something and was ready to talk about it, if I'd just asked the right question and gave her space to answer. But maybe she just wanted to talk about me and Riley, and what was wrong with us being together—and so I didn't ask. I smiled and pretended not to understand or care, then made a pathetic joke about Riley's taste in shoes, or lack thereof, and then she was gone, back to wherever she went to get away. And I went back to Riley.

We didn't do anything more than kiss—nor did we talk about the fact that we weren't doing any more than that. I didn't ask how much he'd experimented since the download. In all the talking we did about the past, I didn't tell him about the night with Walker, when we'd tried to go backward. When I'd touched him and felt nothing, felt nothing when he touched me. Cringed from his hands on my body and from the repulsion in his eyes.

Sometimes I felt something when Riley touched me, when he ran a finger down my spine or his lips found a hollow at the base of my neck.

Sometimes it was the same nothing as always.

We were designed to simulate human life. Our brains were wired to emulate hormonal processes, neurotransmitters, all the bells and whistles of feeling, of pain, of pleasure. It wasn't the same.

But it was enough.

I didn't know if he wanted more. We didn't talk about that.

We had time.

"We have a month," Jude said, "then the new legislation passes, and that's it, we're not people, we're property."

"There's nothing about it anywhere on the network," I said. Riley was sitting next to me on the couch, but we weren't touching. Jude looked at Riley occasionally, but his eyes just skimmed over me like I was furniture. Most of the time he kept his gaze fixed on the screen just over our heads, playing a muted vid of an old concert, some what's-his-name who'd long since dosed up and flamed out. Ani sat off to the side, rigid and upright on the edge of her chair, drumming her fingers against the armrest. Quinn's invitation to the inner circle had been revoked; some kind of olive branch, as I understood it, from Jude to Ani. It didn't seem to be working. Still, she'd come when he called.

"I didn't hear about it on the network," Jude said. "But they know about it at BioMax, so I know about it too."

"Of course." I rolled my eyes. "Your infamous 'sources.' If they even exist."

"They exist," he snapped.

"So you just don't trust us enough to tell us who they are."

"Why would you care what his name is?"

"I don't." *It's only a question,* I assured myself. *It doesn't have to mean anything.* "I just don't like that you're keeping us out of the loop."

Jude looked at me, really looked at me, for the first time, then lowered his gaze to the couch, where Riley's hand rested flat against the fabric, a few inches from my own. We had nothing to hide. But we weren't playing show-and-tell either. "There are a lot of loops," he said. "No one can be in all of them."

"You done with the cryptic crap?" Ani snapped. "Some of us have places to be."

Riley's eyes widened. I'd told him about the Quinn thing, but I could tell he hadn't gotten it, not really. In his mind, Jude was the hero of every story, especially Ani's—the poor little broken girl taken under his wing.

"They're calling it the Human Initiative," Jude said, unflappable as ever. "Paid off a few senators so that the thing looks like a result of public outcry, but everyone knows it's coming from the Brotherhood. From Auden, specifically, since Savona's never known how to work the system like this."

"Who cares?" I said. "So we're unpeople in the eyes of the government."

"*Who cares?*" Jude repeated incredulously.

"Yeah, it sucks, but who cares? It only matters what the corps think, and—"

"Whatever the corps want to do, the letter of the law is still in our favor," Jude cut in. "If we lose that . . ."

"So we *do* something," I said. "Instead of just sitting around here whining about it."

Jude scowled. "Funny, that's exactly my point."

"We need to sway public opinion," I said. "Maybe stop hiding on this estate, get out there. *Talk* to people. Show them they have nothing to fear."

"You'll be great at that. As far as the orgs are concerned, your face is the definition of 'scary.'"

I stiffened.

"Watch it," Riley said.

"No need to defend your girlfriend's honor," Jude drawled. "I'm just stating a fact."

"No one needs to defend me," I said, touching Riley's arm. He moved away. "And you're right, it can't be me. But that doesn't mean we can't get out there. Rally the people who believe in us. They do exist." I thought of my father. "Maybe we can start some kind of petition—"

Jude barked out a harsh laugh. "You're joking, right?"

"Uh, no."

"*Petition?* What next, you want to write a *manifesto* that we can all sign? 'We hold these truths to be self-evident that all mechs are created equal'? Brilliant. Let's get right on that."

"I'm not hearing a better suggestion."

"We stop talking," Jude said. "The orgs are never going to accept us. You heard your boy— I'm sorry, *ex*-boyfriend. We're a threat to them just by existing. They see our strength, they know they're weak. They know they're going to weaken. Sicken. *Die*. We're everything that they're not, and we scare them. No one wants to be scared. They'd rather be angry."

"Thanks for the life lesson," I said, "but I still don't see how that translates into action."

"Action," Jude said. "That's exactly my point. We don't ask for our rights. We *take* them."

"You want a war," I said in a low voice.

And he knew exactly what I was thinking.

"Not a war," he said. "But I'm not afraid to fight."

"Fighting is something you do when talking doesn't work," I said. "It's a last resort, not a first one."

"You learn a lot about fighting in your little org school, in your happy little org home?" Jude snarled. "You fight a lot of battles, defending your estate from the encroaching barbarians, the hordes trying to burn down your mansion and drain your indoor pool?"

"So because I'm not from the city, I don't get a vote? I don't know what I'm talking about?" I turned to Riley. "Tell him there's nothing wrong with trying to *talk* to people."

Riley tilted his head down, his chin skimming his chest. "Sometimes talking makes you look weak," he said quietly.

Thanks for backing me up.

"Especially when no one wants to listen," Jude said, smiling at his best friend. Obedient as ever, loyalties undivided.

"I have a suggestion," Ani said, voice sweet and timid again, almost like it used to be. "If anyone wants to hear it."

"Of course we do," Jude said. There was something soft in his voice when he spoke to her. Like an apology. I wondered if he'd given her a real one or if this was the best she'd get.

"It's the corp-town attack," Ani said. "That's why they hate us, right?"

Jude, always quick to shoot down a restatement of the obvious, just nodded approvingly.

It fell to me: "So what?"

"So we all know the Brotherhood had something to do with it," Ani said.

Do we? I thought, glancing at Jude. *Do we* know?

Jude didn't do anything that wouldn't advance his cause, and the attack had, rather spectacularly, done the opposite. So I believed him that he was innocent. This time. But that didn't make me feel much better. Because I had believed it was possible—and what was I doing here with someone who I believed capable of *that*? So he hadn't attacked the corp-town. Probably. What *would* he do? I told myself that was a good enough reason to stick around: to stop him. But if it came to that, what's to say I would get the chance?

"It doesn't matter what we 'know,'" Jude said. "Not without proof."

"Exactly." Ani looked pleased with herself. "So we get proof. I've heard things. I think I know where we can find what we need."

"You can get us evidence?" Jude asked.

"If we go in at night, when no one's around, and we can get into Savona's office?" Ani paused, then grinned. "Yeah, I think I can. Their security's pathetic, and it's mostly biobased. Not set up to keep us out."

"That's unexpected," Jude said.

More than unexpected, I thought. Unlikely. Savona was assembling an army—why wouldn't he protect his power base from the enemy?

"They're all about being open to everyone, right?" Ani shrugged. "I don't think electric fences really say welcome, you know? I've asked around—"

"They *talk* to you?" I asked, remembering how the mob had nearly torn us to pieces at the rally.

"They're not so bad," Ani said. "I mean, for orgs who hate us," she added quickly. "They think they've convinced me I'm evil, and I'm going to . . . I don't know. Get all my friends to just give up. So they're pretty nice to me. They let me see things I shouldn't, and what I've seen is that they're planning something big. Maybe even bigger than the corp-town. They want to turn people against us once and for all."

Jude shook his head. "I knew it," he said in disgust.

"They lock everything up at night," Ani said. "But I know the code to Savona's office."

"This is perfect," Jude said, beaming at Ani. She looked away. "We'll send a few people in, dig up the dirt on Savona—I say we go tomorrow."

"Just like that?" I said. "No more discussion?"

"What's to discuss?" Jude said. "It's a good plan. Unless you have a problem with it because it's not *your* plan."

"Maybe I have a problem with breaking the *law*," I retorted.

"Savona kills forty-two people and you get squeamish about a little unlawful trespassing?" Jude asked. "Aren't you worried about what he may do next? Or maybe you don't care who dies, because they're 'just orgs,' is that it?" He smirked, knowing that was exactly the same accusation I'd been silently leveling at him.

I didn't take the bait. "You don't think it's all a little too easy? Ani just *happens* to stumble onto rumors about the corp-town attacks, just *happens* to hear about security details? That doesn't make you wonder?"

Ani stood up, her posture rigid. "Are you accusing me of something?" she asked stiffly.

"Ignore her," Jude said. "None of us would ever question your judgment."

"Shut up!" she snapped. "I don't need you to protect me anymore. I'm a big girl now, aren't I? And if Lia wants to accuse me of something, she can go ahead. But say it to me, Lia. Not *him*."

"I know you're trying to help," I said slowly. "But what if they're just showing you what they want you to see?"

Ani sucked in her lip like she was biting down hard to stop herself from spitting out the first thing that came to mind. When she spoke again, her voice was low and deliberate, laced with anger. "So you're just accusing me of being a moron," she said.

"No, of course not—"

"You think I'm oblivious, is that it? I just see what I want to see. I don't *understand* what people are really like. I'm too *stupid* to know what's really going on?" She shook her head, hard. "Whatever." Glaring at me, she stalked to the door. "Let me know when you're ready to make a plan," she said, and although she refused to look at Jude, it was clear the words were for him. "Or listen to her if you want. I don't care anymore."

By the time she slammed the door behind her, I was already halfway across the room, determined to go after her and make things right. Not just the fight but the last several weeks, the conversations I should have forced her to have but didn't, because it was easier just to leave her alone.

"Don't," Jude said. "Trust me, it's better you don't. Not right now." He jerked his head at Riley. "Can you?"

Riley nodded. He flashed me an apologetic look, then slipped out the door after Ani.

"What?" I snapped at Jude. "You'd rather she hate me?"

"I know her better than you," he said. "Give her some time."

"Is that what you've been doing?" I asked. "Giving her time? Hoping she'll forgive you for—"

"Shut up." It wasn't like Jude, always so restrained, every word measured, calculated for maximum impact. That one had just slipped through the defenses, popped out. And we both knew it. "Besides," he said, returning to an even tone. "We're not done here. You want to convince me that raiding the Temple is a bad idea? Go ahead. Convince."

"You're telling me you don't think it's possible that Ani's being misled? Or . . ."

"Or misleading us?" he said.

"I didn't say that . . ." I couldn't look at him. I felt too guilty to even be saying it out loud. Especially with Ani thinking I didn't trust her. "Tell me you don't think it's possible."

"I don't think it's possible," he said without hesitation. "And like I say, I know her better than you do. If she says she's sure, if she says she can do this, then she can."

"Jude, she's . . ." I flicked my eyes to the door. "Fine, you know her. You don't think she's acting a little . . . erratic?"

"No. I don't."

"And you accuse *me* of denying reality?"

"I trust her," he said, loud and slow. "And if you trust *me*, that should be enough. But that's the problem, am I right? You don't."

"I . . . trust that you think you're doing what's best," I said, choosing my words carefully.

"No, you think I'm still hiding things from you," he said. "Even after I told you the truth about the trackers. And about everything else you ever wanted to know. I may keep some things from some people, but all I've ever told *you* was the truth."

I had to acknowledge that, as far as I knew, he was right. I'd never thought to wonder why. "I *think* I'm tired of you telling me what I think."

"Reagan Wood," he said.

"Are your language circuits malfunctioning?" I asked. "Because that wasn't a sentence."

"The name of my source at BioMax. That's what you've been burning to know, right?"

"Why are you telling me this?"

He smiled so fakely that he couldn't have intended it to look sincere. It was a game for him, just like everything else. "Think of it as an act of good faith."

"My faith in you?" I asked. "It's dwindling."

"My faith in *you*," he said. "No secrets. Starting now." He flicked a hand through the air and grinned, knowing how much I hated the fearless-leader thing. It made him all the happier to act the part. "You may go."

I gave Ben a name.

It just wasn't the name he wanted.

It wasn't until I had the real name, Ben's zone keyed into my ViM, staring at his ugly, lifelike av, that I finally decided what to do: lie.

So I sent Ben the information. William Dreyson, the name of the doctor who'd first treated me after the download, the one responsible for transplanting my brain into a new body. He had personal contact with all the mechs he worked on, and the technical skills to know which upgrades were test-run ready. The perfect candidate for a rat—and, added bonus, he even looked like one.

Ben would buy it and leave me alone. Riley would never know I'd considered betraying Jude. And Jude would never have to know any of it.

Things could go back to normal, whatever that meant. And they did—for about six hours.

I was sitting on the sidelines of the skate park, a wide plain of concrete just left of the poolhouse. It was the perfect spot for rollerslam, a game some of the newbie mechs had invented when one of them stumbled across some retro skates on the network. Spinning out of control while a fleet of wheeled mechs sped toward you and smashed you into a cement wall wasn't quite my thing, but Sloane had become slightly addicted, and I'd promised her I'd at least give it a try. I was just gearing up the nerve to strap on a pair of wheels when Jude grabbed my arm and yanked me to my feet.

"What do you want?" I said, shaking him off.

He shook his head. "Not here."

"You better come back!" Sloane shouted as she saw me follow him into the nearby orchard. "You promised!"

"In a minute!" I called back. Then glared at Jude. "This better be good. *What?*"

Once we were safely shielded from the others by a thick crop of trees, he stopped. "I just didn't think you'd want the others to hear what we're about to discuss."

"And what's that?"

"Your true colors."

I decided to take the chance, however unlikely, that he didn't know anything. Bluff it out. "Color doesn't matter to a mech, right, Jude? One of the many valuable lessons I learned from you."

"And what did you learn from BioMax?"

So much for bluffing.

He was watching me carefully. And once he was sure I'd given up the game, he began a slow clap, the smirk creeping across his face. "Just wanted to say congratulations. You can always be trusted to live down to expectations."

"Spying on me?" I guessed. "What, you bugged my ViM? Hacked my zone somehow?"

Jude shook his head. "Didn't have to. Haven't you heard? I have a source on the inside. Oh, that's right," he said, playfully slapping the side of his head, as if to jar loose the memory. "You *do* know. And you just couldn't *wait* to tell your friends at Bio-Max."

"I didn't tell them," I pointed out, without bothering to excuse myself with the circumstances, the blackmail. Either he knew or he didn't, and most likely, he wouldn't care. Much as I didn't care what he thought of me.

But Riley will.

"I know," Jude said. "That's why I'm here. Or why you still are, to be more precise. Points off for not telling me about this Ben guy to begin with. But in the end, you picked the right team. Passing grade, just barely."

"You were *testing* me?"

"Don't play dumb," Jude snapped. "You figured that out the moment I showed up."

"Get away from me."

"Don't tell me you're *offended*." Jude started to laugh again. "You're the one who was considering passing information to BioMax."

"*You're* the one who said they're not the enemy," I reminded him.

"And what are you?"

I didn't reward that one with an answer.

"Now I see why you were so determined to convince me that Ani can't be trusted. It's because *you* can't be trusted. No wonder you don't trust the rest of us. Projection—you think everyone's as craven as you."

"Maybe some of them are," I said.

"*She's* not."

I raised my eyebrows. "I wasn't talking about her."

"I know how to read people," Jude said, ignoring the implication. "I know her. And I guess now this proves that I know *you*."

"Get away from me," I said again. He took a step toward me, then another. I wasn't about to back away from him.

"I'm not angry," he said. "You did what you needed to do. You looked out for yourself." Jude grabbed my wrist, forcing our palms together. "See? We're the same," he said. "That still scares you. But you can't make it disappear."

I tried to pull away, but he was holding on too tight. So

instead I closed my hand into a fist. He wrapped his fingers around mine. "I'm not scared of anything."

"Then remember this," he said, squeezing my fist. His other hand tightened around my wrist, nails digging into the skin. "Remember what you are and where your loyalties should lie."

"I don't need you reminding me. And I *don't* need you testing me. *I'd* never betray one of us. Not to BioMax, not to anyone."

"Not even to save yourself."

"Not even."

His eyes were golden, his lips turned down, missing their smirk. Strands of silvery hair swept across his forehead, nearly brushing his long lashes. His face was cold. His eyes were cold.

His hands, though made from the same material as mine, fueled by the same energy as mine, identical to mine, were warm.

He leaned toward me, his two hands still clasping my one.

I put my free hand on his chest.

To push him away. But I didn't.

"We're the same," he said again.

"Not in any way that matters," I whispered.

"In the only way that matters." He drew closer and dropped his voice so low, I couldn't hear it anymore. I could only watch his lips move. "You know it."

I pushed him away.

Ripped my hand out of his. "You're disgusting," I said. Shouted.

Surprise skittered across his face, and then was gone. Composure, perfect control, returned. "You're confused," he said.

"You want to talk about loyalty?" *Space,* I thought. It was important to put space between us. But I *would not* back away from him. "Riley's supposed to be your best friend."

Jude nodded. "Your point?"

"That doesn't mean anything to you?" I wanted to throw something at him. But the tree branches were bare. "No, don't tell me, that was just another test of my loyalty. Guess I passed, right?"

"You don't know what you're talking about."

"I wonder if that's what Riley would say."

For a moment, I thought he was going to lunge at me. But he stayed where he was, unnaturally still. "Riley knows who I am and what I would do—and what I would *never* do."

"Never betray a friend?" I laughed. "Tell that to Ani."

"That was a mistake," he said quietly.

I shot an exaggerated look of horror up at the night sky. "You're admitting you were *wrong*? Is the world about to end? Should I take cover from the storm of lightning and the rain of fire?"

"And suddenly you're so perfect?" He sneered. "So you gave your buddy at BioMax the wrong name—what do you think's going to happen to that guy now that BioMax thinks he's their leak?"

I hadn't thought about it at all.

And Jude knew it.

"And then there's poor, sad Ariana Croft," he said with a slow shake of his head.

"Sad she didn't kill more orgs, you mean," I muttered.

"If she killed any."

"You think they got the wrong mech?" I asked, surprised. The vids had made it sound like they had iron-clad evidence against her.

"I *think* that if BioMax could forge evidence to get you *out*, they could just as easily forge evidence framing someone else to take your place. And I *think* that's occurred to you too. You're not stupid. Just selfish."

"Are you guessing, or do you know something?" I asked in a low voice.

"Guessing that you're not stupid? Well—"

"Guessing that they framed her!" I shouted. "Just shut up and tell me."

He let me hang for a long moment. "Just a guess," he admitted. "But what if I knew for sure, what then? Would you go crying to BioMax? Would you risk turning yourself in if it meant clearing her?"

"I didn't do anything wrong."

"And you didn't answer the question," he pointed out.

"Because I don't owe you any answers."

"I told you once that you were in denial, because you were afraid of facing the truth about yourself. You didn't listen to me then," he said. "And someone got hurt."

"You don't have to remind me."

"I guess I do. Because you haven't changed at all."

He was still too close to me.

"Shut up." I took a step forward.

"Still running away," he said. But *he* was the one who took a step back, then another, until his back pressed against bark.

"Shut up." Another step forward.

"Still picking the easy choice, the *safe* choice over the *right* choice."

"Shut! Up!" I forced my anger down. I was close enough to grab him. To make him stop. *Control.*

"Your clever comebacks are getting harder and harder to rebut," he taunted.

"I'm not hurting anyone I care about. Never again."

"Tell it to Riley," he said.

I was close enough to press a hand over his mouth, to force his words back inside.

"Like you care about him."

"I care about what you're doing to him," Jude said. "Picking him because you're scared and you think he's safe. Instead of—"

"You?" I forced laughter. "You know what I miss about having an org body? The ability to puke."

Jude's mouth twisted into something that wasn't quite a smile. "I won't let you ruin him the way you ruin everything else."

"Funny. That's exactly what I've been meaning to say to *you*."

Jude just laughed without mirth. "The irony in all this is that Riley's about as far from safe as you can get." He reached up a hand as if he was about to touch me, my hair, my hand, my face. I slapped him away. Turned my back on him.

"Like I'd believe anything you said about him," I said, already walking away.

"Believe whatever you want," he said. "You always do."

TRESPASS

"People don't change just because you want them to."

The Temple of Man was a dark, hulking shadow against the night. Overhead, a smear of moonlight filtered through the cloud cover, our only light beyond the pinprick beams that guided our footsteps. There were five of us hiking the mile between our hidden car and the southernmost entrance of the Temple, a team of volunteers, handpicked by Ani: Sloane, maybe figuring this for another suicide mission. Brahm, who'd been hanging around Quinn like a lost puppy ever since she'd gifted him with his d-day tongue bath. And Ty, the fuchsia-haired newbie mech I'd once done my best to woo, who was already on her second body—in a fit of grief-fueled rage, her mother had gone after the first one with a carving knife. Jude, of course, was nowhere to be seen—the general doesn't fight alongside his foot soldiers. It was agreed: Jude couldn't put himself at risk, not if getting caught meant implicating all of us in the operation, not to mention depriving the mechs of his wit and wisdom going forward. Quinn, whose credit kept us all afloat, was similarly indispensable. The rest of us, apparently, less so.

Riley had wanted to come too, but Ani had vetoed it. "Too distracting," she'd said. "You'll be too focused on protecting each other, not focused on the mission." Ever since Jude had officially put her in charge, she'd started tossing around words like "mission" and "raid," like we were soldiers and she was leading us into battle. So it was one or the other of us, and I'd gotten Riley to agree that I could be of more use—after all, I'd been to the Temple, I knew Auden, I'd be better for the *mission*. He was forced to accept it, because the mission was all that mattered to Jude, and Jude was all that mattered to Riley.

But I wasn't there for the "mission." I was there because it was the only thing that guaranteed Riley wouldn't be. And because when things went wrong, I would be ready.

Ani and I fell into step together, leading the way toward the Temple. The other three clumped together a few feet behind.

"I'm sorry about before," Ani murmured as we tromped through the dark. It was the first thing she'd said directly to me since our fight.

"I didn't meant to call you stupid," I said quickly. I'd tried to apologize several times already, and she'd refused to listen. I wanted to get this out before she changed her mind again. "I just wanted to make sure we covered all possibilities."

"I know." Ani gave me an embarrassed smile. "It just . . . threw me off, having him there."

"Jude."

"Yeah. It made me a little crazy." She raised her hands, palms up, a silent capitulation: *What can you do?* "But I shouldn't have taken it out on you."

"I shouldn't have—"

"Please don't," she said. "You were right to ask the questions, I was wrong to shoot you down, that's it. Can this just officially be over now?"

It felt weird, letting it go without getting out a real apology. But I didn't push it.

"So what happened with Jude yesterday?" Ani asked, shooting me a mischievous grin.

"What?"

She laughed. "Everyone heard you two last night."

"Everyone?"

"Don't look so horrified," she said, giggling. "It was only Sloane, and she couldn't even hear what you two were fighting about."

You, I thought, and suddenly felt like crap. I'd been so sure that Ani had changed, that since the Quinn thing, she'd turned into this angry, distant person—but talking like this, it was just the same as always. It was just Ani, tentative and soft, with just enough unexpected edge to make her interesting. And I started to wonder if I'd imagined the distance between us—or worse, inserted it, because it was easier to believe she was running away. Because it was convenient for me, freeing me up for Riley.

"We weren't fighting," I said. "Jude was just being obnoxious."

"Shocking," she said, laughing again. It was an incongruous sound here, at the moonlit edges of the Temple of Man.

"You won't believe what he tried to tell me," I confided, repeating everything he'd claimed about Riley, waiting for the inevitable flood of derision, the *He's jealous, he's spiteful, he's slime.*

It didn't come.

"Is he right?" Ani asked. "Is Riley your safe choice?"

"Of course not!"

"Then why are you so mad about it?"

"Because Jude's being an asshole!" I snapped, too loudly. Ani shushed me. We were nearing the perimeter of the main Temple buildings, which according to Ani were guarded at night by an electrified field. We slowed down to let Sloane, Brahm, and Ty catch up with us. All Temple personnel had been issued ID chips that allowed them to pass through the field without harm—Ani had gotten her hands on one and we were pretty sure that if we stayed in physical contact with one another while passing through, one chip would do the trick.

"If Jude's the one you really want—"

"He's not," I insisted.

"But if he is—"

"Did you hear the word 'not'?"

"I'm just saying that if you're just playing around with Riley until you get bored and drop him, it's one thing. But it would be such an evil bitch move to drop him for Jude that you would deserve any fucking thing that happened to you."

There it was again, a flash of something dark and angry, like a shadow gliding below the surface of still water.

"What would . . . happen to me?" I asked carefully.

"I'm just saying, maybe Riley isn't as safe as you think he is."

"If you're trying to tell me something, just say it. Otherwise, you should stop." And for a few moments, she did. We walked silently, our footsteps slapping against the asphalt, our flashlight beams casting narrow tunnels of light. Behind us, the other mechs were just twinkling flashes in the dark.

"You don't know who he used to be," Ani said.

"It doesn't *matter*," I reminded her. "It doesn't matter who any of us used to be." It wasn't just a line I'd borrowed from Jude, something useful to reel in the newbies. I believed it, or I wouldn't be sneaking through weeds at two a.m., breaking into the Temple of Man; I'd be at home, at Lia Kahn's house with Lia Kahn's doting parents, tucked safely away in Lia Kahn's comfy bed.

"People don't change just because you want them to," Ani said. "Trust me."

She sped up, gaining several feet on me. I jogged to join her, reminding myself not to let it get to me. That it wasn't even about me, not really.

"Ani, wait."

She kept walking. I touched her shoulder.

She scowled at me.

"You want to talk about it? Quinn?"

"Here?" We'd reached the electrified perimeter. Once we made it through—if we made it through—there'd be org guards prowling, and we would need to be silent and invisible.

"Fine. But if you ever do, you know where to find me."

"Riley's room," she muttered. Then she sighed and gave me a tired smile. "Sorry. Again."

"Forgotten."

Mostly.

As the others caught up with us, we switched off our lights and went to infrared. The other mechs glowed a dull purple in my sights, nearly the same color as the pavement. Ani pulled out her ID chip.

"You sure this is going to work?" Ty asked, clasping Sloane's hand. I reached out for Brahm's hand, and Ani took my other, squeezing tight. The ID chip was pressed between our palms.

"If it doesn't, we're mechs, right?" Sloane asked, sounding like she was expending a considerable effort to seem carefree about the whole thing. "Electrocution could be exciting. Aren't you curious?"

"Not particularly," Ani said. "So let's get this right. Ready?"

"Ready," I agreed. The word rippled down the line and, as one, we took a step forward.

Nothing can happen to me, I thought, waiting for 50,000 volts to sizzle through me as I crossed the field. It wouldn't be enough to kill an org, but who knew what a shock like that would do to a mech body, a mech brain. We were nothing but electricity, elaborately wired computers, and surely it would take less than 50,000 volts to fry the circuitry—maybe enough to send us careening into a brand-new body, but maybe just enough to warp our brains. When the wiring inside your head fused into a tangled knot, would you notice, or just think it was the outside world that had gone askew?

And then I took another step, and I was across.

Nothing happened.

"That's it," Ani said, dropping my hand. "We're safe."

"You sure?" I asked. She pointed to the faded etchings on the pavement, marking off the electrified area.

"Anticlimactic, right?" Sloane said. "Tell me a little piece of you wasn't hoping—"

"No piece," I cut her off. "Not even a little one. I'll be happy for the whole night to be anticlimactic."

The Temple loomed over us, white stone black in the night.

"It's *huge*," Brahm said, staring up at its imposing face. In the dark, he didn't squint, nor did he move like the rest of us, careful and timid, afraid with each step. He moved like he could see.

"I heard them talking about expanding," Ani said. "There's not enough room for everyone who wants to come."

Sloane rolled her extinguished flashlight between her palms, keeping her head averted from the Temple. "How can there be that many morons in the world?"

"You know, Savona and Jude aren't so different," Ani said.

"How can you *say* that?" Brahm asked.

I knew how she could say it.

"Jude's always telling us that we're not human and we should just accept it, right?" Ani said. "They're orgs, we're *machines*. How's that any different from what Savona's trying to say?"

I'd asked myself the same question.

"It just *is*," Brahm said.

It was a pathetic answer. But none of us had anything better.

The Temple defenses were even more meager than Ani let on. Aside from the electrified perimeter, they were nearly non-existent—no patrols, no guard posts or ID checks. And at the main Temple, nothing but a few easily tricked locks, nothing more than you'd find at the entrance of any organization matching the Brotherhood's self-description—open, accessible, *innocent*. Silent and single file, we followed Ani into the building. Instead of taking the moving sidewalk through the silver tunnel to Savona's staging area, we went the opposite way, slipping through an unmarked door into a labyrinthine zone of beige corridors. I recognized it from my last trip to the Temple—Auden's office lay along one of these hallways. Maybe he was in there, hunched over a desk, plotting his next strike on the skinners . . . or maybe staring out the window, watching the night, wondering how he'd ended up here. Because that's what I was wondering, sneaking like a thief, draped in black and raiding a nest of God-fearing vipers who'd prefer me erased, in body and mind. The night had a dreamlike quality, and I half expected to wake up to find that Auden and I had rendezvoused at our favorite grassy hiding spot behind the high school and fallen asleep, dreaming up a new and horrible life.

But machines don't dream. Not that kind of dream, at least, the kind that ends in a gasping, blissful, sweat-stained *and then I woke up.*

Motion-sensitive lights in the floor cast the hallways in a dim glow as we passed, but apparently, foolishly, weren't tied into any kind of central security processor. Because the hallways stayed empty, our path to Savona's office was free and clear. Ani stopped in front of a door that looked no different from any of the others. "This is it," she VM'd. There was a slim key panel along the frame. She keyed in a code.

I was wrong, I thought as the door swung open. *This is actually going to work.*

An alarm screamed.

The hallway flashed blue.

Blue, not red like the corp-town, but for a moment, in the keening wail of the alarm and the faces lighting up in the dark, I was back there again, hearing their screams, though there had never been any screams.

The Brothers approached from both ends of the hallway and streamed through the open office door. We were surrounded.

Five of us, ten of them, all in Brotherhood robes. All with guns raised, glinting in the flashing blue light.

"Don't you pay attention in *church*?" Sloane snarled at the one closest to her. "We're machines. You can't hurt us."

"Don't test us," he said.

"Whatever." Sloane muscled past the guy and took off running down the hall.

The gun didn't make a sound. And neither did Sloane.

It happened nearly in silence: The guard took aim, depressed the trigger. And Sloane went rigid. Her body convulsed, then thumped to the floor. It convulsed once more, her head slapping against the tile, then lay still.

"Sloane!" Ty screamed. But she didn't move to help her. None of us did.

"She'll be fine," the guard said. I had more time to examine his weapon now, and I realized what I'd first taken for an ordinary gun was more like a modified stunshot, like the kind the secops carried. The abbreviated barrel ended in a flat black plate with a narrow blue spark dancing between two metal prongs. "Turns out one little electric pulse is all it takes to temporarily disable your neural systems. I hear it hurts like hell. But you freaks are into that, right?" He scooped Sloane off the floor and tossed her limp body over his shoulder like it was nothing. Then, with a jaunty wave, he carried her down the hall, around the corner, and out of sight. Nine of them left; four of us.

"So who's next?" the largest of the men barked.

Next was Brahm, without warning. A different guard, barely pausing to aim, flicking his gun at Brahm like he was making a conversational point. Brahm collapsed, his body shuddering and shaking for several moments before going still. His eyes were open. I knelt, wanting to . . . I didn't even know. Cradle his head, maybe. Just touch him. Make sure he was still alive.

Not that there would have been any way to prove it. No pulse. No breath. Just a body with a deactivated brain.

"I wouldn't," the guard closest to me said. "Charge might still be live. And it's not your turn yet."

At his words, Ty lunged at her guard, fist making contact with the guy's bulbous nose. She made it about ten steps before the shock took her down.

Unlike the other two, she screamed.

"I'm not going to run," I said with a confidence I didn't feel.

"Not her," Ani said. "That was part of the deal."

She wasn't talking to me.

"What deal?" But as I looked back and forth between them, as I took in the expression on Ani's face—nervous but not scared and not surprised—the way the guards parted to make way for her, the way they lowered their weapons, all except the one who kept pointing his gun at me, I got my answer. *Guess you'll finally have to admit you were wrong,* I said silently to Jude. Too bad I wouldn't be around to hear it. "Stupid question, I guess."

"I'm sorry," Ani said, not particularly sounding it. "I didn't think you'd volunteer to come. You didn't even think this was a good idea."

"Imagine that." I wanted to shake her. I thought I'd been suspicious, but now I knew I hadn't doubted her, not really. I'd thought the Brotherhood was setting her up. The thought of her working *with* them disgusted me. It was inconceivable that she'd changed this much, equally unlikely that this had been the real her all along. There was no reality palatable enough to accept.

I was no better than Jude, I thought. Blind.

"Is this really worth it? You hate Jude this much?"

"This isn't about him," she snapped.

"Right."

"You wouldn't understand."

"Then make me." I glared over her at the guard holding the gun. It was strange, how many of these I'd faced since becoming a mech. Before the download, guns were just something slummers played with in cities and whatever random countries were still playing their ridiculous war games. Now I could stare at one and pretend not to care.

"What we're doing is wrong," Ani said. "What we *are* is wrong. It's not our fault—we didn't *ask* to be this way. But we have to accept the truth. We don't belong here. We're *wrong*."

"Don't tell me you actually *buy* that bullshit."

I shouldn't have let her come back here, I thought. *Not by herself.*

Quinn and Jude left her broken—and I left her alone. Too busy with Riley to see that she was getting sucked in. Too busy, too obliviously happy to notice that she was drifting away.

"I told you before," she said. "Brother Savona, Auden, Jude, they're all saying the same thing. We're machines. But that's what Jude doesn't get—what none of you get. *Machines* are supposed to be *things*. Not people. We don't belong."

And there it was, the answer to the question she'd fired at us before, the difference between Jude and Savona. Both of them believed we were machines. Both of them believed we shouldn't pretend to be human. But Jude believed we were something new, something of value, something *alive*. Savona didn't.

"You can't actually believe that about yourself," I argued. "These people think you don't really think for yourself, or *feel*. You know that's wrong."

Ani smiled sadly. "They programmed us well," she said. "They fooled us into believing we were real. But we're not. We're computers. Copies of dead people. Everything about us is a lie."

"It's not too late," I said, VM. Knowing it was. "We can still get out of here." Knowing we couldn't.

"Enough," she said, nodding at the guard aiming at me. I braced for the shock. *Nothing to fear.* Just a little pain, and not very far to fall.

I'm not afraid of the dark.

But he didn't fire. Instead he grabbed my shoulder.

"He'll take you outside," Ani said. "Go back to Jude, tell him that if he cares about the others, he'll stay away from us. Tell him that even if he doesn't care, he'd better stay away. This is just a taste. He can't beat us."

"*Us?*" I asked incredulously. "You think you're one of them? These orgs are just using you!"

"I'm a machine," Ani said flatly. "That's what I'm built for. And besides, I'm used to it."

"Come on, skinner," the guard grunted. As he yanked my arm, the hood slipped from his head. And I saw his face for the first time.

I knew that face.

At the Brotherhood rally, I had seen them in the crowd, faces of the corp-town dead, the old woman, the mother. The child. And I had assumed I was imagining it. Like I'd imagined Zo—except Zo's face had turned out to be real.

But here was the guard, with the same shaggy eyebrows, bulbous nose, scruffy chin, a face I'd seen only for a second in real life—but I'd watched those vids over and over again. I'd memorized the faces of the victims.

I knew that face.

"I know you."

He turned his face away and let go, jerking his head. Two of the other guards flanked me and seized my arms, holding me in place. I kicked at them, no longer caring about their guns or the electric charge that could leave me twitching on the ground with my friends. I drove my foot into a shin, slammed my knee into a groin, and the grip on my left arm loosened. I yanked my arm free, whacking the guy in the face. Something hard and sharp cracked across my shoulder blades, and as I lurched forward, a fist caught me across the chin. I went flying backward, my head slamming back against the wall. "Stay down!" the guard shouted as I slumped to the floor. "Last chance. Then we shock you and dump you on the highway."

The man, the one who was supposed to be dead, stood frozen a few feet away, watching.

There was pain—in my head, in my back, on my face—artificial nerves alerting me to damage, neural impulses flashing a message that radiated across my body: *Broken*.

But it was the kind of damage that would heal, and it wasn't the kind of pain that made anything clearer. Instead, the opposite: Everything faded away, blotted out, everything but the face of the dead man. "You were there," I said quietly. Then again, shouting. "At the corp-town. You're supposed to be dead." But he was finally backing away from me, into the darkness.

I didn't follow. Because I was on the ground. Because even if the pain was all fake, as fake as everything else, it hurt. Because of the guns.

The gun that slashed through the air, so fast I hadn't seen the guard raise his arm, only saw it coming at me, then felt it smash my face, smash my head back into the wall with another resounding crack. I raised my hands over my head, squeezed my eyes shut. Couldn't stop the next blow, striking the side of my head, knocking me flat. I curled tight in a ball, knees drawn in, head hunched against my chest, fetal and helpless against the kicks and blows. A boot driven into my stomach, my skull, the soft exposed flesh at the nape of my neck, crunching against my spine.

"No!" Ani screamed. "Stop!"

"That's for the kick in the balls, skinner," the man grunted.

I waited for another blow, but it didn't come.

And when I opened my eyes, the guards had retreated, lined up a safe distance away, weapons aimed. Ani knelt at my side. "You're fine," she said. "You'll be fine."

I touched my fingers to my face, lightly, half expecting to feel a crater of dented flesh. But mech bones were tough. My face was still there. I was still there.

"Just get out of here, Lia," Ani pleaded. "They won't hurt you if you just *go*."

"Oh, I don't think she's ready to go just yet." Rai Savona melted out of the shadows, his black eyes flashing with the pulses of blue light. "If you don't mind stepping into my office for a moment?" he said politely, as if I'd arrived for a business meeting.

Ani's eyes narrowed, accusing. "You said she'd be *safe*."

"And you thought you could *trust* him?" I VM'd, disgusted.

"She'll be with me," Savona assured her. His voice was the same one, honeyed and smooth, that he'd been using for years to woo Faithers. His eyes were the same ice. "What could be safer than that?" I followed his glance to the guards, whose weapons were still at the ready. Whose eyes were on Ani.

She grabbed my arm, trying to hoist me off the ground.

"Get off." I knocked her away. I didn't need her to lean on.

One step at a time: I pushed myself up onto my hands and knees, waited for the world to balance. I imagined I could feel my brain knocking around loose in my head, wires frayed and jangling. But that was an indulgence. That was the ghost of org weakness, refusing to die. I was a mech, and I was intact. I rose to my knees, planted one foot on the ground, then, with effort, pushed myself upright on two feet. Gravity defeated.

Ani wouldn't look at me. Savona wouldn't look away. "If you're done with the melodrama, we have a few things to discuss."

"After you," I said, forcing myself not to stare in the direction that the dead man had disappeared. That wasn't important now. What mattered was getting through this, and getting out.

Except I no longer believed that was going to happen.

Ani touched my arm. "Lia—," she began and stopped. She just stared at me, eyes wide.

I waited.

Nothing.

I shook my head, then followed Savona into his office. Left her behind.

Savona's office was nothing like Auden's. The latter had been simple, almost austere, its only ostentation the antique desk at the center of the room. Savona's desk was twice the size and state-of-the-art, a wide, nearly transparent slab with network vids and zones dancing across its surface. The walls were illuminated with pics of Savona with his wealthy patrons and starving acolytes, interspersed with golden plaques and tributes. I was surprised he hadn't equipped the room with the same glowbars that lit up his stage, so that he could labor beneath a golden aura.

The door locked behind us with an audible click.

"Taking a risk, aren't you?" I asked. "Trapping us in here alone together? My body's replaceable. How about yours?"

"I don't expect you to attack me. You're too curious about what I have to say." He settled onto one of the couches and gestured for me to take a seat on the other.

I stood.

"If you think you can turn me like you turned Ani—"

"Not worth my time," he said. His dark eyes gave nothing away. There was something familiar in his expression, I thought. It was the lazy pleasure of a cat batting a mouse between its paws, gauging whether the rodent would be more fun dead or alive. "Now, don't you have a question for me?"

"I don't need to ask you anything," I snarled. "I know what you did."

"Oh, really?" He chuckled lightly. "I highly doubt that."

"That man out there—"

"Jackson?" Savona's lips widened into a predatory smile. "Good man. Works himself to the bone in the Synapsis mining operation."

"He's supposed to be dead."

"His lovely wife and four children will be disappointed to hear that," Savona said wryly.

"How?" I asked. "That's all I want to know."

"Why should I care what you want to know? If I'm this diabolical genius you imagine, do you expect me to just confess?"

Mostly, I didn't expect that I'd be leaving the Temple any time soon. I imagined myself locked in a room again, access to the network jammed—maybe my own brain jammed, neural network overwhelmed by high-voltage shocks, lying on a dirty floor, eyes open, brain closed, hidden away long enough that anyone who might care to look for me would forget to bother.

But without hope, there's no point in fear.

"Deny it all you want," I told him. "But I'm going to find out what's going on. What you did."

"You saw what was done to your friends," he said.

I shrugged.

"But you're not afraid."

"Machines don't feel fear," I said. "They don't feel anything. Remember?"

"I seem to recall your father's a rather powerful man," he said. "Maybe you suspect he won't allow anything bad to happen to you. You're thinking to yourself that your skinner friends know you're here, and if I attempt to hold you here, your loving father will intercede." He gave me a thin, knowing smile. "Or maybe you expect your poor friend *Auden* will save you."

"You don't know me very well," I said coldly. He wanted an unfeeling machine? He could have one. "So I should probably mention that I hate people telling me what I'm thinking."

"Hate's such an ugly emotion."

"Funny, then, that you spend so much time spreading it around."

"I wouldn't expect something like you to understand the nuances of human emotional experience." The preacher tones were back. "The Brotherhood of Man is an organization of love. We embrace that which is noble in the human spirit. Ours is a mission of purification and distillation. Elimination of corrupting elements and parasites clinging to the social organism."

"But you don't hate," I said sarcastically. "Because *that* would be wrong."

"I've told you before, Lia," he said. "I bear no ill will against you—any of you. Not every problem is its own cause. Hating the symptoms won't help us cure the disease."

"Tell me whatever it is you want to tell me, or let me out of here," I said. "Since I can't actually *die* of boredom, my options are pretty limited."

"Fine, let's talk about the unfortunate attack at Synapsis." Savona stretched out on the couch, lacing his hands behind his head.

"Fine. Talk."

"Let's say, hypothetically, there was no attack." He closed his eyes, smiling like he was having a particularly pleasant day-dream. "Or not a serious one, at least. Let's say the toxin was plain old Naxophedrine, causing discomfort and unconsciousness but no fatalities."

"But I—" I stopped myself, suddenly realizing how stupid I'd been, revealing the thing I'd tried so hard to hide. That I had been present for the attack.

"But I was there!" he cried in a high, mocking falsetto. "I saw them die!" He opened his eyes and sat up, leaning toward me. "Did you? Did you *really*?" He pressed a hand to his eyes. "You can't always believe what you see." And when he pulled his hand away, his eyes were bleeding, a trickle of red running down each cheek.

I was proud of myself for not screaming.

Savona wiped away the blood or whatever it was. "It's a brave new world, Lia. Anything's possible. You should know that."

"They worked for you." I said it, but I couldn't believe it. I'd *seen* them. Stepped on them. *Mourned* them.

"No one works for me," Savona corrected me. "The Brotherhood is composed of volunteers, serving the people not *me*. But let's say, hypothetically, that the so-called casualties of the Synapsis attack were affiliated with the Brotherhood. That perhaps the video, the one with your face so inconveniently plastered all over it, was doctored."

And suddenly, in a unexpectedly visceral way—visceral, like I could feel it in my nonexistent gut, like for a moment I could taste what fear used to mean, in all its shivering, hair-raising, stomach-twisting glory—I was afraid. Because I knew how this story ended. The supervillain exposed his crimes, but only before offing the hero. In the story it was a mistake, giving the hero time to escape and shout his discovery to the world. It was a ridiculous roadblock placed in the path of inevitable success.

But I was no hero, and I didn't have an escape plan. "Why are you telling me this?"

I am not afraid, I thought, repeating the lie in a trembling mental voice, twice, three times. Faithers had left blood vengeance behind them. They talked a good game, but they didn't do violence, lunatics or not.

Of course, Savona was an *ex*-Faither.

"You asked," he said.

"Now what?"

"Now you leave," Savona said.

"Leave? Just like that?"

"Just like that. I won't have your father"—his lip curled in distaste—"snooping around my facility. So you run home, and you tell everyone how the big, bad Rai Savona didn't desecrate a hair on your godforsaken head. And you keep our little conversation to yourself."

I didn't bother asking if he was insane. It seemed self-evident. "Why would I do that? So you can enjoy your war between orgs and mechs without the inconvenient truth getting in the way?"

"You're glad that those forty-two people are alive," Savona said. "Each and every one of them. Even though they deceived you? Each and every one of them?"

"Surprised?"

"I can only assume you'll want to ensure they stay alive," Savona said. "Your silence buys them life. But if you choose to break my confidence . . ." He let the threat dangle in the silence.

"You'd *kill* your own followers?" I finally said, unwilling to believe it.

"I won't have to do anything. They do what I tell them to do," he said steadily. "They're willing to give anything for our cause."

"You're bluffing."

"Maybe." He smiled. "Care to test me? If you'd like a demonstration, I can call your friend Jackson in here—although his wife and children may not thank you for it." He shook his head in mock sadness. "So many Brothers and Sisters beyond that door, willing to do anything to protect their families."

"By dying?"

"By ensuring that your kind doesn't destroy us."

Savona paused, waiting for me to spit something back at him. But I could see the crazy in his eyes. I'd seen what he did to Ani—this was a man who could talk people into things. Maybe he was right, and he could talk people to their death. He folded his hands together on his lap, almost as if he were praying. "I've given you this information because I can't have you poking around here, out of control, trying to dig up the truth. And I can't risk keeping you here. This seemed the quickest way to shut you up. I'm sending you back out into the world. With a promise. The Synapsis attack was not your fault—those 'deaths' were not on your conscience. But if you say anything to *anyone*, I'll know. These deaths will be real—and they'll be on *you*."

"You don't think I have a soul," I reminded him. "What makes you think I have a conscience? Maybe I don't care how many orgs have to die."

"Maybe," he said. "And maybe even if you go to the authorities without any proof, you'll be able to convince someone to trust the word of a skinner over that of Brother Rai Savona. Certainly it would be to your advantage to try. I suppose it will be an interesting experiment. I'm willing to take the risk—I *know* what I'm willing to sacrifice for my cause. The question is, how much are you willing to sacrifice for yours?"

"You're disgusting."

He offered up a humble smile. "Our flaws are what make us human. You wouldn't understand." Savona stood. "We're done here."

"Wait." Asking was a show of weakness, but maybe I was weak. "What about Auden. Where does he fit into this?"

"You mean does he know I'm speaking to you tonight? Does he know about the attack? All of it?"

"Any of it."

"Why would you believe anything I had to say?" Savona asked, sounding genuinely curious.

"I won't."

"And yet you still want to know." He was looking at me like I was a science experiment, one he'd written off as a failure that had suddenly produced some unexpectedly intriguing results. "After everything you've done to him—and everything you've seen—you still believe he's on your side."

"Just tell me."

Savona raised his eyebrows. "Ask yourself, Lia, why was it *your* face on that video, declaring war on the mechs? Why would I choose *you*? Especially since your father's connections, his ludicrous campaign, make you a particular liability. Certainly compared to a skinner from a city, with no connections, no family, no power. Why would I go after *you*?"

"I have no idea why the hell you'd do anything."

"I wouldn't," he said. "And *I* didn't."

It was a long, dark walk back to the car. Alone.

The kind of walk that gave you time to think. A silent night, a mile of cement and weeds. A face in my head, a dead man walking.

And Sloane, Ty, and Brahm left behind.

Ani left behind.

Why was I always the one that got away?

Not that I'd gotten away with anything. Not if I believed Savona's threats, his deal. Their lives for my silence.

How was I supposed to let the mechs be blamed for what he'd done—for what he *hadn't* done, for the deaths of orgs who were more alive than I was? What if people kept believing that we were dangerous, if the Human Initiative passed, if we lost our rights, lost our credit, our personhood, everything—and all because I'd stayed silent? Hid what I knew, to protect insane orgs willing to die to prove how much they hated me?

If they were the ones with the choice, they wouldn't save me.

But I couldn't die. That was the difference, right? The bright line marking off "acceptable losses" from "tragedy"? Whatever the mechs lost, it couldn't be worth as much as a single org life.

That's what the orgs would say, anyway.

I didn't want to think.

I linked in to the network, and there was a message waiting for me at my zone. Not from Jude, pestering me for details; not from Ani, apologizing, recanting, atoning.

From Zo.

Her av was draped in black, as always, its oversize dark eyes lined in blood red. It spoke in her voice.

I know what happened, Zo's voice said, her av staring straight out of the screen, straight at me, the way she never did, not since the accident. *We need to talk.*

THE GUILTY ONES

"Here is our enemy."

If three people had broken into the Temple in the dead of night, with intent to vandalize a sacred space and plunder its sacred secrets, perhaps Savona would have been obligated to turn them over to the secops. But the trespassers were mechs—three of them, as it was announced in every vid, on every news zone, no mention of the one released or the one who chose to stay. And the secops wanted nothing to do with them. Savona was on his own. So were the mechs—they were his mechs now.

When it came to rights, we were in a liminal zone. No one's property, not yet—but not quite our own, not anymore. Ani had chosen her team wisely: three mechs whose parents had given up on them, who had no remaining ties to the org world. No one to care if they disappeared. BioMax refused to get involved, given the "criminal nature" of the circumstances under which they'd been acquired.

Not taken, not kidnapped. Acquired.

Call-me-Ben wasn't taking my calls.

And the network was wild with support for the Brotherhood of Man, horror at the narrowly averted attack. Three mechs surely headed toward a ventilation shaft or somewhere worse. Three mechs with deadly intent, headed off in the nick of time.

Three mechs, strapped to three tall, sturdy posts, made from freshly cut pine. Posts drilled into the stage at the front of the Temple's largest auditorium. Directly behind the central podium. The perfect visual backdrop to the next Brotherhood rally.

Three mechs, their hands bound, their heads shaved, their mouths gagged, their eyes open.

Confirmation that the electric shock hadn't completely shattered their systems. But who knew whether the shock had incapacitated them, fried the connections between the neural network and the body, leaving them trapped inside their own heads, plastoid lumps for the Brotherhood to pin up like ornaments. Or whether they'd been left broken inside, half there, half absent, damaged remnants of their old selves, gibbering wild-eyed nonsense, missing reason, missing themselves. What would it look like, madness in a mech?

"Here is our enemy," Savona said, his back to his audience, to the cameras, preaching to his prisoners. "Crept into the very heart of our Temple, just as the skinners have wormed their way into the heart of society. Here is our enemy, the barbarians at our gates, just as the skinners will struggle to defeat our measures, the boundaries we draw for our own protection. Here is our enemy, and here they will stay, for them and for you. For your benefit, so you can look upon them and truly see. For *their* benefit, so they can understand their crime, their trespass. Not breaking into the Temple—the Temple is an open door to any in need. *Any*." He paused there and I waited for the camera to pan across to her, as it often did—her blue-black hair peeking over the crowd—Savona's prize mech, his pet mech, the one who'd seen the light. I should have been grateful that he so loved parading her across the vids—it was the only proof I had that my story was true, that I hadn't led the others to the slaughter, struck my own deal with Savona and Auden to guarantee my escape. After all, I was the one that walked away, free and clear.

I should have been grateful, but I couldn't stand to see her there, glowing under Savona's warm approval. I couldn't stand her expression, coldly serene, empty of doubt or regret. Empty.

But this time the camera didn't move. It stayed on Savona, leaving the fourth mech, *his* mech, just another invisible face in the crowd. And I was relieved.

"They would trespass *here*," Savona boomed. "Here, where they're not wanted, as they don't belong, trespass without a thought, because their very existence is a trespass upon humanity."

He bowed his head and raised his arms out to his sides as if flourishing invisible wings. "We bear them no ill will. But we will hold them here, like this, until BioMax agrees to stop creating new skinners, until the government recognizes that those already built must not be allowed to maintain their stolen identities, living among us, carrying the names and faces of the dead. They will be a symbol, a reminder that our fight continues. And when we have achieved our goal, we will release them." He raised his head then, staring up at the mechs dangling from their posts, unable to respond, unable to look away. "We will release you," he said, like it was a solemn vow.

Then, for the first time, he faced his audience. "They may never understand," he assured them. "They are machines, prisoners to their programming. We can't let their confusion sway us. We can't let their delusions fool us. We can't rest until the skinners are forced to accept what you all know in your hearts. Men make machines. *Objects*. Complicated, remarkable, sometimes wondrous objects. But objects nonetheless. Only God can make a life."

"You were supposed to be her best friend," Quinn told me when she heard. "And you want to blame *me*? Where were you when all this was happening? Where were *you*?"

I hadn't blamed her. Not out loud, at least.

Just told her what had happened, just the facts. Just what Ani had said and done.

Just that Ani had decided betrayal was what mechs did, so why shouldn't she join the party.

"What makes you think I was her best friend?"

"She told me," Quinn said.

She told me you *actually cared about her,* I thought. *She was wrong about a lot.*

But I didn't say that. Didn't ask how we could be best friends when I barely knew her. Or how anyone would want to be my best friend after seeing what had happened to the last one.

"You were supposed to look out for her," Quinn said, angry as Quinn ever got.

And I didn't say anything to that either. Because buried beneath all the reasons that she was wrong—I *wasn't* Ani's best friend, I *wasn't* the one who'd broken my promises or broken her heart, I *wasn't* under any obligations—she was also right. As right as Quinn ever got, at least.

I'd let her think she was my friend, I'd let her tell me things, secrets, let her listen to mine, asked about her like I cared, *had* cared, and maybe I'd let myself think we were friends too—and then I'd shut my eyes and looked away.

My fault, not my fault, all of our faults, no one's fault. And then I linked into the network, saw those mechs, none of them friends, each of them one of us, and all I saw in that moment was that Ani was to blame for what Ani had done.

"Why'd you even do it?" I asked Quinn. "Just couldn't stay away from Jude, even though you knew it was the one thing that would—" I shook my head. "That's it, right? Nothing so sweet as forbidden fruit and all that?"

"What am I, a child?" Quinn snapped. "Or Jude's some god of love I couldn't resist? Please."

"What's the point, then? You just wanted to hurt her?"

"Maybe I don't need a reason for what I do," Quinn said. "I do what I want. Maybe that's the point."

I didn't answer.

"You'll never understand what it was like for me," Quinn said. "Before the download."

I wondered—was that what Jude heard when I talked, *After everything I've lost, I deserve whatever I can get?* Was that why he always threw them in my face, words like "spoiled" and "naive" and "childish"?

So you were a damaged orphan, strapped to a bed for fifteen years, trapped inside a wasted body, I wanted to say. *So what?*

We're all damaged, I wanted to say. *And we're all here now. Stuck. It doesn't mean we get to do whatever we want. Or hurt whoever we want.*

But I didn't.

I wanted to believe that she went to Jude not because she wanted him, not even because she chafed at anyone telling her what she could and couldn't have, but because she *didn't* want him, suddenly didn't want anyone but Ani, and the idea of that, chaining herself to a person when she'd finally gotten free of her cage, losing the freedom to want what she was supposed to want, freaked her out so badly that she pounced on Jude, did it practically in public, did it and would have done it again and again until she got caught.

I wanted to believe that about her and pity her rather than blame her, but I couldn't, not quite. And so instead of asking the question and getting the answer I didn't want, I left.

After it happened, Jude took to sitting in the greenhouse, cross-legged on the floor beneath the tables bursting with purple and golden blossoms, hidden from the hothouse lights by the wide fronds of an anthurium plant overhanging its pot.

"She liked to come here," Jude said, squinting up at me when I found him there. It was two days after the failed raid, and the glass building blazed in the sun. From his perch in the leaf-shaded dark, I must have been a silhouette to him, backlit by the light. "She'd just sit. Said it kept her calm."

"I didn't know that." I sat down across from him.

I'd come to accuse him. And it seemed fitting here, at the greenhouse, where Jude had once explained to me that when it came to hurting people, motives didn't matter.

He looked past me, eyes flitting from plant to flower, set-tling on the windows. Cyclones of dust whirled in the pale beams of morning light. "This was her favorite part about being a mech," he said. It didn't feel like he was talking to me; it felt like he would be saying it if I were there or not. "No more sick-ness. No more death. As much credit as she could want. No more—" He shook his head, jaw clenched. "All the shit we got past, and *this* was still her favorite."

"The greenhouse?"

"The flowers. Trees. All this nature crap. She never saw any of it before. The city's all concrete. We used to laugh about it. How we never really got nature until we turned into machines."

"She's not dead, Jude."

"What?" He looked at me, confused for a moment, as if he'd forgotten I was there.

"Ani," I said. "You're talking about her in the past tense. She's not dead."

"Might as well be."

"Don't say that!"

"Like you care." Jude scooped up some loose soil by his feet, building it into a low mound. "You left her there."

"You weren't there," I reminded him. Driving the knife in. "You don't know what it was like. I couldn't have gotten her out. Even if she'd wanted to come back."

"I know you," he said nastily. "Always looking for an excuse to give in. Run away."

"Run away?" I spit the words out. "You're the coward who didn't go in the first place! No, too risky for *you*, so we should all suffer in your place. None of us should have been there that night, Jude. Not us, not *Ani*—and you knew it. You just didn't want to believe it."

"I wanted . . ." His voice drifted off.

"You wanted to pretend you didn't hurt her, like it never happened!" I fired the words like bullets, knowing they couldn't hurt him, nothing could hurt the mighty Jude. "You wanted to just pretend she was fine and everything was fine, and it wasn't. It's *not!*"

"*Shut up!*" he shouted. Startling us both. "You think I don't know this is my fault?" His voice was ragged. "You think I need you to tell me that?"

"This is Ani's fault," I said quietly. It slipped out, not at all what I'd been intending to say. "She did this."

"*I* did this," Jude said. "Just me." He cupped his hands, sweeping more soil into his pile, packing it hard, smoothing his mound into a tower. "She ever tell you how we met?"

I shook my head, not really expecting him to continue. But he did, like he talked about the past all the time. Like he didn't care anymore.

"We were in there together for almost a month," he said. "Me, Ani, a few others. They never told us what they were testing us for. Or why the ones who disappeared never came back. I was the only one who knew what we were doing there—"

"How?"

A ghost of the old cocky smile crossed his lips. "Knowing things is something of a hobby for me. I'm rather good at it," he said. Not boasting, just stating a fact. "But the rest of them, no idea. You don't tell the lab rats why you're putting them through the maze, right?"

"I thought Riley knew too," I said hesitantly, feeling like I was breaking Riley's confidence by admitting what he'd said. "I thought you got him into the program?"

"He told you that?" Jude asked, surprised. "I didn't think he'd . . . huh."

"What?"

"He tell you the rest? About what he was doing there?"

"He got shot," I said.

"Right, and . . . ?"

"And what?"

Jude nodded with approval. "I didn't think so."

"What?"

"Ask your boyfriend," he said. "If he wants you to know, he'll tell you."

But I wasn't asking Riley much of anything at the moment. All I wanted was his arms around me, his voice in my ear, telling me—

Well, that was the problem. Riley would tell me it was going to be all right. That I'd done nothing wrong. That I couldn't have stopped Ani, couldn't have saved any of them. That we'd find a way.

He wouldn't judge me, and he wouldn't question me.

He wouldn't guess that I had a secret from him, from everyone, that Savona had given me a piece of poisonous knowledge, forced me to swallow it. That everything I told him about that night was infected by the lie of what I couldn't say.

So I avoided him.

And instead sought out Jude, who couldn't judge me but also couldn't trust me, because he knew better. We were both liars, both cowards, in our own way. The same.

He turned back to his small pile of dirt, reaching into one of the plant pots to scoop out a fresh supply. "Anyway, Riley wasn't there, not at first. I got him in at the end, when it seemed like they had figured out what they were doing, and it was going to work. At the beginning, when they were still screwing around, throwing stuff at the wall to see what would stick? I was on my own."

"With Ani." I tried to picture it, the two of them with their old faces, their wheelchairs, two people who had nothing in common with the mechs I knew, and everything in common with each other.

"Yeah. She was from a different city, hung with a different crowd the first week we were in there. But most of them were gone after the first week anyway, so . . . anyway. There was this girl, Jeri. From the same city as Ani. And they were— I don't know. I never knew if they were together, or what. But one day Jeri just wasn't there anymore. And Ani—I'd seen her around by then, you know. There weren't that many of us left, so you pretty much knew everyone. That day, she was just kind of empty. Like she was there, but not there anymore, you know? Nothing behind the eyes."

"And you took pity on her? Decided you were going to rescue her from her misery?" I'd intended sarcasm, but it didn't come out quite right.

He shook his head. "I was . . ." His face twisted. "Preoccupied. You've got to understand, these tests they were doing— we're not talking your standard med-check. They had to figure out how our bodies worked, how our brains controlled our bodies. That's medical research, right? You give a little electric shock to your lab rat's brain, see which part of his body shuts off. You carve open your lab rat, see how things are working, play around a little, sew him back up, watch what happens." He tapped his temple. "You know how they figured out how this stuff works? They study damage. Damaged brains, damaged bodies. Zap a lab rat in the right place, and it forgets how to run the maze—presto, you know where rat memory lives. You can build your rat brain piece by piece, just by taking his apart. Piece by piece. Ever think about that? That's their model. Damage. So you tell me, what does that make us? How are we supposed to be *normal*, when everything they know, everything we're based on, was wrong?"

We're not supposed to be normal, I thought.

"Never thought about it before, did you?" he asked. "How they perfected it."

"I . . ."

"Didn't think so." He shrugged. "They needed to figure out how we were put together, make sure they could replicate it. And they didn't want anything that would corrupt the purity of their experimental results. Muddy the neurological waters. Things like anesthesia. Pain meds."

"So they just . . . ?"

Jude watched me, waiting for me to react. Not wincing at the memory, not inviting my pity, but not flinching from it.

"I didn't know," I said.

"Nothing new about pain," Jude said flatly. "I got used to that a long time ago. But that day that Ani's girlfriend disappeared, that was . . . a bad day. It was hard for me to, uh, get around back then." He paused, as close as he'd ever come to acknowledging who he'd once been. "But that day, I couldn't even—"

He rested his palm on the top of his tower of soil. Then he bore down and crushed it flat. "It was a bad day. And she stayed there with me. Barely knew me, and still had that empty look, because by that point we knew when someone disappeared, they weren't coming back, but she just ignored it, she got *me* through the night, fed me, kept me from—" He waved a hand, like he was brushing away the memory. "I don't like being helpless," he said. "I don't believe in it."

"But you let her help you."

It was as if he hadn't heard me. "I looked out for her after that. Made sure they didn't take her in for the download until they knew what they were doing. She thought *she* owed *me*. Thought she could trust me."

I'd been trying to figure out why Ani hadn't tried any harder to snare Jude in her trap. But maybe she'd known what I never would have guessed. That this—the powerlessness, the guilt, knowing that he could have, should have vetoed the raid, fore-seen the trap, saved the day, knowing he had failed—this would be worse. Maybe she was right all along: She had known a part of him no one else was allowed to see.

"Why are you telling me this, Jude?"

"So you get it. You don't have to tell me what I did." He closed his eyes. "I know what I did."

I didn't ask him why he'd done it.

I touched his hand. He drew it away.

"Why don't you come back inside with me," I suggested. "We can figure out—"

"You go," he said. "I'm sure Riley's looking for you. He's always looking for you."

I wanted to tell him something true, to trade confidence for confidence, secret for secret. But I couldn't tell him the real secret. Because Savona might have been telling the truth. He might have been ready to kill all those orgs. I cared enough to be afraid of him; afraid for them.

Jude might not.

"I got a message from my sister," I said. A smaller, safer secret. "She says there's something we need to know. She wants to help."

"Right," Jude said wryly. "And it was so important that she couldn't just *tell* you? She had to send you a cryptic message and then, let me guess, have you meet her somewhere? Alone?"

"I think she means it," I said.

He stood up abruptly, brushing the soil off his hands. "Of course that's what you want to believe," he snapped, and it was like the conversation had never happened, like I'd imagined everything. "But you can't seriously be considering it. After everything that's happened? After—" He chuckled harshly. Fakely. "You think you can trust *anyone*? You think you can trust an *org*?"

I stood up too. "She's not just any org. She's my sister."

"*She* doesn't think so," he reminded me. "She thinks you're a skinner who stole her sister's identity. She thinks you're the enemy. Maybe she's right."

"It's easier for you to think that," I shot back. "Like everything's so simple, us versus them, orgs versus mechs."

"You're telling me it's not? After seeing what Savona did to his *prisoners*? What the whole org world *let* him do? They think we're *things*, Lia. Not people. Not sisters. *Things*. I don't *want* it to be us against them. It just is. How many times does the truth need to bite you in the ass before you stop turning your back on it?"

"Ani's a mech," I said quietly. "It didn't stop her from joining them. So maybe Zo . . ."

He choked out a pained laugh. "Are you *kidding* me? You warned me, Lia, remember? But I ignored you. I should have known—*I knew*—but I didn't listen. And now—" He stiffened, drawing himself up, still and straight. "Do what you want. Believe what you want. Let me know how that works out for you." Jude pushed past me, pausing for a moment as our shoulders met. "You had more to lose. I get it," he said, flexing his arm, stretching his fingers wide, then curling them into a fist, staring at the muscles working as if he still couldn't quite believe they responded to his command. "But that doesn't change the fact that you lost it. I really thought you'd figured that out." He let his arm drop, and his fingertips brushed mine. Then he was in motion again, past me, out of the greenhouse, and I was on my own.

He wasn't the only one who'd thought I had figured that out.

I'd told myself that I wasn't the same person anymore. That the old Lia Kahn didn't matter. But if I really believed that, then I would have deleted Zo's message from my zone and accepted that she wasn't my sister, just an org related to the org I used to be.

I would have let it go.

We lay side by side in the grass, our hands linked, watching the clouds. They were always thicker in the afternoon, or maybe it just seemed that way on the rare days when the morning sun peeked through the cloud cover and gray gave way to blue— only to inevitably fade away again within hours, the dark chill of daily life returning.

"I don't want you to go," Riley said. He squeezed my hand.

I'd gone to Riley after Jude. I hadn't told him what we'd said, hadn't told him anything. I'd just sagged against him, let him hold me up. I let myself be weak. But that was temporary, and now it was done.

"I have to," I said.

"If it's a trap—"

"I have to know. And besides, what would be the point of a trap? They had me—they let me go. If Savona had wanted me . . ."

"Maybe it's not Savona," he said. "Maybe it's just your sister. Or maybe it's him."

Riley didn't like to say Auden's name.

"I guess I'll find out."

"Then let me go with you," he said, even though I'd already told him no, and told him again.

"I'm not leading you into a trap."

"Maybe you don't get to tell me what to do," he said.

I let go of him and sat up, angry that he didn't understand. "This is my stupid decision," I said. "Not yours. I'm not going to let you pay for it. I'm not going to let you get hurt because I made the wrong choice."

He sat up too, facing me, resolute. "I'm not going to let you get hurt, period. The last time I let you go to the Temple—"

"*Let* me? Since when do you *let* me do anything?"

"Since when do *you*? You can't stop me from going with you."

"And what happens if something goes wrong?" I shouted. "And you end up in that Temple, stapled to one of those posts. Just because you were stupidly trying to protect me? How am I supposed to live with that?"

Riley took my hand and pressed it against his chest. "Feel that?" he asked.

"What the hell are you talking about?" I tried to pull away. He held fast.

"Heartbeat."

"Energy converters don't beat," I snapped.

"Exactly." He let go. "And I'm not Auden."

"Who's talking about him?"

"The accident," Riley said. "He was trying to protect you. He forgot that you were strong, and he was weak. I'm not weak."

"I don't want you there," I lied. "And maybe I don't want you here either. Not if you're going to start telling me what I'm thinking, like everyone else."

"Take me with you, or I'll follow you. I don't care what you tell me. That's the way it is."

"I don't know what's going to happen," I said.

"We'll find out." He leaned forward, hands gentle on my face, and kissed me.

We spent the rest of the day there, in the grass, together, hands and lips and bodies searching for a way to feel, our clothes on, our touches confined, restrained, not wanting to find out what would happen if we pushed too far, if we tried to feel something our artificial receptors couldn't convey, if we let ourselves remember what our bodies used to be.

Whenever we went flying, when I stood at the edge of the sky, beneath the fear of falling, of crashing, there was the taste of something else, the fear that nothing would happen, that I would feel nothing, that the rush of speed, the terror of gravity, would be such old news that the drop would offer no release. It happened eventually, it always happened. Everything we tried got tired, and we would move on to something else. The waterfall. The cliffs. The plane. Maybe even the dreamers. Eventually, perhaps, we would run out of ideas and options and be left with nothing to jolt us into a moment of genuine release. We would be dead inside, for real this time, machines from the inside out.

Usually, I would ignore my fear or use it to kindle the fire I needed, and the rush would hit the moment my feet left the solid ground of the plane and the wind carried me away.

But sometimes I decided not to jump.

Zo sent me the coordinates of a point on the southern perimeter of the Temple campus. It was on the opposite side of the grounds from the main building, but it still felt strange to be there, knowing that Sloane and the others were less than a mile away, waiting for us to save them. Stranger still: knowing what was nestled in the pocket of Riley's bulky coat.

He'd insisted on bringing the gun.

I would never let him hurt my sister.

But if this was a trap, if she showed up with a horde of her newfound Brothers and Sisters, all of them armed with pulse-guns and eager for two new prisoners, I couldn't let them hurt Riley. Not when it was my fault he was here.

The gun was a good compromise, a way of ensuring that we kept a little power, no matter what. We wouldn't use it. That was why he carried it, because he knew guns, he understood guns, and he knew that the safest way to use a gun was to make sure you never had to use it. We would all be safer this way, including Zo. That was Riley's point, at least.

But I didn't want him to bring it.

And I didn't want to hear that he understood guns. Or know why.

"Didn't think you'd show," Zo said flatly when we joined her at the rendezvous point, just beyond the electrified border of the Temple grounds. It was just past midnight, but the main Temple blazed brightly on the horizon, and I realized the other night's darkness must have been part of the plan. Make it look empty and abandoned, so that the foolish, trusting mechs would spring the trap without thinking twice.

And here I was again. "You said it was important."

She glared at Riley. "I also said come alone."

He reached out and took my hand. Zo nodded. "I should have figured." She gave him a nasty smile. "Watch yourself," she suggested. "Lia's never without a guy for too long—but she's also never *with* anyone for very long."

"You say that like you believe I'm Lia," I pointed out.

"No," she said. "Like *you* believe you're Lia. Same nasty habits."

"Why are we here, Zo?" Obviously not for hugs and warm reminiscences of our halcyon youth.

She jerked her head at a flat, domed building just beyond an outcrop of trees. A smattering of rusty, broken machinery marked it as some kind of industrial space, one that seemed likely to have been abandoned long ago.

"They do it out here, away from the central areas," she said. "They don't want anyone to know."

"Know what?"

She didn't answer. Just crept silently toward the building, gesturing for us to follow. At the electrified zone, she held out her hand, waiting. I watched her face as our fingers touched, but it remained blank, no disgust, no curiosity, nothing. I couldn't remember the last time we'd touched.

With Riley's hand firmly gripped in my own, we made it through the invisible fence. She took us on a circuitous route through the industrial zone, skirting motion detectors and, at one point, yanking us back into a shadow just as a flood-light swept across the pavement. Zo nodded to the source of the light, a bulky pillar stretching up from a nearby building, rotating slowly, painting a wide arc with its blinding beam. "AI targeters up there," she whispered. "Coded to face recognition. If the light hits you and you're here without authorization . . ."

The use of deadly force was strictly prohibited in private security—which everyone knew meant it was tacitly allowed if the "private" in "private security" privately paid enough credit to make it worth someone's while to look the other way. Still, if Savona was risking it at the Temple, it must have meant he was protecting something big. I could see from the intent expression on Riley's face and from the way his eyes darted wildly across the landscape that he was constructing a mental inventory of the threats and weaknesses, like he already knew we'd be coming back—on our own.

Creeping slowly, in fits and starts, Zo led us to the edge of the large domed building—judging from the retractable front wall of frosted glass and the decaying, wingless fuselage parked outside, it must have been a hangar for private planes. The glass was too thick to see through, but there were a couple broken panes near ground level. "Just don't let them catch you spying on them," Zo suggested, nestling herself in the shadow of one of the old planes.

I hesitated. If we went for the windows, we'd be in plain sight, target practice for anyone who happened to walk by—or anyone who spotted us from within.

"You came all this way," Zo whispered loudly. "You want to puss out *now*?"

So Riley and I knelt on the cement, peeking through the broken pane. We watched silently, ready to run. But there was only a handful of orgs inside, and none of them seemed likely to notice us. They were a little busy.

Bustling back and forth through a room stuffed with equipment—and at the center, four pallets with four bodies stretched across them, nude, motionless, the skin on their bare skulls stripped, exposing the wiring within. Wiring that was connected to machines, piping data to oversize monitors. Four mechs, and even though the telltale blue hair was gone and we were too far to see her face, I knew. *Ani,* I mouthed, and Riley nodded, his fingers tightening around the sill.

And hovering at her side, anxiously watching the man whose hand was shoved in her skull: the Honored Rai Savona.

We watched for long minutes, as if time was going to give us some glimmer of understanding. But it didn't, and eventually Zo released a long, low whistle. Time to go.

"They cart them back to the Temple every morning," Zo said once we were a safe distance away. "For the vids. Then back here every night. If it helps, I'm pretty sure the skinners have no idea what's happening. I saw them up close once—they're long gone. Totally checked out."

It didn't help.

I wanted to charge through the glass and throw them all over my shoulder, carrying them to safety. It was a fantasy. But maybe that made sense: This was a nightmare. "What the hell is he *doing*?"

"He's trying to figure out a way to kill them," Zo said once we were a safe distance away. "All of you."

"Not possible," Riley said. "Not for long, at least. Our minds are backed up."

"Savona turned on her," I said, barely listening to the two of them, still seeing the mechs laid bare on those gurneys. Remembering what Jude had said about lab rats. "She threw herself away for him, and he did *that* to her."

"What? Your former friend, the Brotherhood's newest recruit?" Zo shook her head. "Not exactly. She's a volunteer. Savona talked her into offering herself up for 'the Cause.'"

"Which is?" Riley prompted her.

"I repeat: He's looking for a way to get rid of you, for good," Zo said. "And he's getting close."

"And you're helping him," I said.

"Right. I'm helping him. By bringing you here." Zo shook her head. "This isn't what the Brotherhood's supposed to be about. This isn't why I joined."

"Don't tell me you're surprised?" I asked incredulously. "The whole point of the Brotherhood is to get rid of the mechs."

"No! We don't want any more of them to be created. And we want to make sure the ones who still exist can't hurt us. Restrictions. Sanctions. We don't want to *kill* them."

"You can't kill a machine," I reminded her. "You just shut it off. I'm not human, right? I'm not your sister. That's what you said."

"You're not," Zo said. "But . . ." She rubbed her hands furiously over her face. "I don't know. You're *something*, okay? You talk like her and you act like her and . . ." Zo sighed. "It's just enough. Enough death. *Enough.*" Her voice hardened. "You should get out of here," she said. "Before someone sees you."

You don't even see me, I thought.

"Come on." Riley looped an arm around me, tugged me toward him. "Let's go."

"Auden doesn't know," Zo said suddenly. Awkwardly, with the same shamefaced half smile she used to flash on my birthday, when she would shove a gift in my face, then run away before I could open it.

"Know what?"

"What Savona's doing. I'm not supposed to either. But Auden's clueless. Thought you'd want to know."

"Thanks, Zo." I wanted to hug her.

Not because of what she'd done tonight or what she'd just said or because when I had last hugged my father, I had let go too soon. Like I let go of everything too soon.

Because she was still my sister, even if I wasn't hers.

Because she still didn't want me. But she wanted me to live.

WHAT HAPPENED

"This isn't my skin."

It was Jude's idea to fly. *Anyone could be listening,* he said, glancing up at the ceiling, where we all knew cameras were hidden behind the plaster. *No one can be trusted.* He didn't have to say her name; we were all thinking it. If Ani could turn—Ani, who'd been with Jude from the beginning, who had been beyond suspicion, who knew all our secrets—then maybe anyone could.

So we went to the mountains. Just the three of us, Jude, Riley, and I, in Quinn's plane. Jude had somehow managed to cut Quinn out with just enough subtlety that she hadn't tried to fight him on it, or maybe she'd just run out of fight. We found an untouched landing spot, a snow-covered valley between the low, rolling peaks, miles from civilization, miles from anything but more mountains and more snow. And we jumped.

Once we were in the air, surfing the wind, nothing mattered but the thunder in my ears and the pressure shifts that buoyed me up and down, the frigid slipstream flowing past, the ground hurtling closer as I angled my body down, coming in safely this time, not too fast, not to steep, no more recklessness than necessary, time slowing down as I plummeted and floated at the same time, and everything else—Zo and Ani and Auden and the Brotherhood—floating away from me as surely as Riley and Jude were, black and violet blots against a gray sky, disappearing into the clouds.

I landed soft and shallow, kicking up a mushroom cloud of snow. Jude and Riley were already down, wriggling out of their flight suits. By silent agreement, we gave ourselves a moment to recover from the flight, to ease back into ourselves, exchange the freedom of release for the strictures of restraint, to absorb the fact that the subzero temperatures, the snow beneath us and fluttering around us, the frost already forming on our eyelashes, provided no discomfort. The *awareness* of cold, the *knowledge* of it, but with no more discomfort than a thermometer might feel. Registering the sensation without experiencing it, that's what it meant to remember ourselves and so we sat there under the heavy gray sky, staring up at the dingy white slopes, our bare fingers plunged into the snow, remembering.

And then I told Jude everything.

And not just about what we'd seen with Zo. Jude had to know what Savona was capable of; he had to know what Savona had done in the corp-town and what he'd threatened to do next. I told him the truth. All of it.

"No one died," I said, keeping my eyes on Riley's face, begging him not to be angry that I hadn't told him sooner. "Savona was behind the attack, just like we thought, but the deaths were staged."

Riley didn't move, didn't speak, but his hand closed over mine with a gentle pressure. Jude didn't react.

"We can't go public," I said quickly, before he jumped to the obvious conclusion. "We can't let him kill all those people."

It was like Jude hadn't heard me.

"You're sure Ani was in there?" he asked. "Did she see you?"

"I told you, no one saw us," I said, exasperated, not wanting to repeat what I'd told him about Ani's condition or remind him that she probably wasn't seeing anything anymore.

"How do you know it wasn't a setup?" he asked after making Riley run through everything Zo had told us a second time. "The org might have just been showing you what they wanted you to see."

"The 'org' is my sister. And she was telling the truth," I said. "I can tell."

"Oh, you can tell? Why didn't you say so." Jude groaned and let himself flop back into the snow. "You dragged me all the way out here for this?"

"*You* dragged us out here," I reminded him. "And I'm telling you I trust her."

"I don't."

"Trust *me*."

He laughed. "I don't do that either."

"Then trust *me*," Riley said. "I was there, I saw it. Whether it's a setup or not, that part's real: They're experimenting on them."

"They opened up their brains," I said, wishing I could talk about it without *seeing* it, without imagining that it was happening to me. "And Zo said there's . . . damage."

"You start treating people like toys, playing with their insides, there's always damage," Jude said darkly. He swept his arms out to his sides, carving an angel in the fresh powder.

"I just don't get the point," Riley said. "They've got to know whatever they do to us, we can download from storage."

I'd spent the last day thinking of little else, and I was afraid I understood what Savona was trying to do—afraid because it seemed like it could work, and because it was *smart*.

Auden's kind of smart.

"What if he's going after the backups?" I said. "Wipe those out, and he can do whatever he wants with our bodies."

"The backups are stored on the central servers," Jude pointed out. "The same ones that store all the network data. They're impossible to get to. You'd need an army."

"I know that," I snapped. "I'm not an idiot."

"And neither is Savona," he shot back. "So where does that leave us?"

"With the daily backups," I said, and here's where it got scary. "What if he's trying to find a way to get to the storage servers through *us*? We access the server every time we do a memory dump. If they could find a way in through that . . ."

Jude looked thoughtful; Riley looked stricken. "We have to get them out," he said. *"Now."*

Jude packed a handful of snow into a tight snowball, tossing it up and down as he thought everything through. Then he smiled. "No, we don't."

"Aren't you listening?" I shouted. It felt like there should be an echo in a place like this, filled with so much emptiness, but my voice was just carried away by the wind. "We have to help them."

"I didn't say we wouldn't *help* them," Jude said. "Just that we wouldn't get them out." He threw the snowball up as high as he could. It fell apart in midair, showering us with snow. "Think about it: We have two objectives, right? Rescue our friends— and destroy the lab."

He said it like it was obvious. "I don't know," I said.

"If you're right, and they're working on a way to wipe us out, then we have to stop them," Jude said. "So unless you want to change your story, and now you think the org was lying . . ."

"No."

"Then we have to get rid of the lab. So we do them both in one shot. Look, they've got heavy security in place, and if the hostages are . . . *damaged*, that means they might not be able to run, or walk. Or even understand what's happening. How do you expect the three of us to get in and get out—get *all* of us out, without getting caught ourselves?"

"Maybe I could convince Zo to help with the—"

"No. No orgs. If we do this, *we* do it. We don't rely on someone who can screw us over at the last minute. Ruin everything." He shook his head. "But I don't see how we get them out—get past the guards, the fence, the security AIs. *Maybe* we can get ourselves in. But we'd need more firepower or . . . I don't know, more *something* to get everyone out."

I don't know—it was a phrase I was pretty sure I'd never heard him say before. Perfect timing for the all-knowing Jude's knowledge to run out. "It doesn't have to be just the three of us," I said, afraid I already knew exactly what he'd think of that. "Plenty of other mechs would—"

"I can't trust anyone," Jude said, his voice laced with steel. "Not anymore. I trust Riley. Riley trusts you. But that's it. We're done."

"Just get to the point," Riley said. Something in his voice made it sound like he already knew where Jude was headed.

"After what's been done to them, we don't even know if they can be fixed," Jude said. "What we *do* know is that they've got perfectly good, intact copies in storage. If something happened to their bodies, they could just be downloaded again. Start fresh. So we make it happen. We don't rescue them—we destroy the lab, and we destroy them with it."

Riley was nodding.

Just one problem. "How do *we* get out?"

Jude shrugged. "Same way we get in—it'll probably be easier, all the Faither freaks running around trying to save their precious lab. They won't even notice us. And if that doesn't work . . ."

"What?"

"We go out the same way the others do," Jude said. "Destruction. Download. Simple."

Right. Simple. Just blow up our friends—and ourselves along with them. Die, and wake up miles away in some Bio-Max lab with no idea how we ended up there. Shoved into new bodies, and forced to pay whatever price for crimes we couldn't remember committing. If anything went wrong . . . *But that's not what you're afraid of,* I told myself. No more avoiding the truth.

Death meant nothing anymore. But I was still afraid of it.

"Even if we could do it . . ." I hesitated, unsure how to put words to what I was feeling. The idea made sense . . . but it felt wrong. "We just let them die?"

"It's not death," Jude reminded me. "It's just their bodies, not their minds. Their minds are safe in storage."

"*Copies* of their minds," I said.

"You're a copy," he pointed out. "Feels real, though, doesn't it?"

I am what I remember, I told myself. *I am what I think. How I think.*

And all that was bits of electronic data, coded into a computer. It didn't matter if the data was in my head or on a server. It didn't matter *which* head the data was in, or how many times it had been duplicated. Maybe I wasn't an exact copy of the old Lia Kahn, because you always lost something going from analog to digital, from org to mech. But the *next* me would be just as mechanical as this one. The next me would be a perfect replication. The next me would be me. And if it was true for me, it was true for all of them.

"We do it this way, they start fresh," Jude said. "Whatever Savona's done to them, they won't have to remember it. It'll be like none of this ever happened. And Ani . . . who knows when she last backed up. It could all disappear."

And she could come back like nothing happened, I thought, hearing in his voice how much he wanted it.

"I have a guy who can get some explosives," Jude said. "Riley and I know how to rig them."

Like it was just a trivial errand, a grocery list. Pick up apples, two pounds of chicken . . . and enough explosives to blow up a secret laboratory and everything inside.

"We get in, blow the lab, get out—if we're lucky, no one will even know we were there. As a bonus, it looks like the Brotherhood blew up its own hostages. Can't hurt with public opinion—and since there's nothing we can do, *yet*, about the Synapsis attack . . ."

There was something surreal about this whole thing. Like I'd become someone unrecognizable; we all had. But: "It actually sounds like it could work."

Riley frowned. "You're not saying all of it," he told Jude.

Jude wasted half a second on a wide-eyed *Who, me?* stare, then gave in. He never said no to Riley, not in the end. "You said they're never alone in the lab?" Jude asked me.

I nodded. "As soon as they're done with the experiments for the night, they take the mechs back to the Temple, string them back up on the posts. Zo says there are usually people in the lab working all night—" I finally got it. "No. No, we get them out first. Sound some kind of alarm. Send a warning. Something."

"The whole point is that it has to be a total surprise," Jude said. "If they knew we were there, we'd have to fight our way out. And we'd lose. There's no way to alert the orgs without giving ourselves away."

"Then we come up with another plan!" I insisted. "I'm not—" I didn't even want to say it out loud. The words would have sounded ludicrous coming out of my mouth. *I'm not killing anyone.* As if I was the type of person for whom that was even an option. Unrecognizable was one thing. This was alien. This was unthinkable. "Tell him, Riley. Tell him we can't do this."

I waited for Riley to take Jude's side or keep his mouth shut. But he shook his head. "No," he said firmly. Not to me, to Jude. "She's right. We don't do this."

"It's not like they're innocent. They're not in there having a tea party. *They're* trying to kill *us*. We'd just be striking first. Self-defense isn't a crime."

"You want to turn us into monsters?" I asked. "You want to confirm everything they say about us? You want to make it all *true*?"

"You want to *die*?" Jude snapped. "This isn't just about Sloane and Ani and all the rest of them, not after what you saw. We didn't turn this into a war, they did. And in a war, you fight. Self-defense is not murder."

"Dead is still dead," I told him. "And if you knew anything about what it was like when people—"

"Lia, don't," Riley said, his voice quiet but insistent.

"No!" I cried. "If he understood what it's like when people fall, when they stop breathing, and their eyes . . . if he'd seen what we saw, he wouldn't . . ."

"That was fake," Jude said tightly. "So maybe you're the one who doesn't get it. I've seen death. The *real* kind. And I've seen people die because they couldn't protect themselves." He shot a glance at Riley, who looked away. "Or because other people refused to do what was necessary to protect them."

"It doesn't make it okay," I insisted. "It doesn't mean we shouldn't find another way."

"Stop being such a child!" Jude yelled. "Sometimes there just *isn't* another way."

"And sometimes there is," Riley said. "So we find one."

"Zo could be in that building," I said.

"You said she's not allowed in there," Jude reminded me.

"Fine. So someone else's sister could be in there."

"You're right," Jude said. "*Sloane*. Sister of an eight-year-old kid named Max. And Ty's got two little brothers. Brahm has an older one, who doesn't acknowledge his existence."

I couldn't believe he'd bothered to find out about anyone's families, much less remembered the details.

"Then there's Ani. Who doesn't have anyone," Jude continued. "Does that make her less valuable? Does that mean we should sacrifice her so the orgs trying to kill her get to live?"

"I don't want to sacrifice *anyone*," I said.

"You want. *You* want. Like that matters." Jude shook his head, plainly disgusted. "Reminder: They're *orgs*. They're going to die sooner or later, so what's the difference if it's a little sooner than later?"

"You don't mean that," Riley said.

Jude shrugged. "Maybe I do, maybe I don't. Here's what I know. Sometimes it's necessary to sacrifice. Isn't that the bedrock of our wonderful society? Isn't that why the masses get shoved into the cities, why they live in the dark, eating synthetic garbage, dying without med-tech? So that the few can enjoy their cars and their network and their organic, free-range beef? Pollution stays under control, population stays under control, everyone's happy—everyone who counts, at least. Every day, we sacrifice the many for the good of the few. So why not, just this once, sacrifice a few for the good of the many?"

"And it's just a coincidence that in this case, the 'many' is us," I said sarcastically.

"It's no coincidence," Jude snapped. "It's self-preservation. In case you haven't noticed, we're in trouble. It's not just the Brotherhood. It's the government restrictions. It's the corps turning on us. It's *BioMax* claiming to be on our side but holding the keys to the kingdom. What happens if they suddenly decide that mech tech is too much trouble for them? What if they don't want to give us new bodies anymore and just let the old ones break down? Let us disappear? We have *no control*," Jude hissed. "And you may be okay with that, but I'm not. At some point, we have to start standing up for ourselves. I say we start now."

"Listen to yourself," I said. "Orgs. Mechs. Us. Them. Like they're so different from us—like *you're* so different from Savona. As if you don't sound just like him, ranting and raving and not caring who gets hurt. You're both so convinced that you're right—"

"The difference is I *am* right!"

"I'm sure he thinks so too."

"Wake up, Lia! Some people are right and some people are wrong. Some *things* are right. And if you're too cowardly to admit that, if you're too scared to face up to the truth and do what needs to be done, then you're just as wrong as they are. Maybe more so. At least they believe in what they're doing. You're just being willfully stupid."

"Don't call her stupid," Riley said.

"I can speak for myself," I told him, putting a hand on his shoulder so he would know I appreciated it, even if I didn't need it. Then turned back to Jude. "Don't call me stupid."

"Go ahead," Jude told Riley. "Nod along with your girl-friend. Let her tell you what to think."

"That's not what I'm doing," Riley said. "She's right. You're wrong. That's it."

"Oh, really?" Jude sneered. "Since when do you care who gets hurt? As long as you get what you want, right? Take care of what's yours, and never—"

"Shut up," Riley said, a warning in his voice.

"You think he's going to choose *you*?" Jude asked me. "Think again. He knows what he owes me. He's never going to forget that."

"You owe each other," I said. "And now he's paying up by stopping you from doing something stupid. Why don't you stop being so pigheaded and paranoid and *listen*? We're not your enemy."

"*We?*" Jude rolled his eyes. "I love how she talks like she knows you. But she doesn't know anything, does she? Not about who you really are. What you're willing to do."

"I'm telling you to shut up—"

"He doesn't have to tell me anything," I said loudly. Like shouting would make it true. "I know what I need to know."

"So do I," Jude said. "This is the only way to rescue our people. And to stop these psychos from doing any more damage. I'd rather do it with you, but if I have to, I'll do it alone."

We argued with him. We kept arguing until there was nothing left to say—until it was clear that Jude was convinced this was the only way. And every time Riley spoke, every time he exchanged one of his looks with Jude or trailed off in the middle of a sentence, knowing Jude would understand and I wouldn't, I wondered. I hated myself for it. But I heard Jude's voice, his unspoken expectations, and I wondered. *Who were you, Riley?* I thought. *What did you do?*

The argument drained us all, and in the end we were still left with no alternatives, no compromises, no resolution. We all agreed: Ani, Sloane, Ty, and Brahm needed to be rescued.

We agreed that the lab was dangerous and should be destroyed.

And we agreed there was no way we could accomplish those tasks without getting caught, not if we gave the Brotherhood any kind of warning.

We agreed that time was running out. Maybe they were closing in on the answer they needed, the way to destroy us all. Maybe they weren't and they were just torturing their prisoners, every day, every night. Either way, it had to end.

But I couldn't turn myself into a murderer.

Jude took the plane back to the estate, agreeing to send it back for us later, so that we could have time alone in the snow to think. Time alone for me to pretend I didn't care who Riley used to be or whatever lurked in the silence between him and his best friend.

"He wants us to agree he's right," Riley said. "But he really will do it himself if he has to."

We couldn't talk him out of it. And we couldn't warn the Brotherhood ahead of time. Or the scoops.

"*I can't*," Riley said. "I can't do that to him. And there's always a chance . . ."

A chance he might change his mind. Innocent until proven guilty, until his finger slipped onto a detonator, until someone died. So we would go along with him—until we couldn't go along with him anymore. We would find a way to get the hostages out, blow up the lab, save the day, without more bloodshed. And if that didn't work, we would call in reinforcements.

Would there be time, between thought and action, time to stop him—to talk him out of it, or to do whatever else, anything else it took?

We decided to bet there would.

But we weren't betting with our own lives.

"I've never gone against him," Riley said. He hugged me from behind, his chin resting on my shoulder. "Never thought I would."

"Are you sure—?"

"I can't let him do this. I owe him too much."

I twisted to face him, without breaking free of his embrace. Our faces were almost touching. "What is it?" I asked. "What do you owe him?"

He let go. Looked away. Sank back into the snow. "It scared you. What he said."

I shook my head. No.

All I did anymore was lie.

"It should have," he said. "It would, if you knew."

I didn't want to know.

"Then you tell me," I said. "Go ahead. Scare me."

He didn't speak, just stared down at the snow. Sleet spattered down on us, streaking our faces like the tears we couldn't cry. I reached out, touched his cheek. He grabbed my wrist. "Just tell me," I said. "Why do you owe him? What did you do?"

"I told you what happened to Jude, how he got hurt," Riley began. He wouldn't look at me. I put my hands over his. *Cold,*

I thought, registering the thin layer of ice crystals coating our skin, without caring.

I nodded. "Some kids beat him up."

"Because of something I did," Riley said, so quietly I almost didn't hear him. "I stole this kid's chillers. That was back when there were still some b-mods floating around. But it was tough to get your hands on them. I didn't even like that crap. I was going to sell them. But . . ."

"They caught you."

"They caught Jude. There were five of them. Older than us, and bigger. They came looking for me, and Jude told them he was the one who stole the chillers. They believed him. And they—" He choked down the words.

I squeezed his hand. "You didn't make them do anything."

"I didn't stop them either. I was there. Hiding."

"You were smaller. You were outnumbered."

"So was Jude," he said, his face twisting in self-disgust. "But he didn't tell them where I was hiding. Or that I was the one. He just let it happen. Like I let it happen. I . . . I just watched."

"You were a kid!"

He ripped his hands away. "Why are you making excuses?"

"Because . . . I . . ." But if he didn't already know, I couldn't say it out loud. "So now you owe him. That's why you took care of him all those years."

He scowled, angry that I didn't understand. "I told you, we looked out for *each other*. And when he wasn't there—when they took him away for all those tests or whatever—"

"BioMax?" I said.

He nodded. "I told you, he's smart."

"You're smart."

"Not like Jude. He knew how to get stuff, how to get out of stuff. And when he wasn't around . . ." Riley finally met my eyes. "You really want to hear it? All of it?"

No. "Yes."

He recited it in a calm, flat voice, like a kid giving a history report, a kid describing a scene long past, holding no interest for him, bearing no relevance. "That guy Wynn you met in the city, the one that took you. He's one of the ones that did it to Jude. When we were kids," he said. "And after Jude disappeared, I got mad. Guess I freaked out. And I decided to get him some payback."

"But you changed your mind," I said hopefully. I'd seen Wynn alive. Healthy. At least before the secops showed up.

"Didn't change my mind," Riley said mechanically. "Missed. Hit someone else instead. Wynn's brother. Little kid, eight or nine."

I stood up. I didn't even know I was doing it. I was barely aware of my legs in motion, rising, pushing me away from the ground, away from him. I just needed to be upright, feet planted on something stable. "What happened? To the kid?"

"What do you think happened?" Riley said harshly. "Blood loss. Infection. Took a couple days, I think. But then he died. That's what I hear."

"You weren't around anymore."

He shook his head.

"Because you got shot."

He nodded.

"For revenge."

He nodded again, still on the ground. I felt like I was looking down at him from very far away. "It's why Wynn was so angry. He thinks I won. That Jude and I get to live forever, and his kid brother's dead."

"He thinks that because it's true," I said flatly.

"Yeah. So that's why he took you," Riley said. "That's my fault too. It all is."

I shouldn't judge him, I thought, staring down at this boy I'd thought I knew. *I wasn't there, I didn't live like that. I don't know what it took to survive.*

But maybe it didn't matter. Maybe death was death.

"I didn't want you to know," Riley said. "I wanted to start clean."

Because we were different now.

People change, I thought. Auden had changed, more than I wanted to admit. Zo had changed, and changed again.

But then, they were people; we were mechs. Our brains were frozen, sliced, scanned, downloaded.

Maybe everything was frozen.

Stand up, I begged him silently. *Convince me. Make me understand.*

But he didn't move. He was looking past me, maybe thinking about the kid. I wondered what he had looked like. What his name was. Whether he'd seen it coming.

How much it had hurt.

"It's why I can't let Jude do this," he said.

I'd almost forgotten why we were here, why we'd started talking about this. The present had receded into the background, pale and colorless. While the past was bleeding red over the snow.

"I promised," he said. "Never again."

"Promised who?"

"Myself." He whispered. "The kid."

This is still Riley, I thought.

Jude was wrong: The past wasn't irrelevant.

But it was past.

I let myself drop into the snow beside him.

"I told you I deserved it," he said, rubbing his fingers against his arm, against the artificial skin. "And it's still not enough."

I couldn't picture him holding a gun, lining up a target. Pulling a trigger. Any more than I could picture him watching his best friend get kicked and pummeled, Jude's body broken, flopping helplessly on the ground, while Riley hid, safe and scared. I couldn't picture him scared or vengeful or anything but what he'd been to me—solid, bold, kind. Riley.

You believe what you want to believe. Jude's voice. Always Jude's voice in my head. *Too scared to face the truth.*

So I faced this. I faced him, Riley, all of him. What he'd done, what he was, who he wanted to be.

I put my cold hands on his cold face, and I drew him toward me.

"I'm sorry," he whispered. He wasn't saying it to me.

"I forgive you," I whispered back, even though I wasn't the one with something to forgive, even though my forgiveness wasn't what he needed.

We stopped talking.

Later.

His fingers, like ice, trickling down my spine. Snow against our skin, snow filling the spaces between us, melting in the crush of flesh on flesh. His eyes drinking in my skin, the body that would never be my body.

"Don't," he whispered, feeling me tense, pull away.

"Close your eyes." My lips brushed his lids, shutting him away. I closed my own, hiding in the dark. Pretending we could be something else.

His hands, cold, his skin, soft. His voice, softer, in my ear. "Open them. *Look.*"

Backs against the ground, eyes to the sky, he linked our fingers, raised our joined hands toward the gray clouds. Traced his fingers down my wrist, down my arm, down my skin.

It felt like nothing.

His skin, pale against the snow, white on white.

"It's all wrong," I said. Imagined a face with hooded brown eyes, a body with narrower shoulders, longer legs, skin the color of weathered oak, a boy I'd never known, a boy who gathered me in, rolled me over in the snow, sugaring our bodies in white.

Remembered a body that shivered in the wind, fingertips brushing lightly against skin, touches painful with promise.

Another body, another life. "You shouldn't look like this. I shouldn't look like this."

"But this is us. This is it."

I didn't want to look. I didn't want him to see.

"This isn't my skin." Riley let the words drift into the wind. "This isn't how it should be. He said it doesn't matter anymore."

Jude said.

Jude said nothing mattered, we were what we were. Bodies and minds.

"He's wrong," Riley said. "It matters. Every day, every time I look—" He passed his hand in front of his eyes, pale fingers spread wide. "It matters. Except now. Here. It's just me. Us."

Just us. Not machines built by human hands, not minds whirring with data. Not eyes that didn't blink or hearts that didn't beat. Not bodies that didn't move the way bodies were supposed to move, not skin that didn't feel the way skin was supposed to feel. Not something ugly, not something wrong.

Just him, his arms, strong. His skin, soft. His lips, cold. His eyes on my body, not turning away.

Just me, folded up in his arms. The sensation of his hands, the pressure, the temperature, the properties of closeness, the elements of touch, not like it used to be—not like it mattered.

Not pain, not passion, not abandon. Just a promise.

Just us.

NO ONE DIES

"One way or another, we would always be fine."

Preparing seemed to take forever as Riley and Jude gathered equipment—that was their word for it, not weapons, not explosives, just *equipment*—from their contacts in the city, as we mapped out entry points and contingency plans, as we cold-shouldered Quinn, pretending that nothing was going on, as Riley and I huddled in dark corners of the orchard, rifling through our backup options and last-minute, last-ditch possibilities to stop the bloodshed. As I learned, just in case, to aim a gun, learned how it was heavier than it looked but not as heavy as it should have been, how my hand fit perfectly around its grip but its holster rested awkwardly at my waist. As three mechs hung on three posts, carried in every morning, carried out every evening, staring blindly over a roaring crowd, their faces pale and twitchy in the vids, waiting for a rescue that was never going to come.

Riley and Jude prepared their way, and I prepared mine. Riley was convinced that he'd be able to talk Jude down before it was too late. I was in charge of the just in case.

It all seemed to take forever—but it took only three days.

Before we set out, I got Riley alone. "You sure about this?"

"We've got to get them out," he said.

"No. I mean, are you sure we'll be able to stop him before . . ."

There was no warmth in Riley's expression, no hesitation in his voice. "No one's dying tonight."

All mech eyes were cold, strangely blank, their flat color only accentuated by the pinprick of light flashing at their centers. But even beyond that, Riley's gaze was steel. For the first time, I could imagine those eyes set in another face, from another lifetime, surviving in a city the only way he knew how.

Then he rested a hand on my lower back and kissed the top of my head and whispered that it would be all right, we'd all be fine, and the look was gone.

And then we began.

True to his word, Jude's secrecy on the BioMax tracking tech had come in handy. As far as anyone at BioMax knew from the doctored stream of data, the three of us were safe and sound in bed—when in fact we were crossing the deserted grounds of an expired airport, insane plan in hand and weapons in tow. We set out after midnight, picking our way along the route Zo had marked out. Safely through the electrified perimeter—thanks to a grounding strip passed along by one of Jude's city contacts—and through the shadows of hangars and warehouses, darting back each time the sweeping floodlights threatened to cross our path. The grounds were too large to cover every corner with cameras—unless Savona had sprung for a military-grade sat-cam, but if he'd gone that far, what little chance we had of success was pretty much gone, so there was no point in worrying. We had to assume that someone, man or machine, was deployed to watch the area around Savona's secret playpen, cameras that Zo hadn't known about, that weren't visible to the naked eye. Which meant we had to assume that they knew we'd been here before and were prepared for our return. Another justification, as far as Jude was concerned, for the surprise attack. Another reason for the guns.

But Riley had jury-rigged a signal jammer, a small-scale model of what they used in the cities to block the wi-fi and energy nets, ensuring that—if it worked—any cameras we passed in range of would report back scrambled, useless data to their central servers. It was a half-assed solution to a problem we weren't sure even existed—and there was a small, hateful piece of me that hoped it wouldn't work. That was the thought I tried to ignore as we crept toward the hangar: *Come and get us.* A silent missive to Savona's security forces. *Stop us before we can't stop ourselves.*

I could have stopped us at any time—by setting off an alarm. Or with one swipe across my ViM, setting the last-minute backup plan in motion long before the last minute. But I'd promised Riley I would wait.

And I'd promised Sloane, Ty, and Brahm—and even Ani— that we would come back for them. We would get them out.

"This it?" Jude asked as we reached the hangar. It was starting to snow, fat, dirty flakes, floating over our heads. We crouched beneath the rusted fuselage of a small plane, one wing missing and the other hanging cockeyed by a snake of heavy-gauge cable and a bent steel frame. Riley began laying out the equipment as Jude tiptoed over to the hangar, kneeling before the broken pane. I watched the play of light and shadow through the frosted glass—it was thick enough to disguise the shapes that moved within, but I had an indelible record playing across my mind every time I made the mistake of closing my eyes. Jude spent only a few seconds at the window, then returned to us, nearly invisible in his black camo gear. Hands shoved in his pockets, shoulders hunched, a fine dusting of snow coating his hair, he scooped up an armful of explosives, his face blank. "It's just like you said," he said tonelessly.

"So we ready?" Riley slipped the detonator into his coat pocket. It was a small gray box with a keypad; the correct code would send a wireless signal to the explosives. Riley had programmed it, so Riley held on to it, which would leave Jude free to do most of the heavy lifting without fear of jostling the switch. Riley would focus on the more delicate wiring. And as for me— too clueless to help with the explosives, too untrustworthy to hold the detonator—I was the one to stay behind. I would be the lookout.

Jude nodded, looking grim. "Now we tear this place down."

It was maddening, having nothing to do but watch: Jude adhering the packets of secondary explosives to the walls of the hangar, Riley following behind him with the highly sensitive primary explosives, carefully weaving them together to ensure a few sparks would bloom into a fiery chain reaction. The blurry figures inside the hangar played with their life-size toys, oblivious. And as I'd been instructed, I watched the perimeter. I leaned against the plane, wet snow pattering against my face, ice congealing at my feet, and watched the ground turn white and the buildings around me disappear into a white mist. I didn't expect I'd have to use the gun.

I wasn't sure it was him at first, when he appeared in the distance. Or at least, I didn't want to be sure—the snow masked his face, so there was at least a possibility it could have been someone else. It could have been anyone. That's what I told myself, as my grip tightened around the gun.

"Someone's coming," I VM'd Jude and Riley. They pressed themselves against the building, and I retreated farther into the shadow of the fuselage, and we waited. That was the plan: If anyone came alone, without reinforcements, it was most likely they were there for the lab, not for us, and we would let them pass. The snow was working to our advantage—the explosives Riley and Jude had laid were already covered by a thin layer of powder, and the whirling flakes made it difficult to see anything clearly.

But I recognized his limp.

"It's Auden¬" I VM'd.

"Stick to the plan¬" Jude cautioned me. "Just let him go inside. You're totally out of sight. If you keep quiet¬ he won't see you."

But I wasn't worried about him catching me.

I told myself that it was safe for him, that no one was dying tonight, that Riley and I had a plan. But I couldn't risk Auden, not again.

He could change his mind and turn back, I thought. *Or he could be going somewhere else.*

But according to Zo, the laboratory had been intentionally positioned at the edge of nowhere. He wasn't going anywhere else; there wasn't anywhere else for him to go.

Before I knew what I was doing, the gun was aimed, and someone's voice, my voice, issued an order.

"Stop."

He stopped.

"What's going on over there?" Jude. I ignored him.

"Hands up."

They went up.

This isn't me, I thought, staring at hands that were holding a gun, hands that felt as alien as they had right after the download, when they'd sat dead and useless in my lap, inanimate objects belonging to someone else.

"*Lia?* What the hell?" Auden's voice broke the spell.

They were my hands; it was my gun. And at the other end of the barrel, that was Auden, the same Auden who'd stood up for me when Bliss Tanzen had called me a skinner in front of our Persuasive Speaking class, who'd carried me away from a jeering crowd the day I'd frozen in the quad, who'd confessed that he would never get his nearsighted eyes fixed because their weakness reminded him of his dead mother.

Jude and Riley were at my side. "Give me the gun," Jude murmured.

I shook my head and held the weapon steady.

"*You,*" Auden spit out in disgust, glaring at Jude. "Of course."

"Finish what you're doing," I told them. "I won't let him call for help."

And I wouldn't let him go inside.

"You go with Jude," Riley said. "I'll babysit."

"Jude needs you," I said. "I don't. Go."

"She'll deal with it," Jude said, glaring at me, and I got his message: *This is your screwup, and you damn well better fix it.*

Riley shook his head no, but he listened to Jude, as he always listened to Jude, and followed his best friend, backing toward the hangar so he could keep his eyes on me, but the distance and the snow got in our way and soon he was just a hunched shadow and Auden and I were alone.

"What are they doing?" Auden asked. I didn't answer. "What are *you* doing?" he said, more urgently. "What is this?"

The gun was heavy, but mech arms don't get tired. I could point it at him forever.

"You *knew*?" I said. "You knew what he was doing in here? You *let* him?"

He glanced involuntarily toward the hangar, his eyebrows quirking, and then his face went blank again. It was an easy expression to read, a mixture of confusion and surprise. But this wasn't the same Auden, and as much as I wanted to believe he hadn't sanctioned the experimentation, I couldn't afford the luxury.

Not that it mattered. One way or another, I would keep him safe. Whatever he'd done.

"You going to shoot me, Lia?"

"You going to shoot *me*?" I asked, nodding toward the weapon at *his* side, one of the electric pulseguns his guards had used to put Sloane, Ty, and Brahm to the ground. "Or is that in case your *prisoners* get out of control?"

"You want to give me a lecture?" Auden asked. "You're trespassing, holding a gun on me, and you want to make it sound like *I'm* the one doing something wrong?"

He took a step toward me.

"Stop."

"You're not going to hurt me, Lia." Another step. His voice was even, his gait less so.

"I'm a monster, remember?"

"I remember a lot of things." He kept coming.

I released the safety, just as Riley had shown me. *"Stop."*

Never aim a gun you're not prepared to fire, Riley had warned me.

And I could fire: Down at the snow, over his head, into the plane. I could squeeze the trigger, I told myself. If I had to.

He wouldn't stop coming at me. He wouldn't stop talking. "This isn't you, Lia," he said. "You don't want to be here. You don't want to be doing this. You don't—"

"Shut up and get back!"

But it was too late, he was within reach, his arm smashing down in a hatchet sweep to knock the gun out of my hands, but I was fast and he was clumsy and I dodged out of the way. He stumbled, throwing his weight against me, and we both toppled to the ground, rolling in the snow, his legs spasming beneath me, his arms flailing, hands grasping for the gun, and I pinned him beneath me, trying not to hurt him, aware, with every sec ond, that his bones were brittle, his muscles weak, and he *would not stop.* For a moment, he lay still beneath me, panting with exhaustion, shivering, shuddering, his hair soaked, his face coated with melting snow, and I remembered the night before, lying in another field of snow with another body beneath mine, a body impervious to the elements, to the touch. I stared down at Auden, at this quivering, sopping, heaving, dripping *mess*; I stared at him, barely seeing his face, and in that moment, he wasn't Auden, he was any org, *every* org, weak and pathetic and alive.

Natural is hell, I'd preached to the mech recruits, believing every word, *willing* myself to believe, and here it was pinned beneath me, words made real. And here, beneath me, the corollary I'd willed myself to forget: *Natural is hell. But hell is* life.

It was just a single moment that I lost focus, the lightning flash of envy banished almost as soon as it struck, but a moment was enough for Auden to lash out with his weak but well-aimed kick, to knock me off balance and make one final, desperate lunge for the gun, for our hands to mash together on cold metal, for a barrel to twist and a trigger to fall and a muffled shot to sound.

And a moment, the next moment, was enough to meet his gaze, see my own expression reflected on his face, his jaw dropped theatrically, his lip trembling, his eyes wide. *What have I done?* Like we'd thought it together, like in just that one moment we didn't need a chip to translate thought to silent speech, because we both knew—and then the moment passed and we fell backward from each other, action and reaction, shooter and shot.

All I could think was: *Thank you.* To the universe, to luck or physics or whatever unseen force of fate had twisted the barrel one way and not the other, had left a raw, jagged hole in my right thigh, a hole that didn't bleed but just gaped, snow fizzling on the exposed wiring, singed synflesh curling back at its edges, a synthetic pain shooting down my leg, up my spine, a rush like jumping out an airplane or over a waterfall clearing out my brain. And Auden, intact, the gun in the snow between us, untouched.

And then Riley was there, his fist smashing into Auden's face, and somehow it was Jude's arms beneath me, lifting me up. "You're okay, it's okay," Jude murmured, as Riley pulled his arm back, slammed it down again, Auden's head snapping back, a soft moan escaping with flecks of blood. "You're okay."

"Stop!" I screamed. Jude slapped a hand over my mouth,

met my eyes, and nodded when he saw I'd gotten the point, remembered myself and where we were. Then he leaped at Riley, grabbed his waist and pulled him off Auden. Riley struggled, but Jude whispered something in his ear, and he went limp. Jude scooped the gun off the ground, holding it trained on Auden. Riley replaced him at my side, slipping his hand into mine.

"I'm fine," I whispered, and I was. I let Riley help me into a standing position, gingerly rested a little weight on the leg to see if it would hold. It did. Damaged or not, it still functioned. "It's fine."

Auden was staring at me. At us, as Riley brushed my hair out of my face, pressed his lips to my forehead. I shook him off. Back to business.

"I'm sorry," Auden said quietly. "I didn't mean—"

"Shut up," Jude barked. "You don't talk to her. In fact, you don't talk at all."

"I'm fine," I said again, louder this time.

"Of course you are," Jude snapped. "But we've still got *him* to deal with."

"This could work for us," I VM'd. And suddenly I saw it all clearly, how we could all win our happy ending. "Now we have a hostage."

"I noticed," Jude said dryly. He jerked his head at Riley. "Take the org's weapon."

Riley yanked the pulsegun out of Auden's holster, looking as if he'd like to smash it into Auden's head.

"Riley," I VM'd. "Just let it go. Please." He

tucked the pulsegun into his pocket and backed away, returning to my side. Auden kept looking back and forth between us, a familiar expression on his face—embittered satisfaction at solving a puzzle with the answer he'd been expecting, even if it was one he'd hoped against.

"Don't you get it?" I asked Jude. "We can use him as leverage, to get us safe passage off the property."

"We won't *need* leverage," Jude said, "because no one's going to know we're here."

"We can evacuate the building before we blow it," I said. "Tell them if they do anything to stop us, we'll kill him."

Auden shook his head slowly. "You won't do that."

"Really?" I glanced pointedly at the wound in my thigh. He winced. "You want to test us? You're the one who said we were capable of anything." I needed him to shut up. I had to make Jude believe that I didn't care about Auden, any more than I cared about the other orgs. That this was just a smarter plan.

"Thanks for proving my point," Auden said, adopting a toughness to match my own. "This'll play great on the vids tomorrow."

"There won't be any vids," Jude said. "We're not changing the plan. If we have to, we'll take him back to the estate with us. You're right, leverage could be a good thing."

"We can make this work, *tonight*," I insisted. "We don't have to kill anyone."

"She's right," Riley said.

"She's living in a fantasy world," Jude snapped. "You think

Savona cares what happens to his little puppet? You don't think he'd make a better martyr dead than alive? Poor, pathetic Auden, slaughtered by a bunch of mechs. We try to use him as leverage and give the Brotherhood *any* warning? Then that's it. We're done."

"Savona needs me," Auden said in a high, tight voice. "Listen to Lia. I don't care what you do to the building, but those people inside—let me get them out. No one will hurt you as long as you've got me."

"See?" I said.

Jude laughed. "What else is he supposed to say?"

"What if I'm right?" I asked, switching to VM. Jude would never back down in front of Auden. "What if this is our chance to do what we need to do, without killing anyone, and we pass it up?"

"What if you *are* right?" Jude retorted. "You want to let Savona just walk away? Along with all his researchers, their brains filled with nasty little tricks to wipe us out? What if this is our chance to stop Savona before he's unstoppable? Like killing Hitler before he turned into Hitler? Stalin? Zomabi? Ever think it's our moral obligation to stop him? Here. Now. *Tonight.*"

"Are you crazy? You actually want to kill these people? Even if we have another option?" Maybe I was as naive as he said. Because it wasn't until that moment that I got it. We weren't going to be able to argue him out of this.

"There is no other option," Jude said aloud. "And I'm not going to let you risk everything on some childish wish that things were different." He held out his hand. "Give me the detonator. Let's just get this done."

Riley shook his head. "No."

"*What?*" Jude looked back and forth between us. "We all agreed this was the only way."

Riley watched him carefully. "And now there's another way."

"Don't do this," Jude said, and it sounded half like a threat and half like a plea. "Don't choose her."

"This is for you," Riley said, and then, as I stood frozen between them, everything fell apart. It happened fast and slow at the same time—so fast I could barely understand what was happening; slow, like a series of freeze frames, flashes of action trapped in amber.

Jude lunging at Riley.

Riley grabbing the electric pulsegun from its holster.

Riley saying, "I'm sorry." Pulling the trigger.

Jude screaming in rage.

Jude screaming in pain.

Jude on the ground, body twitching.

Body still.

"Get the orgs out," Riley told me, kneeling at Jude's body, looking like a frightened child. "We'll blow the lab and get out of here before—"

A siren cut through the night.

Auden's hand was in his pocket.

Riley seized the gun from Jude's limp grip and held it pointed at Auden. "Hands up!" he shouted.

Auden gave us a faint smile. "Too late," he said, holding out his ViM. "The Brotherhood knows you're here. This is over."

"You fucking idiot!" Riley growled.

"Now what?" I shouted over the alarm

"Make the call!" Riley shouted back.

But it was simpler than that—I just skimmed a finger across my nanoViM, linking in and sending the message, all in one motion. Call-me-Ben and the BioMax reinforcements were waiting for my signal. I'd told call-me-Ben we were going to blow something up. I'd told him orgs were going to die. And I'd told him if he acted quickly, did his job right, and kept the operation in house with BioMax secops whose discretion he could trust, he might learn something about the Synapsis Corp-Town attack that could change everything.

I just hadn't told him the where and the when, and thanks to Jude's GPS jamming patch, he had no way of knowing.

Until now.

BioMax had been unwilling to stage a rescue operation, but I'd guessed they would be willing to do anything to protect their image, which had taken a huge blow after Synapsis. And Ben had proved me right, eager to strike a deal that would prevent his precious mechs from committing a mass murder that the public would never forgive and for which, I reminded him, BioMax could ultimately be held to blame. Maybe they *were* partly to blame—but I was gambling on the chance that, whatever role BioMax may have played in all this, Ben wasn't a part of it.

He couldn't be trusted to be on our side, but he would get us away from the Brotherhood, one way or another. If he showed up in time.

"Get him inside!" Riley shouted, forcing Auden at gunpoint toward the laboratory.

He didn't have to explain. Now that the Brotherhood knew we were here, we had two options: Blow the lab with ourselves inside. Or barricade ourselves inside the hangar with Auden as a hostage, keeping ourselves safe until BioMax arrived.

If call-me-Ben was true to his word.

And if Savona and his people really cared enough about Auden to keep him alive.

A river of people streamed out, screaming, as Riley held a gun to Auden's left temple and shouted over the chaos, urging them to run if they wanted their precious martyr to live. I grabbed Jude's wrist, struggling to drag his body into the hangar, but it was heavy, too heavy. Riley shoved the gun at me, and I trained it on Auden. *They should be shaking,* I thought, staring at my hands.

But they didn't do that anymore.

I expected Auden to lunge at me again, take advantage of the chaos to escape and leave us at the Brotherhood's mercy, but he kept his head down and trudged through the snow as I pressed the muzzle to the back of his neck, safety on, knowing that if I was tested, I'd drop the weapon and let him go. Knowing that was the only thing that kept me moving forward, one foot in front of the other.

Riley hoisted Jude's body off the ground and cradled it in his arms, Jude's head resting on his chest, Jude's eyes open and sightless. And somehow we made it inside the laboratory, safe behind a locked door and shaded windows, alone with the damaged mechs, with Jude's still body, alone with Auden.

"Tell them to leave us alone if they want you to stay alive," Riley ordered Auden. We had retreated to the far corner of the hangar, putting as much space between us and the entrance as we could, just in case.

With a trembling finger, Auden activated his ViM and spoke into it. "They want me to say they'll kill me if you move on them. Just wait for my signal. And tell Savona—"

Riley snatched the ViM out of his hands and threw it across the room. "Enough." He forced Auden down into a chair and sent me on a hunt for something that could be used to tie him up. There was a roll of duct tape in one of the cabinets. I tossed it to Riley. With a cool competency, Riley bound Auden's wrists behind his back, then lashed him to the chair at his waist and ankles.

"Do you have to?" I VM'd. I knew how it felt to be bound. Riley didn't answer, just kept going until the job was done. It scared me, how good he was, his movements sure and efficient, his expression determined and free of doubt. It scared me most because this was still, plainly, the Riley I knew, not some alien part of himself that he'd kept hidden from me. This was a strength, a ruthlessness that had been beneath the surface all along. But I understood now that I'd always known it was there.

Jude lay on the floor beside them, faceup, arms splayed.

And when Auden was secured, Riley stood over Jude's body, hands clenched into fists, nothing left to do but wait. I touched his shoulder lightly. "I can't believe I did it," he whispered.

"You had no choice," I reminded him.

"There's always a choice," Riley said. "I was supposed to choose him."

He turned away from me. "I'm going to take a look around," he said, voice rough. "Keep an eye on him and"—he nodded at the four gurneys—"them."

"Okay."

The hangar had been cleared of anything left over from its aeronautic days, and much of it was still empty. The walls were lined with screens and the far side of the room was littered with unidentifiable spare parts and long, empty tables—waiting for more experimental subjects to fill them up?

Only a few feet away from us, four mechs lay prostrate on four gurneys, surrounded by unwieldy equipment I recognized from my early days in the BioMax rehab unit, when I'd lain in a hospital bed, frozen, wires like tentacles hooking me to the machines, their sensors feeding into my exposed brain. Ani's gurney was the closest, and as I drew near, I could hear her murmuring something. A ceaseless string of incomprehensible babble, like a baby testing its tongue. Her head was shaved, tangles of wires connected to a series of monitors disappearing into her open skull. I brushed the back of my hand against her cheek. Her eyes were open, staring past me. And her lips kept moving, spilling out the stream of whispered nonsense syllables.

"How could you do this to yourself?" I murmured. Then forced myself to look past her to Sloane, to Ty, to Brahm, the three of them in the same or worse condition. The fingers of Sloane's right hand twitched uncontrollably. The skin on Brahm's chest had been flayed, the wiring left exposed. His eyes roamed wildly, randomly, skidding from one side to the other, pupils contracting to a point, then periodically expanding in a flush of black that flooded his irises. Ty just moaned. At least her eyes were closed. "How could you do this to *them*?"

"What's wrong with them?" Auden asked, straining to see.

"You tell us," I said. "You did it. You and your *Brothers*."

"I don't know anything about this," Auden said. "Tonight was the first I even heard about this place."

"Right."

"I was on my way here to find out what was going on. I never thought . . ." Auden scowled. "Believe whatever you want."

He twisted around in his chair, watching the door. Outside, everything was quiet. For all I knew, the Brotherhood had us surrounded, their pulseguns drawn. If they called our bluff and broke down the door, what then? We could end up on those gurneys too, right next to Ani. Or we could finish this right now. Send Auden outside and blow the place up—blow ourselves up with it.

It's not death, I reminded myself.

And it was infinitely better than whatever lifeless madness awaited us on those gurneys.

"They'll come for you, you know," Auden said. "Holding me hostage isn't going to get you out of here. You'll never get off the property."

"We're not worried about that," I lied.

"Will they be okay?" Auden asked. "Your friends?"

"What do you care?"

"Will they?"

"They're just machines, right?" I said. Hating him for the fact that I *couldn't* hate him, even here, surrounded by the fruits of what he'd accomplished. "No souls, no consciences. Not alive. So honestly, what do you care?"

"This was never about anyone getting hurt," Auden said, his eyes involuntarily flickering to the hole his bullet had torn through my thigh.

"Tell that to your partner," I said. Then pointed to Ani. "Tell that to her."

"You two are the ones with the guns and the explosives," Auden said. "You're just proving that everything we say about the skinners is true."

"Mechs," I said. "Not skinners."

"Whatever you say."

"You used to tell me I was just like everyone else," I said

quietly, searching his eyes for something of the old Auden. "That the download technology was amazing. You said I was just as human as you."

"I said a lot of things."

"Yeah. You did."

He blushed, and I wondered if we were both thinking of the same moment. I wondered how much would have been different if I'd let the kiss continue. Then he shot a glance across the room, where Riley had given up playing with the machinery and was just sitting on the edge of a table, his back to us, his back to Jude.

"Lia, look at yourself," Auden said. "Look where you are. You really think you made the right choice? To be with them? With *him*?"

"I'm not the one who chose." I didn't mean for my voice to sound so small. "You made me walk away."

"No one makes you do anything," Auden said. "You're Lia Kahn, remember? You do what you want. Isn't that what you always told me?"

"You told me to go away," I said. Even smaller. "And never come back."

Auden's face spasmed, then went still. "And you never did."

"So that's why you did it?" I asked "Tried to turn me into a murderer?"

"You're the one with the gun."

"I'm not talking about *this*," I said in a low voice. "Syanpsis. My face in that vid."

"What about it?"

"I know the Temple was behind it," I spit out, getting angry all over again. "Savona told me everything." Surprise flickered across his face. "He didn't *tell* you that I knew?" I asked, tempted to fake a laugh, just so he would know how much his little band of brothers disgusted me. "And he told me it was your idea," I added. "To set me up. Make me a killer."

He pressed his lips together, tight, like he was holding in the answer.

Tell me I'm wrong, I begged him silently. *Tell me Savona lied.*

"So? Maybe it was my idea," he said hoarsely. Before, I would have known—whether he was admitting the truth or lying to sound tough. Whether he was proud or guilty. I would have read it on his face, because he was a horrible liar, and because I knew him. But I didn't know him anymore. He shook his head. "You think that would make us even?"

"Do *you*?"

But before he could answer, a rolling peal of thunder shook the building. The night filled with shouts and screams, and the windows blazed, illuminated by sweeping spotlights. "They're coming for me," Auden said, going pale. "Tell your friend to put the gun away. I won't let them hurt you."

"We're just machines, remember?" I said. "Nothing can hurt us."

"I'll protect you," Auden said firmly, absurdly, his ravaged body strapped to a chair. "You won't end up . . . like that." Neither of us looked at Ani; we both knew what he meant.

"Riley?" I called. "You ready? If we have to . . ."

He nodded, mouth set in a grim line, hand clutching the detonator in his pocket. We'd have to move fast to get Auden to safety. *No one dies tonight.*

Except maybe us.

The thunder roared from above, drawing closer. Not thunder at all, I realized, but a helicopter swooping down on us, or, from the sound of it, a fleet of them.

"Put down your weapons!" a voice boomed from the sky. I wondered if the ex-Faithers out there in the dark thought they were hearing the word of God. *Tough luck, psychos,* I thought. *It's not your ultimate Creator.*

It's mine.

"They're not coming for you," I told Auden, hoping I was right. "They're coming for us." He looked confused and frightened and something else—something sorry and sad that we'd ended up here, with duct tape and a gun between us and an armed helicopter overhead.

The windows shattered. BioMax had arrived.

At least twenty of them in green uniforms with the BioMax logo striped across the back stormed through the shattered glass, guns raised—both the electric-pulse kind and the ones that shot real, org-piercing bullets. Riley and I flung our hands into the air, allowed the BioMax grunts to restrain us and search us while the others secured the building, insuring there were no mechs (or Faithers) hiding beneath the bulky equipment. Rough hands pinned my arms behind my back. I didn't struggle. Riley too went along quietly. He handed over his weapons voluntarily, and though they gave him a cursory pat down, they missed the most dangerous one of all: the harmless-looking detonator bulging in his coat pocket.

"All clear!" one of the men shouted. Only then did call-me-Ben deign to enter, his gray heart-pulsing suit as smooth and unrumpled as his hair and face.

"Quite a mess of things you've made here, Lia," he said, jerking his head in my direction. The man holding me let go.

"Once you see what they're up to in this lab, you'll thank me," I told him, joining Riley, putting my arms around his waist, my head against his shoulder. Still tied to the chair, pearls of sweat beading on his face, Auden pretended not to watch. *It's over,* I thought.

Ben himself slit the tape binding Auden to the chair. Auden tried to stand, and one of his legs buckled. A BioMax guy swooped in to hold him up, but Auden shook off his help, then limped toward the nearest wall, leaning against it for support, chest heaving.

Two of the men lined the three of us up against the wall, weapons loosely trained on us. The others swarmed the hangar, examining equipment and beginning to load it onto a series of large dollies. Ben just watched us for a moment, hands on hips, head cocked in amusement. He nudged a toe into Jude's body and raised an eyebrow. "Tell me, Lia, does betraying your friends get easier the more you do it?"

Riley glanced quickly between me and Ben. I kept my face

blank, knew that even Riley wouldn't be able to read anything from it. But I didn't like what I'd seen flickering in his eyes for that brief moment. The questions.

"I trust you won't mind sticking around for a bit?" Ben said, as if we had any choice. "I'm sure we'll have a few questions."

"I haven't done anything wrong!" Auden protested.

Ben did a slow turn in place, taking in the machinery, the mechs on their gurneys, then faced Auden again. "You'll stick around," he said, not a question this time. "You'll answer for what you've done."

So the three of us stood there, watching and waiting, as the BioMax men bustled around us as if we were invisible, examining the equipment, studiously adjusting the machinery that monitored Ani and the others. Riley wrapped an arm around my shoulders, and I let him. Auden kept a foot of space between us, watching the BioMax men go to work on our damaged friends.

"Will they be okay?" I asked as one by one the mechs were carried out of the building, their lips still moving in nearly soundless nonsense.

"One way or another," call-me-Ben said.

Life as a mech: One way or another, we would always be fine.

We waited as a BioMax medic examined Auden to be sure we'd done no permanent damage, as she forced Auden to sit, to breathe into a mask that would infuse his weakened lungs with a supply of oxygen. "I'm okay," he choked out, knocking the mask away. Standing up again on wobbling legs.

"We'll get you a wheelchair," the medic said.

Auden shook his head furiously, eyes meeting mine. "I have another hour, at least," he insisted.

"The nerve-impulse electrodes give you four hours of mobility under *optimal* conditions," the medic said. "This much physical and emotional stress, it's not unusual your system would be overwhelmed, need a rest. You have to remember that for someone in your condition—"

"I'm *fine!*" he snapped, pushing the woman away. One foot dragged noticeably behind as he limped back to his place beside us. "Contact Rai Savona," he ordered Ben. "He can explain to you what all this is—"

"I'm afraid your friend Savona has disappeared," call-me-Ben said serenely. "Slipped off the property as soon as you were taken hostage. Seems he didn't want to stick around to see how things played out. So why don't *you* tell me what it is the Brotherhood was doing out here?"

"I don't have to explain anything to you," Auden said. "This is private property. BioMax has no authority here."

"And yet here I am," Ben said. "And here you are. Your loyal followers have all been encouraged, strongly encouraged, to go home for the night. Your loyal partner has fled the scene. It seems like it's just the two of us."

Auden pointed a shaky finger at Riley and me. "They broke into a private facility, tried to blow it up, and when *that* didn't work, they took an innocent human being hostage. And you want to interrogate *me?*"

Ben smiled. "Apparently."

"You can't do this," Auden said, furious. He was already starting to sound less like the boy I'd known and more like the man I'd seen up on that stage, preaching to his masses. "By this time tomorrow, I'll make sure the whole network knows that you and your corp have chosen the skinners over the welfare of fellow humans."

"Tomorrow's tomorrow," Ben said flatly. "I don't deal in predictions. Tonight, your welfare is in *my* hands, and I'll make whatever choices I want."

Ben drove his foot into Jude's side. The body didn't move. "I can wake him up now," he offered us. "Or wait until you're long gone if you'd prefer. Avoid the messy meet-and-greet?"

Later, I wanted to say.

"Now," Riley said, before I could.

Ben did it himself, accessing a panel beneath Jude's armpit. Whatever he did next, he made sure to shield it from our view—preserving his trade secrets, the functions of our bodies that we weren't allowed to know about. Jude's eyes closed, then opened again, aware. He sat up slowly, shaking away the fog, gingerly testing first his arms, then his legs, then climbing to his feet and staring at us, indictment plain on his face. He took in the scene calmly, without question, as if there could be no doubt as to how events had played out while he was down.

"Take him," Ben ordered two of his men.

It had been part of the deal. I had saved myself and Riley, but I couldn't save Jude. "We can't have him running wild anymore," Ben had told me. "Now that you know what he's capable of, you should understand that."

We didn't have a choice, I reminded myself. *We waited until the last possible minute. We tried.*

"Let me just say good-bye to my friends," Jude said, imperious, as if he were still in charge.

Ben nodded, and Jude was released, allowed to approach us, as Ben remained a short distance away, making an ostentatious show of turning his back, leaving us to say our good-byes among ourselves.

Riley disengaged from my arms, stepping away, meeting Jude alone. For a long moment, they didn't speak.

Riley began. "We didn't want to."

"Don't," Jude said quietly. He leaned in close, folded Riley into a loose embrace, whispered something in his ear. Riley glanced at me, his eyes narrowed, then backed away, down the wall, to the other side of Auden and as far as the BioMax men would let him go without raising their weapons again in warning.

He just feels guilty, I thought. *He doesn't want me comforting him.*

I told myself that was it, and that it had nothing to do with the way he'd looked at me before, when Ben started needling me about betrayals.

"What did you say to him?" I asked Jude.

"Just the truth," Jude said.

Just lies, I thought. *And whatever Jude said about me, Riley wouldn't believe it.*

"I'm not apologizing," I said.

"Good. Because I'm not forgiving. Or forgetting."

Jude stepped toward me, grabbed my wrist, hard. The BioMax guys approached, but I waved them away. "I was trying to do the right thing," he said. "One day you'll figure that out."

"You stole my line," I said, trying to pull my arm away, but he held fast. His voice was angry, but his face was something else. Lost, like I'd stolen something from him, the thing at his center that told him what he was. He yanked me toward him, until his lips brushed my ear.

"You want to save your precious orgs?" he whispered. "Three minutes, starting now." Then he dropped my arm and stepped away. "You can do whatever you want with me now," he called out. "Just get me away from these *skinners.*" Flanked by an entourage of BioMax thugs, call-me-Ben took Jude's arm, personally escorting him away. Of course: Riley and I were toys, fun to play with while he had nothing better to do. Jude was the real point, the grand prize.

One minute passed as a security cadre walked Jude out of the building, as I let his words play through my brain, as, without processing what I was doing, I glanced at Riley—at Riley's pocket, checking for the telltale bulge of the detonator. It was gone.

And that's when I screamed.

"Everybody get out!" I shouted. "Explosives!"

Riley shoved a hand in his pocket. Then he started shouting too.

The BioMax guys took off running for the exit. Riley ran. I

ran. And Auden ran—but only a few steps. Then he stumbled and crashed to the floor.

One minute left.

I turned back for him, screaming his name, feeling like I'd been thrown back in time, like the air was water and I was swimming toward him again, the current carrying him away, and somewhere, dimly, I heard Riley shouting for me, and I grabbed Auden's hands and hauled him to his feet, forcing his arm around my shoulder, forcing him to lean on me, as Riley ran in the wrong direction, not toward the door, but toward me, and then everything got very loud—then very silent.

Time's up.

The explosions were like gunshots, close range, and in their wake the world fell quiet, and the building shook.

The building shook, and a chunk of the wall blew out, slamming into Riley, knocking him down in a cloud of plaster and twisted steel.

"Riley!" I shrieked.

There was no answering call.

Flames licked the walls, smoke turned the air heavy and opaque, and Auden buried his face in his shirt as we lurched toward the door, gasping for breath. This time I couldn't breathe for him. I could only get him out.

The walls were crumbling.

Riley's head and torso jutted out from the pile of debris, and he was shouting something I couldn't understand, arms waving in an unmistakable gesture. *Go. Go, get out.*

Get Auden out.

And that was what I thought, as I turned my back on Riley, as I held Auden up, grabbing on as he slipped away from me, as his head nodded drowsily, eyes clouding and lungs filling with smoke. *Not him, not again*, I thought, as I stumbled through the smoky black in the direction I imagined the door to be, sound returning to the world in the form of smaller, secondary explosions, ceilings collapsing, equipment imploding, as we pushed through an opening in the wall, into the cool fresh air of night, and left Riley behind.

No one dies tonight, I thought as the BioMax troops dragged us away from the flames, dragged me away, as I kicked and screamed and lunged toward the flickering storm of fire, and they held me back, because they were stronger. They were in control. And Auden sucked in oxygen as I watched, now silent and still, no breath and no heartbeat, helpless and useless, as a geyser of fire spurted through the roof, and the laboratory—and the machinery and the research and Riley—disintegrated in a crash of thunder and a plume of blue-orange flame.

FLOATING HOME

"I would be his memory."

When life isn't life, death isn't death.

No one died that night.

That's what I told myself.

Bodies break. Brains burn. But memories can be stored, and memories are life. An exact copy is the same as an original in every meaningful way. Mechs are minds. Minds are patterns, data. And data is transferable. So when they transferred Riley's backed-up memories into the new body, it was a logical, inescapable truth: *This is Riley.* A Riley who had never burned, a Riley who had never set foot onto the Temple grounds, never betrayed his best friend, never disappeared in a storm of fire. Never shuddered at something Jude whispered in his ear or looked at me like I might be the enemy. A Riley who had backed up his neural network one last time, one last night, then ceased to exist.

He was the same, and he was alive, as if none of it had ever happened—and for him, it hadn't. A fresh start. A new beginning, same as the old one.

That's what I told myself.

Jude escaped in the chaos. No one knew where he'd gone. Including me, though BioMax seemed not to believe it.

Sloane, Ani, Ty, and Brahm remained at BioMax, under observation. The corp had determined the damage couldn't be reversed, but refused to terminate their bodies and start afresh until they knew exactly what the Brotherhood had done—and exactly how far they had gotten in their research. Ani and the others were in no discernable pain, were likely unaware of their condition, trapped in a dreamless sleep rather than a waking nightmare. *Likely.* Less likely, but still possible, they were awake inside their madness. It was a chance BioMax had elected to take, without objection from the mechs' families, without doubt. Call-me-Ben told me that.

Studying their condition, prolonging their dead-end lives, was for our own good.

Ben told me that too.

And when they woke up in new bodies, they wouldn't remember any of it—they wouldn't be the same mechs who'd gone into the Temple and hung from those posts, so what did it matter what happened to them in the meantime?

If the memories would eventually be ground into dust along with the bodies, then maybe it was as if it hadn't happened at all.

For mechs, even the earliest involuntary volunteers, a new body to replace the old was part of the deal. It was the BioMax guarantee, and so far, the corp had always honored it.

But they didn't have to. It was one of the things I hadn't thought of before, had just accepted, because my new body, and the one after that and the one after that, was already bought and paid for, and because my father sat on the BioMax board. But I thought of it after the explosion, with Riley's body gone and his mind sitting in storage—I let myself think about what would happen if BioMax reneged, because it was easier than thinking about where Riley was now, whether his mind was somehow alive in the storage server in the same way it would be in a body, or if he was just gone, erased from the world, until they brought him back.

We have no control, Jude had said, naming, as was his compulsion, a truth it would have been easier to ignore. Alive only as long as they let us live. Just another funny little perk of mech life: Machines were objects, and objects had owners.

Which meant Jude had been right. BioMax wasn't the enemy, yet. But it would be, eventually, inevitably.

And eventually, inevitably, we would find a way to reclaim ourselves.

In the meantime, the corp delivered our bodies. Riley was

slated to get another generic model, a duplicate of the one he'd lost.

I had a better idea.

"This is important to you," my father said.

I nodded.

We met in his office, at my request, to make it clear this wasn't a homecoming, the prodigal daughter returns. This was a transaction. Or it would be, if he granted my request.

"I assume it's important, or you wouldn't have come to me," my father said.

I nodded again. Because if I had lied, acted repentant, he would have known.

"It won't be cheap," he said. "This is a lot of credit you're talking about here."

I knew that. More credit than Quinn had been willing to spare—though these days, Quinn wasn't much in the mood for handouts. Not for me, at least. As far as she was concerned, Jude and Ani had both abandoned her, leaving me behind as an unwanted consolation prize. She hadn't thrown me off the estate, not yet, but she was doing a pretty effective job of freezing me out.

"And what do I get in return?" my father asked.

"Whatever you want," I said. "I *will* pay you back someday." Somehow.

He didn't even pause. It was like he'd been waiting for me, like he knew I'd eventually need something big, so big that I'd be willing to do anything in return, and he was ready. "I want you to come home. To stay."

"Okay."

I didn't pause either.

I wasn't there when Riley woke up in his new body. And I didn't visit him in rehab as he learned how to use it.

I left him a message on his zone, explaining what had happened, how he had ended up on the thirteenth floor of BioMax, waking up all over again. Except I didn't explain all of it, or really any of it. I told him we had gone through with our plans, that we had rescued our friends, that no one had died. That the lab was destroyed and he'd been caught in the explosion.

That I would tell him more when I saw him. And I would see him, I would come to visit, if he wanted me to.

I promised him that, although I couldn't imagine going back to the thirteenth floor—much as I couldn't face the thought of sitting by a bed, next to another broken body, another person that I'd left behind. But I would have come, if he'd asked.

Don't, he'd texted me, when he finally woke. *You shouldn't have to be here. Or see me like this.*

And for one month, that was all I heard from him.

One month, back at Chez Kahn, removing the metallic streaks from my skin and hair, trying to fit the org mold so I could live an org life, pretending that nothing had changed, that I didn't notice the way my mother always left the room moments after I entered, or that my father no longer gave me orders, like ordering me home had emptied him of commands, or like as long as I was there, he no longer cared what I did. Zo and I lived under a wary silent truce, circling each other like caged animals, exhausted but afraid to sleep lest the other strike. She'd left the Brotherhood—I learned this from her zone, not from her. Neither she nor my parents ever spoke of her time at the Temple. But a frost had congealed over her relationship with my father. Now he watched her from a safe distance, just as he watched me, maintaining a careful formality when circumstances forced them together. We coexisted without comingling, one big happy family of strangers.

I left the cat with Quinn. He'd be happier there, without the stench of orgs to shatter his feline composure. And whatever comfort he might have been to me, nuzzling his wet nose into my synthetic flesh, I didn't need and I didn't deserve. Until Riley was made whole again, I wanted to be alone.

It took months to adjust to the first download, teaching your brain to accommodate itself to its new surroundings. But subsequent downloads, in most cases, were easier. Your brain was already wired for mech life. It knew how to flex the artificial muscles, it knew how to work the artificial larynx and maneuver the artificial tongue.

Ben gave me reports: Riley was awake one week after the download, mobile the week after that. Talking no more than was required, spending his days in his room, scanning the network for accounts of the Brotherhood raid and the explosion, to fill the hole in his memory, the empty space left behind. But I'd

413

scanned the network too and knew what he'd find and what he wouldn't. I had to make sure he was safe from the truth.

He wouldn't find what he wanted on the network—he would have to come to me.

One month later, he did.

We met by the flood zone. I got there early, stared out at the calm blue-red surface, imagining the sunken city that lay rotting below. I'd forgotten about the crowds at the Windows of Memory, and the way the orgs would glare at me as I slipped through, shrinking away from any accidental touch. The restrictions on mechs had loosened slightly, thanks to an upswing of public support after the Brotherhood's role in the Synapsis attack had been made public. Not that the Brotherhood lacked its fair share of conspiracy nuts, now flocking in even greater numbers to the Temple's doors. Savona was presumed dead in the explosion, martyred to his cause, slain by his mechanical enemy. I was convinced he'd just gone to ground, waiting for the optimal moment for his triumphant resurrection.

Meanwhile, Auden had taken over, promising a kinder, gentler Brotherhood of Man. But he hadn't done much to stop the Brotherhood's unofficial campaign of persecution against mechs all over the country or the official one still being waged in the back rooms of every corp, as they inched forward, lockstep, in defining us out of existence.

Everything will make sense again when Riley's back, I had promised myself. *We'll know what to do.*

But when he appeared on the horizon, inching his way down the hill with the tight, cautious steps of someone still uncertain of his control over his body, I just wanted to run away.

The custom body had been made to fit precise specifications, the face molded to match a pic on file at BioMax, stored alongside all the other physical and mental attributes of their initial slate of "volunteers." It wasn't a perfect replica—from a distance he looked like the boy in the picture, but as he drew closer, it was easy to pick out the tight and smooth synflesh, the unnatural combination of grace and awkwardness in his step, the lifeless eyes. He would never be mistaken for an org—but maybe, looking in the mirror, he would no longer be such a stranger to himself.

Like he was a stranger to me.

This is Riley, I told myself. The *real* Riley.

But it wasn't. The deep-set brown eyes, the lips that curled up instead of down, slightly oversize ears and a slightly undersize nose, a square chin with a shallow cleft at its center, rich brown skin stretched taut across thick muscles, a crease in his forehead where his eyebrows knit together in concern. He was a stranger.

He drew closer, and I searched for something familiar, some ghost of the Riley I knew, in the way he walked, the way he held himself, some trace of Riley in his smile, in his eyes.

But there was nothing.

And when he reached me, and it was too late to run, and he said my name, that was different too. A differently sized throat, differently shaped mouth, differently spaced teeth—it meant different acoustics, and so a different voice. This one was lower, made him sound older, but there was almost something melodic about it, like he was singing as he spoke. Not that it mattered. A voice wasn't a soul, it was just a set of vibrations in the air, just physics. As his body was just a machine, his features just molded plastic. None of it should have mattered. None of it was *him*, except the patterns inside his head, the data arranged into feelings and memories—but that was nothing I could see. Nothing I could touch.

He reached for me, and without thinking, I pulled away.

In that moment, I finally understood what had happened after my accident, why my friends, my boyfriend, my family, couldn't see that beneath the wiring and the synflesh I was still *me*, no matter how I looked, no matter how I sounded. Because knowing something to be true is different than believing it.

This is Riley, I told myself. But you can't force yourself to believe.

"What is it?" the stranger asked in a stranger's voice.

I shook my head. What if I couldn't do it? What if I just walked away from him, like everyone had walked away from me? What if, after helping him destroy his best friend, I left him alone?

He held out his hand, palm up, an invitation. "It's still me," he said.

I put my hand on his, palm to palm.

"It's still us," he said.

His arms felt different around my body. We didn't fit

together the same way, folded into the same curves and hollows. He was taller, slimmer. Even his lips were the wrong shape, the wrong size. But his hands cupping my face, slipping down my neck, my back, different and the same, all at once, and the feel of someone holding me up, a chest to lean against, a hand to hold—it was still him.

It was still us.

"Tell me what happened," he said when we lay in the damp grass, in each other's arms. "Help me remember."

"BioMax lied," I told him, launching into a well-rehearsed narrative. "They didn't wait for my signal—they just showed up, busted us as we were laying the explosives. The explosion was an accident."

"Jude wouldn't have done it," he said. "Not in the end. We would have talked him out of it. I wouldn't have let him do that to himself."

"I know. He's your best friend," I murmured, and tightened my grip on his hand.

"He'll make contact when he can," Riley said. "When he needs us. He knows we'll help. He'll be back."

I hope not, I thought.

Because if he came back, then Riley would have to know what we'd done. Except that *this* Riley hadn't done anything. He'd committed no betrayal, and given the opportunity, he might have chosen differently. In that one way—*and* only *that one way,* I told myself—the old Riley was dead. I'd left him behind and watched him die. This new one couldn't be held accountable for someone else's sins; this Riley was innocent.

It's not a lie, I thought, telling him a story of what should have happened, where he was a hero and Jude was still his friend and happily ever after was still in reach for someone, someday. *It's a gift.*

I would be his memory.

"It seems like a long time ago," he said as we stood at the edge of the water, clothes in two neat piles on the ground, feet bare. "Since we were here."

"It was," I said to the stranger who wasn't a stranger, with a hand that looked so wrong in my own.

We stood with our backs to the hill and everything it led to. Somewhere up there, beyond the horizon: the Brotherhood regrouping, Savona lying in wait, orgs hating us, orgs fearing us, BioMax holding us under absolute control, pretending we walked free, Auden knowing I'd saved him all over again and knowing I was the reason he'd needed to be saved. Somewhere up there: a home, my father asking God to forgive him for creating me, expecting me to be someone long dead, my sister, wanting to be anyone but my sister, not wanting me to die. Somewhere up there: Jude, who knew the truth.

All behind us. And ahead of us, nothing but a stretch of murky blue. We couldn't run away. Or hide, like children, behind wishes and lies. We wouldn't fight like Jude—but we would fight.

We would, but only when we climbed the hill, trekked to

the road, returned to the world, where we were mechs and they were orgs and nothing made sense. Here, now, alone, we joined hands, and it didn't matter what we were or what was waiting for us. We stepped forward, water lapping at our ankles, our knees, our thighs, our waists. We stepped forward together and let ourselves drift, the muddy seabed dropping out beneath our feet, the water carrying us toward a buried ruin, carrying us away from the noise and chaos waiting for us onshore, and together, we dipped below the surface and let our bodies sink into the silent deep.

LOOK FOR THE STUNNING CONCLUSION
TO LIA'S STORY:

TORN

*T*his *is not real.*

"This is real," I said, because the voice in my head ordered me to say it.

Because machines follow orders, and I am a machine.

This is not me.

"This is me," I said. Because I was programmed to lie.

You see everything, but you get nothing.

"What you see is what you get," I said, and I smiled.

You see: Perfect lips drawn back in a perfect smile. Perfect skin pulled taut over a perfect body.

You see: Hands that grasp, legs that stretch, eyes that understand.

You see a machine that plays the part she was built to play. You see a dead girl walking. You see a freak, a transgression, a sin, a hero. You see a mech; you see a skinner. You see what you want to see.

You don't see me.

"So it doesn't bother you, millions of people watching your every move?" the interviewer asked. She was sweating under the camera lights. I wasn't. Machines neither sweat nor shiver; we endure. This interviewer had a reputation for wringing tears from all her interview subjects, but in my case it would be easier to get a toaster to cry. So something else was needed. Extra feeling from her, to make up for my lack. Shining eyes welling with liquid, rosy cheeks at opportune moments for anger or passion, a shudder for effect when we passed through the really gory parts: the aftermath of the accident, the uploading of spongy brain matter into sterile hardware, the death and reawakening. I had to admit her act was better than mine. But then, pretending to be human is easier when you actually are.

"You don't feel like you need to put on an act for us? Keep something private, something only for you?"

Artificial neural synapses fired, and electrical impulses shot through artificial conduits, zapped artificial nerves. My perfect shoulders shrugged. My perfect forehead wrinkled in the perfect approximation of human emotion.

"Why would I?" I said.

It had been fifteen days. Fifteen days of posing and preening under their cameras, mouthing their words, following their orders. Burrowing deeper into my own head, desperate for some hidden refuge that their cameras couldn't penetrate, somewhere dark and empty and safe that belonged only to me.

Widen eyes.

Tilt head.

Smile.

"After all, I have nothing to hide."

Day one.

"The commands will feed directly into your auditory system, and it'll sound like the voice is coming from inside your head," Ben said, giving the equipment one final check like the perpetual employee-of-the-week I knew him to be. BioMax's best mender of broken mechs—mender, fixer, occasionally builder, but, as he was always careful to clarify, not doctor. Doctors tended to real, live orgs, and Ben fixed broken-down machines who only looked human. These last six months, every single thing in my life had changed and changed again, everything except for Ben, who was a constant: same tacky flash suits, same waxy hair, same plastic good looks. Same fake-modesty shtick, as in *Aw, shucks, I'm no one important, no one to be afraid of, certainly no one who'd keep secrets from you and manipulate you and blackmail you and hold the power of life and death over your remarkably lifelike head; I'm just a guy, like any other, so you can call me Ben.* "Some people get disoriented by the voice—"

"I'll be fine," I said flatly. I'd had voices in my head before. One of the many perks of being a machine: the potential for "improvements." Like a neural implant that would let me speak silently to other mechs, and hear their voices in my head. Like infrared vision and internal GPS and all the other inhuman modifications I'd had stripped away when I moved back in with my org parents and my org sister and pretended to return to my org life. Like I could close my eyes, make a wish, and suddenly be *organic* again, suddenly be the living, breathing Lia Kahn that had gotten into that car a year ago, pulled onto the highway, slammed into a shipping truck, and been blown into a million burned, bloody pieces.

"I want to make sure you understand how everything's going to work," call-me-Ben said, always pushing. "Once things start, we're not going to have a chance to talk like this."

"What a shame."

He ignored me. "So if you have any questions, it's best to ask—"

"If Lia says she'll be fine, she'll be *fine*." That was Kiri Napoor, director of public relations and my own personal liaison to the Bio-Max powers that be. She caught my eye and winked, Kiri-speak for *I know he's lame; just go with it.*

Kiri was my watchdog, assigned to make sure I kept both feet on the company line. When they'd first told me about her, I'd imagined a female version of call-me-Ben, some puffbag of hot air with a tacky weave and skin pulled watertight from one too many lift-tucks, a nag who would follow me around all day, tattling back to her BioMax overlords every time I opened my mouth. Instead she turned out to be *Kiri*, with her sleek purple hair, perma-smirk, impeccable taste (retroslum shift dress paired with networked boots flashing mangarock vids, that first time I saw her), and enough of a punk twist to make her look cool without even trying.

"You say you want to help the mechs," she'd said, that first day. "So I trust you to do that. I'm not here to spy on you; I'm here to help you."

It was pretty much the same line call-me-Ben had been feeding me ever since I'd signed on to the BioMax cause. But when Kiri said it, something in her voice suggested she thought as little of the corp as I did, and felt the same about the crap spewing out of her mouth. Then she'd kicked call-me-Ben out of the room, telling him that from now on if he wanted to bother me, he'd have to bother her first. That sealed the deal.

Kiri was the only reason I'd gone along with this stupid idea to begin with. It had been hers, which meant it couldn't be all bad. At least that's what I'd let myself believe when she talked me into it.

Guesting in a vidlife meant wiring myself with micro-cams and mics, ensuring that anyone who wanted could track my every move. Worse, it meant playing whatever part my audience wanted to give me. The perfect blend of scripted melodrama and absolute 24/7 reality, that's how they had advertised it when vidlifes first started popping up. Your favorite characters mouthing *your* lines, dosing on *your* favorite b-mod, hooking up with *your* choice of guy, running their lives by your rules and ruining their lives for your personal entertainment.

I told myself that it wasn't any different from what I'd been doing for the last six months as BioMax's poster child for the happy, healthy mech, doing what they told me to do, saying what they told me to say, bowing and scraping for board meetings and press conferences and legislative committees, dangling on their strings. I'd started because my father had asked me to, and I was still playing nice, honoring the letter of our bargain—I got all the credit I needed to help Riley, and my father got his daughter back. Or at least a reasonable simulacrum thereof. But once I'd made the obligatory appearances he'd asked of me, I stuck around. I'd always been good at acting the part, and at least this time the act would be for a good cause.

Baby steps, that was the plan. Persuade the orgs that the mechs offered no threat, meant no harm. That we were just like them. That we were young and foolish—yet also mature. Carefree, yet responsible. Predictable, yet prone to petty spats and parties like the orgs our age. It meant walking a fine line, and singing different songs to different audiences. Kiri customized the sober lectures I delivered to boardrooms, the grinning idiot I made myself into for pop-up ads, each persona carefully crafted to suit its circumstances—irrelevant, apparently, that none of them suited me.

The vidlife took the act one step further. We would offer them proof—24/7, in living color—that I was no more harmless and no less vapid than your average rich-bitch wild child. We would sucker them into caring about my fights and flings, sacred pacts and romantic treasons, and without realizing it, they would come to believe that *I* cared, that *I* felt. That I was, in my petty melodramas of daily life, no different from them. Or at least no different from the other people they watched on the vids. There were those at BioMax who couldn't understand how acting a part would convince anyone of anything about the "real" me—but they were the ones who didn't watch vidlifes. Those of us who did knew the shameful truth: No matter how much you *knew* you were watching live-action puppets play out the fantasies of the masses, the more you watched the vidlifers, the more you believed in them. That was, after all, the whole point of the vidlife: to forget the fantasy and accept the reality. To ignore the distinction between "reality" and "real."

"Ready?" call-me-Ben asked.

I nodded, and he exchanged a cryptic set of gestures with the vidlife rep, then gave me a thumbs-up. That was it. *This* was it.

Nothing seemed different. Nothing *felt* different. The buzzing of the micro-cam hovering over my shoulder could have been a fly.

Just make them love you, I reminded myself, waiting for something to happen. Preparing myself to be bright and sparkly, harmless and irresistible, to be the old Lia Kahn, the one who didn't run on rechargeable batteries. *We're the same people we used to be,* I'd said at meeting after meeting, lying through my porcelain teeth. *We're perfect copies of our old selves. We're exactly like you.*

The voice, when it finally spoke, was inflectionless and personality-free.

There's a party at the Wilding, the voice said. From what I'd heard, there was always a party at the Wilding. The club ran full speed from dusk till dawn and round to dusk again, the dancers and dosers locking themselves in a nonstop fantasy. *Find something to wear and check it out.*

"You know what?" I said brightly. "I feel like dancing. Maybe I'll go find myself a party."

And without waiting for a response, I skipped out of the bunkered office, already mentally running through my wardrobe, wondering what would be suitable for the Wilding, wondering what the voice would make me do once I got in.

Wondering who would be watching.

∙ ∙ ∙

Day three.

Mechs don't get tired. We don't, technically, need to sleep. And obviously there's no need to eat or drink or rest our legs from hour after hour of whirling beneath spinning neon lights, arms twirling, head thrown back, bass-pumping music shaking the walls, floor undulating beneath our feet, bodies on bodies pressed together, sticky, sweaty, salty flesh grinding against flesh, and in the center, me. Seventy-two hours at the Wilding, watching dancers flow in and out, like jellyfish washing up on the beach, then dragged out again by the rising tide, ragged and desiccated by their hours in the sun. Except here in the Wilding there was no sun, no hint of anything that might mark the time passing, or the daylight world beyond its midnight walls.

It turned out the Wilding had only one rule, anything goes, which was good for me since I'd heard one too many stories about mechs trying to slip into org-only clubs and getting the shit pounded out of them. But here the wasted masses were too lost in their dancing, their shockers, their threesomes and foursomes, their licking and tonguing and whipping, to notice what I really was, or to care.

"You need a guy," Felicity shouted in my ear, with a giggle that sounded almost sincere. Everything she said sounded almost sincere—the same went for Pria and Cally, the other two vidlife regulars who'd swept me into their circle as soon as I stepped into the club. The fly cams buzzing over our heads glowed as they came within range of one another, and on cue the lifers laughed and shrieked, stroked my hair, whipped me in wild loops across the packed dance floor, and didn't seem to care that I was a mech—which of course only meant that their characters didn't care, and they were playing their parts.

Cally grabbed my shoulders and kneaded her thumbs into the synflesh. "Definitely need a guy," she agreed. "You're way too tense."

"I'm just tired," I shouted back, my body still rippling in time with the music, arms, legs, hips on autopilot as we bobbed on the synthmetal waves. "Don't you ever get . . . tired?" I didn't mean tired of dancing. And they knew it.

"Never," Felicity said, twirling in place. Her red hair furled around her head like a cloud of fire.

"But don't you ever . . ." I chose my words carefully. No mention of cameras or privacy, nothing that would burst the delicate vidlife bubble. ". . . feel like a break?"

"Break from what? This is life." Pria giggled. She threw her arms in the air, where they flickered and whorled like ribbons in the wind. She'd been vidlifing for two years without a day off, and I wondered if she even knew the difference anymore. What would she do if the voice in her head went silent and left her on her own?

"Come on, pick someone," Pria urged me. She twisted me in a slow circle, her pointed finger hopping from a weeper with huge biceps and teary hangdog eyes to an albino blond to an artfully scruffed guy, bare from the waist up and dosed out on Xers, who happened to be a dead ringer for Walker, my org ex. Not going to happen.

"Look, I already have—" I stopped, reminding myself that for these fifteen days Riley—or, more specifically, Riley-and-me—did not exist. No one wanted their vidlifers tied down, at least not with an outsider, and certainly not with another mech, a random from a *city* who'd never been to a club and, if he had, would have spent the night sitting in a corner, still and silent as his chair. It would be different if Riley had agreed to go on the vidlife with me. It might have been an appealing novelty act, he-and-she mechs, a matched set ready and willing to show off how anatomically correct—how lustful, how passionate, how *human*—the walking dead could be. But Riley never would have agreed to something like that, so I hadn't asked.

Him, the voice in my head decided for me, as my eyes settled on a punkish banger a few years older than me, his spiked hair tipped with metal studs, silver bangles ringing both arms from wrist to elbow. The silver decals striping his neck marked him as a skinnerhead, one of those fetishists who claimed to crave eternal life as a mech—but didn't crave it enough to actually cut open their brains and download them into a computer. Covering yourself in mech-tech was the newest trend, at least among those who weren't trolling the streets looking for a mech to bash, and sometimes—fine line between love and hate and all that—among those who were. This loser clearly considered himself on the cutting edge. Someone out there on the network apparently thought that made him my perfect match. *Go for it.*

It didn't take much.

My come-hither glance was rusty, but it got the job done. Or maybe it was the pinpricks of golden light at the center of my pupils, the dead mech eyes flashing under the neon strobes, the taunting glimpses of synflesh beneath the on-and-off transparent material of the flash shirt. What skinnerhead could resist a skinner?

I love Riley, I thought, as the skinnerhead began to grind his hips against mine.

But: *Tell him you want him*, the voice in my head commanded.

"I want you," I breathed. The skinnerhead smiled like a wolf.

He pressed his left hand—nails coated in metallic silver, of course—to my bare shoulder. His fingers spidered down my back, and I hoped it was too dark for the cameras to see my face. He twisted me around, pressing his sweaty chest against my back, his groin against my ass, and wrapped his arms around me, one hand cupping my breast, the other squeezing my waist, his lips at the curve where my neck met my shoulders, breathing in my artificial skin.

Riley and I had talked about this. We'd discussed the obligations, weighed pros and cons, set boundaries. But boundaries were hard to specify in advance. No nudity, fine. But what about a skirt that barely covered the curve of my thigh, what about silver-tipped fingers creeping beneath the netsilk, what about legs tangled in legs . . . arms encircling chests . . . what about lips?

It's just an act, I had said, we had agreed, I reminded myself now. *Means nothing.*

His lips were on mine. Sucking. Slobbering. His tongue in my mouth, something wet and alien, probing soft places it didn't belong. I counted to ten. Ignored the squishing and smacking sounds, focused on the music. Counted to twenty, closed my eyes as his tongue slurped down my chin, up my cheek, explored the caverns of my ear, his body still grinding against mine, slow, slow, slow even as the music gathered strength and speed, a hurricane of beats. We were the calm at the center. I counted to thirty. Thought about the big picture, the message it would send, another divide between mechs and orgs crumbling to the ground, another thing we had in common: desire, need, want. Thought about the computer that was my brain and the body that was only a body, mechanical limbs woven through with wires, fake nerves that let me feel but made nothing feel real. Counted to forty, and his tongue had no taste, because I couldn't taste; his hair, his neck, his sweat had no smell, because I couldn't smell. I counted to fifty, and when his lips moved down my breastbone to the dark shadow beyond, I threw my head back and tried to smile.

And then I got to sixty and pushed him away, so hard that he stumbled backward, wheeled his arms for balance, and toppled into a klatch of lip-locked vamp-tramps. "Can't spend it all in one place!" I shouted, and let the crowd fill the spaces around me, so by the time he got to his feet, I was gone.

"Let's talk about the Brotherhood of Man." The interviewer flashed a saccharine smile. "Unless it's too difficult for you."

I shook my head. After two weeks in the vidlife, "difficult" had taken on a new meaning; this didn't qualify. "I'm here to talk," I said. "About whatever you'd like."

"We all know the story of how the Brotherhood began," the interviewer said, then immediately disregarded her own words by regaling us with the gory details: the Honored Rai Savona's noble quest to preserve the sanctity of human life, his abdication of the Faither throne in favor of a small, grassroots, antiskinner organization that helped the poor, fed the hungry, and, incidentally, advocated for the eradication of those of us with artificial blood running through our artificial veins. As the interviewer moved onto the "tragic downfall" portion of events, the vidscreen behind her flashed images: kidnapped mechs strung up on poles at the altar of Savona's temple, the "mysterious" explosion at the edge of the temple complex, the destruction of a facility that was never supposed to have existed in the first place—and then the final image, Savona's right-hand man standing before the adoring masses, apologizing for the transgressions of the supreme leader. Promising a kinder, gentler Brotherhood under his new kinder, gentler leadership. Auden Heller, the best weapon the Brotherhood had against the skinners, because his ruined body, his artificial limbs and dented organs, were all permanent reminders of the damage we could wreak.

"Lia, how did it *feel*—"

I steeled myself, waiting for her to ask me about Auden, though she'd been told he was off-limits.

Or about Riley, who had burned in the explosion but was back now, a different body but the same mind, containing an exact copy of all the memories of the previous Riley, every memory but the memory of how he died. Every mech had an uplinker, and we used them daily to upload a copy of our memories to a secure server, just in case. But unless you were uploading at the moment your body was destroyed, that memory would be gone.

"—when Brother Savona came out of hiding and surrendered himself to BioMax?" she concluded. Then she leaned forward, as if—misinformed about my technical specifications—waiting for waterworks.

"I was surprised."

"Because you were among those who believed that he'd died in the explosion?"

Sure, we'd go with that.

I nodded, wishing I were free to answer honestly. The only surprise was that a cowardly nut job like Savona would deposit himself on BioMax's front doorstep and beg for judgment. The only thing I *felt* was disappointment that he was still breathing.

"And how did you *feel*"—insert predatory smile here—"when corp security operations officially pardoned him for any role he may have played in the unpleasantries at the temple?"

BioMax had released its own official account of "the unpleasantries," one in which Brotherhood fanatics had nearly slaughtered a building full of their own, not to mention a handful of innocent mechs. (Of course it was the *mechs* who had nearly massacred all those orgs. But that kind of truth was counterproductive, and so we all kept our mouths shut.)

"You have to weigh Brother Savona's past behavior against his expressed willingness to repair the damage." The script had been easier to memorize than it was to choke out. "Brother Savona's voice obviously has a wide reach, and now that he's had his revelations—"

"You're referring, I assume, to his statements expressing regret for the way he treated the skinners, and his pledges of tolerance? You believe he means what he says?"

I believed that there was nothing anyone could do to Savona now that BioMax had decided he made a better savior than he did a martyr. He'd signed back on to the Brotherhood as an unofficial consultant—right-hand man to his former right-hand man—and the rest of us were supposed to forgive and forget.

"We prefer to be called mechs," I told the interviewer. "'Skinner' is derogatory." Out of the corner of my eye, and just beyond the camera's sightline, I saw Kiri raise a hand in silent warning.

"Of course," the interviewer said. "I'm sorry. I didn't mean—"

"I know." No one ever *meant*. "And to answer your question, Brother Savona and Brother Auden have a message of tolerance and equality that I'd like to think we can all believe in. All I want is to show people that mechs are no different from anyone else—we're regular people. If the Brotherhood can help get that message out, then I'm all for it."

"You're a very big-hearted girl," the interviewer said.

I could have reminded her about the wireless power converter nestled where my heart should be. But I didn't.

Day seven.

Halfway there.

Not going to make it.

"You skank!" Cally shouted, and launched herself at Pria.

"Not my fault you couldn't give him what he wanted!" Pria screeched, squaring off to face the charging blonde. She crouched and grabbed Cally around the knees, flipping her head over heels. Which put Cally in perfect position to gnaw on her thigh.

Pria went down.

Hands clutched at tangles of blond hair, yanked. Violet nails raked across pale skin. They hissed, they slapped; teeth were bared, backs were arched, saliva was sprayed. There was some very unladylike grunting. Soon the two interlocked, writhing bodies rolled across the mansion's marble floor, a monstrous eight-legged beast.

Sometimes these fights ended at the hospital; sometimes they ended in bed. (Or in the closet, the pool, the shower, the rug—any and every conceivable surface.) Whatever the audience wanted.

Now, the voice commanded. *Tell them.*

"You're both brainburned," I said. "You want to kill yourselves over Caleb? Go for it." The voice gave me the storyline, but—usually—I made up the words myself. A miniature measure of freedom in my zombie life. "You know who'll really love that? Felicity. Because then she gets him all to herself."

The writhing creature froze, then separated itself into two discrete bodies again, every eye, ear, and molecule trained on my next words.

"Of course, she's already got him," I said.

"That bitch!"

"That skank!"

"That tramper!"

"I'll kill her."

"Not if I kill her first."

"I'll kill *you* first, if you try that."

The truth: Felicity had never touched Caleb. I didn't know if I was lying because I wanted him for myself, because I wanted Cally or Pria for myself, or because I wanted trouble. The voice would tell me, soon enough, and then that would be the new truth.

The fight temporarily over, and Felicity marked for death, we were free to move on to more pressing concerns.

"Mini or maxi?" Pria demanded, hanging the two dresses over her curvy frame. "There's a rage at Chaos tonight and we are *there*."

"Maxi," I said. "Definitely." Because that day I was supposed to be hating on Pria, and the billowing black and white gown made her look like a pregnant cow.

"That's *my dress*!" Cally spit, grabbing it out of her hand.

Pria looked clueless, but only for a moment. Then her face transformed—narrowed eyes, tensed muscles, slight upturn in her puffy lips. A masterful dose of pure spite. "So what if it is?" she snarled. "Looks better on me, anyway."

It's your *dress,* the voice decided.

So that's what I said.

Then I added the part about the pregnant cow.

And then I was on the ground, with my hair in Pria's hands and my artificial flesh beneath her nails.

Good luck breaking the skin, I thought, gifting her with a light sucker punch that would give her plenty of material for the cameras.

It had been made clear to me that the audience loved a fight.

Especially when the skinner lost.

"Every skinner—I'm sorry, mech—has an understandably conflicted relationship with the Brotherhood, but I think it's safe to say that yours is more conflicted, or certainly more *complicated,* than most," the interviewer said. "After all, its current leader, Auden Heller, is a former classmate of yours, isn't that right?"

You know it's right, you disingenuous bitch.

I should have known better than to believe Kiri when she said the interviewer had agreed to my terms. Easy to declare a subject off-limits when you're backstage—so much the better to launch a sneak attack once the cameras are rolling.

I smiled.

"Yes. We were in school together for about ten years."

"And you were close?" she said.

"Briefly."

"Until that day at the waterfall—"

"I don't talk about that."

"That's understandable," she said, sounding sympathetic. She patted my knee.

I let her. I even let her regurgitate the story of the waterfall, and how Auden had nearly died trying to save me, the skinner who didn't need saving. My fault, and so—in his mind, and the minds of the Brotherhood's brainwashed masses—the fault of every skinner.

"It must be *so hard* for you," she said. "I'm sure you wish you could talk to him, apologize for everything that's happened. Is there anything you'd like to say to him now?" she asked, eyes hungry. "Anything at all?"

I wasn't about to ruin everything by exploding on camera. Two weeks of misery were *not* going in the garbage just to give myself the luxury of self-pity. Or privacy. I'd given the latter up for fifteen days, and the former up for good. But I couldn't play along.

I glanced off camera. Kiri's lips were moving, and, like a ventriloquist's dummy, the interviewer began to speak. "Looks like we're out of time," she said, stiffly. I was surprised the sweat running down her face didn't harden to ice. "It's been a pleasure to have you with us. Please come again."

I smiled like I meant it. "Anytime."

Maybe I was the better actor after all.

Day fifteen.

"You survived." Kiri swept me off as the interview ended. That was code for *You didn't screw up.* I didn't know whether she meant the interview or the whole two weeks; I was too tired to care.

One more night and I was free.

I couldn't thank her for the save—not without revealing her interference to the vidlife audience. So I just raised an eyebrow, and she mirrored the gesture with her own. *You're welcome.*

"She wanted me to talk about myself," I chirped. "What's better than that?" Code for *I know I'm already dead . . . but kill me now. Please.*

"Ah, the Lia Kahn we all know and love," she said. "Sure you're not too tired to hit this gala tonight?"

A star-studded night with the crème de la crème of high society, pretending not to notice that the crème was made with soured milk? We both knew there was only one acceptable response.

"Me? Miss a party? As if."

No one told me the party was underwater.

A transparent bubble sucked us below sea level. The orgs were intrigued, pressed against the clear walls, watching fish meander by and algae lick at the glass. This was all new to them, an adventure. But I'd stroked through the deep; I knew what it was like to lose myself in the silent dark of the water.

I knew what was hiding beneath the ocean's surface—I'd seen the dead cities and their bloated bodies, and I knew that only algae and jellyfish could survive in the bath of toxic sludge. But the transparent dome was surrounded by an elaborately fake ecosystem, sparkling water clear enough to show off rainbow coral reefs and fluorescent schools of fish. It was the perfect match for the garish undersea spectacle that lay *within* the dome, synthetic algae undulating from the floor, sparkling lights floating in midair, stars hung so low you could flick them with a finger and watch them float across the room, as if we were all buoyant, gravity temporarily suspended. Holographic reefs and ridges projected from every surface, the illusion broken only when the occasional dancing couple floated right through it. Literally floated, thanks to the buoyancy generators beneath the floor that lifted them on a cushion of air. The party was a gala, which normally would have meant fairy-tale finery but this time, apparently—for those more in the know than I—demanded a more nautical touch. Mermaids drifted by on hovering platforms, their hair architectured to float above their heads. There were org-sized sharks with gnashing teeth and of course the obligatory skanked-up efforts, in this case nude body stockings wired to project shimmering scales across bare abs, chests, and asses.

I wandered, waiting for my orders, wondering what all these people would do if they saw what life underwater was really like, how the ocean had transformed the org world: the pale, swollen flesh, the rusted cars and broken windows, and all the detritus of life interrupted. And then I imagined the transparent dome over our heads cracking, a spiderweb of broken glass spreading across our sky, the water trickling down, like rain, and then breaking through, a hail of glass and a gush of water washing everything away. I imagined the costumed mermaids writhing and flailing, trapped in their tangled hair, their cheeks puffing with one final breath, bubbles streaming out of their mouths and noses until there were none left. I imagined their corpses floating slowly to the surface, leaving me, one by one until I was alone with the wreckage. It would be like being the only person left at the end of the world.

I shoved the vision from my mind. That wasn't my fantasy; that was *his*. Jude's. A world purged of orgs. *Purified,* he would have said. I didn't want to think about the things he would have said, or the things he'd dreamed about, but I did, more than I would have liked to admit.

Which is probably why, at first, I thought it was my imagination.

A shock of silver hair bobbing over the crowd. The razor-sharp cheekbones, the unbearable smirk. Slitted golden eyes, resting on mine for an impossible second, flickering away, and then he was gone.

Never there, I told myself, and danced. My mech mind processed music as little more than syncopated noise. There was none of that wild abandon I'd once felt, the loss of body and self in throbbing notes. Only silent commands, from brain to limbs. *Twist. Turn.*

Jump. Wave. Shuffle. Shimmy. The motions looked seamless; I knew, because I'd practiced in a mirror. It turned out there was nothing too hard about building a smooth surface for yourself. If you knew the steps, if you knew which muscles to move, if you knew how to smile and how to speak, if you knew your lines and played your part, then it didn't matter what lay behind the pose.

The hands that slipped over my eyes were cold.

The whisper in my ear was familiar.

"Miss me?"

Remember they're watching.

I grabbed his wrists, dug in my nails. Knowing it would make him smile. Then turned around slowly, fake smile fixed on my face. He had one to match.

"Didn't expect to see you anytime soon," I said casually, lightly.

Because he was a fugitive, accused of trying to blow up a laboratory full of orgs. He was guilty; I knew, because I'd helped him— and because I'd stopped him. Not exactly the safe, harmless face I wanted to present to the world.

He nodded, his eyes flickering toward the fly cam hovering above my shoulder, and his full lips curled upward.

"I've been around," he said. "Maybe you haven't been looking."

Riley would be watching this, I realized, keeping my face blank. Riley, who knew only the story I'd told him, a fairy tale in which he'd never betrayed Jude, never seen cold hatred in his best friend's eyes.

You were supposed to stay gone forever, I thought.

The skank fish spotted him and began to swarm. Girls distinguishable only by their hair color rubbed up against him, and he let it stretch on, grinning at the lame flirtations, complimenting one on her scales and another on her elaborate wings, forgoing what I would have thought would be the irresistible urge to point out that fish don't fly. He was weirdly good at it, juggling them with an oozing grace, meeting their eyes with a gaze intense enough to convince them of their special place in his heart, fleeting enough to leave hope beating in the hearts of the rest.

He's what you want tonight, the voice commanded me. Then it gave me my first line.

"Want to dance?"

Before I finished the question, Jude's arms were around me, and we were floating across the dance floor.

"So you've decided the high life isn't so bad after all," I said carefully. Jude twirled me out, our fingers linked tightly so I couldn't escape.

"What's not to love?" We turned and turned. Lights flickered overhead, mimicking the effect of sunlight on water. "I can see how glad you are to have me back."

I couldn't see anything in those cat-orange eyes. I only knew that he wanted something, because Jude always did.

This is all for us, he'd always said. The good of the mechs, not the good of Jude. Just a coincidence, then, that they were so often the same thing.

"We've got a lot to talk about." He dipped me so low that my hair brushed the floor.

"I'm not much for talking these days." I shot a mischievous glance directly into the camera buzzing over our heads.

"And the world sighs in relief."

"Well, you know what they say; talking's overrated."

Which meant *shut up*.

Not an instruction he'd ever been inclined to follow. "When you're feeling chattier, let me know. I'll be a mile past human sorrow, where nature rises again."

"You're an enigma, wrapped in a moron, shrouded in pretension," I said, sweetly as I could muster.

"I aim to please. And, since I gather you do too—" He shot another look at the hovering cameras, and I stiffened, waiting for him to spout some anti-org drivel that would ruin all my work.

He leaned toward me, one hand tight around my waist, the other latched on to my shoulder. His voice was low, but the mics would catch it, as they caught everything, and he knew it. "Let's give the people what they want."

Maybe if I'd known it was coming, I could have ducked out of the way.

Maybe I did know it was coming.

I didn't duck.

Just for the cameras, I told myself.

His lips were as cold as mine, his eyes open, watching me.

No different from any of the others, I told myself.

His lips were so soft.

His chest was silent, an empty cavity pressed against the emptiness of my own. A perfect fit.

This is harmless, I told myself.

It couldn't have lasted more than a few seconds. And then I

remembered what fifteen days had almost made me forget: that I could act, that sometimes the puppet could pull her own strings—and that the people liked a fight.

I slapped him.

He saw it coming, like I did; and he let me, like I did. There was a sharp crack, but he didn't flinch. There was no angry red welt left behind on the synthetic flesh. Like nothing had happened.

"When you want me, you'll know where to find me," he whispered. And let go. He melted into the crowd before I could stop him. Not that I would have tried. I told myself I wanted him gone, for good this time.

I almost believed it.

ROBIN WASSERMAN is the author of the Cold Awakening trilogy (*Frozen*, *Shattered*, *Torn*), *Hacking Harvard*, the Seven Deadly Sins series, and the Chasing Yesterday trilogy. She lives in Brooklyn, New York.

Vi knows the Rules.
But Rules are made to be broken.

"*Possession* held me completely captivated from beginning to end.
And what an end! I fell in love with the characters and had countless moments of 'Wow.'"
—JAMES DASHNER, bestselling author of *The Maze Runner* and *The Scorch Trials*

POSSESSION

Elana Johnson